# UNMOORED

The Stranger Trilogy: Book One

## SONIA ORIN LYRIS

Knotted Road Press

**Want all the maps?**
https://lyris.org/seer-saga-maps/unmoored

**Want the entire trilogy? Get your copies here:**
*Unmoored*
*Maelstrom*
*Landfall*

**It's True. Reviews Help.**

If you liked this book, please consider giving a rating and a review. Even a short "Can't wait for the next one!" will do nicely, and help the author to make more books for you.

**A note from Sonia:**

Thank you for being part of my creative process. I have regular chats for subscribers, on my Patreon account, here:

**https://www.patreon.com/lyris**

**Never miss a release!**

I announce new projects on my Facebook feed:

https://www.facebook.com/authorlyris

You can also sign up for my newsletter:

https://lyris.org/subscribe/

Also by Sonia Orin Lyris

*The Stranger Trilogy*

*The Seer*

*Touchstone*

*Mirror Test*

*It Might be Sunlight*

*The Angel's Share*

*Blades*

Chapter One

INNEL'S EYES adjusted to the dimly lit warehouse room, longer than it was wide. Barrels and boxes lined the walls.

His second in command, Nalas, pressed a woman toward him.

"The spice merchant, ser. Her cart wheel broke near Carpuna." His tone softened a bit. "Go on, woman. Tell him what you told me. About the boy."

At the far end of the room sat a boy, perhaps seven.

"Be quick about it," Innel said. He looked the woman over. An occasional informant, travel jacket and trousers caked with the mud of the season, her face weathered.

"Ya, your—" she began.

"No titles," interjected Nalas.

She nodded nervously and Innel stifled impatience. He could not afford the time it had taken to come here from the palace, or the effort to depart unseen. But if it had to do with House Etallan…

"Last I was here in Yarpin," the woman said. "Last season, ser. I heard about the…" She trailed off, her eyes sliding away from Innel's face.

It wasn't a hard guess. "The Queen's Justice," he said.

"Ya, ser," she said, clearly relieved not to need another name for the event. "I brought the boy, to show you. You been so good to me before."

Meaning that he'd paid her well, and she expected him to do it again. "We'll see what it's worth, what you've got. What about the boy?"

"His name, ser."

"Which is?"

"Ask him," she said in a bare whisper.

Innel gave an exhale that came out as a growl. "Tell me his name."

She cringed, lips moving silently to shape a word. Innel had been raised in the Royal Cohort, where lip-reading was a matter of survival.

"Eregin?" he asked.

She nodded mutely.

The name of a dead man, born to House Etallan, whose head Innel had removed not long ago, during the very event that the woman had not wanted to name.

It had not been a private matter, happening as it did in front of the queen, House Etallan's eparch and high family, and countless guards. The story of Innel's actions had spread like wildfire.

*In one motion, Innel stepped forward, right foot touching back exactly as the blade found its target. Metal sliced through neck and vertebrae, and Eregin's head came clean off. His knees buckled, back arched, and the bloody, open neck sprayed backward across Etallan's eparch, Minister of Chimes, and Tokerae, spattering their faces and clothes with red.*

It had been one of Innel's finest moments. He had done the nearly impossible: an off-hand stroke. An ideal cut. The head had gone flying.

In truth, the cut was closer to impossible than he would

admit aloud. If he had not had the seer's advice well in advance, it could never have happened. The seer, who for reasons that now escaped him, he had released.

Well, he still had the seer's sister, Dirina—Nalas's betrothed—and Dirina's son, Pas. Sooner or later, Amarta dua Seer al Arunkel would return to see her family.

As for the beheading—the reprimand to the House of Metal—as far as Innel was concerned, that was barely a start on the debt that House owed the crown for their treason.

Innel looked at the child at the end of the room. Eregin was a House name. Unusual for a town-child, but not unheard of.

"So?" he asked the woman.

"His brother has the same name, ser."

That was beyond unusual. Innel walked the room and stood over the seated child.

"Your name?"

The child looked up and trembled.

"Eregin, ser."

"Your brother?"

"Eregin as well, ser."

"How did you come by this name?"

"Some men visited. A few months ago. All the boys got the name, ser, not only us."

"I see. Were these men wearing gray and orange livery?"

A furtive nod.

"Gave coin to your parents, did they?"

Another nod.

House Etallan, then, both coin and colors, and no attempt to hide it.

Innel walked back, and to his steward and most trusted servant, Srel.

"Who holds Carpuna's charters?" he asked. House

charters were complicated enough that the paperwork describing them could fill a large room, and often did.

"The crown, ser," answered Srel. "Assessment warrant."

"Ours, then." He turned to the woman. "Your back cart wheel. This happen often?"

"Never. Damned wheelwright," she muttered, annoyance overtaking fear. "Knows the roads up river well enough to sketch me a map, but couldn't keep my wheels on. Be having a talk with him when I get back to Dalgo, see if I don't."

"Don't."

She twitched. "Ya, ser."

Innel made eye contact with Srel, who raised an eyebrow inquiringly. No accident, that wheel. "Get the wheelwright's name," Innel told him, knowing Srel was good with people in ways Innel sometimes wasn't.

Srel took the woman's arm, patting it, and took her a handful of strides away as he murmured about how happy the Lord Commander was with her service.

Nalas tilted his head closer. "What is this, ser? Bribes to change names? A tribute to a headless man?"

Innel shook his head. "A message."

For a long moment, Innel considered sending the boy's head to House Etallan, to join the original Eregin's. A somewhat poetic reply, perhaps.

But the child's head would mean nothing compared to the weightier head Innel had already provided.

"Just the boys?" Innel asked the spice merchant.

The woman looked up from her conversation with Srel. "Na. The girls, too. Didn't the boy say, ser?"

Innel strode to her, took her shoulders, stared down into her eyes. "To what, damn you?"

Her mouth hung open and he gripped harder.

"Sachare," she yelped. "Sachare."

*Sachare.* Just as Innel stood between queen Cern and all

external threats, Sachare—Cern's chamberlain—was the final defense of the monarch of the Arunkel empire.

And Innel's unborn child.

In anger, he thrust the woman away. She stumbled backward. Srel caught her by the arm, keeping her from falling.

Now the pieces fell into place. House Etallan was drawing an equivalence between Eregin's head and Sachare's. But Sachare was still alive.

It was a threat.

Innel gestured abruptly, and Srel hastily ushered the woman out of the room.

Nalas stepped to his side. "What now, ser?"

Innel considered the message.

"Signpost the town," he said. "With the children."

Nalas blinked. "Ser? They are surely blameless in this."

"Irrelevant. Etallan has sent a message and a message must be returned."

"But, ser…" Nalas's voice was quiet.

"What?"

Nalas stared at the boy at the other end of the room. "He's the same age as Pas. Once I marry Dirina, Pas is my son. But really, he's my son already."

Innel turned to face his second and made a dismissive sound. "That boy is nothing like Pas. Listen, Nalas." He put a hand on the other man's shoulder. "The Houses are not yet secure in Cern's grasp, and Etallan has every reason to rock her throne. Much will stabilize after the heir is born. Protect the queen, you protect your son. You know this."

Nalas nodded. "But could we not simply bribe Carpuna to change the children's names back?"

"A weak response. If I could send troops to House Etallan's front door to smelt the entire House to slag, I would." That was the message he really wanted to send, but that would mean a civil war, one that the monarchy could not win.

Yet.

The problem was that House Etallan was nearly as powerful as the monarchy itself, a problem Innel intended to solve. He just needed some time.

He wished he had not so willingly parted with his best weapon. What an odd mood he'd been in that day, when he released the seer from the contract he'd worked so hard to bind her to. Innel had just found out that his brother, Pohut —dead at Innel's hand—had not betrayed him. In that profoundly unsettled frame of mind, Amarta had come to him.

*Release me, she had said. It will be worth a great deal to you to have done so.*

Now he weighed this vague promise against his current need, and wondered if he'd been taken in. If anything happened to Cern, and the seer could have prevented it…

No. Such thoughts led in circles.

He turned to Nalas, who he judged needed more convincing.

"They threaten my Cohort sister Sachare, and thus the queen, and my child, the presumptive Anandynar heir. Our response must make it clear how far we will go to defend her. A well-phrased reply, Nalas—written in blood—cannot be misunderstood."

Nalas appeared to struggle with this. After a long moment, he nodded soberly. "Rope or stakes, ser?"

Etallan, the House of Metal, took pride in the precision of their casting and smelting. They would keenly note the details.

"Stakes. Make them iron." Innel imagined dozens of children, nailed up as signposts. "Paint their names on their foreheads. Only the boys. Perhaps the screams and blood of their children will make the townspeople wiser about taking coin to convey a threat to the queen."

Nalas let out a weighty sigh, and looked at the boy. "And this one?"

"Send him home to join the rest."

Innel's thoughts returned to Cern. In the catalog of threats arrayed against her, Etallan was only first of many. But she was occupied, mind and body, making a child, so it fell to him to make sure nothing could reach her.

He must bring Etallan to heel. And he would.

---

INNEL STRODE THE PALACE HALLS, footfalls landing loudly enough to give those ahead of him notice to flatten themselves to the walls as his entourage passed.

He must get to the queen's wing, assure himself that Cern was well, and talk with Sachare. Nothing could be more important.

"Lord Commander?" A messenger dashed along to catch up, holding out a blue envelope. Srel took it, clasping the woman's shoulder briefly as he hurried to catch up with Innel.

"Lord Commander, I need—" From the other side, Nalas muttered fast words to a captain, accepting a scroll, sealed in red and black, marking it as crown business.

Innel's gaze swept across those lining the walls. A pair of green-liveried servants, a blond work-slave at their side. A triad of gray-clad clerks, skullcaps trimmed in red. A House liaison from Great House Helata, dressed in formal green-and-blue. Here, Innel had no doubt, to discuss the crown's shipbuilding contracts. An important discussion, and Innel should be there. But no—it must all wait.

"Lord Commander."

A gaunt old man stood in the center of the hallway, white hair braided into a tight tail down the back of his red-and-black livery. His stance was wide, as if he actually thought he might be able to block Innel's path.

He was the queen's seneschal, and had served her father the old king before that. He might even be ancient enough to have served the Grandmother Queen.

Anger flashed through Innel at the seneschal's audacity. For a moment he thought to barrel through the old man, who seemed little more substantial than a desiccated reed.

He considered how that story would sound across the palace, and instead came to a stop. They locked gazes.

"What?" Innel demanded.

The seneschal gave him a thin-lipped look. "You ignore my messages, Royal Consort."

Innel noted the pointed use of his other title. "I'm a bit busy."

"The Houses are about to have a number of weddings."

"Excellent," Innel said. "I approve."

"You'll care more, Consort, when the Charter Courts begin."

House weddings were one of the many ways aristos built mutual dependencies, preparing for the real battles of the Charter Courts. But the frenzy didn't usually start this early.

"The Courts are five years hence," Innel said. "This matter can wait."

"Four years and five months," corrected the seneschal. "I would be most pleased to spare your attention and take this directly to the Queen. Is that your will, ser?"

A pointed comment, as the seneschal had been kept away from the queen's wing, along with countless others. It was not a good time for Cern to be visible and talked about. Not until she looked healthier.

Not flattering, the comparisons between Cern and her

great-grandmother, Queen Niala, who when similarly pregnant, some four months in, had led Arunkel troops into battle.

"This is not hallway conversation, Seneschal."

"No it is not, Consort," the seneschal agreed. "To judge by your unattractive expression, I am no more amused by the necessity of tracking you down to have it than you are."

Innel's voice dropped. "Srel will address."

The seneschal managed a derisive laugh, with no hint of a smile. "The queen will address, Consort. She should attend these weddings, or have someone suitable represent her."

Which would not be Innel, no one needed to say. Innel scanned the onlookers at the walls to see who might understand more than was being spoken.

"I go to see her now," Innel said. "I will discuss it with her, then with you."

"I eagerly await your informed guidance, Consort," said the seneschal, somewhat sourly, but he moved out of Innel's way, allowing the entourage to press forward to the queen's wing.

Once there, Innel paused briefly to assess the queensguards, then those at the next door, and the next, until he and his men stood outside the queen's antechamber.

"Double the guards here," he said softly to Nalas.

Then he entered, his mind far from the painted silks and woven geometries of cascading gemstones that adorned the walls.

"Where have you been?" Sachare asked, grabbing him by the arm, not waiting for an answer. "Go in. She wants you."

His Cohort sister was tall for a woman, yet shorter than Innel by a head. A child of Great House Nital—the House of Wood—Sachare had long ago sworn to serve the Anandynar princess instead.

She wore the queen's colors. Magenta and black robes of

heavy silk brushed the tops of her slippered feet, the gold brocade on the collar and shoulders a repeating pattern of the royal crest.

At her neck glinted a chain of rubies, the color of blood. Innel gaped, thinking of the message from Carpuna.

"You'd better be clean, boy," Sachare said. "Her sense of smell's quite good these days."

"I need to talk to you," Innel said, but Sachare firmly herded him toward the door that led to the queen's chambers. "Am I clean enough?"

She leaned in close, took a sniff, sighed. "Barely. Don't bore her."

"I never do."

Sachare snickered, and pressed him forward.

Innel went inside.

---

AN ORNATE STONE-TOPPED stove kept the room warm. Near by on the floor lounged the two large dichu dogs.

Innel remembered a time when Cern would not even have considered letting the dogs in her room. Then they had saved her life.

The dark-muzzled Chula opened one gold eye to see who had entered. Tashu raised his brindled head. They recognized Innel. The eye shut, the head dropped.

"Your majesty," Innel said.

From a nest of pillows, the queen of the Arunkel empire reached out a hand toward Innel.

"Come here."

He did. She took his fingers, pulled him close for a kiss. He let himself down on the edge of the bed, careful not to put any weight on her belly.

Her tongue found its way into his mouth, her hand to the back of his neck. Her touch was hungry, her breath hard.

His hand went to her breast, and hers to his pants. Pregnancy, apparently, was an excellent aphrodisiac.

Suddenly she yelped. He pulled back, alarmed. She curled onto her side, around her stomach, and whimpered.

"What?" he breathed. "Did I—"

She shook her head, clutching her abdomen.

He was on his feet. "I'll call the doctors."

"No, no. Just a little discomfort." She inhaled sharply. "Entirely normal, they tell me."

"They'll give another answer when they hurt as much as you do, Your Grace," he said darkly.

"Innel. Stop that. There, see? It's passed." She rolled over on to her back, still breathing hard.

His amorousness of moments ago had dissolved in the heat of terror.

"Your Grace."

She sat up in the bed, held his look. "See? I'm entirely well."

She wasn't, he could tell at a glance. The dark hollows around her eyes and paleness of her skin did nothing to change his mind. He slowly shook his head.

"The first one is hardest, they tell me," she said. "*The winter child is never mild.*" She snorted at the aphorism. "The next one will be easier."

The next?

Innel felt abruptly light-headed, as if he'd just swallowed the finest of adept wines. Traditionally served in thimble-sized cups, he felt as if he'd quaffed a mug of it.

Strangely, it had not occurred to him until just this moment to think beyond one child. Without considering, he laid a light touch on the gentle curve of her belly. Her hand covered his. She smiled. A tired smile, but it seemed genuine.

"Not tonight, after all," she said, releasing his hand.

He stood from the bed. "At your service, my queen."

Wearily she asked, "Is there anything that requires my attention?"

"Nothing that can't wait."

"What about Etallan?"

"I'll take care of Etallan," he said flatly.

"Their path must be smoothed, Innel. They have been chastised and must be redeemed."

Innel nodded slowly. Now was not the time to explain about the threat Etallan had just sent.

"See what you can do to repair the rift, hmm? Too soon, perhaps, for a friendly visit with Tok, though." She laughed slightly.

Tokerae dele Etallan, their Cohort sibling, and eparch-heir of House Etallan.

Also Eregin's cousin.

"Too soon, Your Grace," he replied at the joke, smiling at the hope it gave him, to see her laugh.

She drew herself straighter in the bed, wincing slightly. "The Houses must be juggled with care, like the sharp knives they are. Etallan must be handled cautiously." As she exhaled, he listened for the raggedness in her breath. "It is a test of my rule, how well the Charter Courts go."

"Yes, but first, my lady…" He glanced at her belly and then her face. "Your health. The child's health." He hesitated. "I could find another mage."

She shook her head. "We must not do that again. Against our laws, still. My laws."

"Times are changing."

"Not as fast as we might like." Her stare was distant. "Niala expanded the borders of Arunkel when she was pregnant. Each of the four times. Surely I can have just this one without so much fuss."

"The doctors, then."

"No. I'm tired, is all. Let me sleep." She sounded cross and waved him away, sinking back among the pillows, burrowing her head under the covers.

"Your Grace," he muttered, staring at the slight curve of her belly through the blankets.

Innel had come to the palace as a child with his older brother, Pohut. Inducted into the Princess's Cohort, they had studied and struggled, faced insults and brutal bullying. Then years seducing Cern.

Staring at his child-to-be, it came to Innel that in all his learning about the Arunkel monarchy and blood lines and ascendancies, he had never really grasped that someday he might be part of that lineage.

Not until now.

---

"THAT WAS FAST," Sachare said.

"She's tired and sleeps. Sacha, I must tell you something. I have a message from Etallan."

"Oh?"

"The first part of it was 'Eregin'."

"Ah? Has he lost something?" She snickered.

"The second part was your name."

Her smile faded as she gathered the meaning. Then she shook her head. "None of us who are this close to her—" a nod at the door "—expect otherwise. But they did try before." She touched a fist to her chest, in the very spot that she had taken a spear to stand between it and Cern. "Let them try again."

Them. It was still not known who orchestrated the attack on Cern that day in the kennels. Nothing linked it to Etallan, of course.

"I am doubling the queensguards," Innel said.

"Oh, by the Hells—I'm already tripping over them. This is Cohort games, nothing more. The move is to get you to react, Innel. And behold." She gestured at him with both hands. "You react."

He ignored this, walking the room, making a survey of the adjoining closet, full of Cern's many red, gold, and black cloaks. He ran eyes over the antechamber ceiling and fingers across the baseboards.

"Guards in here as well," he said.

"What? No. We've never had guards this close in."

"We will now. The queen's security comes first."

"What do you think I am, Innel?"

He turned to face her. "Insufficient?"

A guttural sound came from her throat. She made an abrupt, inviting gesture. "Come on. See if you can take me, Cohort-brother. I win, I decide."

Sachare was a tall woman, but had nowhere near Innel's bulk. He was tempted—it would end the argument quickly.

"This is no game, Sacha," he said, deciding against it. If he so much as bruised her, Cern would be livid.

She smirked. "While you were training with wooden swords, I was taken aside to learn to protect her, close in. Come on, Innel, you've never seen what I can do. Aren't you even a little curious?"

He was, actually. She read it in his expression, her smile going wide. "Innel, I want to say that you—" she began. Then, faster than he expected, she had sunk the fingers of a rigid hand into his stomach.

Nothing more than painful, a point scored. He snapped out to grab her arm, his hand closing on empty air.

"You're slow, Innel. I decide about the guards."

"I'm Lord Commander, Sacha. Did no one tell you?"

"In title only?" she taunted.

From anyone else, an unforgivable insult. But the Cohort was groomed by fierce competition, from the earliest years. This was familiar ground.

They both crouched slightly, gazes sweeping each other for nuances of balance and tension, the signs of movement to come.

She grinned with pleasure. He wondered how fast he could get a choke hold on her.

From the next room, Cern screamed.

A DAY BECAME TWO, then three, then four. One doctor, a second. A third was brought. A fourth. The best in the empire's capital, by reputation and standing.

But still Cern weakened.

Innel spoke to each one, taking their measure, then described to them in detail how tightly entwined their futures were to that of the queen.

Innel slept only when he could no longer stand. The rest of the time, he waited in the antechamber, pacing.

This morning, he stumbled from his room. Sachare diverted him from his near sprint to the queen's door.

"Stop threatening the doctors," she hissed. "You terrify them, Innel."

"Good. Let me show them Execution Square, while I'm about it. It'll sharpen their wits."

"They tell me you won't let them leave the queen's wing."

He met her look. "No one must know, Sacha. No one must even guess."

She nodded grudgingly. "Give them time to work, Innel."

But Cern was running out of time. And if the worst happened?

Sachare could go home to House Nital. Innel had no House to return to, and no one but Cern to catch him if he fell.

He looked to Cern's door, aching to go inside to see with his own eyes that she still breathed. But a thought had come to him, and then a decision. He turned to leave.

Sachare must have read something in his face. "Innel? Where are you—"

He was out the door before she could finish the question.

———

THE MOMENT he exited the queen's wing, Innel was faced with a crowd of messengers and liaisons. He pressed through them, hurrying to his office.

On Innel's large desk sat neat piles of petitions and correspondences, all requiring attention.

Srel turned to look at him.

Innel's gaze slid to what was on top of the pile, presumably the most urgent. A petition for water rights, by the Lesser House Keramos, vassal to Etallan. He slid it to the bottom of the pile.

"What do they say, Srel?" he asked, mind already on his plans. He must go into the city unseen, and soon.

"They wonder, ser: is it serious?"

"And?"

"Most believe she is recovering from a minor illness, the many doctors an abundance of concern by a nervous Consort."

"Good." The best deceptions were built on splinters of truth. "Anything else?"

"They wonder if she will snub the weddings."

The weddings. If she recovered, no one need ever know how bad it had been, but only if appearances were kept now.

In his mind's eye, he saw the upside-down tree of the Anandynar line that had produced in Cern esse Arunkel. The leaves were sparse, but Cern's aunt Lismar had made a few branches.

Who among Cern's second and third cousins might usefully be pressed into the service of representing the crown?

"Citriona Anandynar," Innel said, seating himself at his desk. "Twelve?"

"Thirteen, ser."

"See if she can be managed."

"Yes, ser."

A knock at the door. Srel opened it, but before he could issue a greeting, the queen's seneschal pushed past.

The old man stomped to Innel's desk and glared, his face twisting into barely contained fury.

"Do you know how many lies I have told for you this last five-day, Lord Commander? No, because you have shut me out. You play a dangerous game, Lord Commander. A fool's game."

"How dare you speak to me—" Innel began, half out of his chair.

The old man's eyes suddenly went wide and his mouth contorted in pain. It was such an uncharacteristic expression that Innel's next words died on his lips.

The seneschal put hands on the desk and leaned forward. He whispered hoarsely. "I have served three generations of Anandynar monarchs. You came to your position—what? Four years ago? Four whole years?" The old man was trembling.

"Yes," Innel said uncertainly.

The seneschal made a sound in his throat, a swallowed sob. "She is my queen, too, Consort. Tell me what is happening. Let me help."

Innel lowered himself into his chair and contemplated the man in front of him.

"We need a mage," Innel said softly. "Keyretura, if you can find him. And fast."

In a blink, the seneschal's expression changed. He gave Innel a smug smile and tapped a knuckle on the wood.

"Consider it done, Consort. Consider it done."

———

"DO NOT DISTURB ME," the mage Keyretura had said, as he went Cern's room.

How long ago had that been?

Innel would give a great deal to know the future right now, and what it would take to make it the one he wanted it to be. The seer…if he hadn't let her go…

She would probably be telling him the many ways in which his life was about to crumble. Those futures he needed no help envisioning.

"Stop it," Sachare snapped at him. Then, more softly, "Innel, please."

He found that he had been pacing the length of the antechamber, as fast as his long legs would carry him, making it a short walk in each direction.

"How long has it been?" he asked, facing her.

Neither of them had slept in days. She looked drawn and haggard. He probably did, too.

"Six bells."

They were both whispering, but for no good reason; the door to Cern's bedchamber was heavy enough to muffle all but the loudest sounds. In any case, the mage could hear them right through it if he wanted to.

In the days it had taken for the seneschal to find Keyretura and quietly bring him to the palace, Cern had gone from poor to worse. Truly, it had been a miracle that the mage was in-city at all, and willing to come, after last time.

Credit to the seneschal for that. Innel would not exclude him again.

His thoughts churned. No more missteps. Innel's every action must be meticulously unassailable. Because if Cern…

He would not even think it. The mage would heal her and would save Innel's winter child. He must.

But if he could not, then…

He realized that he had been staring at Sachare, and she at him, statue-like, their gazes locked.

The door to Cern's bedchamber opened. Out stepped the dark-skinned black-robed Perripin mage. He closed the door behind himself and looked at them.

"This is not good," he said.

The words swam through Innel's mind like starlings in a windstorm. He tried to corral them into some order so that they might mean something different, but could not.

"But you can heal her," Innel said, suddenly hoarse. Not a question. It could not be a question.

"No," answered Keyretura.

Innel felt the blood drain from his face. Sachare's mouth dropped open.

"More money?" Innel croaked. "What do you need? Anything."

Keyretura made a sound that might have been amusement or disgust. "I came when your man called, *Iliban*, something that does not much please me. Coin for my trouble, yes, but you mistake my meaning. It is this: the tangled patterns of your queen's pregnancy go deep. I do not have a solution."

"Who has done this to her?" Innel demanded.

"Her body has done this to her," Keyretura answered blandly. "Nothing more."

Sachare seemed to crumple. She slid to her knees. "High One, we beg you. Is there anything at all that we can—"

"You must try," Innel said, cutting her off. "She is..." Irreplaceable, he thought, but it was not the right word. "The child is..."

Irreplaceable.

"Silence," Keyretura snapped, making a short, abrupt gesture with one finger.

Innel's throat suddenly constricted. He could barely breathe, let alone speak. On her knees, Sachare gasped like a fish.

"You listen poorly, Iliban. Do I have your attention now?"

Innel and Sachare both nodded vigorously.

"Your queen's best chance lies with my *uslata*, Marisel. She knows the subtle patterns of pregnancy and how to resolve its fragile complexities."

Innel swallowed, found that he could speak again. "Marisel dua Mage? But she..." Innel and Marisel had not parted on the best of terms. "Are you certain?"

Keyretura turned to Innel. Suddenly the room felt very bright, and entirely too warm. "Am I *certain*?"

"I apologize, High One," Innel said quickly. "If you say it is so, it is so. I will send for her. Will she come?"

"That is another matter. I'll pen a letter for you. Your release of Amarta dua Seer may also work in your favor. But you have no choice. Your queen is weak. If you do nothing, the pregnancy disorder will draw both child and mother through death's door."

Innel's heart pounded in his chest, his pulse surged in his ears. "A messenger. Our fastest horses—"

"A messenger will not convince her."

"You, then. High One, You could persuade her."

"Certainly. But Marisel is a hard ride and many days away. Who will keep your queen alive while you travel?"

Innel's mouth opened and closed.

"Yes, you, Lord Commander," the mage said, now clearly amused. "Go. Perhaps you can convince my uslata of your profound need and abject humility."

At the moment, that did not seem hard. Innel had never felt so desperate.

These last months had been floor-to-ceiling problems, and Innel had spread himself across them all, like bridges of silk holding together ships in a storm, while pretending that Cern was only mildly incapacitated. He had needed to comport himself across the palace with confidence, knowing that his world might come crashing down at any moment.

Now the clutter in his mind cleared. The prospect of useful action was a powerful tonic.

"I'll assemble riders and be away within a bell." Innel was already sketching what he would say to Maris and who he could trust at his side.

A few men only. Ride light, ride fast.

"Absent her willingness to aid your cause," Keyretura said, "the sensible course might be to offer yourself to her *taslata* for his study of anatomy."

Innel gave the clearly amused mage a startled look. "What?"

"Should your petition fail, Iliban, your queen dies. You might be better off to surrender your life there than return for a stay in Execution Square, which I observe to be conveniently unoccupied. No less painful, to be used for such a study, but perhaps the lesser of the two disgraces. What do you think, Lord Commander?"

Innel decided that the mage's question didn't require an answer. He lurched for the door.

Chapter Two

AMARTA'S EYE was caught by a shimmering shell on a vendor's table. She went to it eagerly, fingertips tracing its bright green curve.

She had seen it before, she was nearly positive. A dream or a vision—a moment ago, a lifetime hence, she wasn't sure. An echo from some possible future? *The glinting, rainbow iridescence rippled across a field.* Then it was gone: another mysterious glimpse of what might yet be.

"Tell your fortune, foreign miss?"

So much of Amarta's foresight was like this very shell, she reflected. The emerald glint in sunlight befuddled the eye. Did she see this shell before her, true? Or was it to come, and still only possible in the world?

The eye and mind could be confused. Touch was more certain. Her fingers brushed the hard surface again.

"Your future? Good sera? I to tell you?"

Amarta blinked, realizing that these spoken words were now, here, in this busy market. And further, were spoken in her own language. No future vision, this.

She looked for the source, across tables heaped with trays

of still-twitching sea creatures, past piles of oddly shaped fruits with fingers like the limbs of lovers entwined—but no —that didn't bear thinking about.

Beyond the seawall, the crashing of waves cut through the market chatter every few moments, the hush of the sea weaving through the high laughter of children, who darted and dodged around haggling adults. Suddenly, a few paces away, a table leg collapsed, skeins of yarn tumbling to the dirt and cobbles. A sharp, outraged yell. Children scattered in all directions.

A young boy ran in front of Amarta and stopped, gaping and pointing at her. A scowling shopkeeper lurched for the child who dashed out of reach and was gone, sliding through a narrow opening of brick and barrels.

"Sera? Your fortune you want?"

Amarta at last thought to look down. On the ground, from under a tattered awning, its fabric faded to colorlessness, an aged hand reached out and up. She leaned into view, the old woman, her face lined, dark skin blotched pale, her white hair a ragged fuzz.

"What did you say, grandmother?" Amarta asked her in the language and dialect of this land.

"Ah, you speak Perripin! And so well," said the old woman, grinning toothlessly. "I would hardly know you for a foreigner, miss, but for your sickly pale skin. Do you wish your fortune, this fine, bright market day? I was trained in the auguring ways by the Monks of Revelation, so I can tell your future true."

Amarta felt a hand close on her arm. A gentle grip, but it might as well have been steel. He leaned in close.

"She can't, Amarta."

The scent of him warred with the mingling smoke of frying fish and the heavy brine of the sea, and won. An ache swirled through her.

"And if you keep walking away from me," he breathed into her ear, "you will seem an Arunkin woman traveling the coast of Perripur alone, rather than a back-country couple, here to shop. In these lands, that is worthy of note."

Amarta brushed back the tail of the long scarf he'd wrapped around her head that morning. The local style, the scarf and blouse. They dressed the part of poor rural inlanders. The scarf tangled, and she tugged at it, frustrated.

"I'll do better," she said.

"Try to seem at ease with me," he said gently. "Or annoyed, if you prefer. Act familiar, in any case, as if we've been together for years. Yes?"

"Yes."

*Together for years.* Which they had been, in a way. Years in which he had hunted her relentlessly. A lifetime ago. A world away.

"It comes to my eyes," the old woman said, fanning fingers before her face, looking up at Amarta. "Good miss, will you know what I see?"

"Yes," Amarta replied eagerly, pulling her arm from Tayre's light grip. "Give her a coin, won't you—" she searched her mind for some appropriate local slang. "—my starfish?"

He sighed deeply, ending it with a short laugh. "You have persuaded her." His indulgent tone and amused expression told the story of their pretend relationship perfectly. He dropped an octagonal sorin-ga coin into the old woman's outstretched hand.

"So generous, ser," said the old woman, the coin vanishing into her grimy caftan. She brought out a tangle of thick, faded red yarn and shook the bundle in her hands and then over her head.

She chanted a children's rhyme. No invocation of the

serpent moon or some other Perripin piety, but a simple litany about collecting precious stones on an island.

Amarta watched, fascinated. She had never chanted while foreseeing. Perhaps the monks who had trained the woman knew something that Amarta did not?

Or, Tayre might say, the woman didn't expect Amarta's grasp of the language to be so good and was intending to enhance her performance with what came readily to mind.

Amarta watched Tayre while he scanned the crowd in seemingly idle boredom. What a knack he had for appearing to be doing something other than he really was: watching. Always watching.

Where did he keep it, Amarta wondered, the cheap *nals* coin she had given him? In a hidden pocket? In one of his many stashes, across who knew how many lands?

Or maybe he'd already spent it. For a moment she imagined him purchasing something practical, that small nals among a handful of coins, casually tossed in as an afterthought.

But no—somehow she knew that wherever it was, Tayre still owned the four-part copper coin that had sealed the contract between them, that marked the moment in which he would never hunt her again.

His gaze came to her. Before looking on, he smiled at her, an expression so fond and familiar that her stomach dropped.

Pretense. All pretense.

The old woman stopped chanting. She threw the tangled yarn to the dusty ground, peering at it closely. It was intended to resemble intestines, Amarta realized, her hope sinking.

"Fame and fortune!" the old woman cried, as if surprised, her smile stretching and going slack by turns as she watched Amarta for a response. "The adoration of many!" She looked at Tayre. Then, with less certainty: "Children and family?"

"What about my sister?" Amarta found herself asking.

Tayre's hand was firm on Amarta's shoulder, his touch both reassuring and unnerving. "Never mind that, grandmother. What about her father? He's been terribly sick. We need him back at the mill. Will he be restored to health?"

His tone, the ache in his eyes—it was a riveting performance. Amarta herself was nearly convinced that Tayre cared deeply for her father, a man dead nearly twenty years, whom Tayre had never met.

The old woman's gaze flickered between them. "Most treasured, is it not, that which is gone? He will be strong again, your father, come the delinquent sun returned to the northern lands."

Amarta puzzled over these words. She had learned so much of the language with Tayre, but as he had pointed out many times, it was one thing to understand a language, and another to understand the speaker. Was the old woman saying Amarta's dead father would recover in the Spring?

"I see your confusion, foreign lady," said the old woman. "With another coin, more might be revealed. You have questions. I have answers."

"Enough answers," Tayre said, taking Amarta's arm. "The market closes soon, darling, and we have much to do." He tapped Amarta's shoulder in a silent signal: *We go.*

Amarta let him draw her along the street. As they passed tents and tables, buckets of crabs and boxes of orange and magenta fruit, she stifled annoyance. "I wanted to hear that. What if she is true?"

"She's a fraud, Amarta."

"You don't know that."

"The Monks of Revelation are a men's-only order," he said. "Make of that what you will. Also, know this: a sailor at the dock pointed at you, then turned to speak to a man at his side. Best we move on."

Protecting her, she realized with mild surprise. So unnecessary. Amarta could not count the hunters she had evaded across the years. If someone truly threatened her, vision would warn. It always did.

Perhaps she should remind him of the years he himself had not been able to catch her.

No, perhaps not that.

Was his protection part of this contract? *Help you learn about yourself and the world.* Months with him, and yet she still did not know what was between them.

She did know what he thought of the old woman on the ground behind them, that such a ragged, poor creature, sitting on the street of a small seaside town, could not be offering true fortunes.

Amarta's own past taught her otherwise: she and her sister Dirina had been just this poor and desperate, begging small coins from strangers in exchange for Amarta's answers. It was too easy to imagine herself, years hence, as that old woman.

With that thought, vision flickered at the edges of her mind, trying to answer the half-asked question. Murky flashes. Cobwebs of maybe. The smell of a rank, open sewer. Hard cobblestones beneath her.

And it was gone.

*Unique beyond reckoning,* Maris had said of Amarta.

Tayre was right, she decided: the old woman was a fraud. Someday Amarta might find someone like herself, from whom she could learn more about what she was.

But not today.

Disappointment settled on her like a heavy shawl.

TAYRE LED them along the hot, dusty Perripin street, past the final stalls of market row. Dark-skinned Perripin faces turned to watch them go. Suspicion? Curiosity? She could not tell.

They were heading toward the inn, she realized.

"Do you mean us to leave Mutarka?" she asked.

"Yes."

From within stacked wicker cages, small hens clucked, their heads tilted as they eyed baskets out of reach, piled high with multicolored eggs.

"Because one man pointed at me?"

"It was not idle curiosity."

"No. He wouldn't come after me." No need to name him, the Lord Commander of Arunkel, the man who had hired the hunters Amarta and her sister and nephew had evaded these many years. "He released me from the contract. He let me go. Willingly."

"Minds have been known to change."

She shook her head. "But he gave me a horse. A horse!"

A beautiful bay mare who responded so easily to every touch that Amarta felt comforted just putting her hand on the golden animal's hide. She had named her Souver, after the golden coin of her homeland, because the mare was a treasure, and Amarta felt rich every time she rode her.

"An expensive horse, making you even easier to find."

"We were to stay the night," Amarta said, hearing the whine in her own voice.

Not on the ground and separate pallets. At an inn. Together. In one room. One bed.

He glanced sidelong at her, appeared to consider. "All right. Tell me, Seer: if we stay the night, what might happen?"

Exactly what she had been wondering. She held the question within, letting images form.

*He slept. She watched him, caught in indecision. Thinking to move closer. If she brought her lips to his, might he turn to her and respond in kind?*

*You're a fool, she would tell herself. He'll say no, again, is what.*

She blinked herself back to the present, puzzling at this —what?—vision of vision? Vision of speculation?

Regardless, it was not what he meant, and she knew it.

She held the question again, drawing it wide. Possibilities splayed before her by the tens, by the hundreds, by the uncountable many. With her intention she reached inside, as if pawing through a huge bag of thread, fumbling for the twine of the most likely outcomes.

*A quiet night at an inn. One without his touch, but also without intrusion.*

Back in the present she found herself staring at her feet, at the worn turnshoes, the dirt, the cobblestones.

"Nothing happens," she said, struggling to keep bitterness from her tone, turning her head so that he might not see the disappointment. On a side street, laughing children drew adults to some late-day entertainment. She envied them.

"Spoken fast for certainty," he said. "No danger? It is not even possible?"

If anyone else had asked—but no, it was him. She looked again, this time at the edges of the possible, the thinnest strands.

*A spreading fire in the inn's kitchens. An improbable windstorm that tore off shutters and battered down doors. A drunken couple mistaking the room for their own, pounding on the door.*

Pressure in her head bordered on pain. She groped for spider-silk trails of what might be.

*The door slammed open. Four hulking shapes. Tayre moving*

*fast. A shout. A pained cry. Down went one, then another. A quick exchange with the third. Tayre swept to the floor. Amarta gasped, but a moment later, he was standing. Alone.*

So remote. So unlikely. Hardly worth mentioning.

"Nothing," she repeated, head down, throbbing. Could she convincingly end the prediction there? Probably not. "Most likely," she amended. "A small chance." her voice dropped to a bare whisper. "Four men. Hardly possible."

"Not worth the risk. We go back."

Back to the gentle prison of the mage's land, where Amarta had foreseen the mage soon returning from Arunkel.

Overhead, seagulls screeched. Ahead, a sheep bleated. Somewhere, a dog barked. It all seemed too loud.

"But you and Maris," Amarta said.

"I'll stay off the mage's land and out of her path."

He no longer referred to Maris by name, not since the four of them—Amarta, Tayre, Maris, and her new apprentice Samnt—had ridden south from Arunkel to Perripur, where Maris had made it clear that Tayre was not welcome. Then she'd left. *He'd better not be here when I return, Amarta.*

It gave Amarta a sick feeling, that the two people she trusted most in the world were at odds with each other. There must be a way to reconcile them.

"Be sure of the timing, Seer. You should be there when the mage arrives."

*A large envelope. Pale red linen. A message carrying grief.*

"I will."

He glanced at her. "You foresee something. What?"

Amarta's head ached. From the side street, a flute began to play, trilling and high.

"Make way for the Arunkel queen! Make way!" someone yelled in Perripin.

Amarta dashed to the edge of the crowd, craning her neck to see. Around her, townspeople nudged each other, pointing at her, at Tayre who had followed. They whispered to each other, laughed in surprise, and in a rippling fashion, moved aside to make a pathway for them to the center.

"Your queen, Arunkin," one said, laughing. "Go on."

At the center of the crowd was a puppet theater, purple curtains pulled aside. Two dark-skinned wooden puppets, breathtakingly lifelike, peered across the stage to where a light-skinned puppet lurched from side to side, her huge belly protruding from long red and black robes, a crown on her head.

"Cern esse Arunkel!" shouted one of the puppets, waving at her. "Welcome to Mutarka's market day. Is that a baby in your tummy?"

"Or a bag of pineapples?" called out the second puppet to the crowd.

The crowd chuckled.

"I am joyful!" the Cern puppet said, throwing her arms wide. "But I am despondent!" She closed her arms over her belly, looking down in sorrow.

"What? Surely all rejoice at the birth of the Arunkin heir! What is wrong, oh queen?"

"I think there is only one inside me."

"You can have more!" shouted the second puppet.

The Cern puppet's head tilted in confusion. "Are they not all born together?"

The two Perripin puppets gawked at each other, then at the audience, then back at the Cern puppet.

"No, queen. You are thinking of puppies."

The crowd tittered.

"I love my dogs!"

"Yes, but babies…" began one puppet.

"Are born one at a time," continued the other. "After the first, if you want another, you simply…ah…how to explain?"

He looked at the first puppet, who made a crude thrusting motion with his hips.

The audience laughed and cheered, gazes going back and forth, from the stage to Amarta.

His hand was on Amarta's shoulder, his mouth to her ear. "Compose yourself."

Amarta had not realized she was scowling. She swallowed, ignoring the looks, attempting a neutral expression.

The Cern puppet danced around the stage, singing an off-key Arunkin lullaby.

Tayre leaned close to whisper. "Notice what is not being said. They don't know the truth of the matter, or we would see it played out here."

Amarta nodded. Were it known that a Perripin mage had gone to aid the Arunkel queen, that would be huge news. No Perripin would pass up a chance to mock Arunkel's attitudes about magic.

"Should we remind her who the father is?" asked the first puppet.

"You mean Innel, The Mutt? No no—she might become confused again."

"But if she doesn't understand how babies are made," said the first, "We must—"

"—send her a Perripin *anknapa*!" finished the second.

Anknapas were teachers who ministered to the powerful and wealthy, preparing young elites for adult life. Cern would have been done with such instruction long ago.

Laughter, shouts of agreement. "La la la!" "Yes! Send two!" "Three!" "She can have mine!"

"Sorin coins, fellow Perripin," said one puppet. "It will take many sorins to send a good Perripin anknapa to the queen, to teach her how babies are made!"

Coins flew, thunked, and spun into the trough before the puppet theater.

Amarta clenched her mouth on the words she wanted to say.

"By the Dragon Sun, I'm hungry!" shouted the Cern puppet. "I could eat a city!"

"Oh, no!" cried one of the puppets. "Feed her quick, lest she gnaw our borders again. Someone hand me a mountain!"

From the side of the stage came a huge cutout of a snow-topped mountain. The two puppets, grunting and groaning, dragged it onto the stage where they dropped it with a bang in front of the Cern puppet, who began to chew loudly at the edges.

Amarta's face went hot as the audience trilled and laughed and threw more coins.

*We go*, Tayre tapped on her shoulder, very clearly. When Amarta didn't respond, he turned her away from the stage and pressed her to walk through the crowd. A gentle but firm suggestion.

The crowd let them pass, but the faces laughed and pointed, some cheering, as if Amarta and Tayre were part of the show.

"How many children will I have?" asked the Cern puppet from behind.

"Ask a fortune teller!"

Amarta slowed, and Tayre's arm slid around her shoulders.

"Yes!" cried the Cern puppet. "I have a collection of them in the kennels. With the dogs. All my precious pets together!"

"No, she doesn't—" Amarta began, starting to turn, to tell them how absurd they were, but Tayre's hold on her shoulders was solid, and he kept her moving forward, past the jeering crowd.

It was nothing like a suggestion.

---

*SILENCE,* he tapped with a hand on her shoulders, the arm still holding her tight, forcing her forward.

She held her tongue until they reached the inn. Then up the stairs and into the room, the door closing behind.

"They insult her!" Amarta spat, no longer containing her outrage. "Make her seem foolish. A child. How dare they?"

Tayre set down the bags he'd been carrying. She watched while he began to repack produce and dried goods into saddlebags.

She took a breath, trying to still her storm of emotion. "Why?"

"Because Arunkel has a history of crossing borders and claiming lands," he answered. "Cern and the number and status of her children matter here." He looked at Amarta. "And it is Perripin to laugh at what is feared."

"Let them laugh at their own leaders, then."

"They do. Watch some more puppet shows. Why do you care? Is the queen such a good friend?"

"You know she is not."

"I do?" He looked at her again. "I was not the only one curious to know what you and the queen talked about that one afternoon, behind closed doors."

Amarta gaped. "How do you even know that much?"

"Information travels. I make sure it travels to me. I also know the answer: you rolled dice for her, to prove your ability."

Amarta nodded slowly, still stunned. There had been only three people in that room that day: Amarta, the queen, and Sachare, the queen's chamberlain.

Well, maybe a guard or two.

Of course Tayre would somehow know.

He pulled up a pants cuff, adjusted a knife sheath tight against his leg. "That you were held prisoner in the palace, many would be aware, but questions would remain. Whether you were the seer of rumor, or the Lord Commander's wayward cousin, as he claimed, it was clear that you were important. Where are you now? What stories might you have to tell, if the right questions were asked?"

*The right questions.* In memory, a candle lit a dark room. Amarta's heart and breath sped. Her gaze skittered across the room to find something to look at besides him. The fingers of her left hand ached.

"There is no reason to believe that there is not still a price on your head, Amarta, whoever is paying the bill. As there was before."

When he was her hunter, he meant.

Her gaze seemed stuck on the empty, unused bed.

"But I have you now," she whispered.

The softest of laughs. "I am only one man."

She thought of the years in which she had barely escaped his grasp, and the futures she had just witnessed in which he had laid out four attackers in fewer moments than it would take to tell him. The hundreds and thousands of futures in which four large men could not best him.

"No, you are..." She trailed off, her mouth moving, unable to find the words. "But we already paid for the room."

"Coin is cheaper than blood." He adjusted a buckle, tightened a strap, then stood, hefting the packs. "Ready?"

She wasn't. Not ready to go back to Maris's land. Not ready to open the red linen envelope.

Not ready to give up on her hopes.

He had been her first time. Her only time, thus far. She remembered it keenly. She wanted it again.

At last she nodded, slung her own pack over her

shoulder, and followed him to the door. She paused a moment to look back at the lone bed and the two untouched feather pillows.

Then to the stables outside the inn where Amarta helped him set and attach saddlebags on her mare, Souver, and his chestnut-brown gelding, who met her look with a sweet brown-eyed stare. He nosed her, as if to see if she were all right.

For a moment her eyes stung. He was beautiful, Tayre's horse.

"You need a new name," she told him.

---

"WHAT'S HIS NAME?" she had asked Tayre, some months ago.

"That depends," Tayre had answered. "When I'm in Arunkel, I call him 'Faithful'. In the back country, 'Whiskey' works better. In Perripur he's 'Coffee Bean' or 'Mouse.'"

She absorbed this and what it told her about the respective cultures.

"But what's his real name?"

Tayre laughed softly, then made a clicking sound with his tongue. The chestnut-brown animal walked to him, eagerly lipping from his hand the honeyball Tayre offered.

"He has many names," Amarta said, watching this moment between them, and feeling oddly moved. "Like you. But what was his first one?" *And what was yours?*

"Horse."

"Horse? That's it?"

"Yes."

"That's no name at all."

Tayre gave her an amused look. "Rename him, then. I doubt he'll object."

THEY RODE Horse and Souver out of Mutarka, past the tumbled-down walls that marked the town's edge. At a crossroads, one way led up into hills of thick inland forests, the other along the coast. Behind them, the sun set, dusting the tops of the inland trees with gold.

Back. They were going back. Amarta to the mage's house to await her return. Tayre to his camp. Frustration gnawed at her.

"Let's take the coastal road," she said suddenly. "A few days more will make no difference."

Another town, another inn, another bed. Another chance?

Half-images flickered, jittered, refused to resolve. She tried again, tightening her focus, narrowing the question.

"Be certain, Seer. If the mage returns home and you're not there, she'll assume I've abducted you. I see no wisdom in angering an already annoyed mage."

Amarta nodded, not really listening. She had found a faint trail. *His fingers slowly stroked her cheek.* Then she lost it, found it again, taking hold of the slippery line. Almost. She almost had it. *In the moonlight his expression said maybe. He reached over to her, opening his mouth to speak. He said—*

"We're being followed." His tone was quiet but sharp. "One rider, two on foot."

Amarta blinked back into the present, following his gaze to a gully of trees back the way they'd come. She squinted into the sun and saw nothing.

She was about to ask him how he could be so certain, either of the count of followers, or the number of horses, when she herself could see nothing, when foresight exploded in warning.

*A searing pain through her shoulder.*

Amarta twitched and curled, rolling her shoulder just so.

A hiss—the sound of a huge, flying insect—mere inches away. She gasped.

Tayre was turning, Horse bunching under him, readying a sprint. He reached over to slap Souver's rump.

"Ride!"

Under her, Souver's neck gathered and stretched, a small toss to shift weight. With a powerful motion, she launched herself forward and uphill.

Again, foresight gave alarm. Amarta hunched.

A fast line grazed her back, like the faintest brush of a whip's tail.

Souver was now climbing the hill with an eager stride that quickly turned into a gallop. Tayre rode down in the other direction. Everything shook as Souver pounded upwards. Amarta grasped for the reins. Unable to find them, she instead took tight hold of Souver's mane, her mind nearly blank with shock at the future pain that vision was serving up as warning.

*It came again: a piercing cut across her cheek.*

Amarta whimpered, dropping to wrap arms around Souver's neck.

Another arrow hissed by her, slicing only air.

She passed trees and fields as Souver pounded up the incline, her hooves consuming the road as if it were flat. An expensive horse, Tayre had said. Now Amarta understood why.

Numbly, Amarta wondered how far was far enough. In the many months of Tayre's tutelage, he had somehow failed to teach her about the range of an arrow shot at a moving target in the confusing light of sunset.

But it didn't matter: Amarta only needed to know what to do in the next moment. That, vision would provide.

Souver reached the top of the rise. At last Amarta found

reins and sense, slowing Souver, turning them both to face the way they'd come. She gulped air as she looked down and across the shadowy trees and gullies below, the half-lit fields and dark tangles of brush.

Nothing moved.

Vision assured her that she was safe. Her mind knew, but her body still felt the attack, the cuts and piercings that had never happened. She shuddered, her galloping heart taking a long time to come to rest.

Where was Tayre? What was he doing? Her near futures held him beside her, a quiet, intense presence. But what he was doing now, she could not even guess.

As always, some part of her worried that he might not come back, contract or no. Then the nightmares would return. By her side, his hunter's face was well-lit, even if the contract was balanced on the edge of a single nals coin.

Overhead, the stars brightened. The night came on.

Amarta waited.

---

AMARTA SAT ATOP SOUVER, watching. Through high, distant trees behind her, the moon was a bright luminescence. It slowly freed itself of the dark tangle of silhouetted branches and crawled up into the night sky.

Despite everything—despite knowing that he would return, and then knowing it would be soon—he arrived quietly, behind her, from the other side of the rise. Souver knew it before Amarta did, and was already turning to meet her equine companion.

How anyone could train a full-sized horse to walk so silently, Amarta had no idea.

Now at her side, Tayre scanned the moonlit forest and fields below, then looked her over.

"Are you all right?"

His concern touched her more deeply than any of the times he'd laid hands on her today.

"I'm fine."

"Well done, then," he said, turning Horse and leading them forward along the road that went into the mountains.

Not the coastal road, as she had hoped. She clung instead to the praise. *Well done.*

"What happened?" she asked.

"Every appearance of being a simple, poorly executed pillage," he answered. "But I have doubts—they aimed too well, and knew that coin was being offered for reports of an Arunkin woman."

"Me?"

He shrugged. "It was a vague description."

"Will they report?"

"No. They've been discouraged from that action."

Despite still feeling shaken, Amarta laughed a little. She had seen this before, how compelling Tayre could be. When he told a story, as he had done to teach her language, history, and politics, he could make the tales come alive.

"A good time for you to vanish again," he said, "into the mage's protected lands. Another season, two—even three— and those hunting you may look elsewhere."

"Another season?" She gave him an incredulous look. "I have waited long enough to see the world. I—" Amarta's eye caught on something: a long bundle, tied alongside Horse's saddlebags. It had not been there before, when they left Mutarka. "What is that?"

"Bows. knives. Whatever was of value."

It took her a moment to understand. Tayre had robbed the thieves in return. Well, good: that seemed just.

As they rode, she thought about it some more, and

realized that she hadn't understood at all. As she tensed, Souver glanced back at her.

Tayre would not have taken the time to persuade the attackers. There would be no clever story. No convincing words to get them to go their way without speaking of the Arunkin woman they had found. He would simply have ended them.

No, not simply. First he would have forced them to tell him everything they knew. *A dark room. A single candle.*

A small, wordless sound emerged from her throat. "If I had not stepped away from you in the market…if I had not shown anger at the puppet show…"

"Does foresight tell you what might have been?"

He knew it did not. She shook her head.

"Then we can only speculate. They were thieves, Amarta, not slaves. They chose their course freely."

*As did you.*

Even now, his tone was so pleasant and reasonable that she found herself reconsidering. Maybe he had only frightened them. Wounded them, perhaps, but then let them go.

She opened her mouth to ask, and for a long moment it stayed that way.

Then she closed it again. To ask a question was to invite an answer.

For a long while they rode in silence. Overhead, the moon lent the road before them a silvery glow.

At last she spoke. "Maris is coming home. That must mean that Cern and her child are well."

"Or dead," he replied. "All we can be sure of is that the situation is resolved beyond the mage's ability to affect, whatever has happened."

It had not even occurred to Amarta that Maris might fail

to save Cern and the child. A stab of grief went through her at the thought.

Tayre glanced at her. "In time, the news of the Arunkel queen and child will reach us from all quarters. But if you want to know sooner, could you not look for a future in which you speak with the mage? Surely the matter would come up in conversation."

Of course it would. But then Amarta would also know what was in the red envelope, and that grief she could wait for.

She considered the many, many moments that led from here into the future, but did not contain his unpretended touch.

"I see no point," she said tightly, "in knowing a future that can't be changed."

## Chapter Three

"A RARE DELIGHT TO see you, cousin," Bolah said, closing the door behind him.

Her tone was warm, yet subtly sharp. Natun felt a blossom of guilt. Earned, no doubt; it had been years since his last visit.

The room was small and snug, walls heavy with expensive tapestries. Red and black velvet drapes dampened sound.

Bolah gestured to chairs at a small center table. Natun sat, passing his fingertips over the wood. Perripin mahogany, and that worthy of his scowl. But the inlaid marquetry of sigils of the Lesser Houses was good Arunkel wood—birch and amardide, if his old eyes didn't steer him wrong—and balanced the insult.

He examined the room. Cut-glass and shelves revealed all manner of beautiful items. Some were heirlooms and quite expensive. A few, he was nearly certain, were mage-wrought and priceless.

"I meant to come sooner," he said. "But I can hardly slip from the palace without my absence being noted."

"So I hear." He gave her a sharp look to see if this was humor, but her face showed nothing. "Wine? Twunta? Tea?"

"Tea," he said primly.

In truth, he would welcome something stronger, to soften the edge of this visit and the times that compelled it, but he could not return to the palace with smoke on his jacket, or wine on his breath.

What would it be like, he wondered, to indulge whatever whim took him, without regard to the many who watched him so keenly, seeking his corruptibility? A different life, that, certainly.

Bolah moved about the room, setting a kettle of water on her iron cookstove, adjusting the stovepipe flue. She brushed a spot of ash from her silk sleeve. Natun noted the worn fabric and a short thread where it should not be.

For a moment, annoyance flashed through him at this fashion breach—in his own staff, an unacceptable lapse. But no, with Bolah, it was deliberate. She cultivated a look of worn elegance, of cast-off wealth. It put her exclusive clients at ease and assured them that she was still entirely beneath them.

A familiar task, he thought sourly, and that thought led him to another: should he even be here? He gripped the sides of his chair, pushing himself to stand, to leave.

"How is our excellent queen, cousin?" Bolah asked smoothly.

At this, he eased himself back into his seat. That's why he was here: the queen. And, as annoying as he was, her Consort. They both needed him, even if they did not know it yet.

Yet. It was surely his duty as the queen's seneschal to know when *yet* was too close.

Bolah set a porcelain tea cylinder on a side table, her movements unhurried.

The queen's pregnancy had only just been announced, but Natun had been watching her closely. The signs were there. Trouble was brewing.

"She is most excellent," he said.

"Ah," Bolah said, drawing out the sound, as if this explained everything.

Natun narrowed his eyes at this sarcasm. "I can only say so much."

"You need something from me, Natun, or you wouldn't be here."

He caught himself raising and lowering his pressed lips over his teeth, a nervous habit he had long tried to break, and forced himself to a less mobile scowl.

"Yes," he managed.

"Then I think you can say a little more."

"What have you heard?" he demanded.

Bolah selected an ornately carved box from a shelf. Black gum wood, if Natun didn't miss his guess, and clearly House Nital's detailed work. With polished silver tongs that sported a filigreed handle, she pinched out a small tangle of deep red leaves, holding them over the center of the open tea cylinder, releasing them to fall into the hot water.

Again, she dipped the tongs into the box. Again, the slow motions, the release, and the fall of tea leaves into water.

Very slow. She was making him wait, and making the point that he had come to her, and not the other way around.

He exhaled. "I must rely on your absolute confidence."

"Yes, I think you must."

If they hadn't known each other since childhood, he might have missed her quiet rebuke.

"I have no choice," he said, "but to be discreet in every word." Which, for the most part, meant saying nothing.

"The crown's honor is paramount. My loyalty must be unquestionable."

When the young queen Cern had taken the throne, Natun had entertained the idea of relinquishing his position to one of his apprentices. Surely, he thought, he had earned a respite. The old king had needed him, and he had served that great monarch gladly. But when Cern ascended, it became clear that Restarn's daughter needed him just as much.

Bolah placed before him a short cup that matched the cylinder, and gestured for him to continue.

"Tell me," Natun said, "who has spoken to you about the queen. The Consort, perhaps?"

She snorted, amusement and irritation across her aged face. "You think I live this well…" she gestured around the room, "because I am the village minstrel?"

"No," he muttered, his lips moving over his teeth again. "These are hard times, cousin. If my words come edged, it is because I am…" He inhaled, let it out slowly. "Afraid."

She seemed moved by his confession. He met her eyes, hoping that she would read there his desperation.

"You think the Consort would speak to me, but not to the queen's seneschal?" she asked gently.

"He doesn't trust me."

"Ah."

"It's not my fault," Natun said, feeling he must explain. "He's Cohort." Natun thought of young Emand's fall so many years ago, and Yandesa, sent back to House Kincel to die. Pohut's body on the king's audience chamber floor, which of course had fallen to Natun to clean up. "In the Cohort, too much trust is deadly."

So many of them, gone so young.

She nodded. "I can tell you this: The Houses maneuver early for control of the Charter Courts. They see the opportunity…" She paused, as if weighing her words. "For circumstances to shift."

*Circumstances.*

The queen's fragile rule, Bolah meant, made more fragile by Cern's recent withdrawal. It was too early in the pregnancy for this.

"They test for weak boards in the fence," Bolah added.

He knew who she meant. Risen fast and harsh, Innel sev Cern esse Arunkel, his brother's lifeblood on his hands, and now a House Etallan head as well, an act that Etallan would not forgive or forget. Innel took great risks. He made great enemies.

"Strong, for a weak board," Natun said. "The mining shipments are back on schedule. The rebellions are quelled."

"Do these not count in his favor?"

"Some say he takes credit that is not his," Natun replied.

"The battle of Otevan? The Teva treaty? Surely those are his to claim?"

Natun spread his hands. "Others say that General Lismar Anandynar brokered the treaty, while Innel lay wounded in his tent. But we cannot know the truth."

"We cannot," agreed Bolah.

Natun looked down at his hands on the table, a fair match to her own, a map of the hills and valleys and landmarks of age.

How many palace doors had these hands opened? How many ambassadors had he placated with some gesture, royals soothed as he pointed out a tapestry or sculpture as they waited to see the monarch?

From secrets to dispatches, from quills to trays, keys to coins, Natun had carried anything and everything that could not be entrusted to mere servants, his hands conveying some of the most important affairs of the Anandynar royals.

A shepherd, that's what he was, shepherding the

monarchy across days and decades, from the blood-red and ebony-black robes of state to the pages of the Histories. It was not too much to say, were he of a mind to boast, that some of the things he had touched on behalf of the monarchy had great consequence.

As this one might.

Unless he was wrong. Could he be wrong?

Just yesterday Natun had seen a second doctor rush into the queen's quarters. Later that day, to his shock, Natun himself had been excluded from the quarter.

Bolah poured from the steaming tea cylinder into his cup, a slight trembling in her aged hand.

No, he was right.

"The queen," he said.

"Trouble with the pregnancy?"

Natun blinked slowly, forcing his breath to be steady. The work of a lifetime, this cultivation of a controlled demeanor.

"What do you mean?"

"I only guess, cousin. You would not be here if it were not so very important."

His voice dropped. "In times past, the Consort has come to you to secure the services of the High One called Keyretura."

"I cannot say."

"I was not asking. I know who is in the palace and who is not, and mages are no exception." He took a breath. "My service to the crown, Bolah—my life's work, if anything is. That High One healed Sachare sev Cern after she stood between our queen and certain death. We need him to be close by, in Yarpin, so that when the Consort realizes that he needs a mage to save the queen, it will not be..." his mouth moved silently, struggling to force out the words. "Too late."

*Too late.* The queen dead, no named heir, no child, no

succession—at best a political melee among the royals. At worst, the Houses would begin to think the unthinkable.

No. At worst, it could be the end of his beloved country, Arunkel.

"Send for him," Natun urged.

"You want a mage of Keyretura's standing *sent for*?"

Natun made a vague gesture. "Petitioned, then? However it is done."

Illegally, was how it was done. If it came out that the queen's seneschal had initiated this—no. He must seem irreproachable. Hence this visit.

Bolah gestured. "Drink, cousin. A fine brew. It will not stay warm forever."

"What does?" he muttered, putting the tea cup to his lips.

A subtle, many-layered taste met his tongue. He sighed in satisfaction at this salutary pleasure. There seemed to be fewer and fewer of them as the years piled up, the reward for long life a kind of curse. His joints ached. He moved slowly. Names he knew sometimes flitted away like uncatchable butterflies.

He looked down into the small bits of leaves at the bottom of the cup. "I never expected to serve so long. Does it not seem astonishing to you, cousin, what we have survived?"

She snorted gentle agreement.

He thought of the closed door to the queen's quarters, of what might yet happen. "Sometimes I wish…"

"Yes?"

"Green pastures on which to roam. Flowers. Grasses, where I might eat my fill, without being milked quite so… vigorously. Do you ever wish for such things?"

"Until my clients stop pressing embarrassingly large purses upon me, I can hardly turn them away." She eyed him. "The Anandynars have asked much of you."

"It is my work, to be asked much of."

"Released to green pastures," she mused, staring distantly. "It would need to be a very long way away, to be sure we were not drawn back into service. When I think of how much we both know…" She shook her head. "There are many ways not to be milked, cousin. We must take care to be sure it is to pastures we are being led, and not the butcher's table."

He nodded glumly. For a time they sat together in silence.

His thoughts circled. What would his life be about, in a world where the only daughter of the great king Restarn died with her unborn child still within?

Nothing. His life would be about nothing.

His chest felt tight, and his swallow was painful. He blinked, snuffled, scowled, then looked around the room, seeing little. Eyes damp, his gaze returned to meet his cousin's.

"We can't let her die, Bolah."

She took his hands in hers. "No, cousin. We can't."

---

"MAGES," spat the eparch of House Etallan, as if it were a curse.

Good, Tokerae thought. Better to have his mother's displeasure directed somewhere else. Anywhere else.

"Mother," he said, bowing deeply. He had not seen his mother in—had it really been months?

It had.

Tokerae keenly regretted having slept at home last night, and worse, having slept late enough that his mother could summon him before he was already gone.

He should have approached her first, months ago. He knew this. But each day his resolve rotted further.

She would demand an account of his whereabouts and actions. *Engaged in the business of the House, mother*, he would say, with a slightly affronted tone, quenching her doubt, his voice confident, his stance certain. He was eparch-heir, after all.

Now, facing her withering look, he found himself instead examining his feet. And she hadn't even spoken.

Well, the one word. *Mages.*

Tokerae regretted forgoing a swallow of wine. His reasoning had been sound—clear thought, clear breath, give her no cause for complaint. But the craving nagged. Which itself was a distraction. Next time he'd allow temptation a hand in his decision.

He made a show of examining the new set of lenses that dangled in the window facing the spring garden, spreading rainbows across the metallic filigreed walls. Lenses from House Glass, one of Etallan's vassal Houses.

Damn, but Tok's thoughts felt muddled. He cleared his throat. Mages. What could he say about the magi?

"I must assume," she said in a tone he knew presaged a cutting comment, "that you've been busy engaging with various and relevant persons these last months, your Cohort among them, and not merely indulging yourself in smoke and drink and body sweat. Have you heard anything useful, my dear son, or have you simply been improving your already impressive capacity for excess?"

*Oh, I've heard things, mother. If you knew what they say about our House—vile jokes about losing our heads, and changing our colors to dried blood.*

"Yes," he managed after a moment, hoping that was the right answer. "You'll be pleased." He took a wider stance and at last met her gaze.

She gestured for him to continue.

"Mages," Tokerae said, echoing the derisive edge of her voice, "have been seen, in-city. Black robed. Walking our streets, as if our laws mattered not at all."

She made a long, guttural sound he finally deciphered as disappointment. She strolled to the long mantel atop the wide hearth and examined a set of ten silver bells resting in a carved amardide and ebony stand. They had been bestowed upon House Etallan a generation ago by Niala esse Arunkel, the Grandmother Queen. Niala the Conqueror.

The bells had been a token of monarchical favor, one that Etallan was rightly proud of, given to commemorate the House's acquisition of the Lesser House Bell at the Charter Courts. Etallan had held House Bell ever since.

"I'm fond of these," his mother said, gracing him with a fast, bright smile that he did not for a moment mistake for affection. "So well-cast. Cleverly tuned, the set of them, to sound in harmony. A fine example to us all, don't you think?"

"Yes, mother," he said, pretty sure that was the right answer. He pushed his sluggish mind to find the trap.

She took the middle bell, shook it, cocked her head to listen. A high, pure sound filled the room, ending abruptly as she returned it to the stand. She took another, shook it—a higher sound yet—set it back again.

"Ah, but this one—this is my favorite." She took hold of the largest of the bells, turned it upside down to examine the inside. "The clapper is made of bronze, tin, and nickel, blended to achieve an unusually resonant tone." She rang it sharply, then again. The deep pealing sound hinted at multiples of tones as it echoed off the high ceilings.

With an abrupt motion, she hurled it into the unlit fireplace, the reverberating sound abruptly muffled in a puff of ash. "If I never see it again, I will be sad, Tokerae. I truly will. But…" Her smile hardened, showing teeth. "I have other bells."

Ah, that was today's game: to put him in his place. She had named him Eparch-Heir of House Etallan, but it was not etched in stone. Drawn in ash, perhaps.

They both knew that if he wanted to be eparch someday, he would play any game she put before him.

She stepped very close to him. Full grown, he topped her by a head and a half. Why did it feel the other way around?

Reaching up, she put a hand on the side of his face. From anyone else, a tender gesture. He felt dread.

"What else have you heard, my son?"

Jibes and mockery, whispered snickers. Outrageous quips.

Tokerae had been spending nights with a particular woman, named Lilsla. Her half-sister's uncle's wife worked in the palace and relayed news back down the chain to Lilsla. Tokerae had put the Cohort's royal anknapa teachings to good use, and had convinced Lilsla that she had charmed and bedazzled him beyond sense. She told him everything.

Thus Tokerae had information that he'd been saving for this very moment, to quell his mother's accusations.

"The queen," he said, in a tone he'd gained from years from the Cohort, proximity to the old king—and yes, his mother. "Is withdrawn from sight, beyond her innermost circle and a new doctor."

A troubled pregnancy for the only scion of a dead king? How ironic, if the greatest threat the Anandynars faced came from within.

Across the empire's centuries, Etallan was the only House that kept the Anandynars in check. Unsaid outside the House, but whispered within, was that but for a small accident of history, the monarchy's name would be Etallan.

Said more quietly was that this might yet be corrected.

His mother's look went blank, and he felt a dawning elation. Had he surprised her? He began to smile.

"Yes," she said. "The old doctor has been withdrawn, a second brought in, to be watched by a third. A fourth waits in the wings. Very well, you found this out on your own. I suppose it's a start. Do you know about the mutt's woman, then?"

Tokerae's smile vanished. "Rumors about Innel's women dissolve upon approach, Mother. He keeps his snake sheathed. He is exceedingly—" Clean was not the right word. As Cohort sibs, Tokerae had seen Innel grow into abilities and ambition, and Innel was nothing like clean. Rather, he managed to surround himself with people who stayed clean for him. His brother Pohut, for example, until Innel had murdered him, that act somehow forgiven by the old king.

Now the mutt was Royal Consort and Lord Commander both, and had an even greater shield to hide his stains: the queen.

For a moment, Tokerae imagined Innel's crumbling world should the queen die in childbirth. An enticing vision. "Devoted," he finished at last.

"Devoted," his mother said. "I see. What of that young woman he kept chained in a cell, then in a wagon at Otevan? The one the soldiers laughingly called his whore?"

Tokerae took a breath. "Ah," he said. "That was Innel's father's sister's child, from the slime-puddle his family crawled out of to come to Yarpin. She was spouting dirt about his father, and he wanted…" He trailed off at his mother's widening smirk. "He wanted…"

"There is no such cousin."

"Respectfully, mother. I have it from Mulack who had it direct from Innel when he spoke with him before Otevan." Tok faltered to a stop. Since when had he trusted anything

Mulack said? He felt as foolish as his mother's look said he was. He summoned irritation, waved a hand. "How can you be sure of this?"

"Because I sent people into that river valley slime-puddle to find out. My informants are better than yours. I don't fuck them. I pay them."

He felt his face go hot. "I know things from my… informant…that no amount of money could have gained me."

She snorted. "When you're older, you'll understand how much more reliable are the hard chains of coin than the slippery silks of sex."

This was not going well. Time to resort to dignified deference.

"Mother. If I have failed you in any way, allow me to make it right. Tell me what you want me to do and I will do it."

The honest annoyance on her face was an improvement. "Get yourself back to the palace. You're the queen's Cohort, damn it; they can't turn you away. I want to know what is going on."

But Tokerae heard nothing past "the palace."

He could still see his cousin's Eregin's head as it flew through the air, blood spraying across everyone who had the wretched fortune to be standing close to Innel and his impossibly fast sword.

The head bounced across the stone floor in three soft, meaty thuds. It seemed so wrong that the moment did not make a great deal more noise.

Tokerae was no stranger to such things. Old king Restarn had required Cohort education to include the observation and study of questionings and executions. There was an art to dealing death, the old king said, and they would learn it. While only the odd Putar of House Kincel was truly passionate about the subject, no one in the Cohort dared retreat from the lessons.

But not one of those experiences had made Tokerae so desperate to wipe the images from his mind.

These last months, Tokerae had consumed an astonishing variety of elixirs. Twunta and kanna were easily obtained. Seuan qualan white was much harder to find, but find it he did, then cut it paper-thin from a small, translucent brick, and tucked it up inside his cheeks. The qualan had cleared the haunting images in swirls of joy, bringing welcome relief, but it didn't last.

Then Tokerae scraped off small chunks of the green resinous floral-scented phapha into a pipe, and smoked it alongside the twunta. That helped for a time, but sleeplessness returned. He poured powdered duca and kanna into his wine.

The mix proved a potent combination. Tokerae woke to discover that he had lost whole days. Only when he saw Lilsla's expression did he realize how far he'd slipped, and that if this continued, he would never become eparch.

He stopped. The nightmares came back, along with the worst breath of his life. He considered consuming the rest of everything he had, all at once, to make it stop for good. Lilsla kept him alive.

His cousin Eregin had been an innocent man. Offered to the queen, to make right House Etallan's revealed transgression—not treason, despite the mutt's outrageous accusation.

Eregin, born to the Great House Etallan, was meant to pay for the House's overstep. He should have been imprisoned a short time in the tower, perhaps a light whipping, allowing the crown to demonstrate her displeasure. That was how such things were properly handled, giving everyone a chance to save face, to reset the balance. The offering should have been accepted and honored.

Instead, Innel had murdered the man in front of his family and the queen. House Etallan was shamed beyond measure.

Tokerae had burned the clothes he'd worn that day. He still felt the smear of Eregin's blood on his face, and washed obsessively. Every night, mid-sleep, he woke from the nightmare. The headless body, the knees buckling, the torso crumpling to the stone floor like some slaughtered animal.

"Yes, Mother," he said bleakly, belatedly.

"He's not going to lop your head off right there in the hallway," his mother snapped, too clearly reading his thoughts.

"No?" Tokerae demanded. "What would stop him?"

His eparch-mother's expression went dark. "Eregin was not my heir. That is a line even the mutt dare not cross. It would be war." She exhaled slowly, banking—not dousing—her fury. Tokerae found it oddly comforting that his eparch-mother might consider his death less acceptable than his cousin's. "Get yourself back in play, boy. Pull your tail out from between your legs and start sniffing some palace ass."

*Palace.*

What a strange procession they had made that day, his family shuffling their way out of the palace, down the front steps, to where the sun shone hot and bright on the ground. Nothing rushed in any of their motions. Nothing to reveal dishevelment or lack of dignity.

Nothing but a dripping head, held tight in his father's chalk-white grip.

"Go and make nice with your Cohort siblings," his mother was saying as the familiar images played through Tokerae's mind. "Find out if our ransomed Sutarnan has recovered enough wits to tell us what happened at Garaya.

I'm going to punish those putrid traitors, the moment we have things in hand."

*Things in hand.*

At the bottom of the palace steps, his father dropped the head, bent double, and began to retch. His mother gave him a disgusted look and snapped at Tokerae to pick it up.

Such a simple thing. He meant to obey. He told himself to. Step forward, reach down, grab the hair of his cousin's head.

But as his father continued to spew bits of food, Tokerae felt frozen. Eregin's face stared up at him, one eye bizarrely open and the other shut, as if winking at him in some shared grisly joke.

His mother had been furious. The eparch of the most powerful Great House of the Arunkel empire, who had named him eparch-heir, was displeased with him.

That had not changed.

"The woman he had in chains at Otevan," his mother was now saying. "Is she the seer everyone was talking about? Is that what the cursed dog Innel thought he had?"

Innel, fool enough to believe in fortune tellers?

"He knows better than to credit such things."

"Does he? You've proven you don't know him nearly as well as you think. Who said, 'Best we go to Cern, before she sends for us'? Who said, 'She's my Cohort sister—she'll understand'? And we carried Eregin home in pieces."

His father had slowly stood, wiped his mouth with the back of his hand, and picked up Eregin's head again by the thick mop of hair. Only that morning his cousin had been pressed into a carriage for the family's hastily arranged audience with the queen.

"The rain of gold at Otevan," his mother said. "No trivial magic, that. Who arranged for magi to be there? It's time we had one of our own. Find us one."

"What? Me?" Tokerae squeaked.

"You want to be eparch, start earning your place at my table."

*Start earning?* He considered the years in the Cohort, the agonizing and careful work of befriending Innel, the dangerous travel to Otevan and back—all at his eparch-mother's direction. He swallowed angry words.

"Be discreet," she continued. "The royals embarrass themselves. The palace might as well be an inn for mages. Revolting."

"I understand, mother." Not really—he didn't have the first idea of how to hire a mage. Not quite the sort of thing he could ask his Cohort sibs over drinks. "Perhaps I can even find one less expensive than our new foundry." A small joke.

"Don't be a fool," she snarled. "No cheap mages. Find us the best."

"How am I to know that?" Frustration leaked into his tone.

"Discuss with those who know, eparch-heir. Find out who they recommend but can't obtain. That's who we want."

Reveal his House's intention to break Arunkel law?

No, just his own. She was dangling him out in the wind, giving him the risk. If he failed, she could disown him. But if he succeeded…

"And Innel's woman," she said. "What does she look like? I want a portrait. Where is she? Find out."

His mother inspected him for flaws as if he was a black-market iron ingot. "And I don't care that you sleep with trash, boy, but this fixation on one piece of it makes you look like trash yourself. Spread your seed. If you can't find legs to spread, I will arrange them for you."

With a sick feeling, he realized that his mother knew exactly who Lilsla was.

"I don't need you to find whores for me, mother."

"I am gratified to hear it. Now go."

He held his breath and his tongue until he had left and was well on his way back to his own room, where a carafe of wine waited. He wondered how much of it he would need to wash away the taste of his mother.

———

TOKERAE STOOD outside the front door of the Boar and Bull.

*Go on in*, he told himself. Having anticipated his own reluctance, he had refused himself drink until now. Desire nagged. *There's drink within.* Yet there he stood, hand on the door.

Then he remembered the bell in the fireplace.

The door yielded to his press. He took the outer hallway to the back room, which the Cohort had long ago dubbed the Pig's Ass. He leaned on that heavy, familiar door a moment, composed himself, took a breath, and pushed inside.

The table was full of Great House scions.

"Well, well," said Taba--the only woman there, and one of the few to finish out the Cohort's formal and final years. Her captain's green-and-blue jacket stretched across wide shoulders. A smile showed teeth. She and her cousin Fadrel-- away at sea--had been House Helata's presence in the Cohort.

"Look what's staggered into the barn." This from Mulack, Eparch-Heir of House Murice. Mulack's hands, thick with rings, were held high in a dramatic gesture, a smoldering reed tucked between two fingers. His starched white double-folded cuffs set off rich purple sleeves. Murice—House of Dye and Weave—was proud of their colors, and Mulack's clothes were always immaculate. He let out a long, loud belch.

Tokerae smirked, nodded at Taba, gave a head tilt to the brothers Dil and Putar of House Kincel, in their beige and dark gray colors. Thinking better of it, he gave a nearly respectful inclination to Putar, the oddest of their Cohort sibs, in deference to his new position as assistant Minister of Justice.

The last of them was Ilmach del House Passare. Nearly as tall as Tokerae, who still loomed above his Cohort sibs, Ilmach's Passare grays and greens were mottled with road dirt. "Business," Ilmach said, answering Tokerae's wordless question.

Business between Passare and Kincel, he meant. Passare's Roads, bridges, and wayhouses, and Kincel's stone and brothels. Their business was as old as the empire.

It had occurred to Tokerae the other night, while twirling Lilsla's curls of honey-colored hair around his fingers, that Cohort was nothing except business. No moment unguarded, no word that did not affect future arrangements, understandings, and contracts. The trick was to make it seem personal.

To business, then.

Tokerae found an open chair, doing his best to act as if the scrutinizing looks of his Cohort sibs meant nothing. He leaned his long frame back in the chair and took the full mug to his right, which happened to be Mulack's, and downed it entirely, earning a sour look from the smaller man, who snapped fingers at a servant, who obediently loped off.

Taba put her wide hands on the table. "We thought perhaps your esteemed mother was keeping you abed a time, to recover from your shock." Her smile deepened the taunt.

"I've had business to attend to," Tokerae said, hoping his forceful tone might carry across the emptiness of the statement.

Mulack gave him a raised eyebrow. "A side-gig as an

anknapa?"

"Taste-master for Elupene's twunta crop?" Taba asked, following Mulack's lead.

Mulack tapped ash from his reed into a small plate, then took a drag. "Food. Drink. Smoke. Why do our Elupene sibs not host us for tastings?"

"Armand died in that fall, remember?" said Ilmach.

"Not exactly clever, dueling on the palace roof," said Dil.

"Sutarnan was only half Elupene, anyway," Taba said. "A mess, they say."

"Lucky to be alive," said Dil.

"Ransom, not luck," Mulack said, waving the pungent reed in two fingers. "A child of two Houses—Garaya would be foolish to pluck a hair from his head, with what each one is worth."

"What you say makes no sense." This from Putar, who stared at them, his tone prim. "As Eparch Heir, Tokerae would never be employed to teach fornication or to opine on the quality of twunta cultivars. Your words are either foolish or erroneous."

Putar's cup, Tokerae noticed, was untouched.

"It's a joke, brother," Dil muttered.

"Explain it to me," Putar said flatly, his look falling first on his brother, then on Mulack, then on Tokerae.

A silence took the table, as fast looks assigning responsibility were tossed back and forth, finally settling on Dil, who looked distinctly uncomfortable.

Putar almost never came to these gatherings, which could be because he was rarely invited. In years past, the Cohort had managed the odd Putar by the simple means of ignoring him.

Then Cern esse Arunkel had made the mutt the Lord Commander and Royal Consort, and Innel—in a move that was either stunningly clever or deadly stupid—had made

Putar assistant Minister of Justice. The Minister of Justice oversaw criminal assessments and executions.

Putar's knack for unsettling even his Cohort sibs was now backed by this newly minted power. From the looks on the others' faces, Tokerae suspected that they were musing on how astonishingly creative and breathtaking the last few executions had been. No one wondered if Putar had a hand in designing them. His touch was obvious.

Dil, well on his way to becoming House Kincel's official palace liaison, due to his agreeable and diplomatic nature, put a casual touch on Putar's arm.

Suddenly Putar gave his brother's hand a great deal of attention. Dil snatched it back, cleared his throat. "We have all, ah, heard that Tokerae has been sexing and imbibing rather a lot since the… " he looked sideways at Tokerae, "event."

"The event? What event? You mean the beheading?" Putar asked. He waved a hand around the table. "This is exactly what's always been wrong with the Cohort: words get stuck in your throats behind your gaudy, jeweled chokers. It's as if you can't think at all. I suspect inbreeding."

A new silence settled on them all. Taba was grinning, as if this were a great joke. Mulack tongued and sucked at his teeth, as if trying to dislodge a seed. Ilmach looked around the table, eyebrows raised.

Behind Putar's back, Dil gestured urgently at Mulack's servant, who had just returned with a carafe of wine. The servant allowed Dil's motions to sway him from his intended target, his master, Mulack. Dil took hold of the servant's sleeve in one hand, downed his drink with the other, and gestured for a refill.

Tokerae could well imagine that being Putar's brother might make intoxicants necessary. He himself wanted more. A lot more.

Mulack, his empty cup held high, growled at his servant, who pretended not to notice as he filled the mug and fled. Mulack moved the full cup to the side away from Tokerae.

All this was, Tokerae reflected, probably not quite what his mother had meant when she told him to make nice with the Cohort. He took a deep breath, readying himself to speak. That was all it took: he had everyone's attention.

"Well," he began, "Yes. I've been…Some indulgences were…" he worked his mouth, "necessary."

While Mulack was momentarily looking elsewhere, and Tokerae demonstrated the length of his arm by reaching across him to again take his drink. Tokerae sipped the thick, dark red liquid, nodding appreciatively, and gave Mulack an abbreviated toast.

Mulack scowled and shouted at his departed servant. "Two carafes. Hells, make it three."

"Indulgences?" Putar asked, giving Tokerae an unwavering stare. "Do you mean sex and drugs, yes? Or is there something else?"

In a stage-whisper, Dil said to his brother: "You do know he's Etallan's eparch-heir, right?"

"So?"

This was all getting a bit out of control. Tokerae decided to try Putar's direct approach.

"Putar doesn't care who the eparch-heir is," Tokerae said, smiling, "Because he will, eventually, oversee all our executions."

While everyone digested this unsettling notion, Putar asked, with sudden and startled surprise, "Is that what this is about? What, you think being polite to me now will change anything about how you die?"

It was Putar's astonished expression that did it. Taba, who had just taken a mouthful of ale into her mouth, sprayed it across the table, the wet of it managing to reach all the way to Tokerae's face. Mulack choked on whatever was in his throat. For a moment, Dil held tight to his composure, his face twisting in failing control, then he broke into snickers. Ilmach began the donkey-bray laugh that he was famous for.

In moments, Mulack was wheezing for air, pointing at Putar's deeply confused expression, and Taba was flat-out bellowing, pounding her now quite empty mug on the table. Around the table, all the Cohort sibs save Putar were helplessly in the grip of loud mirth.

Tokerae was not immune. He wiped his nose, snorting as the tide of humor rose, crested, and began to ease. It had been a long time since he'd laughed like this. It almost made him miss the Cohort.

A wide-eyed servant at the doorway—Dil or Putar's, from the livery—looked to see what the noise was about, then quickly backed out.

As the laughter died down, Mulack raised his mug. "To our brother Putar, may his great and noble art amuse us all into our quite doddering old ages."

"To Putar!"

"Huzzah!"

"Old age!"

Dil smiled, but his eyes were on his brother and edged with concern. Even Dil was not confident that his blood ties would protect him from his brother.

With the release of tension, Tokerae judged it a good time to test the waters.

"While we're toasting," Tokerae said, "let's drink to our sister and queen: Cern esse Arunkel and her winter child." He raised his mug. Everyone followed.

"The queen!"

"The heir!"

Did they know the rumors about Cern's troubled pregnancy? If they did, they hid it well.

Tokerae smiled even more widely, and raised his mug again. "And the Lord Commander, hero of Otevan and quencher of rebellions."

The table stuttered to silence. Tokerae licked his lips, feeling out the looks, not entirely liking the temperature.

"Look here," he said, gesturing around the table. "We're all Cohort—we understand: Innel did what he had to do. I don't…" Could he pull this off? He let some small splash from the ocean of fury he felt slip out as a short, bitter laugh. "What choice did he have? Standing in his place, I would have done the same." He smiled wryly. "Were I as good a swordsman, that is. What a stroke that was, eh?"

His stomach churned sourly. It took all his years of Cohort training to pull off this act.

But they looked convinced, easing back into the usual guarded, sardonic expressions.

Except for Putar, who was nodding with rare enthusiasm. "Yes! I heard all about it from the guards, but they don't have Cohort eyes. Fates, I wish I'd seen it. What I'd give…" His eyes were hard and bright on Tokerae. "They told me—" he shook off Dil's quelling hand—"told me not to ask you. As if you were a child of delicate sensibilities. An impossible cut! What did Innel do? Describe it to me, Tok."

Tokerae swallowed bile, the sharp pain in his stomach clearing his head. He met Putar's hungry look.

"No."

Tokerae heard his own breath, felt his pulse speed. For a long moment, the Eparch-Heir of House Etallan and the probable future Minister of Justice locked hard gazes. Whatever it was that Putar saw in his face, it was enough; Putar looked away, his features etched in disappointment.

Dil exhaled slowly in relief, gave Tokerae a tiny, apologetic eyebrow raise.

"But never mind all that," Tokerae said, struggling to

recover the semblance of his previous joviality. "I've been remiss, not keeping company with you, my good sibs. Now that we're all achieving our positions, we should be working together."

"How do you mean?" Ilmach asked.

"The Charter Courts are coming," Tokerae said.

Mulack favored this with a long belch. "The Charter Courts are always coming."

"Or have just come," Putar said, annoyed. "They happen every fifteen years. No one should be surprised."

"Even so," Tokerae said. "Much is possible this time that might have not always been."

"I can stomach no more of these mush words," Putar said, standing. "You cannot seem to speak clearly."

Dil sighed heavily, looking as if he'd far prefer to stay, but he stood, too, and followed Putar with a longing glance back, then the two of them were gone.

"How interesting, Tok," Mulack said, stubbing out his reed, and sorting through his mugs and glasses, sniffing at the smallest of them. "Do continue."

Tokerae considered the four Great Houses represented here.

Mulack was uncontested Eparch-Heir of House Murice. Mulack's eparch-mother, unlike Tokerae's, seemed to have no desire to put his title in question, a certainty Tokerae envied.

Taba had steadfastly refused to take any title beyond ship's captain, but it was widely known that she held far more sway in House Helata than the position would imply.

Ilmach's eparch-father had yet to name an heir, but Ilmach was steady and sensible and was widely seen as his father's first choice for House Passare.

And Tokerae intended to be Etallan's eparch, his mother's bells notwithstanding.

He looked earnestly at each of them as he calculated the

connecting forces between their Houses. The understandings and compromises. The long-held grudges.

"Since the last Courts, we've all reached our majority. The next is a scant handful of years hence. Must we bicker among ourselves? Do we really need the crown to adjudicate our struggles, as if we were unruly children? We are the most powerful Cohort in three generations. Surely we can agree among ourselves who will take each contract, and ratify the Lesser Houses without help. For that matter, perhaps it's time to reconsider the institution itself."

That last was a step too far. He could tell from their faces.

"Funny," Taba said, though for a change, she wasn't smiling.

"Etallan feeling a royal chill?" asked Mulack.

Tokerae shook his head. "We all feel it. When we fight over the Charters, no one wins."

"Except the Houses that actually do," Taba said. She shut her eyes, then opened them to slits, staring at Tokerae. "Which might not be Etallan, this time, hmm? But I have the idea you're leading somewhere. Go on."

Tokerae exhaled, spread his long fingers atop the table, looking at the one ring he wore, the one with the emblem of his house, bright brass worked into black silver. "Innel."

"Ah," said Mulack, punctuating it with a shrug. "Seems to be doing serviceable work. Got her pregnant, which was surely his first duty."

Taba gave a dismissive snort. "For a boy to make a pup is a moment's distraction."

"Not so clear with the Anandynars," Ilmach said.

A few years ago, that statement would have been whispered. Times were indeed changing.

Mulack made a hurry-up gesture. "Get to it, Tok."

"The mutt has too much to do," Tokerae said. "He cannot hold all the fish he's netted. Overwhelmed.

Distracted. All his convoluted treaties. I blame the hard knock to the head he took at the battle of Otevan."

"What hard knock?" Ilmach asked.

Tokerae shrugged. "I see no other explanation. Best education in the empire and all he's done since Otevan is talk and look under the bed for monsters. Why is the actual treason of Garaya allowed to stand? Where is the force of the crown?"

"And yet," Mulack said, "The rails are no longer under attack, and your House's ore is flowing. Yes?"

Tokerae waved this away. "Nothing to do with Innel. Confidence in the monarchy, with the queen about to produce an heir. Meanwhile, the borderlands grow arrogant, while the mutt invents treasons, and spies on his Cohort sibs, instead of holding the provinces to account."

"Spies on you, you mean," said Taba.

"All of us," Tokerae said firmly.

"Perhaps Etallan got off easy, all things considered," Mulack said.

Tokerae's tamped down the rage he felt. "I was splattered with my kinsman's death-blood," he said. "The mutt derided my House's colors. My House's colors! What price did you pay for similar work, House Murice?" He looked at Taba. "House Helata? Do you remember what we said to each other in the amardide forests, beyond all hearing?"

Taba's lips thinned, her eyes flashed.

No, this was wrong—he must shift to another path, if he wanted cooperation.

With effort, he steadied his breathing, adjusted his tone. "He killed my cousin, siblings. No minor insult. What happens the next time the mutt is allowed to decide the queen's justice with the stroke of a blade? Who in your House will suffer a bloody humiliation?"

"Do you know something, Etallan?" Taba asked softly.

He met her look. "Nothing was said to implicate you, Helata. Not a word." Though saying that now implied plenty, which from her ugly expression was clear to her as well.

Well, he was in it now. Might as well go all the way.

"Let me be blunt, brothers and sister: the mutt does not understand the business of the realm as we do. Doesn't have our history. Our investment. This common, House-less man, who has impregnated our queen, who looks for plots everywhere—give him a chance and he'll put his clumsy fingers into the already tangled Charters Courts—you know he will—and make of them a disaster." Then, slowly, and with a look at each of them. "If we let him."

Ilmach sat back, arms crossed, watching intently.

A noncommittal sound issued from Mulack's throat. "And you suggest…what?"

"Encourage him to keep his focus on the queen. Pleasing her in the bedroom. Smoothing the way for the child. Rather than putting his nose in our business." Tokerae dropped his voice. "Our time is coming, siblings. Day by day our Houses hand the reins to us. If we are not allied in purpose, we will be divided, and more House blood will flow."

"Prophecy, brother?" laughed Mulack.

"Simple observation of evidence. But if we work together…look up, my friends." He gestured overhead at box beams and a grime-speckled, whitewashed ceiling. "This cannot hold us. We break through. We rise above." There, that was suitably picturesque, yet deniably unspecific.

He searched the faces around the table, far more sober than the multitudes of near-empty glasses, mugs, and ashtrays would suggest. Tokerae's words were landing.

He reached again for Mulack's drink. This time, the eparch-heir of House Murice spread his hands wide in a gesture of welcome.

## Chapter Four

THE DAY that Amarta escaped the capital city of the Arunkel empire was beyond strange.

What she had done at Otevan was beyond anything she could have imagined. In a rain of gold, she had saved the Lord Commander's life and reputation, and averted the full-out slaughter of his queen's army by the smaller Teva force. She had sat by his side as he lay dying, and told him why he must live.

Returning to the capital, he allowed Amarta to ride a horse rather than inside a windowless guarded wagon.

She saw it in his look. Something like respect.

But his gratitude would only stretch so far. Amarta had no hope that he would willingly release her, not after he'd worked so many years to get her in hand.

Amarta returned to a locked, guarded palace room, and resolved herself to spend her life here. He might let Dirina and Pas visit, at least.

Then, one morning, she glimpsed a hairline crack in the future. Thin as breath, unlikely as a falling star in the midday sun. A tangled bramble of timing.

It couldn't work.

It might.

Now, she told her guards, somehow persuading them to take her to see him. At the Lord Commander's office, Srel was just bowing out of the room a group in brown and gray livery. Srel gave her a warm smile, held her with a gesture, slipped inside, then ushered her within.

"Seer," Innel said, surprised. "Come in. What is it?"

She knew that she must be bold. Hesitation would cut the gossamer strand instantly. A wrong word would dissolve the chance.

"My freedom from the contract, Lord Commander," she said, straddling the future and the present, a tenuous hold on both. *Flickers of light and darkness, of blood and death.* "Release me. It will be worth a great deal to you to have done so."

He was silent for a long moment. He looked at her, then at the far wall, where a floor-to-ceiling map showed the Arunkel empire and the Perripin lands south. He looked again at her.

The future did not reassure. It was still unlikely, and reason told her that he would never free her from the contract. Why should he?

Then he did.

She had nothing to pack and no reason to delay. Her most precious things were Dirina and Pas, and despite everything—the years of running from this very man and his hirelings—despite the freedom that now opened to them— Dirina refused to leave this man named Nalas.

Amarta made every argument, every one that foresight could provide. Dirina would not budge.

Innel might still change his mind. Amarta could not wait.

So it was that hours later Amarta sat atop a beautiful bay

mare that Innel had given her, and took the blue-and-white seashell that he handed up to her, which she had thought lost forever: her mother's last gift.

Then, in a moment odder than any she could remember, the Lord Commander of the Arunkel empire asked her what he could offer her to make her stay.

"Name it," he said.

"I want to be free of all this." Free of him. Free of Arunkel.

And she left. She rode south. With each step away from the capital, she felt liberated from Innel sev Cern esse Arunkel and free of the empire and its grip.

No longer hunted. She could go anywhere, do anything. Find out what she was.

This freedom was a glorious feeling, unlike any she had ever known.

It lasted a day.

---

AMARTA WAS NOT likely to ever forget the moment she sealed the contract with Tayre.

*To learn to live in the world. To understand yourself.*

Along with Maris and her apprentice Samnt, they rode south. Tayre soon dropped back and followed at such a distance that Amarta often lost sight of him. Maris was taciturn with Amarta and impatient with Samnt.

Something, Amarta gathered, had happened between Maris and Tayre. But what?

The trip was long and quiet, and Amarta saw little of the man who was now contract-bound to her.

At Maris's land, Tayre stayed outside the mage's boundary wardstones. Amarta followed Maris and Samnt into the house atop the hill.

Amarta stood in the doorway of the room that she had shared with Dirina and Pas, and wondered what they were doing now in Arunkel. Waiting in some guarded room for Nalas to visit, when he was not too busy being the Arunkel Lord Commander's second? Was Pas being forced to wear the empire's colors? A fury began to swirl inside her. They would have been safe here.

A soft footstep behind her was Maris.

"End the contract, Amarta."

Memory served up a flash of Tayre's hand on hers, their palms touching, a nals coin between. Then the ritual reversal, Amarta's hand on top, the coin in his. The contract made, mage-witnessed, as sacred and secure as a contract could be.

"What?" Amarta asked, stunned. "I only just made it, Maris. You witnessed."

"Witnessed and regretted. Be free of him, Seer."

"No. Why do you say this?"

"I know what he did to you. It is written in the bones of your body."

Almost involuntarily, Amarta's left hand made a fist. She held it to her thigh protectively.

"You don't. You weren't there."

Maris's gaze went distant, and Amarta felt a warmth go through her. The mage had healed her once, years ago, and Amarta recognized the crawling sensation she felt now.

"Stop it," Amarta hissed.

The magic invasion into Amarta's body ceased.

Maris gestured at her fingers. "Let me heal what he has broken."

"No."

"Amarta, listen to me—"

"No!" Amarta tore past Maris and out of the house, descending the hill on foot, to find Tayre's camp.

"I COULD STAY HERE WITH YOU," she said to him.

Tayre secured an oilskin tarpaulin between trees. Large insects hummed in the brush from under broad-leafed trees. Southern Perripur—the wet season. It would rain again soon.

He crouched down, setting large stones into a ring for a cookfire. "That won't improve her regard for me."

"Let's go somewhere else."

He rocked back onto his heels to look at Amarta. "You've been on the road a long time, Seer. Running. Hiding. A mage's protection is not to be discarded lightly. Take it, Amarta. Rest a while."

"For how long?"

A soft chuckle. "Until you are rested."

An infuriated orange-and-yellow bird chattered loudly from a high branch, then launched into the air in a flutter of wings. One tiny, bright orange fluff drifted down to the ground between them. Amarta picked up the small feather. Above, the bird winged south. She watched with longing.

"I have never traveled," she said softly, "but to run."

To flee him, but no need to say that.

"Let the mage care for you. Sleep in a bed while you can."

She stared back at him, wondering what the contract between them meant.

He studied her in return. A slow smile infused his expression and Amarta felt as if the sun caressed her cheek.

"I will be here when you return, Seer."

His words and smile took her breath away, her emotions plucked as if she were a lute.

AMARTA DID AS TAYRE ADVISED, and slept in the mage's house, watching as Samnt began his apprenticeship.

If Amarta had ever imagined what it would be like, a mage's apprenticeship, it would have been nothing like this.

Hours would pass, Maris and Samnt sitting together in silence. They would take slow, wordless walks. Maris rarely spoke. When she did, her tone was sharp, impatient. Samnt must learn to read. He must learn to speak a new language. He must focus.

She wondered if the young man were surprised, or mystified, at the exacting and harsh Maris he saw now, if the mage seemed as strange to him as she did to Amarta.

One night, Amarta was woken by voices through the wall. Samnt's voice was high-pitched, nearly hysterical. Maris's reply was low, implacable.

Amarta slept more than she would have thought possible. Tayre had been right: she was bone-deep exhausted, and found herself shocked at how many hours each day she could spend in slumber.

But some nights she awoke in the dark, with a start, from dreams where a terrifying shadow waited in the bush. His face was hidden, but she knew who he was.

Who he had been.

Each morning, she left, and with each step down the steep road, she felt excitement tinged with apprehension. Past the wardstones, a right at the wild Tamarind, she would take the game trail through colorful snarls and weaves of Perripin jungle, across a footbridge that spanned a small, fast brook. There she would find the clearing of moss and fern where Tayre made his camp.

She refused to look into the future to know if he would be there. She needed to see it with her own eyes.

Each time that she saw Horse grazing and Tayre beyond, cooking or repairing some item, relief washed over her.

THE SUN HAD JUST TOPPED the high eastern rise, turning the overhead canopy into a glowing, emerald green. Amarta settled herself on a half-log to watch Tayre prepare food. She'd timed it just right: he was just scraping food from a pan onto two plates.

Two plates. It filled her with an absurd joy.

They ate in an easy silence. Overhead, three long-necked birds trumpeted loudly, winging their way west.

West. To Senta? To Free Port and Kelerre? Some island across the Nelar Ocean?

Bit by bit Amarta's exhaustion had eased, and Tayre's many and fascinating stories took hold inside her, weaving vivid tales of mountains and cities, of the *magi-khrastos*—the mages' great works—across the world. She learned the Perripin language.

She would tell him that she was rested and ready to travel. He spoke first.

"There is something you should know."

A tingle of dread trickled through her.

"What?"

"How to end this contract."

Her mouth dropped open.

He held up a finger, a second one, then a third. "Say three times: 'I release you.' Then the contract is over, and we are both free of the bond. Do you understand?"

She dropped her spoon onto the plate full of food, and put it aside, appetite gone.

"Why do you tell me this?"

"It is your contract to begin, yours to end."

She stood, feeling inexplicably wounded. He followed her with his eyes. "I don't want to end it."

"You might, someday."

"No."

His eyebrows rose. "Is that a prediction?"

When she did not answer, he took another bite, chewing and swallowing as he watched her. "You must know how to end it."

"Or you could," she snapped back. "It's only a nals coin."

"You asked how long," he said. "Do you remember?"

She nodded, her feelings tangled.

"I said, 'As long as you need me. Until you release me.'"

He continued to eat, as if nothing had happened.

Confused, she sat again, and attempted another bite. He began to tell her a story, in Perripin, about the One, how it broke apart to become the Many, spinning off the Great Worms. The dragon sun, the serpent moon. Before she knew it, she had finished the food. So vividly did he speak that she was captivated and entirely forgot the earlier conversation, until the end of the day, as the sun set, and she walked up the hill to Maris's house.

A comfortable house that was nothing like a home.

Amarta thought of the farm woman who had taken them in for a time, and how at peace Amarta had felt. She remembered the dark halls of Kusan—the hidden city—and the warmth of the Emendi there who had given them sanctuary.

So elusive and fragile, that feeling of belonging. She wondered if she would know it again.

To this half-question, vision attempted answer. A din of splashes, many of them loud, none of them clear. She stopped on the steep road, trying to sort the images into sense.

Finally, in disgust, she brushed it all away, like the small biting flies that had come out with the dusk to swarm around her.

THE MILD PERRIPIN SPRING WARMED, then warmed some more. The land turned hot with summer, the muggy breeze scented with jasmine and lock-vine.

She gained competence with the Perripin language. Tayre taught her a simpler language, one of subtle taps and finger signs. She watched his hands move like a dance.

Fascinated and inspired, she was about to show him some of the Emendi signs that she had learned in Kusan. Her hands were raised when she froze, alarm coursing through her, her pulse speeding.

It took her a long moment to understand why.

He was the reason that she and Dirina and Pas had fled Kusan, abandoned what could have been their home. Him.

Hands lowered, she sat down heavily on the half-log. She felt shaken.

For a time he said nothing. Then he resumed the lesson.

LATE ONE AFTERNOON, feeling bold, Amarta left the mage's house with her bedroll tucked under her arm.

She had timed her departure so that the mage's attention would be deep on Samnt, so Maris scowled at Amarta as she walked through the main room, but did not break whatever mysterious teaching she was engaged with to voice objection.

Nor did Tayre say anything when Amarta laid out her bedroll near his.

Hope dawned as the sun set in a wash of fruit-orange and blood red. Fronds and leaves and vines lost their emerald brilliance, tree trunks turning to washed-out browns and greens against the night's black. The stars came out.

A thin crescent moon hung amid wisps of clouds. The

Serpent Moon, spun to its monthly finest. Near it was a star, bright and lonely. If the star fell, it seemed to Amarta, the bowl of the moon would catch it.

But what if the star were heavier than the moon realized? Would the bowl shatter into a thousand pieces?

Amarta did not even notice when she drifted off, not until she woke to starlight. In her sleep she had inched closer to him, near enough to see his face, his lashes, his hand cradling his head as he slept. She watched the rise and fall of his chest, the hint of pulse at his neck, and marveled at how beautiful he was.

And how close. Close enough to touch.

What would happen, she wondered, if she reached out a finger to trace a line from under his chin, down his neck to where his shirt opened to reveal the top of his collarbone? With trepidation, she edged open the door of vision.

*His eyes opened, narrowed, as he stared at her. Flatly, without invitation.*

Stung, she rolled over on her back, feeling the cold weight of a refusal that had not even happened.

Why did he say no?

Above, the crescent moon—shattered or whole—had fled the sky.

THEY WERE NOW days out of the seaside town of Mutarka, with its puppet show and bright shells and laughing crowds. Here, high in the Shentaret mountains, they rode toward the mage's land.

As the sun began to sink in the sky, they turned the horses from the main road to take a side path that led to the banks of a hushing river. They dismounted at a stretch of sand and rocks surrounded by a tangle of madrone trees adorned with fuzzy webs of fern-vines and snap-flowers.

Tayre unpacked cheese and dried meat, set it out on the rocks for their meal.

"There must be others," Amarta said, watching him. "Not street-corner fortune tellers like that old woman, but those who are known for their seeing."

"Certainly. The Handless of Vilaros, who supposedly feel the weave of the future with their missing fingers. The Saripechi Waterfall where priests read fortunes from the stunned bodies of the fallen fish. The Heart of Seuan who is said to predict Eufalmo swarms. The Stone Lady's tears that make a map of time."

"The Monks of the Revelation," Amarta added, recalling the old woman's words. "But you don't think any of this is true."

"No."

"But if there are so many stories, there must be some truth to some of them, right?"

"Hope makes people easy to fool."

"That's so," she said, thinking of the many she had given visions to across her life, from poor villagers to rich lords, all of whom already knew the answers they wanted from her.

As they set out bedrolls, his scent wafted to her on the breeze, and she wondered how close to put hers to his.

Only then did it occur to her that when he spoke of hope, he was referring to her. Was she easy to fool, because she hoped to find others like herself?

Or did he mean that her desire for him blinded her?

He had once told her that her face was a window, her thoughts were so easy to read. If so, as he sat there, his face was a wall.

"Why will you not touch me?" she blurted. "To learn about myself and the world. Surely that should include this.

The one time that we coupled—" Or was it two times? She wasn't quite sure how such things were counted. "—that cannot have been everything I ought to know about it. Can it?"

"Not everything, no," he said, amusement in his tone. "You should learn more. A good deal more. But perhaps not with me."

"Why not with you?"

In the dark, he considered her a moment, then gestured an invitation to sit closer.

Her breath quickened. She searched the future to see if it led where she wanted to go, and found many moments in which she sat as she was now, looking into the future. While here, in the actual moment, she was still looking.

Exhaling a wordless frustration, she dismissed it all, and moved closer. Close enough to touch, but not touching.

He held out a hand, palm up, and she reached for it. Halfway there she realized that it was her left hand, the one with the fingers that he had broken. In her knuckles the ache flared.

She froze, hand in mid-air. *A dark room. Lamplight flickering on the stone walls. The hard edge of a table.* Before she could stop herself, she snatched back her hand.

His own hand returned to his leg. "Too soon. Your fear of me fades slowly, like a late spring melt."

"I'm not afraid," she said forcefully.

"No?" he asked.

"No."

Ever so slowly, slowly enough that she had plenty of time —time to refuse, to twitch, to recoil—he reached out his hand again, this time to her face, the backs of his fingers passing gently across her cheek.

A caress, light as the brush of a butterfly's wing.

She held her breath, knowing it was a test, determined to pass.

His dark eyes watched. The eyes of a hunter.

Deep inside, something trembled. She shuddered.

A rueful look crossed his face. He drew his hand back again.

"Some parts of you want my touch. Others don't. They must all agree. It needs more time."

*More time.*

Her tone dropped. "If you don't desire me, why don't you just say so, instead of talking about time?"

He took a breath, let it out slow, looked up into the dark canopy of trees. "If I agree with the premise of your question, you'll feel as though I've hit you." He thumped his sternum lightly. "But if I tell you that you're wrong, you'll fight even harder to induce me to say yes. In neither case do you have the chance to catch up to yourself."

"I don't need time. I need—" She swallowed. "That first time, you were—you were competent." Better than competent, she suspected. Those hours had been delicious. "Have you forgotten how it's done? Maybe it was just luck that you got through it at all." She chomped down on the awkward, biting words, rubbing sweaty hands on her trousers, angrily ignoring the ache in the fingers of her left hand.

"That first time," he said, slowly, as if choosing his words, "when you asked me, the contract to which I had then bound myself, and your wish, were in alignment. Now, my contract and your wish are not. At least, not yet."

*Not yet.*

Hope rose in her, as he must surely have known it would.

She shook her head, angry again. "How does this contract work, in which you are supposed to help me understand myself and the world, yet when I ask you to teach me something important, you refuse?"

He nodded. "It's a puzzle. But not every wheel can be made to turn faster. I do what I can. I do what I must."

There seemed nothing else to say.

That night she lay awake for hours, watching the halfmoon crawl across the sky. She considered wheels, seasons, and puzzles.

Finally, she inched her bedroll away. Close enough to be companionable, but not so close that the scent of him would keep her awake.

Late spring melt indeed.

MIDDAY, they reached Maris's land, crossing the ensorcelled watchstones that marked the boundary. Amarta strained to feel anything, even a tingle. But Maris had made her welcome, and the stones knew it.

Tayre could now pass only because Amarta had told Maris, before she'd left, that keeping him away meant he could not protect her if he needed to.

Still, it was not a warm welcome.

"What does it feel like?" she asked.

"A fast fall into an icy stream."

She thought of him naked and wet, but no—he'd be dressed. Wet clothes, then. The image was distracting.

They surged up the incline, eager to get to the stables they knew were there, for water and feed. Amarta and Tayre tended to them, then went into the house to unpack the supplies they had brought for Maris.

Amarta arranged various brightly colored fruit into a bowl. On the windowsill, a spider had curled up to die.

"When?" he asked. Every few hours, he asked when

Maris would return.

Absurd, this rift between them, the two most capable people Amarta knew, both powerful and clever. Until recently, there had been great good will between them.

She still remembered how Maris used to talk about him, as a friend, one she would trust with her life, and had. Maybe if the two of them would just talk—

"Amarta?"

Amarta sighed, slipped open the door to vision, watching the future solidify.

It was not what she expected.

"Something has happened on their journey back." A detour not taken, a ferry caught early…there was no way to know the cause. An unlikely occurrence, in any case.

"Oh no," she breathed.

"Do I have time to leave?"

"I don't think so."

Outside, the sound of horses answered with certainty.

"Dirina and I used to fight. But we made up, every time." Except maybe this last time, she didn't say. "You speak so well. Just talk to her."

The door banged open and in strode Maris. With a glance, she took in the room, her look staying on Tayre.

"Salt air on you both. You take her seaside, where she stands out like a diamond? Whose coin has bought you now, mercenary?" Maris demanded.

"Only hers," Tayre replied.

Amarta spoke. "It was my idea to go to Mutarka, Maris. I wanted to travel. But we are returned safe."

Samnt followed Maris into the room, his eyes flickering between his *aetur* and Tayre and Amarta. He muttered something about the horses and left.

"I'll help," Tayre said, following him out, closing the door behind him.

Maris scowled at the door.

"What of Cern and the child?" Amarta asked, hoping to focus the mage on something else.

"The entire purpose of my unpleasant journey." Maris dropped a pack on the table, and examined Amarta as she spoke. "Queen and daughter are both healthy. The eternal gratitude of Innel al Arunkel is mine."

Amarta was surprised at how much relief she felt to know that Cern and the child had both lived. "Thank you," she breathed.

Maris snorted, shrugged. "Ah, I have something for you." She tugged loose the ties on her pack and took out a large red-and-black envelope, holding it out to Amarta.

Amarta's heart sank. Could she simply refuse?

*Maris opened the envelope, began to read aloud.*

Apparently not.

Still, she delayed, turning it over and over in her hands. The paper was combed amardide textile, the ribbon a thick satin. Expensive. Probably shockingly so. She wondered how many meals the cost of this one envelope would buy.

On the front her name was made elegant by some royal calligrapher. On the other side was the black raised seal of the Arunkel monarchy. So beautiful, this carrier of grief.

At last she broke open the seal and drew out a many-folded thing, its edges dusted with gold. She stared at the script uncomprehendingly. While she could read the complex Perripin pictograms, the convoluted slashes that composed the high-form script of her homeland were still illegible.

"What does it say?" she asked in a small voice.

"It says that Dirina is to be wed to Nalas, deputy Lord Commander of the Arunkel empire. Your presence is most ardently requested."

Amarta's mouth went dry. "No."

At this, Maris chuckled a little. "So often those we care

about fail to choose their companions wisely, don't they?"

"Aristo," Amarta said, staring at the invitation. "Nalas is aristo. Dirina is common. He can't marry her."

Maris made a surprised sound. "She'll have a challenging time of it, surrounded by pompous fools and scheming clods who would doubtless agree with you, but there's nothing preventing this match."

The foreseen grief settled on Amarta like heavy snow. Her sister was marrying into the Arunkel aristocracy, but could never be one of them. While Amarta was still hoping that her sister might come to her senses, Dirina was planning to stay.

So hard. She had worked so hard, across so many years, to keep them safe. It was like losing them all over again. Her chest shuddered with a silent sob.

"Ama," Maris said more gently, "they delayed the marriage so that you could be there. I've a letter of credit for you, to fund your passage north in safety and comfort."

"No."

"I have no more love for the empire than you do, but this is Dirina. Your sister."

"She chose to stay in Arunkel in spite of all sense," Amarta said sharply. "She can marry a soldier without me, too."

Maris walked the room, her gaze momentarily on the bowl of fruit, then turned to Amarta. "Do you know what convinced me to ride to a city I loathe, to sustain a monarchy I decry? Yes, I had a letter penned by my aetur, and Innel's self-abasement was impressive. But neither of those were sufficient. Do you know what tipped the scales?"

Amarta shook her head.

"You, Amarta. Innel set you free from that wretched contract. I went because of that. I've given him three lives now, one of which is his own. He is in my debt and will not come after you again."

*Amarta suddenly remembered her own words: Release me. It will be worth a great deal to you to have done so.*

How strange to know a thing was coming, yet also know nothing about it.

"I am grateful, then," Amarta humbly.

"It grieves me to see you in another ill-conceived contract, one that I witnessed and thus must uphold."

"Maris, Innel gave Tayre his directions, yet you forgave him. How is that just?"

"No one is forgiven," Maris snapped. "But Innel does not change his loyalties with each larger stack of coins. To the mercenary you are merely a wager on the ground of some back-alley Rochi game."

Amarta shook her head in denial, but the image stung. "A single nals for the bond. What stack of coins?"

"Fates, Amarta! You don't know your own worth."

For a fleeting moment, Maris's expression opened, and Amarta thought she saw pain, then it was gone.

Suddenly Amarta nearly understood: the difference between Innel and Tayre was not who had hurt Amarta, or why. It was that Maris had never trusted Innel to begin with, but Tayre had been her friend. Maris felt betrayed.

It came to Amarta, then, how little she really knew about Maris, about her apprenticeship with the mage Keyretura. How young had Maris been?

Her empathy stirred, Amarta searched for the right words to say that she cared about Maris's pain. How to say it without being insulting? *With mages, respect first.* Was there some future in which she said the right thing? She began to foresee.

Maris's voice snapped her back. "What is he to you, Amarta? A lover?"

Amarta blushed, knew it was obvious, blushed further,

shook her head adamantly. "He is to help me learn. You witnessed the words, Maris."

"Meaningless words. I'll find you a suitable companion to warm your bed and sooth your body hungers. I should never have allowed this contract."

"What?" Amarta's empathy for the mage's pain shredded.

"You want to learn? I'll teach you."

"You? Do you mean me to be your—" What was the word? "*taslata*? Your apprentice? To study alongside Samnt?"

Maris's expression was tinged with brief pity. "You are not *udardae*, Amarta. What you are, I don't know. But not that."

Amarta felt a hardening resolve. "Not udardae. I accept this. As you must accept that I decide my fate."

"You are besotted, your judgment unsound. End this contract, Amarta, or I will."

Amarta's mouth opened in outrage. "I will not. I've barely—" Met him, she wanted to say, but that wasn't quite right. "begun."

The door opened. In stepped Samnt, setting down travel bags. Tayre followed him in.

Amarta felt the future warn. She began to look. As if she knew exactly what she was doing, Maris's words cut through.

"Watch, Amarta. Watch closely. Let me show you how weak is this man you so admire." Then, to Tayre: "Mercenary, the amount of coin that Innel al Arunkel paid you to hunt Amarta dua Seer—you must know it to the nals."

Tayre blinked.

"I will pay you twice that amount to end this contract," Maris said. "Name your price."

Amarta gaped, at her, then at him, her breath caught tight in her throat. How much coin was it that Tayre had been paid across the years, to find her? Surely a fortune.

A mage-witnessed contract should be secure. But the mage stood right here, urging him to end it.

If Maris and Tayre agreed, who would hold them to account? No one.

He wouldn't. Not for mere money. Not even for a fortune.

Would he?

He met Amarta's eyes and held her gaze a long moment. He looked back at Maris.

"No," he said.

Amarta exhaled in relief. This was clearly not the answer that Maris expected. The mage lifted her hands.

*Vision came clear: He lay on the floor, gasping.*

"Maris!" Amarta cried. "No!"

Tayre stiffened, stumbled backward, hands flat to the wall, knees buckling as he lowered himself to the floor. Unthinking, Amarta ran at Maris. She had no plan, just a driving need to make the mage stop.

All at once, everything went black. Amarta gasped, coming to a sudden awareness as she stumbled into Maris, who took her by the arm to hold her upright.

On the floor, Tayre was trembling violently. He struggled to rise, collapsed again as he convulsed.

"Stop it," Amarta shouted. "Maris, you have no right!"

"I bought my rights with mage-blood—my own. With what did you buy yours, Amarta?"

*His breath would stop. He would turn waxy pale. Motionless. He would die.*

"Please," Amarta croaked. She yanked her arm, again and again, trying to free herself, but could not break the mage's grip.

"Taslata, attend," Maris said calmly to Samnt, gesturing at Tayre with her free hand. "Put your focus within the Iliban. Do you note the patterns of pain response? Typical, but lacking the expected fear markers. You perceive this, yes?"

Samnt was breathing raggedly, wide-eyed, seeming as

panicked as Amarta felt. "Yes, Aetur."

Tayre was choking. The futures in which he would live another minute were fast dwindling.

He could not die. Amarta would not let him die.

And so she must— what? What must she do?

With a great force of will, Amarta ignored everything, but the one answer she needed. Even his wheezing, and Maris's morbid lesson, she pressed away.

This moment. The next. A future in which Tayre stood whole again.

That future's trail back to the now.

"Do you feel it, Samnt?" Maris was saying. "He moves close to the door. Do you see the land beyond life? Do you feel it?"

The words that could change this moment…

*Will you lose me, too, Maris?*

"Yes, Aetur."

He was no longer moving.

"Maris," Amarta cried, her voice breaking. "Will you lose me, too?"

Maris frowned, very slightly.

"I know the future, Maris. Kill him and you will never see me again."

At last she had the mage's attention. "He's taught you to lie, too, has he?"

"Truth, mage," Amarta hissed, rage fueling her determination. She would create a future in which her words were true. "I will despise you. You will be to me as he is to you."

Maris searched Amarta's face. An unsettling touch of magery went through her body.

Then she released Amarta's arm. Amarta wanted to run to him, to drop to the floor, to assure herself that he lived.

But no. He was close to that door. He must not go

through. With great effort, she turned her back on him to face the mage.

"Restore him, Maris."

"Your bones to heal, Seer."

Amarta made a furious, frustrated sound, clenched her teeth. She held high a trembling left hand, with all but the smallest finger curled tight.

"This one only, mage. The rest are mine."

A flash of heat rushed up through Amarta's hand and she whimpered as her smallest finger shifted under the skin, a grinding sensation, and flare of agony that left the finger red and pulsing.

"Get him out. Out and gone, before I change my mind."

From the floor, Tayre gasped. He rolled onto his back, clutching his chest.

"It hurts, doesn't it, to come back from the edge," Maris said. "But so much more pain is possible. Someday, Iliban, I'll show you."

Samnt struggled to get Tayre to his feet and helped him stagger through the door. Amarta followed them outside, taking over for Samnt.

For a moment Samnt looked as if he wanted to say something. Then he shook his head, squared his shoulders, and went back inside.

Amarta wrapped Tayre's arm across her shoulder as he shuffled forward toward the steep road down.

<hr>

"SHOULD WE RUN?" Amarta asked him about halfway down the road.

The future offered a range of possibilities. Maris must be considering many options, including the one where she changed her mind.

A rueful smile. "I don't think I can."

"How dare she—"

*Silence*, he tapped on her shoulder. "We're not away yet."

He recovered a bit more, every few steps. Their pace improved until he no longer needed to lean on her.

Back at his camp, they assembled packs. Amarta worked the knots of the oilskin tarpaulin attached to the trees.

"Leave it," he said of the oilskin, pans, bags of vegetables suspended from branches. "Leave it all."

Such a familiar moment, to be about to flee, to need to decide too quickly what you could live without, so that you might live at all.

Amarta secured Souver's saddle, tied on the saddlebags, stuffing in what she could.

The sound came from the edge of the clearing, so soft that it took Amarta a moment to realize she was hearing something. She whirled, drew a sharp breath.

Maris stood by a tree, gaze panning across the campsite. From her look, Amarta suspected that this was the first time the mage had been here.

Overhead, a small, chittering creature peered out from dark leafy foliage, then darted back into hiding.

Maris made a thoughtful sound, then spoke. "What have you learned from me today, Amarta? Perhaps how a mage treats those she claims to care for?" A humorless laugh. "Or how potent is the blindness of the powerful? Perhaps I have taught you something of value, after all." Her tone softened to a near whisper, "And perhaps someday you'll forgive me."

"Maris, I—"

The mage raised a hand, her expression stone-like. Amarta bit off the words.

"Listen, Seer, and listen well. It is unknown, for an Iliban to see the future as you do. Dribs and drabs, perhaps. Lucky guesses, more like. Even among the elder mages, foresight like yours is beyond rare. Your worth is…unreckonable." Maris's gaze found Tayre. "Be shrewd in your choice of companions."

"I will," Amarta said softly.

"Go, then. Go well. Where does your path lead?"

Fear made Amarta hesitate, but anger gave her voice. "There must be others like me. I will find them and learn what they know."

"A fruitless search."

"Mine to make."

"I suspect you go west," Maris said. "Forgo the coastal road. Lerpan's Labyrinth is snarled. Some recently created mages are making a mess of the place. Eventually someone will clean it up, but I advise avoiding it now."

"Thank you," Amarta said, a little surprised at this help. Tayre had mentioned Lerpan's Labyrinth in one of his stories. Until this moment, Amarta had thought it only a fable.

"Clear vision to you, Amarta dua Seer al—" Maris paused thoughtfully. "You're not from Arunkel any more, that's certain. Safe journey, Traveler." She walked to the edge of the clearing and paused, facing away. "Enlon."

At the sound of the name by which Maris had first known him, Tayre shifted his stance.

"I listen, High One."

"Whatever befalls Amarta dua Seer, if it displeases me in any portion, I hold you accountable. I swear by my lineage to settle that debt, at leisure and with precision."

It took Amarta a moment to understand that the words were a threat. She opened her mouth to object, but Tayre signed: *silence.*

"I hear," he said.

Maris nodded, then walked away. They stood unmoving until the mage's steps had faded to silence.

"Now," Tayre said, "We must go. While we still can."

## Chapter Five

INNEL CAME AWAKE on his feet, half panicked, groping for his short sword at one hip, then the dagger at the other, not finding either.

There they were, sheathed, on the floor, by the cot on which he'd slept, in this small room of cloaks.

Innel stared at the closet doorway, where stood the reason he had awoken from this exhausted sleep: the queen's seneschal, whose words echoed meaninglessly in his mind.

The seneschal gave Innel a dour look at the lack of sensible response. Innel found this reassuring; the man's expression would doubtless change if disaster ever actually struck.

As it nearly had.

Marisel dua Mage had left the previous day, assuring Innel—repeatedly, and with increasing annoyance—that Cern and the baby were out of mortal danger, that there was nothing more she could—or would?—do, and that rest was all that mother and child needed.

Innel remembered offering her more money, then more, enough that Sachare's eyebrows rose.

Despite everything, the mage left. Then Innel stumbled back into the closet that had become his make-shift bedroom these last months. Judging by how disoriented he felt, he had indeed slept.

But he couldn't bring to mind the seneschal's words.

"What did you say?" he asked, wondering how the man managed to affect such a servile-yet-disapproving look. A lifetime of practice, no doubt.

"The House Passare delegation is here. To discuss the roads, Lord Commander. Again," repeated the seneschal slowly. "I trust that you recall this is the fifth time you have agreed to speak with them, and each time you have required the matter to be rescheduled."

Innel had not left the queen's antechamber in many days. He ran a hand over his unshaven face.

"I'll be along shortly."

"They will be so pleased to hear the good news, Lord Commander, as they wait patiently in the hallway outside your office," the seneschal said. Before he left, he bowed. Not very deeply, Innel noticed.

But never mind: the seneschal had brought Keyretura, who had kept Cern and the infant alive long enough for Innel to ride to the mountains of Perripur where he somehow convinced Marisel dua Mage to help, so Innel was prepared to forgive the old man any slight.

*He blinked, recalling the seer's words: Release me. It will be worth a great deal to you to have done so.*

Was that, somehow, how this had all come together? Surely it could not be coincidence.

Innel brushed aside cloaks to leave the closet. In the antechamber, to the side of the door to the queen's room, blankets lay heaped. When Sachare was not in with Cern, she slept by the door, as if taking over for the dichu dogs, who had not been happy to be returned to the kennels. But after demonstrating their willingness to protect Cern against the doctors, with lethal force, there was no choice.

"Sleeping," Sachare said at his questioning look.

"I have to see," he muttered.

Sachare nodded, opened the door and gestured him inside, closing it behind.

Innel stood at the door and stared at the two of them sleeping. He held his breath until he saw Cern's chest rise and fall.

Once might be wishful thinking. Twice it must be, before he would let himself inhale. No, make it three times. At last he took air.

Cern's eyes were closed. Dark, purpled hollows ringed them, her face tight and thin from months of pain.

But she lived. And in the crook of her arm lay the infant, her mouth open, tiny chest rising and falling with her mother's.

Rising and falling.

Such a near thing, that tiny life. Far too near.

Innel had let so much lapse these last months since that day when Cern had screamed in agony. Without Cern, nothing else mattered.

Drinking in the sight of them both now, Innel felt as if his own life had begun to be restored as well. Cern and the child had survived one near-fatal blow—the pregnancy itself—and Innel must see to it that no other threats came close.

And that meant that he must return to all the other matters that demanded his attention. The roads. The Houses. The tribes. The Charters Courts. The various intrigues and schemes.

House Etallan. The House of Metal had been quiet since that day in the queen's audience chamber, their palace liaison notably absent. Innel had no illusions that they had forgotten. Good—a charge of treason should not be forgotten.

*They have been chastised and must be redeemed.*

Not chastised enough, in Innel's view. But the matter could not be addressed until Cern had fully recovered.

He blinked eyes gritty from lack of sleep, and realized that his daughter was staring back at him.

Roads, Houses, and all the rest vanished from his mind, replaced by a conviction that he must increase the queensguard. He would send for Nalas and do just that, the moment he got back to his office.

No, a whole new contingent was needed. The Princess's Guard. A full set of thirty—no, forty, to be sure not one of them was ever as tired as Innel was right now, their judgment compromised in protection of the most precious child in the empire. His mind was alight with plans.

They would be sworn not only to Cern directly, but also to him, and to the infant child. *Sev Cern. Sev Innel. Sev…*

The unnamed baby girl blinked. Innel felt an unnerving but not entirely unpleasant fluttering in his stomach.

Her name. That was something only the queen could decide.

All at once it landed on him, almost like a hard blow, that she was the presumptive heir to the Arunkel throne, and he the father.

The evidence blinked at him again and he drew in a sharp breath, held it, and found himself unable to exhale until she did. Rise and fall, rise and fall, he only breathed when the infant did.

Innel had nearly failed her. He would not allow himself to fail again.

So much to do. He put a hand on the door behind him, his gaze on the child.

"Innel."

It was a near-shock to hear Cern say his name after so long.

"Your Grace," he whispered.

"Do you want to hold her?" Cern asked hoarsely.

The queen of the Arunkel empire was offering to let him hold her child.

His child.

She was so tiny. Born early, born small. She looked so fragile. What if he accidentally dropped her?

No. It could not be allowed.

"Your Grace, I am…late for a meeting with House Passare."

She nodded. "Go."

He ducked his head in a bow, did it again, and left.

As Innel left the room, then the antechamber, he felt as if a cord were tied from the baby to his own guts, tearing at his most tender insides with every step. His craving to go back was matched by his need to protect them.

He must return to tracking the plots against the queen that crawled and buzzed through the palace. Most were simple and short-lived, once light was shined on them. For the insidious ones, Innel put counter plans in place, with Srel's help, and arms-length hirelings, to contain them until they could be identified, isolated, and removed.

Quietly removed. The standard of law required three pieces of evidence, but acquiring those would slow down the removal of these dangers, and that could not be risked.

And the worst of the plots must be left to run a time. Only a fool yanked a weed, leaving the roots intact for the weed to grow back stronger. Those plots Innel must track to see how deep they stretched and where they led.

Etallan, he would wager.

As he walked the halls to his office, his daughter's gaze haunted him.

INNEL SAT, staring with increasing dismay at the fortifications of paper, envelopes, scrolls, sealed flats, and parchment cubes on his desk. Neatly stacked piles, like a display of some famous battle.

Srel, laden with a large basket of more papers, paused, looking for open space on the wood.

Had Innel really been away so long?

"Not to worry, Lord Commander. I can help."

But what Srel could do, he had already done. Another side table of neat piles and envelopes was testament to this.

"Tell me what they've been saying, Srel."

Srel put a parchment cube on top of the stack, like a child's plaything but for the formal seals on all sides, indicating the Great House and its various vassals.

"The queen has been on post-birth bed-rest longer than any other queen in Arunkel history."

That much was true. "Another few days," Innel muttered.

A few beyond that, more likely.

No one must know how close the empire had come to having the monarchy suddenly vacated with no clear succession. Innel's life would have been worthless. He wondered, if it had come to that, and he had to run, how far he would get.

He dismissed that path of thought. He didn't have time to muse on averted disaster. A miss by an inch was as good as a chasm.

On top of the nearest pile was an Account and Petition from House Elupene. All the Houses would send at least one to the crown. It was the pre-game of the Charters Courts, in which each House described what they had done with the charters granted to them at the last Courts, and the benefits to the queen and the public good of granting them again. It would include their plans going forward with the charters they hoped to keep or gain at the next Courts.

The reports were lengthy affairs, full of ledgers and records, calendars and diagrams. But when to send the document to the crown, and how many to send, was a political decision. Too early, the document might get buried in the mind of the monarch, who was required by the Charters Courts to read and affirm, or acknowledge, each one.

But too late, and she might already be biased toward another House's Account and Petition.

Fortunes were made and lost at the Charters Courts. If negotiations stalled at any point during a Court—and they almost always did—it was the monarch's duty to smooth the way and adjudicate as needed, for which she would be referring to the Accounts and Petitions.

Cern, of course, was not in condition to read any of this.

Next on the pile was a strident letter from Munasee's governor about the Great Road, which she wrote was becoming impassable, upsetting trade and travel.

Innel recalled yesterday's meeting with House Passare, which had not gone well. Between the limits of Innel's actual authority, and Passare's demand for more money, exactly nothing had been agreed to.

First Rider Passare had drummed his fingers on the table. "First Rider" was one of the many unique House titles that Innel must know, made more challenging by the Houses' habit of changing them at every House tiff and make-up kiss.

"It's the higher prices for bitumen and lava, Lord Commander. As you know, repair work is a net loss, one not covered under the current contract with the monarchy."

"I understand entirely, First Rider." Innel affixed what he hoped was a sympathetic look on his face. "The work of roads is essential."

As were a hundred other things.

The Second Rider spoke. "Across the empire, order is kept only by virtue of the roads. What far better work we might do, ser, if we held Lesser House Phaltos."

Ah, Phaltos. Phaltos made adhesives, mortars, and waterproofing compounds, all of which road-building relied upon.

"I understand entirely," Innel said again, "We all look forward to the possibilities that the Charter Court engenders."

It was, he decided, a very good phrase. He planned to use it again.

"Just so," said Passare's First Rider, his disappointed smile showing that he understood the message: Innel would do nothing.

"What else do they say, Srel?" he asked.

"Celebrations across the city for the birth of the heir, Lord Commander. Many follow the Blessing Doctrine."

Innel let out a long stream of air. "Tell me they are not exercising the Doctrine in the streets."

"Enthusiastically."

Well, it kept the people busy. There were worse ways to celebrate.

"Did this happen when Cern was born?"

"Day and night, I'm told," Srel replied. "It slowed only when the king revealed the princess publicly. Because the queen and heir have yet to be seen, the people assume this means they should continue."

"And in the palace and Houses, I assume even more."

"Yes, ser. The Princess's Cohort is on the minds of many."

"More than minds, no doubt," Innel muttered. He stood, took his wine in hand, and walked to the window, looking out at the new construction in Execution Square.

Innel had not yet considered the Princess's Cohort, but of course there would be one.

"What do they say about the provinces? Garaya?"

"Lord Commander, you must eat. Let me send for food, ser. You—"

Innel turned back. "I rely on you to tell me, Srel."

His steward pursed his lips. "Some say that the ore shipments and quieted rebellions are not to your credit, but Garaya..." he trailed off.

But Garaya was his fault. Of course.

But some truth to that. "I should never have sent Sutarnan to lead that force."

Srel snorted in disgust. An unexpected, and decidedly unservile sound.

"Lord Commander, forgive me, but you provided Sutarnan with a wealth of seasoned advisers. Either he ignored them—which would not have been at all unlike him—or there were no means by which the situation in Garaya might be redeemed. You've said it yourself across the years: not all battles can be won."

It was one thing to say it. Another to live it.

"Otevan—you returned from there triumphant, Lord Commander."

Otevan had very nearly been a complete disaster.

"I had help," Innel said quietly. Amarta dua Seer. Marisel dua Mage. The Teva themselves.

"Surely that could be said of any of us, ser?"

Innel looked at his steward's determined expression, and wondered what the small man saw in him. Someone very grand, no doubt. Innel took a large swallow from his wine.

In Garaya, Sutarnan had lost, to a man, the entire army that Innel had sent with him to quell that rebellion. That wretched failure reflected poorly on the queen. More poorly on Innel, of course, but it was his job to deflect blame from her where he could, so that she could protect him.

And now Garaya was trading with the borderlands of Perripur and ignoring taxes and tariffs in outright defiance of the law and crown. Beyond unacceptable. He considered sending another, larger force. A greater disaster in the making, if that were lost—other towns and cities would wonder if they could follow Garaya's lead.

Perhaps it was time to consider the unthinkable: negotiation. Hard to swallow, giving any ground to a rebel city. No matter how secret the arrangement, word would get out, and that would be even worse.

No—any response to Garaya would need Cern's backing, after she was fully restored to health.

He examined Srel a moment. "What aren't you telling me?"

The smaller man swallowed nervously, and looked down for a moment. "Some say that Cern's illness is reminiscent of the old king's."

"Meaning?"

Srel swallowed. "At your hands, ser. To put yourself in line for the throne."

"That," Innel said with a clenched jaw, "is absurd. I have as much chance of ascending the throne as…" he paused. "As you do. Less, really—you haven't made as many enemies." He gave Srel's face another look. "There's more. Something worse. Out with it."

Srel heaved a deep sigh. "Some whisper that a half-commoner child will break under pressure, like an ill-made sword."

Innel felt himself go hot. Srel watching his face, took a half step back.

"No, she will not. She will have every educational advantage that her position both requires and allows, and her

Cohort will be full of the most capable and clever children in the empire. Not only spoiled House brats."

"Yes, ser."

"She'll be protected, every moment, until she is strong enough to rule. Then she will."

"Yes, ser."

Innel let himself sink back in to his chair. He took his cup in hand. It was empty. "More."

"And food, ser."

"And Nalas. We need to discuss a new guard. The Princess's Guard."

---

"IF YOU SAY SO, LORD COMMANDER." Nalas's tone did little to hide his lack of enthusiasm.

Innel examined his second's face. "You don't approve?"

"If you want my opinion, ser."

"Speak."

Nalas shifted weight where he stood, stared into the distance. "You form a new guard out of—who? The old guard? Breaking them into two parts?"

"No, that would diminish the numbers. I want more guards in total, of course." Innel heard the edge in his voice. Wasn't this obvious?

"Going to be tension between the old and new, then."

"So?"

Nalas blew out a stream of air, gave one nod. "Respectfully, ser, not everyone was raised in the Cohort as you were, to compete. We've got truly loyal people in the queensguard, ones we've checked and trained, willing to put their lives between any threat and her majesty and the child. Make a new group, they'll wonder, did I do something wrong? Am I being replaced? Who are these newcomers? Can I trust them?"

"We are concerned about the feelings of the guards?"

"No, ser. Concerned about effectiveness. We replaced nearly the entire queensguard after the kennel attack. Anyone possibly connected to those traitors is gone. The guard is already plenty suspicious of each other."

"That's good."

Nalas tilted his head. "There's a balance between trusting each too much, and suspecting everyone at your side. Bring in new people, and that line changes."

"Then change the line! If there had been more guards around the queen, the kennel attack would never have come close to succeeding. Or happened at all. Quantity has a value all its own. Add more guards, Nalas."

"I will, ser. Of course. It's just that…we can't read hearts and minds, ser. Not really."

"I want the best, Nalas."

"Yes, ser."

"What of the Seer's sister and nephew?"

Nalas clicked his tongue. "The palace is not kind to commoners, ser."

Innel had lived that truth his whole life. The wedding would, he decided, be well-attended. He would tell Srel to make certain of it, and to be sure that they were convincing.

"Pas is good," Nalas continued, "but I think he'd be good anywhere. He always sees the bright side." Nalas grinned but it faded. "Dirina's doing her best, but I know she feels out of place. She must really like me," he said with a rueful smile.

Amarta dua Seer would come to her sister's wedding, and when she did, there could be no question that her sister and nephew were happy, so that she would return again and again.

"We'll see to it that she's content, Nalas."

"Gotta tell you, not sure how to do that, ser."

"I'll put the queen's seneschal on it."

Nalas's eyebrows rose slightly.

Innel met the other man's eyes. "My daughter is the presumptive heir to the throne. We need the best guard the empire has ever known. Make it so."

"Yes, ser."

---

"FIVE, LORD COMMANDER," the Helata general said slowly. "We can have those ships ready by…" He was flipping between pages, then frowned deeply, sea-beaten lines furrowing his brows. "I don't see how we can have them ready by the Charters Court."

An irrelevant deadline, but this was not the first time Innel had encountered it.

"Take longer, then," he said.

The admiral sat back, regarded Innel. "Lord Commander, let me be sailor-direct with you. House Kincel has been lowering the cost of Phaltos's glues and sealants in anticipation of the Charters Court." He stroked one side of his thick mustache with his two smallest fingers. "Prices will rise after the close of the Courts, as they always do. Considerably. Now, if we were certain who would hold Phaltos, after the Courts, we could make accommodations immediately, as well as fashion a mutually favorable contract with the crown."

House Phaltos's adhesives and waterproofing compounds were essential to shipbuilding. Their patron house, Kincel— the House of Stone—would hardly give them up without a fight.

"Kincel has held Phaltos three Courts now," Innel said. "They are not going to…" No, he could not say that.

Everyone knew that he had no standing to make promises about the Courts, but everyone also knew—or assumed—that he had the queen's ear, and could influence her decisions, so he must not say anything now to undercut her rulings in the Charters Courts.

How to be politic? He considered.

"I would be," he said, "unsurprised to find the queen willing to amend this contract in order to allow for changing costs, should circumstances likewise alter."

There, that lacked commitment.

The admiral blinked, making sense of the implication, cautiously pleased. "I will look forward to that conversation with the queen. Which might be when, Lord Consort?"

"Soon."

"The child is what? A month and ten days in life?"

"Yes."

"House Helata knows great joy at the birth of the heir. Does she have a name?"

"No," Innel said, in a tone that he hoped would invite no reply. For a long moment, it didn't.

"Always a pleasure doing business with the crown, Lord Commander," the admiral said at last, but made no move to stand.

"The pleasure is mutual," replied Innel, not pointing out that he was not, in any sense, the crown.

"Ah, one more thing," said the admiral, still sitting. "I admit to being conflicted about passing on what is probably only a jest. And yet…" He dug inside his coat, brought out a folded paper, held it between two fingers. "This note has passed through many hands to arrive in my possession. While it is true that I know what it says, I do not know, as I am certain you will, what veracity it might hold. I have every faith in you and the queen's retinue, and so it, as I say, is likely only good for a laugh, but surely even a laugh is worth—"

"Admiral."

"Yes. Well. Here." The admiral moved his fingers, the paper between them, closer to Innel, but only by a few inches, requiring Innel to come to him.

Innel stifled annoyance—he'd been dealing with such slights since he joined the Cohort. He leaned forward, took it, sat back, opened it, and skimmed.

Another sketch of another plot.

"Where did this come from?"

"Given to me, Lord Commander, by one of my captains. Came to him through another, then another. Sailors are like birds, you see, passing on information like splats of excrement-soaked seeds. Probably nothing, but I deemed it worthy of your attention."

The way the Admiral was smiling, it was clear he thought that Innel had just incurred a debt to him.

The note was specific, mentioning which window in the gallery under the queen's suites would need to be loosened to be opened from the outside gardens, and at what time in the early morning a person dangling there would be unlikely to be seen.

When Cern was eleven, the Cohort had gone on a binge of leaving small gifts for her, outside that very window. The described route had been a favorite to achieve the dangerous climb. Dangerous, but nowhere near impossible, as a good number of the Cohort boys had proved.

Innel remembered a tiny, cleverly woven straw falcon with spread wings. He'd found it in a down-city market. He and Pohut had strung it across her window as if it were in flight.

The next day in the yard, a twelve-year-old Cern looked

at them both, smiled a little, then briefly spread her arms like wings.

They'd given each other a victory grin. He must remind Pohut of that. His brother would laugh. And it had been too long since they had…

His brother was dead.

Innel blinked and looked again at the note. Not a bad plan, but far out of date—Cern hadn't slept in those suites in years.

He thanked the Admiral, assured him that Helata's interest in the queen's safety would be remembered, and showed him firmly to the door.

Whoever had conveyed this set of instructions wanted money. They described how to wash it through a series of contacts, a plan that Innel could break easily, if he cared to put the men on it. Cohort? Maybe, but it was clumsy.

Or Cohort pretending to be clumsy.

Really, it smelled of a simple swindle, rather than a plan with teeth.

He went to the window, pulled back the drapes, and gazed down on Putar's latest work.

It had snowed lightly last night, and swirls continued to fall. A huge set of scales sat in the center of Execution Square, one side designed to shed snow, the other to collect it. Between them, the condemned man looked up at the sky, his face pale in the wan daylight, statue-like. A simple leather cord around his neck tightened, ever so slowly.

For a moment Innel was curious: what was he thinking? Was he remorseful for his crimes, or merely regretting having been caught?

There would be no public executions for the traitors Innel would lay hands on shortly. They were tiny weeds that could be yanked with the smallest finger.

The greatest traitors, though, Innel had every intention of

giving to Putar for his clever extravaganzas. But he would need to accumulate more evidence, and wait for the queen to be healthy and ready to back him.

He wondered if the Eparch of House Etallan would be as quiet and dignified as the man in the square below. He doubted it.

In any case, it must not and could not be rushed. Those truly potent plots had deep roots, sunk far below, under blankets of snow.

INNEL LOOKED in on Cern and the baby as often as he could. Some days every hour, standing and watching them sleep for as long as he dared before returning to work.

He watched the guards in her quarters closely enough that they twitched, and kept watching until they stopped. He observed the quins—the five-men units in which queensguards were trained—replaced each other. He made sure Nalas varied the times.

Gifts arrived for the child. Congratulatory notes penned in high-form script, often with postscripts mentioning subtle —and not-so-subtle—favors that might be granted in return.

He read every one of them and had the gifts sent to a guarded inventory, for inspection, and to await Cern's recovery.

Which surely would not be long now. And then…He imagined Cern holding court, his daughter perched on her lap, and himself at her side.

His daughter. Her baby face swam into his mind's eye again and again. She stared at him. She blinked.

He looked around his office at the room that he nearly lived in. Weapons and maps on the walls.

It stank, he realized suddenly.

No, that was him.

Well, he could now at least see over the piles, and that must be considered a minor triumph. He reached for his wine, downed it.

"More."

Srel poured.

"The other business," Innel said quietly, opening a large drawer in which were bills, names, numbers, addresses. Money offered, demanded, proposed. Anything that had come to him through back-channels.

Anything to do with the queen.

Srel laid out two new piles onto the small open space on Innel's desk.

The first pile was probably nothing, but was kept in Innel's lockbox, in case it later turned into something. The second, Srel would look into, hiring arms-length agents to bring back reports.

The third pile was important enough that even Srel didn't know about it. It remained now in a flat pouch in Innel's vest, on his person at all times.

Innel looked at a new scrap of paper. It contained a tincture recipe.

Innel knew a great deal about poisons, because the rumors about what he had done to the old king were partly true, though he hadn't expected the old man to hoard the dose in quantity sufficient to kill himself. So it was obvious to Innel, at a glance, that this particular elixir would give someone a stomach ache and nothing more. More likely a half-hearted attempt to get back at a former friend or jilted lover, and nothing at all to do with the queen.

"Next?"

"This, ser. Seems a tad expensive for flowers."

Innel knew what it was. More than a tad. Many times too expensive. It had taken Innel some work to obtain the money without its lack being noticed, but Srel had found it anyway.

"A friend of my mother's," Innel said. "A favor. A small thing. I'll take it." He tucked it into his vest.

Most moves against the monarchy were obvious—bribes, attempts to foul food, accusations, lies—but some were more subtle. It was an open secret that some in-palace royals from a line descended from the Grandmother Queen were still nursing the hope they might move themselves up on the rumored succession list. The list Cern had yet to make.

Some of them had been on Restarn's list and felt they had a right to be on Cern's. But were they brazen enough to try to unseat a sitting monarch?

Probably not. Any cut to the monarchical Anandynar line was a cut to their own. Further, few of the royals were Cohort-hardened, so they didn't know how to see such schemes through to their end. Fearful enough not to want to risk what they already had for what they might yet.

Though if they thought Cern's recovery in doubt, they might take a shot.

One of Innel's most reliable down-city informants had delivered a rumor that some of House Elupene was, with serious coin, backing royals fitting this description. The informant had gone one step better and laid hands on someone from Elupene's vassal House Flore, a man discontented and ready to act against his patron house. Ready to talk. He only needed a nudge, said the informant.

So Innel had funded the matter. It began with a quantity of overpriced flowers.

"Where shall I have these flowers sent, ser?" asked Srel.

Innel had not considered the quantity of flowers he was buying at exorbitant prices until this moment.

"Sachare. She'll know what to do with them." She would check every one, is what she would do. Good. Keep her busy.

"Yes, ser." The next item was a plain envelope, addressed to Innel. "Probably another forgery, but you would know."

Innel read it, then again, more slowly. Like the note the admiral had brought, it was an offer to help.

Unlike that note, it referred to him as brother, in the flippant style of the Cohort.

He didn't recognize the handwriting, but at the bottom were a series of numbers that he did: the bell-times at which one quin of the Queen's Guard relieved the next. It was information that only the guards, himself, and Nalas were supposed to have.

The note offered to explain, but only if Innel showed up to meet the unsigned author, at the Broken Prayer, a mid-city inn.

"This I need to go to," Innel said, rubbing his face.

"I'll make arrangements, ser."

HOURS LATER, Innel found himself staring at the many pages of a particular Account and Petition. As plots against the queen went, this one was singularly tedious. He set it down with reluctant admiration.

The rambling report began with a full three pages of praise for the queen, which was two pages longer than typical, then launched into a grindingly dull recounting of the produce of House Sartor since the last Charters Court. Lists and tallies, long descriptions, lengthy sentences.

One sentence spanned an entire page. Innel struggled to keep focus.

Then he'd found the buried nugget and perked right up.

No Account and Petition was binding on the monarch's decisions. But if she did not reject it—or parts of it—it could be used to support a formal argument during the insanity of the months-long Charters Courts, making Cern's job more complicated, which was why she must read every one of them. She could object to portions of them, and would, when it was worth the insult to the House to do so.

Sartor was clearly hoping to have the document approved by the queen, then use it to put a wedge between Kincel and Passare, who, for Houses, got along rather well.

"Clever," he said aloud. "Sartor's attempt to reinterpret Kincel's vassal charter with Phaltos would have the crown paying a hundred times more for every road."

It was hard to understand the Cohort if you hadn't gone through it. Even the families of the Cohort often failed to grasp how grueling and effective the education was.

King Restarn had a team to handle these reports. Cern did not, as of yet. So it fell, like so much else, to Innel. House Sartor probably thought it would slide right past him.

"Tired, not stupid," he muttered.

His head ached. He reached for his wine glass. It was empty. "Srel?"

A soft snoring sound from the cot in the corner told him it was quite late, and that meant it had been hours since he'd last looked at Cern and the baby.

His heart sped. There was too much hallway between his office and the queen's room, but his body felt too heavy to stand.

"Srel."

The smaller man, popped up to his feet, swaying slightly. "Ser?"

"In the morning, I want you to—"

"I think it *is* morning, ser."

Innel glanced at the drawn red drapes. A line of light limned the edges.

"So it is." He reached automatically for the wine, fingers hesitating just short. No—that would not make him feel more awake. Sometimes it was hard to remember that he had money. "I need to think clearly. Can you get me qualan?"

"White or bronze?" Srel asked, stifling a yawn. At Innel's sharply questioning look, he said, "Oh, I don't use it, ser. I could never afford it. But I've been with you through the Cohort, when it was my duty to know what the others were doing when they weren't studying."

Qualan was astonishingly expensive, but Innel had tried the white once, and it had given him a rich sense of easy confidence and clarity that he could use now. Bronze qualan was only rumor. "Where would you get bronze?"

A dismissive gesture. "It doesn't matter, ser. Phapha is what you want, not qualan. I'll find you some. What about that, ser?" he nodded at the document Innel had been reading.

"It's shit with nails," Innel said, too tired to summon more eloquent language. "But must be responded to."

"I will fashion a reply, ser."

Innel looked up. "You?"

"A first draft only," Srel said. "For your review."

"For the queen's review, you mean."

"Yes, of course, ser."

Innel pushed himself to stand. "I go to check on them."

"You should sleep, ser."

"Later."

Chapter Six

BEYOND UNACCEPTABLE, Cern decided, this near inability to get out of bed. She struggled to put herself upright to sit against the pillows. Even the mere task of using the chamberpot in the corner could leave her exhausted.

She was again unpleasantly reminded of her father's incapacitation, then even more unpleasantly reminded of who was its agent. He had told her, Innel had, and credit to him for that confession. A carefully meted-out potion that had kept her father abed for so long.

But if he could do it once…

No. If she began to suspect everyone, who would she rely on? She must look to the future, to her baby and country, both of whom seemed inclined to fuss a great deal.

She shook her head, her thoughts foggy. Still. Again.

How had it come to this?

The usual way, she thought ruefully, looking at the infant at her side, who looked back up at her and began hiccuping. Cern took the baby into her arms and patted her back gently. The child then yawned, and Cern found it impossible not to do likewise.

She had slept all day, and yet she was still tired. At least the pain was receding, thanks to the two mages. Though in truth, Cern barely remembered Keyretura at her side this visit, so far gone was she in agony. It had been a wretched, vile time. But she had survived. But Fates, how it had hurt.

It still hurt.

Enough whining, she told herself. There was work to do, some of which only she could do.

Etallan. Despite the scandal, they must be brought back into the fold.

*Should have married Tokerae*, someone had the bad judgment to whisper, just after the wedding, not entirely out of her hearing. She had him watched closely.

Who had that been? She knew, damn it, she just couldn't bring the name to mind.

She remembered what happened yesterday, at least. An elderly cousin whom Cern had known since childhood had come. While Cern dozed, the cousin attempted to take the child from the bed.

"Only to rock a moment, Your Majesty," The old woman had cried out, hands up, cowering at Cern's howl, cutting her reach short.

On her feet, Cern stumbled and knocked over a water glass on the bedside table, her hand on the wall to steady herself. Sachare and guards came crashing in.

"The baby does not leave my side," Cern shouted.

The elderly cousin quite sensibly had fled. Unlikely to return.

Good.

Cern lay back, nearly as exhausted by the memory itself as the event. She let her eyes close.

Paranoia?

No, prudence. The baby was the heir to Cern's throne.

But *had* Cern made a mistake with Innel? Would the

child's position always be in doubt? When the child grew and took the throne, would she be challenged at every turn, her bloodline questioned, because of the man Cern had chosen to father her?

Sachare entered quietly. Opening her eyes a slit, Cern watched her chamberlain put away folded clothes. Sachare winced slightly as she bent, a hand momentarily to her chest where a spear had nearly taken her life defending Cern.

Sachare, with her mage-healed wound still aching. Cern with her mage-healed pregnancy that still left her barely able to get out of bed.

"We're a fine pair, aren't we," Cern croaked hoarsely.

"Both of us nearly died." Sachare said gently.

"I feel so damned helpless, Sacha."

The baby was fussing, and Cern put a finger into her tiny hand. She was quiet for a moment.

"Give yourself time to heal, Your Grace."

"What news is there? No one tells me," Cern said, feeling cross. "Are you protecting me, too?"

"Never." Sachare gave the smallest of grins.

"Don't mock, Sacha." Sachare's face went instantly sober, as if taking off a mask. Or putting one on? "What of Innel?"

Sachare tilted her head thoughtfully. "He comes to visit when you are asleep."

"Coward. He made her," she gestured to the baby, who wanted to be held, so she did, then wanted to be fed, so she did that. "How is he?"

Sachare hesitated. How interesting.

"Busy," Sachare said, continuing to straighten the room. "The Houses, royals, Ministerial Council—they all want your attention, and Innel makes them talk to him instead."

Cern sighed. "I'll get to it and see them all. Soon."

A sound from Sachare that was anything but agreement.

Cern had known the woman since childhood, and read in her stance and wordless tone that she didn't agree.

"What?" Cern asked.

"There are things you can do from your bed, Your Grace. You could, for example, name her."

"So soon?" Cern muttered, looking down at the face of her baby, who had fallen asleep. Gently, she lay the child down at her side. *Such a burden for you to carry, precious one.*

What name could possibly survive the scrutiny it would beget? Any name that made a reference to Innel was entirely out of the question, a spit in the eye of the Houses, and an insult to the royals.

Yet to name the child after an ancestor monarch was similarly fraught with political traps. Who would be flattered? Appalled? Offended?

Could the child ever live up to the comparison? Cern's father had repeatedly measured Cern against his idolized Grandmother Queen and found her wanting, she thought sourly.

To name her, as tired as Cern felt, was a puzzle that seemed entirely too hard to solve.

"Or," Sachare said evenly, "you could make a start by simply formally recognizing her as the Heir. A succession list. Settle some of the worst of the rumors."

Among all who surrounded her, only Sachare could speak to her this way. Cern's momentary annoyance was fast replaced by the gratitude of knowing that there was someone who could.

"For which she would need a name," Cern said lowly.

"Not at all, Your Grace. 'My firstborn daughter' would do for now."

"No Arunkel monarch has ever done that."

"Be the first."

Cern gently stroked her daughter's soft head, her fine brown hair. The child made a small noise in her sleep.

Cern remembered how her own childhood had been various hells from the very moment she had been proclaimed Heir. How could she do that to this small, beautiful creature she had made so painstakingly?

But of course she must.

"I could bring for you all the necessary papers and seals, Your Grace. All you need do is declare it so and put your hand to the ratification."

Cern snorted in dark amusement at this sketch of how easy it ought to be.

"Then there's the list," Cern said, to which Sachare sensibly said nothing.

Putting the child first on the list made her an instant target, but anyone else in that position would weaken her standing from the very start.

Sachare was right: the child must be named. It was long past time for a succession list, and it was Cern's duty to make it. Really, she should have done it last year, before she'd gotten pregnant, when this small creature by her side was still an imaginary stranger.

It would be some reassurance, to know that someone else stood ready to take over for her.

*Planning your escape already, are you?*

No, death was entirely out of the question. Cern had an empire to attend to. If her life ended today, who would see to her child? To the fabric and sinew of her country?

No one.

It was time to make the list. She would open her father's lockbox, even if she ignored everything her father had left there for her.

Not his lockbox, damn it. Hers.

Cern remembered the first time she had seen the box.

Her Cohort had not yet even been called, so she must have been younger than five.

He had seemed so large, the king-her-father. Imposing and terrifying, a veritable god in his vastness and power. He lifted her up, as if she weighed nothing, set her on his lap, then gestured at the table, where sat the huge metal box, inlaid with pearls and diamonds and gemstones, etched with writing that she could not yet quite read.

"Do you see this, Cern?" he asked.

"Yes, sire."

"It is the monarch's lockbox. When I'm gone, it will be yours. You'll open it. You'll find my instructions. Do you understand, Cern?"

She did not, but she knew the right answer. "Yes, sire."

Her father took Cern's right pointing finger and gripped it hard. She clamped down on a whimper, knowing better than to give voice to pain. He pressed the tip of her finger to the top of the lockbox, to the lock at the front, then held it high, with a nod to a nearby servant.

The servant bowed deeply to the king, then to Cern. Suddenly the servant flashed a thin knife, pricking her firmly held finger.

A surprised cry of pain escaped Cern, quickly swallowed in the displeasure on her father's face. Her father took her finger, tipped with a bead of blood, and pressed it against the lock, holding it there.

A heavy, metallic sound came from within the box. A grinding. It clicked open. For a moment Cern thought she was going to see what was inside, and she was fascinated. Then her father shut the lid again.

"When you have an heir, Cern, you'll do the same as we have just done."

He then handed her off to another servant. As she was

carried from the room, Cern looked over the servant's shoulders and back at the box, still a mystery.

Cern would not see the lockbox again for many years, but she would hear about it often.

It was always strange to have herself and her family talked about by tutors, as if she weren't quite there, right in front of them. In the educational cauldron of the Cohort, the study of histories mentioned the succession list, the lockbox, and the mysterious means by which it was opened. Thrice-locked, it was called.

That the thing was mage-made seemed a well-known secret.

Now the lockbox was hers, and she knew exactly how to open it. It lived under this very bed, as protected as she was, a laden reminder of the past, a weighty demand from the future.

"Your grace," Sachare said slowly, watching her closely, "if you're too tired and weak to open the lockbox, of course we can put it off."

Cern drew herself up to sitting, wincing at all the many parts of her that were still wretchedly sore, and fighting her eyelids which wanted to close. But she knew the tone in her chamberlain's voice.

"You taunt me, Sacha?"

"Never," Sachare said. But between the tone, raised chin, and stoic expression, Cern understood the humor.

She smiled wearily at her oldest companion.

Cern could almost feel the damned thing under the bed, waiting for her. Full of whatever arrogant, vain, and condescending notes her father-the-king had left for her.

*You'll find my instructions.*

"It's heavier than you think," she muttered, feeling herself overcome with exhaustion, and sinking back into the bed. As she drifted off, she heard Sachare let herself out.

## Chapter Seven

*CHILDREN,* Ella thought, exasperated. Why did so many problems seem to come back to children?

But they weren't children, weren't even eager adolescents. Adults, every one of them.

She stifled the sharp rebuke that leapt to her tongue at the House Murice man who was tugging at her sleeve like a five-year-old.

Instead, she mustered a warm look for him—beyond warm—let him hope—and favored the rest—following her like ducklings—with a bright smile.

"This way, my darlings," she called, gesturing to servants carrying huge bags and lugging barrels from wagons to house. Two more lacquered carriages were just now arriving, disgorging various aristos into the street, all chattering and squealing and giving each other lecherous looks.

Excellent.

She waved them over to join her and led them up the steps.

One fellow—a House Helata man—was entirely too eager, so Ella playfully and dramatically gestured him forward. He lunged for the door knocker, but was laughingly shouldered aside by a Passare woman who pounded on the door with a fist instead.

When the door did not immediately open, another woman leaned past Ella—it was now tight quarters up here on the landing—took the knocker in her fingers, and slammed it as befitted its design.

The knocker was a wrought brass bumblebee—good, solid Etallan work—the striker itself a pointed, hard stinger. What an apt symbol.

"Ah, the sweet song of metal," muttered one of Ella's House Etallan cousins.

At last the door opened. A servant's eyes went wide as he took them all in. He made a stammered greeting and was quickly overrun as the vanguard of aristos pressed past and into the antechamber, trailed by Ella's own laden attendants.

"What a cute little place," said a Passare woman pausing in the large entrance way. No one paid any attention to the servant's objections.

Forward they all went, Ella in the lead. To one side, they passed a sitting room.

"Why yes, by all means," Ella said as a couple from Houses Sartor and Nital dashed inside and deliberately fell together onto a couch, kissing.

Sloppily, she noted. What cut-rate *anknapa* were those Houses using?

A disgrace. If she cared. She didn't.

"Come along, come along," she trilled to the rest, leading the laughing, chattering group down the wide hallway, gesturing to the doors of rooms as they passed. "Make yourselves at home."

Four peeled off, taking over a small library.

"Is her dress supposed to come off like that?" Ella's cousin asked, pausing to look.

"Most assuredly," she told him. "And most expensively."

Another set of doors, another set of aristos making good use of a large bed.

Ella's eye snagged momentarily on a House Sartor woman and an aristo girl, her hair loose and long down her now-naked back. Ella felt a sudden longing for Mardra.

Business now. Pleasure later.

The dwindling group ascended a wide staircase to the next level up. Floating to them were the sounds of the knocker at the front door, more startled exclamations from house servants, and more chattering and laughing aristos pushing past to join the festivities.

Another room. Another. With graphic hand motions, Ella urged the remainder of her flock to waste no time. Finally having deployed all her guests, she approached the last door, which was just now opening from the inside.

Half-dressed, mouth agape, and face pinking nicely, Tokerae staggered out, pulling the door not quite closed behind him. Ella could smell the sex on him, along with the wine, though she had to admit that at that very moment he looked quite sober.

Must be the shock.

He turned on Ella a look of such outrage that she had to struggle not to laugh.

Taller than a man should be, her brother Tokerae, and slender, like their father. Ella was tall, too, but they stood nothing like eye to eye.

"I'm going to kill you," he hissed down at her.

"No, you are not. Because I am going to save your eparch-heir reputation from disastrous ruin."

As if on cue, a face appeared at the cracked door from which he had emerged. Big dark eyes looked left and right and settled on Ella, staying there.

Good, the woman had some sense. After Ella was done with her, she'd have even more of it.

"Tok, we must discuss…" Ella paused momentarily to let shrieking a room over subside into mere gasping moans. Downstairs the door knocker slammed again. Delighted voices followed.

Tok grabbed her hand. Ella allowed him to drag her into the bedroom.

"I'm not introducing you," he said angrily, with a half wave at the woman, who was wearing a belted robe.

"No need." Ella stepped forward to inspect her. Pretty, in a trades sort of way—what was it that the girl did again? Cobbler's daughter, Ella recalled, in charge of a tiny down-city shop, until it had been bought by House Chandler.

"I am Ella del Etallan, Tokerae's sister. You are?"

The woman curtsied, dropped her head, held a moment before rising. A solid gesture of respect. Ella gave her brother an approving smile.

He scowled back resentfully, refusing to be mollified.

"Lilsla, at your service, Lady Ella. Shoemaker by training and birth, I was. Now…" her expression flickered through some sober thought, "I don't know."

"You and I will speak of that later and see what might be arranged, but now I must consult with my brother alone. Perhaps you could show my servants," she nodded at the door, "to the kitchen, so that they can make our guests more welcome."

"*Our* guests?" Tokerae demanded, but Ella kept her gaze firmly on Lilsla as the other woman digested this gentle command. Lilsla nodded, bowed again, left the room.

The kitchen was a safe enough place for her, for now. None of the House babies Ella had brought would think to go into that servant's domain.

Alone, Tokerae lunged at Ella, who stepped back, just out of his reach.

"You—" he sputtered.

"I? I?" she taunted, stepping back again. His face reddened further, and she took pity on him, putting a hand on his shoulder. "You manage your affairs with the deftness of a bull in a shop of spun glass. Everyone knows about this girl."

"I'm sexing others, too," he said sullenly, arms crossed.

"The problem with whores, brother, is that they talk. All of yours say you act like a child. A well-mannered child at that. Only one says that you kiss. Very politely and infrequently. And to a woman, they say that you aren't making any *ointment* at all." As she spoke, Ella walked the room, sizing up from the crumpled sheets and scattered clothes the extent of her brother's evening and intoxication. "Plenty of ointment here, though. A bit under her spell, are you?" He opened his mouth, but she cut off whatever he had intended to say. "No one cares, Tok. If you were keeping two or three such women in town, a man or two besides, no one would raise an eyebrow, not with our House's known appetites."

"But—"

"To keep only the one—a commoner—a *tradeswoman*…" She snorted.

He looked around the room, perhaps only now seeing it as Ella might. "I like her," he grumbled.

"Don't sulk. You want to be eparch? Not like this. People will think you're serious about her. Which brings us to my first gift to you."

"I don't want—"

"I will take her out the back, explain a few things, make sure she's comfy somewhere else, and you will stay here and act as if this grand party were all your idea."

His exhale was sharp.

"Then you'll open some windows so that the neighbors can hear better."

As if to illustrate this reasoning, sudden laughter, shrieking, and pounding, came from the room below.

"One gift from you today might be all I can take, sister," Tokerae said.

Ah, he'd found his tongue at last.

"Oh, you'll want the next one, brother. You surely will."

Tok raised an eyebrow, then gave her a wary look. "Why are you helping me, Ella?"

She read the deep mistrust in his face and was unsurprised, given what had happened to their brother Assel.

---

ELLA HAD BEEN BORN into a frenzy of copulation. The instant that word had come from the palace that King Restarn's consort was three months pregnant, every aristo across the empire got very, very busy. Seuan fertility elixirs—already exorbitantly expensive—could not be obtained at any price.

The Great Houses would do anything for a chance to have a promising child in the Cohort. With the connections and proximity to the princess that Cohort life begat, it was worth any cost.

But timing was key. The Cohort would be formally called when the royal heir turned five. At that time, only those children born within two years of the exact day of the heir's birth could be considered for the Cohort.

To guard against argument, every House-born child had a palace-certified birth document on file at the palace, under heavy lock.

By great luck, Ella's mother, the Eparch of House Etallan,

happened to already be pregnant. By the time Cern was five and the Cohort was officially called, House Etallan boasted three children in range: Tokerae, Ella, and their brother Assel.

House Etallan was also in rich favor with king Restarn. He bestowed upon them, as was the monarch's prerogative, the exceptional honor of two places in the Cohort.

Two places. A gift beyond measure.

Ella, capable and clever, had been the clear choice, and had the heir been a boy, she would have grown up in the Cohort.

Alas, the heir was a girl. Thus, the simple calculation: Etallan had two spots and two boys in range. Those Houses who only had qualified girls might reasonably offer them to the Cohort, but to have twice the possibility of becoming Royal Consort? The chance could not be passed up.

Ella could still remember the day her father took four-year-old Ella aside to explain to her how this was best for the House, that she would have as good an education as her brothers. Better, really, because she would get to stay at home, and they would have to live in the palace. Wasn't Ella happy to hear that?

She wasn't.

The years proved right what Ella had known that very day, that Assel was not Cohort material. By the time Assel was fifteen, he'd been returned to the palace after running away for the ninth time.

This time was different, though. Assel had learned enough to know how to cement his escape: he publicly declared that not only didn't he care for the princess, or want the eparchy, but that he would rather be a blacksmith for the rest of his life than to return to the Cohort and all of its ills.

Furthermore, he was quite loud about it, and his carefully punctuated words echoed through the halls of

House Etallan, to be repeated in every bedchamber, balcony, and corner.

By the time their eparch-mother emerged from her suite, her face was expressionless. She spoke calmly as she agreed to grant Assel his wish.

The next day Assel was shipped off to the province of Pelapa, deep in rural forests, and signed into a formal and binding fifteen-year apprenticeship contract with a local smithy.

It was an educational moment for Ella and Tokerae, seeing what their mother would do when truly angry.

With Assel gone, House Etallan had only one boy in the Cohort, only one hope to become Royal Consort. Mother made sure Tokerae was keenly aware of this.

And Tok, for his part, was sturdily loyal—to both House and mother. He did everything she directed, even shepherding through her failed plot to elevate Innel high enough to fall and shatter.

Year by year, their mother dangled the heir-apparency before Tokerae, making sure that he knew that his future depended entirely on the meticulous execution of her will. Year by year, Tokerae became more and more bitter.

And so, Ella reflected now, as she stared into her brother's eyes, Tokerae might be forgiven for mistrusting gifts.

Especially from his own family.

ELLA STEPPED CLOSE TO TOKERAE, and tilted her head toward his.

He mirrored her. Forehead to forehead, they met. It was an old posture between them.

"You want to know why, brother?" she asked softly.

"Because you are Etallan's best chance to recover our honor. You should be eparch, and I intend to see it happen."

His head moved. Barely a twitch. He might not believe her—or not entirely—but he wanted to.

Erigin's death had not been easy for any of them, but Tokerae had taken it very hard indeed. Mother was furious as well, but—as always—cold, like hardened steel. She did not understand her eldest son.

*Etallan needs you, Tok. But mother has no idea what you need.*

Ella did. When she looked at her brother, she saw a lost child. It was time to bring him home.

She gave him a moment to digest her words. A rising tide of orgasmic howls and raucous howling filled the hallways of the house.

At last Tokerae gave a deep sigh. "Is this second gift of yours as loud as the first, sister, and will it require as much cleaning up?"

Ella smiled a little. "That depends on how we use him. Right now, he's in a dark basement, swearing innocence and promising anything, if we only let him live."

Now that she had Tokerae's full attention, she told him what she had brought for him, though not how she'd come by it.

Because that would lead to Mardra, and Mardra was Ella's secret, one she had no intention of sharing.

---

"I HAVE SOMETHING FOR YOU," Mardra had said to Ella, as they lay together on the bed, Mardra's hands clasped behind her head.

Ella drank in the curves of Mardra's body, through the

clinging silk sheets, tracing her fingers from Mardra's forehead slowly down her prominent nose.

All the women of House Kincel had marvelous noses, though in Mardra's case, the rest of her sharp features showed it off like a main dish. Ella took her time traveling down Mardra's elegant beak, pausing on her lips, which pressed into her fingertips with a kiss.

Then the chin, which was its own exquisite land, then down her long, delicious neck and under the sheets and between hills of breast. And beyond.

Mardra put a hand flat atop her belly, trapping Ella's own there, halting Ella's fingers' southward journey.

"I thought you said you had something for me," Ella objected.

"Something else," Mardra said, with a smile.

"What is it?"

Mardra raised her hand, freeing Ella's from captivity, then gave a contented exhale as Ella continued her explorations.

For a time, there were no words. When they were again ready for conversation, Mardra raised an arm to invite Ella closer. Together they looked at the ceiling.

"Remember that red-alabaster and silver rose I brought you, a handful of years back," Mardra asked, "when first we made eyes at each other at Elupene's dance?"

"Of course."

Ella kept the delicately carved stone rose with its silver-wrapped stem and nubs of thorn on her mantel, easily accessible for those times when she could not manage to see Mardra. Then she would roll it between her palms, the cold metal and stone warming fast.

"I bought that lovely thing from a cart man, years ago in a Low-town Yarpin market."

"Dangerous," Ella said. "I don't approve."

"Dressed in my colors? No one touches Kincel. *Stone is forever, and in all places.*"

"Perhaps also because you indulge the flesh peddlers by looking away."

"Sensible enforcement of a Charter requires both prudence and pragmatic flexibility."

Ella snorted, reflecting on her own House's rather more ruthless approach to those who engaged in metallurgy without the House Etallan's blessing. She gestured to Mardra to continue.

"The cart man had almost nothing to sell. Except for a few small cleverly hidden pieces like yours, because his wares had been taken from him by the king's Rusties, in a town called Arteni."

"Oh?"

"Arteni, it seems, went around their royal charter to sell grain direct to someone other than the crown."

"Foolish."

Mardra nodded. "King Restarn was not particularly pleased. He dispatched a young captain, with soldiers, to go and teach Arteni a good lesson. Hangings and piercings and burnings—all manner of excitement. My cart man told the Rusties that he was only passing through, that he had nothing to do with any of it. But that captain? He gave his soldiers permission to ransack the cart, taking everything. My cart man says he'll never forget that captain's face, not even if he lives forever."

"So?"

"So that captain is now our Lord Commander and the queen's Consort."

Ella slowly sat up in the bed. "Go on."

Mardra also drew herself up, her gray eyes on Ella. "I overpaid him lavishly for your lovely rose and invited him to call on me next time he was in our fair city. Some months ago, he did. Had been traveling east through a string of small villages, looking to buy unusual and undervalued items, and made the acquaintance of a man rather down on his luck, looking for any work at all. My cart man hired him to accompany him back to Yarpin, then put him in my care."

Ella frowned her confusion.

"The man has an unforgettable face," Mardra said, smiling smugly.

"What does that mean?"

"In the small villages, far from the capital, not many know the appearance of the Lord Commander and Royal Consort. This man could be his twin. As long as he doesn't speak. It seemed to me that you might have a use for him."

Ella's thoughts spun quickly and in a number of directions. "How is this possible?"

A shrug. "It happens, sometimes, in the random chance of eyes and noses and lips. An accident of fate. Do you want him or don't you?"

Of course she did.

Ella turned a cautious look on her lover. "What is the cost?"

Mardra had a way of curling her lips when offended. She did so now. "Nothing, damn you."

"Nothing? Then why?"

Mardra put her hand to the back of Ella's neck, and gazed into her eyes. "I made this happen, Ella." Then she grabbed Ella's hair in a fist, and shook her head a little. "And you ask why? Because of *you*. Isn't that enough?"

Looking into Mardra's face, her gray eyes lidded against hurt, Ella realized that no matter what Mardra's motivations —desire to please, or something less pure—if Ella took this gift, she would be in Mardra's debt.

Well, she thought, as their lips met, and their hands went

to all the warm places that their fingers liked so much, there were worse places to put it.

———

"AND WHAT WILL this cost me, Ella?" Tokerae asked, bringing her back to the present.

Ella exhaled and turned over in her mind the difficulty of giving gifts.

What she really wanted was for Tokerae to step up and do what was needed for House Etallan, whether it was today's orchestrated revelry, or palace politics, or Cohort games. She wanted what mother's years-long Cohort plot was supposed to have accomplished, but failed to.

She wanted Etallan returned to its previous glory, the House's good name fully restored. She wanted revenge against the man who had sullied her House, taken her cousin Eregin's life, and soiled their queen with his seed.

No, not mere revenge. She wanted Innel ruined. Utterly destroyed.

For this, Etallan needed Tokerae. Needed him strong and needed him now.

But too much like Ella herself, Tokerae would trust an exchange long before he would put faith in her generosity, let alone her belief in him.

So she must ask for something, and it must be of appropriate consequence. What?

"Make me your second, brother," she said urgently. "If you ever willingly give up the eparchy, promise me that you'll take my cause to succeed you." She held up a hand to forestall his reply. "I don't want the eparchy, Tok. You are Etallan's best hope for justice and honor restored. That's what I want. Let me help."

His look passed through surprise to momentary

vulnerability and landed near weak confidence. For a moment she saw a boy who had never known anyone to believe in him.

Then he took her hand in his, and blinked in what had every appearance of emotion. No pretense, she suspected, and that brought a slight stinging to her own eyes.

"I accept," he said quietly. "Show me this creature. I wonder what we might do with him."

"A near-twin to the mutt? It is a find beyond our wildest hopes, far better than that wretched gold mine mother made such a mess of." Ella exhaled a laugh. "If we can't take him down with this gift, we are not the Great House we imagine ourselves to be."

TOKERAE STARED down at the man seated on a wooden box. The terrified man stared back.

"Remarkable," Tokerae said, circling the man, examining him minutely.

Whatever Ella and her assistants had said or done to him had taken any fight out of him. Unbound, he sat as if he were tied, arms to his sides, shoulders tight. He looked from Tokerae to Ella and back again, desperately, as if he might find in their faces the key to his survival.

Bright lamps had been set about, shining a great deal of light on him, making the windowless room nearly bright as day.

Tokerae could see how the man might be confused with Innel. The nose wasn't right. A little large. The ears were at the wrong angle. He was smaller. But only someone who had grown up with Innel, who had fought him in weapons practice as Tokerae had, would know the difference.

The enormity of the opportunity staring back at him began to settle across his shoulders, like the finest of cloaks.

Tokerae summoned a severe tone, though delight was coursing through him. "Do you understand why you're here?"

The man swallowed and nodded. "My Lord, it has been explained to me. Whatever I can do to serve…ah." He didn't know—had no idea—who held him. Good. "You, and, ah —" he looked at Ella, "and you, my lady, of course. Would be my ah—greatest pleasure."

Tokerae stopped in front of him. "Your utter compliance is required."

"Yes, I am only too happy—you have only to say— whatever you—please, allow me to…" the man trailed off, clearly at a complete loss as to what was being asked of him.

But eager.

He was nothing like Innel. In no way was his posture, attitude, or use of words anything like the Lord Commander's and Royal Consort's. He was not a shadow of the man.

But his appearance…

Yes. Oh yes.

Tokerae exchanged a look with his sister. At his expression, her face dimpled with pleasure, followed by a tilt of the head and a small shrug as if to say, no, he's not Innel, but…

As one, the siblings considered the man.

Tokerae smiled wide. House Etallan's luck was about to turn.

He brought himself down a bit, to examine the man's face more closely. Innel's twin. He nearly was.

"How are you with crowds?" Tokerae asked.

Chapter Eight

AMARTA CAUGHT a brief whiff of sea air as it rose up into the coastal foothills.

She and Tayre road the high inland trail west to Senta, the largest Perripin port city on the Northern side of the Temani Gulf. There, Tayre said, he could launch rumors to obscure both where—and who—Amarta really was.

"Especially during the month-long Accord festival that celebrates the Perripin Unity," he said. "It won't take much for us to be lost in the crowds."

And being a port city, they could go anywhere.

As they passed orchards of catthorn and flats of camellia, Amarta recalled the scene with Maris, again and again. He had almost died.

That he could even be hurt was still a shock.

"Why are you not angry?" she asked.

"Angry?"

"At what Maris did."

He exhaled a short laugh. "Should we blame the sky for the wind? The ocean for being wet? Maris is a mage. She acts in accordance with her making."

"What does that mean?"

He tilted his head slightly. "The mage council has some influence on their own kind, I'm told. But when it comes to Iliban…" he shrugged. "The magi do as they wish. Little stops them."

"There is no justice in that."

He made a thoughtful, doubtful sound.

"You don't agree?" she asked.

"From all that I have seen, justice is fashioned and wielded by those who have the power to make others agree with them."

"Fair is what you take," Amarta muttered. "Someone told me that, once."

In the dark corridors of the hidden city of Kusan, when she was hiding from Innel, who was wielding this very hunter.

As they ascending a hill, the horses pressed forward eagerly, knowing from past experience that it was likely they would rest and have a treat at the top.

At the crest, they fed the horses honeyballs, then let them graze on thick Perripin grasses. Tayre and Amarta sat on a large boulder and gazed down on an expansive green valley, distantly limned by a line of gray-blue ocean.

"Angry at me, then," she said quietly.

"You?"

"I didn't think she would act that way. I should have seen it."

"Ah," Tayre said. For a time, the only sound was the soft rustling of leaves. Then he pointed out across the valley. "A bit ago, there was a red hawk circling. It landed on that far tree, there, the one fork upward. Did you see the hawk?"

She squinted at the distant tree to which he pointed. "No."

He pointed east. "A caravan on the coastal road, between those two rises there. Gone now. Did you see it?"

She looked where he pointed, at the winding brown string that was a distant road. She shook her head.

"You didn't," Tayre said. "Because no one sees everything."

"You do."

"Far from it," he said, amused, as he gazed out at the valley, "Sometimes I know where to look, and that can make all the difference."

"But I did look, on the way back from Mutarka. Again and again. But…" She rolled it around in her mind. There wasn't a good way to say it. "I was distracted," she confessed.

He nodded. "Yes."

She took a breath. "I was thinking about you."

"I know."

"You do?"

He nodded again.

"Then—why aren't you angry? You almost died. It's my fault."

He looked at her, blinked slowly. "Is it? I came back inside the mage's house, with the packs, knowing full well that she didn't want me there."

"I suppose you did," Amarta said slowly. "Why?"

"Because I judged that if the situation went badly, your ability had a chance, where mine would be useless. I intended to split the mage's attention between us, to give you time to act. And you saved us both."

"But it was so close. I barely—"

"Amarta," he said, cutting her off. "I survived a mage attack. Do you know how many Iliban can say as much? Not many. I survived. You are the reason." Gazing back out at the valley again, he smiled. "Sometimes, Seer, the victory is being able to walk away."

NOTHING TAYRE HAD TOLD her about Senta prepared Amarta for the Accord Festival.

Amarta had lived in large Arunkel cities. She had worked as a messenger in Munasee, where she had learned to thread her way through packed throngs of people, making her way through markets, and into crowded taverns.

The Accord Festival was something else entirely.

They left the horses outside the city, because, Tayre assured her, there would be no room within. He was right.

For the miles that the city hugged the coastline, the harbor was like a carpet of ships. But the streets were an ocean of people—a din of noise and colors and smells, washing over Amarta in waves.

Clanging. Chanting. Drumming. So thick were the masses that Amarta and Tayre could not see the edges of the street. People from dark Perripin to pale Arunkin, with hues of tan-skinned foreigners. Islanders, tall and thin, short and thick.

And a bewildering range of outfits: layered weaves, gauzy wraps, swirling skirts. Or near-naked. A man in a cape of dried flowers gave her a look as he passed. For a moment, her gaze stuck to his skirts, which hid little.

At head level, hats and parasols bobbed, dwarfed by headdresses that reached two or three feet above their owners. Sedan chairs tangled with foot traffic, leading to shouting and cursing.

Crows clustered around costermongers with carts of baked pockets, fruits, and triangles.

A throng of laughing young women, half-shaved heads painted blue and white, their braids trailing down their backs to their calves, came by, bursting into song. Children in masks made high trilling sounds. A crying baby, soothed by fast-spoken Perripin. A man on stilts, with spirals of raised scars all across his face and chest, hands held to the sky. A huge man, half as wide as he was tall, howled with laughter. A woman clapped a rhythm to another woman, who gave one in return in mysterious conversation.

A few steps forward, then they must change course to go around another knot, or musicians who had stopped to play in the middle of the lane.

Dozens of dialects and languages swirled. A thousand brilliant shades. Smoke and perfume and human odor, all mingling with strange spices, roasting meats, the tang of spilled wine.

Somewhere, something bayed. Overhead, a clock bell rang loudly.

Overwhelmed, she stopped.

Tayre took her arm. "This way."

He pressed her to walk through a narrow opening between two buildings. There, at the front of a brick storefront, he pushed open a heavy door, drew her through.

Amarta blinked into dim light, exhaling into the relative quiet as the door closed behind. Tables, shelves, large baskets. The enticing smell of baked bread.

"Hello, sers." A short Perripin man, head bobbing as he wiped his hands on an apron. He looked at Tayre with delayed recognition. "Ah, yes. Come with me, please."

He left them at a small side-room with a single table, shutting the door. They sat.

"Does everyone know you?" she asked.

On the way to Senta, they had stopped at small towns, staying with people who clearly knew him, or knew something about him, who gave him envelopes. Messages, he explained. Bits of news. Rumors. Offers of work. Letters of credit.

He gave a half-smile. "I hope not."

The baker returned with a basket of spiced rolls, small plates of pepper and sweet oil, and two mugs of frothy, fermented *atolli*, then left again. Tayre dug under the rolls and napkin to extract an oilskin pouch containing papers, which he read as they ate. He held up an envelope, lavender in color and scent.

"This is an invitation to today's naumachia."

"Today's what?"

"A mock sea-battle. One-man ships. An annual event. As close to interstate war as Perripur gets any more. One of the highlights of the Accord festival. Admissions are negotiated and assigned years—decades—in advance, and only to those with exceptional wealth and position. Not available to the likes of us, at any price."

"Arunkin, you mean?"

"Common Arunkin," he said. "There will be Arunkin. Governors. The southernmost ones who have endeared themselves to the Perripin elites, at least. But mostly it's Perripin congredia, statesmen, merchants, money-changers, and the like. Worth a lot, this invitation, if I could sell it, but it doesn't work that way. But it wouldn't be prudent to go."

"Why not?"

"We'd stand out."

Frustration flashed through her. She reined it in, forcing herself to consider.

"Does our contract say anything about safety?" she asked.

His slow smile dazzled her. "No."

She looked down from his smile, suddenly self-conscious, and traced her finger through the residue of sweet oil on her plate to have something to do besides look at him.

"To understand myself and the world, is what it says. I want to see this thing, this—what did you call it?"

"Naumachia." She could feel him watching her closely.

"Amarta, this would require pretext. Yours and mine. Are you certain?"

"Yes."

A moment passed.

"So be it," he said. "We'll be the guests of the merchant Zeted, an old friend of mine."

"An old friend? Like Maris?"

He laughed a little. "No, not like that."

———

THEY PASSED an open area of benches, where a trio of musicians in wide-brimmed hats plucked at lutes and tapped on wooden boxes. From a tower overhead, bells began to sound, so loudly that all conversation ceased. Then another tower, and another. The chords of bells seemed to ripple across the city.

There was a pattern to these hourly bells, Tayre had told her. If one's ears were educated, one could know not only the time of day but the season, the phase of the moon, and one's location in the city.

But it was also loud. She held her hands over her ears.

When the bells were done, the chatter of the crowd resumed. As they walked, Tayre told her how to tell where someone came from by their clothes, paint, tattoos, or scars. What was on their feet—if anything.

Those with drapes over skin-tight silks were Atudakans—northern, not southern. The voluminous blouses clothed deep-country Ventans, but only in beiges and yellows—a similar style in greens and blues indicated the teacher class of Vilaros, a huge university city that lay across the Temani Gulf.

Eyes outlined in red, with spiral scars under the eyes and a serpent tattoo atop shaved heads, were Dulu Snake tribe.

The spiraling whorls of fuzzy hair, like jeweled plants growing skyward, indicated Perripin aristocracy. Or, Tayre whispered as they passed three of them, those who wanted to appear so.

Their stares were returned, but not for long. This was nothing like Mutarka, where they were clearly out of place. Senta was a wealth of variety, and especially during the Accord Festival, two Arunkin mattered not at all.

A band of men in loincloths and bright colors came dancing toward them, hair swept back into wide fins atop their heads. Their faces painted with huge smiles that showed impossible glee and eyes lined outward to make them seem ever-surprised.

"Oh, milky Arunkin!" they half-sang, half-shouted. "Joyous Accord to you!"

Into Tayre's outstretched hand, a painted man dropped something, and danced past. Tayre showed it to her: a knuckle die.

"Always best to take what the Timuros offer," he said. "Lest they give you something worse. We're lucky: frequently their gifts are made of goat droppings."

"Really?"

"Yes. This is Timurung coinage." He gave her the die to examine. "Weighted, so it rolls to the same number."

"How odd."

"The states are proud of their money." He drew out a handful of coins. "A Shentarat coyle," he said of a small metal curl like a flattened snake, then a round coin with a square hold through the center. "An *uum* from Ulawesan, to be strung on cords." He held up the familiar octagonal sorin. "The Taluk sorin is the most stable of the Perripin currencies, so it's the standard by which the rest are held to account."

"This die from Timurung…what's it worth in sorins?"

"Officially, nothing. But the Timuros are well-liked, so

the Perripin Assembly declared them suitable for paying low-stakes gambling debts."

"Is that a joke?"

A small smile. "Perhaps, but on the part of the Assembly, not me. If we look, we might be able to find a Dulu coil, not to be confused with the Shentarat coin of similar name. It's a bracelet, the number of wraps signifying denomination, each being worth twice the last. The Dulus are famous for their arm-wrestling."

She looked at him. "Now you're joking."

"No."

"Why not have just one currency?"

"The states would never agree. And they believe their diversity makes them stronger. The Perripin Unity ended hundreds of years of embattled kingdoms, all of them finally exhausted enough to forge the thus-far-binding Accord, which has lasted some three hundred years. In practical terms, such differences keep the peace."

"Arunkel is nearly a thousand," Amarta said, wondering why she felt any pride at all in a country she had worked so hard to escape.

A loud, sunny voice cut through the din. "I suffer so, my Perripin friends!"

Nearby, Amarta glimpsed a small man dressed in faded blues and reds in front of a small, painted wagon, a rounded hat clutched to his chest. Somehow, at the same time, the performer was balancing a wooden rod on his nose. That was impressive enough, but when Amarta looked up, she gasped: on top of the rod was a spinning metal plate.

She stepped closer, Tayre following. A gathering ring of people thickened fast behind them.

"Such misery!" the small man cried out brightly. Looking up at the spinning plate, he tossed his hat to land at his feet, open side up. Now there were hoops spinning around both his wrists. Where had they come from?

"What is my woe, good people? Why, it is this: there is no sweet pie atop my plate, dripping with Perripin honey!" A spinning hoop flew up, off his hand, then the other.

*Everything in the air, but nothing dropped.*

Impossible.

His whole body seemed to shudder. All at once, everything flew into the air. Grinning, the small man took up a dramatic pose, the toes of one foot cocked.

The hoops fell onto his pointed toe, the plate onto his open palm, and the rod into his other hand.

The crowd gasped. Loud "la las!". Snapping fingers.

"La, la," echoed Tayre at her side, an impressed tone to his voice. Amarta's own delight faded as she took in this secondary performance.

With a metallic bang, a coin hit the performer's plate. More pattered after. Others went into the hat on the ground.

At the edge of the encircling audience, was the painted wagon, that might have been pulled by a small donkey. Or a determined man. Peeling paint, faded wood—it had seen better days. Leaning against it was a tiny table.

"Thank you, good sers! Fine miss! Domina. Seras. Children. Another trick, perhaps? I have just the one! I must warn you: it is very difficult, and not without risk. For me, of course! You are the first audience who will ever see it. Will you permit me?"

"Yes!" "Huzzah!" "Do!"

"Ah—but I am undecided." He gave a torn look, replaced by a slow, mischievous smile, as he made a slow circuit of the open space, holding out the plate to the crowd. He caught their gazes in his own, eyes sparkling. "Terribly difficult." Tayre chuckled as he passed, placing a few tiny kli-coyles on the plate.

At Amarta's side, a tall Perripin couple had three children between them, hands linked. The performer brought his head even with the middle child, a small girl.

"I'm thinking about that sweet pie! Aren't you?"

The girl nodded enthusiastically. The performer looked at the plate with a mournful expression, then back to the girl with a hopeful smile. "The trick is going to be amazing! Don't you want to see it?"

"La, la!" cried the girl, looking up at her mother, tugging her hand, and gesturing to the plate. The tall woman gave the man a reproachful glare, but put sorin-menhas on the plate.

The performer stopped at a trio of large Perripin men, their white headbands and silver chains marking them as festival constables. "Good sers, you'd be horrified to see the scars I have from the last time I tried this trick." They smirked as he walked on. "The last juggler who attempted this trick lost his mind! Had to give up the business entirely. Now he's a gong farmer. I can't do that. I have a very sensitive nose!"

Scattered laughter.

"Yes, we can smell you from here, Vagras!"

"Vagras?" Amarta whispered to Tayre.

"Vagrant. Wanderers. The Unwelcome. The Lost. They have many names, but they call themselves the Farliosan."

The small performer sniffed theatrically at his armpits. "It's true: I smell terrible! Shall I dust myself like a finch, right here?" He made a birdlike motion with his head, then began to unbutton his shirt. "I apologize for the delay and the sickly shade of my naked skin compared to your rich, healthy ones. If only I could afford a bath."

Groans from the crowd. A few coins went onto the plate. Another two hit him directly on the leg. He frowned, but continued to unbutton his shirt.

"Give us the show," said a well-dressed, mustachioed

Perripin man with an embroidered headdress that draped down past his ears, tapering to points. He stepped into the circle, dropped into the plate a large octagonal sorin, then retreated back to the audience.

"The scales have tipped!" the performer cried, re-buttoning his shirt. "Now I exist only to entertain." He bowed deeply. "I am Olessio, Prince of Wanderers, Ambassador of the Farliosan, come from lands distant and exotic—yet ever-so humble—to bring to the exalted Perripin people, at the grand Accord Festival, my modest talents."

Fingersnaps of agreement through the crowd.

"Allow me to introduce my lovely assistant. Tadesh," Olessio called loudly. "Come and show everyone your pretty face." He flourished a hand toward the wagon's small back door, open a crack.

After a moment, Olessio frowned, cleared his throat. "Tadesh?" Then, as if sharing a secret: "She's rather vain. Give her a moment to make ready." Then, louder: "Hurry up, darling! The people are waiting!"

"Show us the damned trick, Vagras," growled someone.

Amarta agreed: while the feat with plate and rod and hoops had been impressive, the festival was rich with astonishing performances. He would lose his crowd if he didn't do something soon.

"Ah! Here is my lovely helpmate now. Tadesh, dearest, find me a volunteer child for this next trick, won't you?"

Something brushed by Amarta's leg. Suddenly everyone was looking at her.

No, they were staring at her feet.

Gazing up at her from the ground were large golden eyes in a tiny, white-and-dark-brown face. A long snout tipped with a quivering black nose tilted up. As Amarta watched, stupefied, the creature's long ears slowly went back, then forward again. It retreated a dainty step from her, then came closer, touching her shoe with a tentative paw.

Children squealed and cooed with delight, struggling in hasty parental grips. Heads craned around to get a better look.

"A child, Tadesh—not a full grown woman!" Olessio said sternly. "Now, for my next trick, not only will I juggle three sharp knives, but also—a child!"

A scattering of uncertain laughter.

"Tadesh, find me a rather small one, won't you?"

Tadesh looked at Olessio, over her shoulder, then up to Amarta. She then shook her long-snouted head, as if to say, can you believe this man?

The crowd tittered. Olessio put hands on hips, bent over and wagged a finger. "You are keeping our magnificent Perripin friends waiting, Tadesh. They have paid for a show. Obey!"

Tadesh opened her mouth, tilted her head, and shook a little—a silent mimicry of laughter. The crowd laughed back, delighted. Enthralled.

Olessio tossed a tidbit to the small creature, who caught it with a graceful hop, landing to face him.

"And this," Olessio said to the audience, "is why I named her 'Tadesh-a-makeem'. It means, in the language of Princes, 'tastes good with butter.' The better to help her stay humble, you see."

Tadesh wrinkled her nose in what might have been, on a less furry face, a scowl.

"You see," Olessio continued, turning slowly, hands extended for emphasis as he nodded at the audience. "There is a natural order to the world. Tadesh, being a mere beast..."

His back now turned, Tadesh raised herself up hind legs, her paws stretched to the side, her head bobbing in time with Olessio's, as she mimicked his motions.

Gasps rippled through the crowd. Children whispered excitedly, pointing.

No one was leaving now.

Olessio continued to turn. "Adorable though she is, Tadesh is not as intelligent as we are, though certainly you Perripin are far more clever than I." Olessio's turn finally brought him to face Tadesh again.

Still on her hind legs, she pulled her paws together, and modestly cocked her head, as if listening attentively. He tossed her another bit of food. A gulp, and it was gone.

Then he turned to the tiny table and pulled away a cloth to reveal three long knives.

*Amarta felt a chill. A darkened room. Lamplight glinted on the flat of blade.*

Around her, smiles faded, expression turned uneasy.

Taking the knives in hand, Olessio tossed each one, end over end, until he was juggling all three. "Very dangerous," he cried, his eyebrows waggling playfully.

He glanced around, only now seeming to notice the crowd's disquiet. Uncertainty flickered across his face.

"Ah, wrong trick!" he said quickly, tossing the knives flat to the dirt, near the wagon. "Tadesh?"

Tayre whispered into her ear. "The Perripin don't like to see knives brandished by foreigners, especially at this festival. They think he might be Arunkin, which makes it worse."

To Amarta, Olessio looked nothing like Arunkin, not with his tan skin and heavy brows.

"Tadesh," Olessio said, toeing the knives under the cart with one foot. "A small child. Now, please?"

Tadesh ran to the three children nearest Amarta. She pointed to the smallest of them, a boy, who began to jump up and down enthusiastically.

"Good choice. Hello, young man." Olessio crouched to come eye level with him. "Are these your parents? Best of the

Accord to you, Perripin sers! Either of you solicitors? No? Excellent! I see you have other children. Even better. Did I mention that Olessio's not my real name?"

Chuckles from the crowd. The boy's mother was frowning, but her husband laughed, gesturing for his son to go ahead. The boy bounded eagerly into the middle of the circle. Olessio took his hand.

"Takes steady courage and nerve to work with a small child—as many of you parents already know! Good thing I have both!" Olessio took the set of hoops and began to juggle. He crouched down a bit, put an arm around the boy's waist, and hefted him up off the ground by a few inches. Down, then up, down, then up.

"And there it is! Hoops and a child, juggled together!" Olessio released the child to return to his family.

There was laughter, finger-snaps. Olessio's hat and plate were fast filling with coins.

"Next, watch me juggle three cups of water, without spilling a drop! Famous throughout the land, my firefly and saucer trick!"

The crowd hooted and la-la-ed, seeming to forget—or perhaps to forgive—the misstep with the knives.

Tayre tapped her shoulder. *We go.*

Across the circle, the constables were watching the two of them rather too closely.

They stepped back into the crowd, the space they left immediately filled.

---

"PROBABLY NO MORE THAN PROFESSIONAL SUSPICION," Tayre said of the constables, as they strode a quiet brick alleyway. "But no need to find out. Remember Caurpana's labyrinth?"

Amarta nodded. They had glimpsed the walls distantly from the road to Senta.

"There's another magi-khrastos on our way. Do you want to see it?"

"Yes!"

They came to a row of shabby tents and tables. Smaller booths. More foreigners. Even some Arunkin. They waved or gave a nod.

"Countrymen!" called a hunched man, who waved them over to his small gray tent. "Come closer! Wouldn't you like to know what fate has in store for you?"

Amarta slowed.

He swept open the grimy tent curtain and a young girl, perhaps six, peered out. "Arunkin seers are the finest! So young—closer to the edge of life, giving her keener powers. She can see…" he made a circling gesture in the air. "What will be!"

"That makes no sense," Amarta said.

"Ah, but it will! Don't pass this chance by, countrymen. Only two falcons."

"Two falcons?" Amarta said, disbelievingly.

Tayre laughed. "Is why we're so poor," he said to the other man. "I make it, she spends it." He wrapped an arm around Amarta's shoulders and shook her a little, giving her a fond smile.

Her furious expression, she realized belatedly, fit his drama perfectly.

Clever.

Tayre gave a frown to the tent. "What's her divination device? We've already seen—and smelled, by the Fates—goat entrails, maggots in meat, scrying glass, and drunken beetles. What does your girl use?"

Drunken beetles? Did he make that up?

The man gave a dismissive snort. "Pah. The cards are the

only true way." He gave them a fast, assessing look. "Wouldn't be at all surprised to see you turn over *The Lovers*, you two. Of course, the girl is the teller, not me. How's this—let's call it one falcon."

"No falcons," Tayre said, holding out a mix of coins. The man looked about to object. "Take it or leave it," Tayre said, his voice hardening.

"Since you're countrymen," The man said, pocketing the offered coins. He pulled back the curtain, gave a flourish. "See what fate has in store for you."

They ducked to enter. The curtain dropped, the light graying. The young girl sat at a small round table, gesturing for Amarta and Tayre to take two small stools.

The girl was not much older than Amarta had been when she first started having visions. She gave them a too-wide smile and took up a Rochi deck, her small hands barely managing a pull-shuffle.

"You must focus, sers," she said, "on your question, so that the reading is true." As she spoke, her words and cadence made it clear that they were memorized. Amarta wondered if she understood what she was saying at all.

So young, Amarta thought with an ache, staring at the girl's face. Was the man outside her father? Where was her mother?

"Have you a question firmly in mind?"

*Can I really be the only one?*

The girl fanned the deck face down across the table. "Choose one."

Amarta touched a card. The girl turned it over.

"Ah, *The Purse*! A fine card!" The picture showed coins and gemstones and shells—wealth spilling across a table. "Choose a second."

Amarta did. The girl turned it over. "Oh, look! *Birth*! A baby to come, perhaps. A relative?"

She had just been talking to Tayre about coins, and there was the birth of Cern's baby. Could this girl be a true seer? Amarta felt her hope rise.

"Show us all the cards," Tayre said quietly.

"Choose one more card, and we will know all!" the girl said.

Amarta touched one tentatively.

The girl turned it over, and clapped in delight. "*The Lovers*! A very fine telling! Wealth and a baby and marriage! So good—so much…"

Tayre held up a sorin between his fingers and the girl fell silent. "For you, only," he breathed. "Let us see the rest of the cards."

The girl glanced anxiously at the drapes, then back at Tayre. She took a breath, and nodded, taking the coin from his fingers.

Tayre then turned over the deck, with a practiced ease, gently fanning the cards on the table with his fingers. Silently, he pointed out a card to Amarta, then another and another.

They were duplicates. She frowned in confusion.

He whispered, "What is missing?" At her bemused headshake, he answered: "Any card that might convey a poor outcome. *Aftermath. Betrayal. Invasion. Catastrophe.*"

Then Amarta understood: it was not a full deck.

It was not a true reading.

Tayre restacked the cards, face down. With a loud exhalation of surprise he said, affably, "A good outcome indeed. Worth a bit more to me and my lady." He got up, pushed aside the drapes. Amarta followed him, saw as he grinned and put another two small coins in the hand of the man outside the tent.

As they walked on, Amarta looked back. The man was counting his coins.

In the tent, the girl was probably trying to figure out how to hide hers.

---

"JUST FOR SHOW, sera, just for show."

Amarta stared into a large glass tank from which clear tubes rose like ghostly branches. Exquisitely small, bright fish swam through the snaking chambers to the top.

The round-faced man smiled at her. "To show what is possible, to the Primeri, who pay me to build tanks in their fine mansions. But aren't they beautiful?"

"Oh, yes," Amarta breathed as a shimmering blue fish flickered upward.

"Watch, now." The man sprinkled crumbs into a funnel at the top. Down below, from under a rock in the tank, a tiny pale creature, no bigger than her fingertip, began to make its way upward through the channels, its many limbs propelling it forward. She looked closely. Tiny tentacles.

"Now these—these are for sale." The man gestured to a display of curved iridescent ovals, some as wide as her palm, some as tiny as a nals coin. Thin strands of cord went through drilled holes at their ends. "Very hard. They make fine adornments. Or spoons."

The shells shimmered in various colors, like bright sun across sand.

Memory tickled. Vision hummed. Amarta blinked, trying to place the image.

"Does it please you, my sweet?" Tayre asked, the term of endearment wrenching her into the moment with an angry ache that swirled through her.

He couldn't have known, could he? Dirina used to call her that. Her sister, about to be irrevocably married into the Arunkin empire.

"This one, I think," Tayre said to the man, paying him and draping the corded shell over her neck. "Lovely." He winked at her, his face precisely positioned for the vendor to see.

At this pretense, a different sort of anger and ache came over her.

He took her arm, and led her along. On another lane, a row of booths was devoted to dolls, made of all imaginable materials, from rags to precious metal. Like real people, the dolls sat on benches, with eyes of glinting gemstones, skin of burnished wood, blouses and jackets of lush velvet and silk.

As they passed, well-dressed children pawed through the dolls, cackling with delight when they found one that echoed their own satin outfits and leather boots. Behind them, parents fished out coins. Many coins. Large coins.

The children delightedly held up their new dolls. The price of any one of them would have fed Amarta and her family for months.

She knew what it was to be poor—to be hungry—but this extraordinary wealth—this she did not know.

At another table, animal figurines. Her mind went to Pas. Would he have toys like these in the Arunkel palace? And Dirina—

*My sweet.*

*Act familiar with me.*

Just how familiar would he let her be, here in the street? She grabbed Tayre's arm and touched her head to his shoulder, then looked at his face.

His smile was so warm and convincing that she felt ill. But it was touch. His touch. Perhaps that was enough, all by itself, whatever the reason.

Another street and another. They stopped to buy skewers of roasted meats and orange roots and sat on bales of hay to eat.

"Those two," she said softly, glancing surreptitiously at two men across the square. "They're watching us."

"Watching you," he replied quietly. "But they have no interest in you beyond lechery."

"What?" she hissed at him. "How can you possibly know that? You're not even looking."

His eyes held suppressed amusement. "I saw them when we sat down. I don't need to see them now. I know how men hold themselves when they're hunting people, and how they hold themselves when they're hunting sex, and the difference is obvious to me."

"Not to me," she said.

"Learn something, then. Go talk to them."

"Why would I do that?"

"To learn to live in a world that includes lecherous men."

"No," she said, not sure if she should feel affronted or not.

He shrugged a little, licking the rest of one stick clean and starting on the next. "Take a step or two toward them, then. What might foresight tell you?"

She considered how Tayre could sometimes change futures just by changing his intention. He made it look easy. It wasn't. But until she was truly resolved to go talk to them, vision would only provide only a messy mash of visages.

The two men noticed her looking at them. They waved, calling and gesturing for her to come closer.

Why not?

Grabbing tight to the trickle of impulse, she took a step toward them, then another. A trio of fast-talking, high-hatted women pushed in front of her, forcing her to pause. She lost the trail, lost the courage, fought to gain it back, took another step.

She would go to the men. To practice her Perripin skills. They would…what? Another step. What would they do?

*One man moved close, his hand on her shoulder, his breath full of spice and garlic. He spoke to her in Perripin and grinned. She understood nearly all the words, but not the meaning, and they could tell. They laughed. Then he made a gesture, and she understood perfectly.*

Tayre was right. They were not hunting her because she was the seer. Only because she was a woman.

She turned back to Tayre, who was waiting for her. He took her arm, and patted it. Laughing, as if at a shared joke. She looked at his hand on her arm.

No, she decided: it wasn't enough.

## Chapter Nine

TAYRE AND AMARTA walked a wide street shaded by huge salap trees, each thick leaf frilled in pale green edging. A wealthier neighborhood, without rows of street stalls or carts. Instead, shops with glass windows, by which stood guards who watched them.

The came to a large square where they joined an oddly hushed crowd that stood some forty feet back from a black, rectangular structure. The stone rose ten or twenty levels high, so high above the tallest buildings of Senta that one could not quite measure it by comparison. Seagulls circled above, crying as if they, too, could not make sense of the thing.

It was black stone, darkly reflecting the surrounding crowd like a poor mirror. No windows or doors were visible. Only a crack, hairline at the top, jagged to the ground, where it gaped open in shadow.

The crowd's feet, Amarta noticed, formed an outline of the foundation of the structure itself, to each corner, as if they stood at an invisible barrier.

A magic barrier.

"Zenectia's Library," Tayre said of the structure. "What it really is, I have not been able to discover, but I do know that someone—possibly Zenectia—pays taxes to Senta for the land on which it sits. Not cheap. Uma-sorins, and a good many of them."

"So, it's a library?"

"Perhaps. It is said that Zenectia's agents purchase books at top value."

"But what makes it a magi-khrastos? That it so… impressive? And mage-made?"

"Yes. And that the work is singular across the world."

Amarta digested this.

"Why?" she asked.

He shrugged. "A rite of passage, perhaps. A demonstration of power. A symbol to remind Iliban of their place? Who knows—perhaps they want to be admired."

"The crack. At the base, it almost looks wide enough to walk through."

"Could be."

Amarta felt a sudden hunger to know, to go to the crack, to peer inside. Would she see books lining the walls? A mage at a table of tomes? An empty room?

Solid rock?

She took a tiny step forward, inching closer to the invisible boundary.

No, she decided, that was a poor idea. She had just tangled with Maris. Tayre had almost died. A terrible idea. One of the worst she'd ever had. Tightness and a sense of dread came over her, and she was reminded of all the times that she had almost died. All the bad decisions she had made.

She felt sick. She inched back. It faded.

"Is this what it felt like to cross Maris's wardstones?" she asked.

He shook his head. "This is far stronger. Zenectia is—or was, who knows—an elder mage. I can't cross it. Can you?"

Vision gave Amarta no future in which she did. "No."

The border was lined with all manner of people. Perripin, Arunkin, Islanders, and more. But there were no wary looks at each other, no curious glimpses, no whispers, no pointing. All eyes were on the magi-khrastos. It was as if all their differences had been put aside.

The magi-khrastos was riches beyond dolls and coins, even mountains of gold. It was something beyond wealth itself.

What must it feel like, Amarta wondered, to have made something like that? Was the mage inside, watching the Iliban marvel at her creation?

Somehow she thought not.

---

"COME to see the Tree of Revelation!"

A stout, swarthy man waved them over. He gestured at a wide, shallow pot before him, from which grew a tree some three feet high. No sapling, though, Amarta realized as she came close. The deep red bark and small leaves had the look of a huge, full-grown tree, somehow made small. From one narrow branch hung a chain that ended in a teardrop-shaped magenta stone.

"Watch." The man tapped the hanging teardrop, setting it to swinging. "The Great Tree in the Xanmelkie Valley is like this, only far larger, and ancient."

"Is that where the Monks are?" Amarta asked.

"You have heard of the holy order! Then you must know that once a year, on the Day, the Tree answers the questions of those querants lucky enough to be chosen."

"The tree answers?" Amarta asked.

"The monks interpret," said Tayre from her side.

The man's eyes flickered to Tayre. "The Monks of Revelation are virtuous and devoted. What's more, each question and answer are written in their Great Book. Thus they have held the trust of the people for generations."

Amarta watched the small pendulum swing back and forth. "Can anyone ask?"

"Oh, no. You must be chosen on the Day of Revelation. For that—" he gestured to a black and chestnut box, the lid halfway open, revealing translucent pink stones, "—you must have a rare and precious monkstone."

"A gift?" asked Tayre with a small smile.

The man's eyes narrowed. "All funds go to sustain the Great Tree and the holy monks who nurture it."

"May I touch one?" Amarta asked.

His smile turned pained. "Alas, sera! The stones are sensitive. I cannot let you touch one unless you are taking it with you."

"How much?" Tayre asked.

"Only five sorin. I have seen them sold for many times that amount. Why, in Zaneke—"

"Five sorin, for a piece of common quartz?" Tayre snorted. "Why, we could purchase a night at the Honey Drizzle for that much."

A deep scowl settled on the man's face. "These are far from common, sir," he said. "And to compare the Honey Drizzle to the sacred work of—"

"I want one," Amarta said, hoping to cut this line of discussion short.

"You'll have one, my dearest," Tayre said adamantly. "But he'll take a lot less."

The two men glared at each other and Amarta opened her mouth to object, but Tayre's hand flashed: *Wait.*

"Please, miss, will you reason with your..." the man seemed at a loss as to how to finish the sentence.

Amarta understood that too well.

Tayre slapped a handful of menha-sorins on the table and stepped back, making a gesture of sardonic welcome.

The man blinked.

"I can see you are no ordinary Arunkin, sera," he said to Amarta. "Though my children will go hungry tonight, and the monks be without shoes this season..." he brushed the coins toward himself, then took from the box a small pink stone, handing it to Amarta. "A sacred monkstone into your hands, good lady."

"Thank you." She held it a moment. "Should I feel something?"

"The monks study their entire lives to achieve holy purity. The likes of you and I can hardly expect to find it in an instant, can we? It may take many turnings of the wheel."

"To which wheel do you refer, exactly?" Tayre asked mildly. "A day? A month? A year?"

"Who can say?"

Amarta sighed. She was learning about the world, all right. Tucking the stone into a pocket, she turned to go, then paused.

"When is this Day of Revelation?"

"The Autumn Equinox."

"Thank you," she said again, and they walked on. Amarta fingered the quartz stone in her pocket. "Have you seen this thing, the Monks and their Day?"

"No," Tayre answered.

"Then how can you be sure that it's not true?"

"Because I know how pretenders predict results—they arrange the causes. I've done it myself. How many tricksters must you examine, Amarta, before you are convinced that they are not like you?"

*All of them*, she didn't say. "The monks keep a book, to prove their predictions."

"Ink and paper do not make the words they hold true."

"But I am true," she said. "So they might be."

He shrugged. "They might."

---

THEY CONTINUED across the city toward the amphitheater. Another street, houses with silver-and-brass doors, and windows that glinted.

Next a wide avenue with trees of long leaves like tongues, that danced in the breeze. It opened into a huge square, where a thick crowd faced a distant, raised platform. To one side, elevated pavilions of brilliant colors shaded elegantly dressed figures.

Through the crowd's hats, hair-towers, and parasols, Amarta caught a glimpse of the distant stage. A man's loud voice reached back to her.

"Number twenty-eight!"

Onto the platform was led a long line of bound, nearly naked, light-skinned figures, the first of which was unlatched from the chain and pressed to the front of the stage. Arunkin, from the looks of him.

He might have been any boy from the villages Amarta had once called home. Or Pas, a handful of years hence.

"Already strong and still growing," the man bellowed. "You can tell from the feet. Show us your feet, boy!" With a stick he tapped the young man's foot, which lifted. "Good people, don't let the forehead brand fool you! His crime was small and he's been retrained. Entirely obedient now. Aren't you, boy?" He nodded at the young man, who nodded back, seemingly dazed.

Amarta wondered if the young man understood a word

of the Perripin being spoken. He was turned. "Look at that back! A fine creature! He'll work hard for you. What am I bid?"

A shout from a pavilion, then from another. A flurry of them. In moments, the young man had been hustled off and another figure brought forward.

This one's hair was as pale as the sun. Amarta's heart raced. No question, even from this distance: he was Emendi.

"Number twenty-nine. Look at this lovely thing. Best of kind—don't see this quality often. Make an excellent in-house servant. You'll be the envy of all your friends and neighbors, as this beautiful creature brings you drinks and food. And anything else that you may desire! A true prize. What am I bid?"

Amarta swallowed a lump in her throat. She had made friends in Kusan who had looked so much like this man. Kusan, which she had nearly let be destroyed, because of him.

She did not look at Tayre. She felt his hand on her shoulder. She stiffened.

The bidding for the Emendi man was fast, loud, and expensive, then he was gone, and another Arunkin man brought to the platform.

Amarta whirled to face Tayre. She should say nothing, not about Kusan, not about her thoughts.

Then he gave her a gentle, questioning look. Somehow it unlocked both voice and fury.

"They did nothing to you," she hissed, "yet you would have destroyed them. Hundreds of good people, turned into slaves to be sold like animals. Children and babies. All to get at me?"

He put an arm around her trembling body, his free hand waving in the air as if to accompany some speech. As if they were a couple, tiffing. A rueful smile played across his face, as if apologizing for some slight. He moved closer and breathed into her ear:

"If you're going to blame me for what I might have done, but didn't, while I was under contract to someone else, will you also praise me for what I might yet do, but haven't, under contract to you?"

Amarta thought of Darad, of Ksava. Of Nidem. Her eyes stung.

She shook her head. "You took them from me. My friends. My home." Her voice cracked. Still he smiled, as if trying to make amends for the supposed fight he was pretending to have. Her chest ached. Did he have no feelings? "Maybe Maris was right about you."

He let her go, holding up his hands as if conceding a point. But he said, "You know how to end this, Seer, if you want to."

She shook her head, furious with him, with herself. With having given voice to this. Foolish of her to mention the Emendi and the hidden city, when they had trusted her with everything.

On the platform, another Emendi, his hair blond-white, went to a new owner. The line of men still waiting to be displayed peered around each other to see the audience. To glimpse their future.

Beyond that line was another. Women, some with long locks, the color of straw.

"I can't bear it," she whispered.

Tayre took her elbow, drawing her away, walking her back from the crowd, and turning into a narrow alleyway.

Boxy, shabby buildings rose on either side. He stopped at an alcove, took her shoulders, turned her to look at him.

"None of them are from Kusan. They are imports from Dalgo. Bred, not captured. They are trained for Perripin state governor's households. Dukes, Primeri, wealthy merchants.

They'll be servants, nursemaids, cooks. They'll clean and care for children and well-loved pets."

"That doesn't make it right."

"I am not making the case for justice, only telling you their origin and probable destination." Then, more gently, "To understand yourself and the world, Amarta, you must see both clearly."

A sudden peal of children's delighted laughter caught her off-guard. For a moment she let herself drink in the sound, a balm for her ache, then she turned to look for the source.

A high, narrow window, less than a hand's-finger-spread wide. Amarta stood on tiptoe, edging up to see inside. There, two children, perhaps eight years old, a boy and a girl. The boy's shirt was off, and the girl held his arm up by the wrist.

"See how strong he is? Make a fist, brother. No, not like that. Like you're showing your big muscles. Yes, that's how."

They were blonde and blue-eyed.

Amarta pulled back from the window as if slapped. "What is this?" she breathed.

"Holding cells for the auction."

"But children?"

"Yes, children."

"What are they doing?"

"Like all children, they play at what they know."

"Selling each other?" She asked in horror. "How can you be so sure they're not from Kusan?"

He turned her back to the window. "Look at the boy's arm. Do you see what's branded there? The first glyph is the Arunkel sigil, and the second is the sign for slave. So that's his status and origin. But if he had been captured anywhere in the countryside, Kusan or not, he would have been treated as an escaped slave and his forehead branded as a criminal."

She imagined everyone in Kusan, branded on the forehead. It must never happen.

"We could rescue them," she said urgently. "Buy them. Do we have that much money?"

He gave her a look that she could not read. "Let us say, for a moment, that we did. We buy them. What then?"

"Give them their freedom, of course."

"Where? Here, in the streets of Senta?" He looked around the alleyway, then cocked his head at her. "In a countryside town, like Mutarka? They are marked as slaves. Once found, they'll be treated as escaped—criminals—and be branded." He touched his forehead.

"We could hide them."

Even as the words left her mouth, she felt hope crumble. An Emendi child with hair the color of straw could not hide. Not in Perripur, not in Arunkel. They could not walk free, not without heavy disguise, and even that was a great risk. She knew this from her time in Kusan. "Bring them to Maris. She would protect them, surely."

"Would she? Do you believe that?"

She thought back on her time with Maris.

"Take them with us, then."

"As slaves?"

"No!"

"What then? Are you assembling a new family to protect, Amarta, because you miss the last one?"

His words were so soft. How could they feel like blows? She wanted to yell at him, tell him how wrong he was, but she could not seem to.

"So they're…what?" she asked bitterly. "Worthless?"

"Worth plenty. The girl is clever and lively. The boy looks like he will grow fair. For someone willing to invest in them, they will be worth a very great deal. The Perripin treat their slaves far better than Arunkin do."

Through the window, the girl was ushering her brother

into the hands of an imaginary buyer. Both were smiling wide.

"I'll sell you, now!" the boy said to her.

Amarta pulled back, strode away. Tayre followed.

She choked down a sob. "We must leave them here?"

"I see no better option."

Unbidden, an image came to Amarta. A memory of a vision. A flash of a thing she had not actually seen, except in foresight, but that had happened, and that she could never forget.

*A girl's body lay on the dirt. An arrow through her, a dark red stain spreading across Amarta's own cloak. Her friend Nidem, who had died in Amarta's place, outside the city of Kusan.*

A sick shock of realization went through her. She herself was surely responsible for Nidem's death, because she'd given her friend her own blue-trimmed cloak, and from a distance and with disguise, the girl had looked like Amarta. But who had actually put the arrow through the girl's chest?

It could have been Tayre. In all the months they had spent together, this possibility had not occurred to her, until just now. She could ask him.

But then she would know.

*We go*, she signed sharply, striding away.

---

THE ENTRANCE to the huge amphitheater was guarded by two large, well-muscled Perripin men wearing the white headbands and silver chains of the congredia's constables. One gave them a look that said that they were surely in the wrong place and had best get along quickly. Then he reluctantly accepted the paper Tayre offered.

The two men conferred over the invitation, one handing

it to a messenger. "Check with Domina to see that this isn't forged," he said in fast Perripin. The boy ran off.

In minutes, the messenger returned, whispering into the constable's ear. The constable gave Amarta and Tayre an unhappy look, handed the invitation back.

"You're late," he said reproachfully, waving them inside. "Behave yourself, Arunkin. We're watching you."

"Yes, ser," Tayre said, hanging his head in supplication.

They followed the boy into the great oval structure of the amphitheater, where a cacophony of color and sound swept over Amarta. Spread out before them, above and below, were broad terraces, like a giant's circular staircase, climbing higher than she'd realized from the walls outside, and down to the flooded arena below.

They climbed a staircase up a level, then another, where huge canopied tents crouched, like houses made of silk, many with curtains pulled back to reveal lavishly furnished rooms and expensively dressed Perripin elites.

Tayre pointed upward and beyond. "That pavilion is the Perripin Congredia itself. Next to it, the twin Arquebusiers of Mundar. See the red booth with the parrot on top? The Duke of Atudaka. There, the ur-kahn of Dulu. That gray booth to the side—that's the Night's Seven, whose membership overlaps with the Congredia. Remember the diagrams?"

She nodded. He'd sketched the Perripin confederacy, by state and family and Assembly in the dirt. Only now, seeing all these booths and people, did she begin to grasp the convoluted enormity of it.

"That's Venta's grand vizier." He gestured to a heavy metal cage, inside of which was an enormous black bull, glaring down. She slowed with astonishment, and he pressed her forward. "Every year Venta demands more area for their vizier, and every year the Assembly says no. Part of what keeps the Perripin peace is that each state gets exactly the same space on this level, the allotment measured to the fingernail width by a conclave of magi." He gestured to a terrace below, where each slice of the circle contained a single, canopied black pavilion, in which sat or stood figures in black robes.

"Mages," she said. "In the open."

"Perripur has a good relationship with the magi. Here, each state has one, to make sure that no state uses magery to win the contest."

Perripin heads swiveled to watch them as they walked the arena's circumference. Few smiled. Some frowned. Many seemed bemused by their presence.

In the flooded arena, brightly painted single-man ships began to ram each other hard enough that Amarta could hear the cracks over the crowd's hooting and calling. One sailor threw a short spear, hitting the raised shield of an opponent.

"That looks dangerous," she whispered.

"Choreographed. A repeat of last year's battle," Tayre said, "a show for the crowd. The actual contest has yet to start. Careful." She looked down, stepping around a huge blue lizard. A girl dashed after it, snatched it up, put it on her shoulders, staring at them as she retreated. "This level is populated by merchants with enough influence to be patrons of ship teams. It's an impressive expense. Here's our destination."

A tent draped in various shades of violet was fronted by six large guards. One nodded at Tayre, pulled back the curtain to allow them inside. There, Perripin servants and guests oriented toward a center settee on which lounged an extremely fat woman, her deep dark skin offset by strands of purple gems and glinting stones that cascaded from ears and hair.

The woman smiled delightedly, gesturing abruptly to

those nearest to her to vacate their chairs, which they scrambled to do.

"Tymon, my excellent boy!" she beckoned Tayre closer. "Some spice to make more delicious my Accord Festival. I didn't think you'd get the invitation in time."

"Zeted, my dear. How fortunate that I did. You are magnificent, as always." He came close and kissed her on each large cheek and forehead, in the Perripin fashion.

But slowly. Very slowly.

Zeted smiled more widely, the smile becoming uncertain when she took in Amarta. "Who is this skinny little creature? Have you had a change in taste? Not like you to take on charity."

Tayre laughed. Loudly. It seemed so genuine, the laugh, that Amarta felt herself warm.

"I call her Kiki." He shrugged. "Got tired of sleeping alone." He gave Amarta a version of the look she'd seen on the faces of the two Perripin men in the festival earlier. She felt dizzied, embarrassed. Her gaze slid away.

"Arunkin?" asked Zeted.

They had rehearsed what to say to this. "No," she began, "I am from the—" Border, she intended to say, but Tayre cut her off.

"Borderello," he said, as if there were a taste in his mouth about which he was undecided. "No training at all, Domina, yet she has a compelling talent for my particular tastes."

"High praise indeed, Tymon, though frankly she looks as if light use would break her. Feed her," Zeted snapped at her retainers.

Suddenly, three bowing men offered Amarta plates of food, along with a mug of what turned out to be a cold, sweet drink that had a pleasant bite to it.

Tayre sat by Zeted, his arm around her large shoulders. He laughed at a joke she was telling.

Amarta had to remind herself that she came willingly—that he had recommended against it—that this was pretense to protect her. That he was sworn to her.

A roar from the crowd and Zeted was standing. "That's not how it happened! Why do I pay such exorbitant amounts? Thieves! Idiots! Weaklings!" She turned a scowl to the man who was suddenly at her side, and whispered hissed instructions to him that sounded like a wager. He left at a dash.

Zeted sat again and gave a long, satisfied belch before putting a paste-filled date into her mouth. She turned another critical look on the watery game down below.

Tayre stood, stretched, and strolled around the booth, greeting various of Zeted's retainers, smiling and nodding, and coming at last to Amarta. Head leaning toward her, hand lightly on her arm, he said, "We're in the Taluk section, their home port is below, because Zeted is the majority patron of that boat team. One pavilion over is Shentaret, then Mundar. Across the way is Dulu, Ulawesan, Atudaka. That flag there, with the grinning face? Take a guess."

"Timurung."

"Well done." A smile, a reassuring touch. While Zeted's back was turned, anyway.

"Here's the best part," Zeted said loudly. "Watch how we turn the tide against those cheating Ventan bastards!"

"I'd guess you already know the outcome, Zeted," called Tayre, chucking, then sat again by her side. She stroked his head as if he were a pet.

"I have large wagers on the fight to come, pretty boy."

Down in the arena, sailor-warriors splashed out of broken boats, wading to engage each other, hitting with whatever they had handy—wood swords, oars, or even parts of boats. One boat was on fire.

"Never did figure out how that happened," Zeted said gleefully.

The show concluded. Taluk's win was followed by what seemed to Amarta an astonishing din of clanging of drums and metal and howling from the crowd.

For a moment Amarta thought the merchant was in pain. But no—she was simply howling with joy at the win of her team, despite it being no surprise. She sat again, wiping her brow with a lavender cloth.

Another drink with brandy-soaked fruit-pieces around the rim found its way into Amarta's hands.

Zeted gave Amarta a long look. "Not Arunkin, you say. You're sure?"

Tayre waved a hand casually. "Back a few generations, who knows. Nature of the border."

"Because," Zeted went on, "I have a third-hand contract offer to acquire a young woman matching her general description. The Houses are offering enough coin to make it worth even my attention. Be convenient if you happened to have her in hand."

Tayre turned around in his seat, to give Amarta an assessing stare. She felt a chill.

"No," he said slowly, tone disappointed. "If only it were so, but she's not who they're looking for. Wouldn't do to sour my reputation by selling bad merchandise."

*Bad merchandise.* Amarta swallowed, wondering what the woman she was pretending to be would be feeling now besides a blushing face.

In the arena, boats were dragged out of the water onto the first level—some in pieces—hoisted overhead, and marched out passageway exits. New teams arrived, carrying new boats, each with the flag of its Perripin state.

More cheering as teams set their boats into the water and readied them for this year's contest.

Then the cheering turned to hissing.

"Oh, not again." Zeted scoffed. "Every year, the same damned thing. Timuros say they can't afford the fee, then at the last minute a patron comes forward. Me, sometimes." She shook her head. "Not a real contest without all the states, though."

The crowd's displeasure was focused on the empty space where the Timurung boat should be. Complaints rang out from across the theater.

At Zaneke's slice of the terrace—across from the empty space—a handful took up the shout, "Timurung! Timurung!"

Suddenly they began to cheer, and everyone craned their heads to try to see the ramp coming into the Timurung area. The crowd was louder and louder, the entire amphitheater roaring.

Out came the Timurung team with a boat on their shoulders.

For a moment, everyone fell silent. Then, across the stadium, people leapt to their feet. Zeted also stood, her expression darkening.

Angry sounds from the terraces. Raucous laughter. Hissing. Banging. Scattered cheers.

At the Timurung booth, wearing animal skins, Timuros were grinning widely, holding both fists high in a gesture of victory.

Tayre was at her side. He whispered in her ear, "The Timurung boat is flying the Arunkel *Gotar* flag alongside their own.

"But Gotar is an Arunkel province."

"Exactly. If Gotar is the Timurung patron, as the flag implies, this is nearly treason—or an even larger joke. Humor is the Timurung shield, but I suspect it only stretches so far. This won't go over well in Arunkel, either, where

Garaya—Gotar's largest city—is already flaunting Arunkel rule."

Zeted was talking hurriedly to her retainers, two of whom left at a near run. "My wagers, damn it," she snapped.

Tayre breathed in Amarta's ear. "Now is the time, Seer: are we in danger? Look for force. Look for weapons."

She did.

*In moments, the Assembly and the Night's Seven would step from their booths to confer. Mages would step out of their canopies, a silent show of power to keep the peace. Constables would begin to walk the circumference, looking in pavilions, asking questions, searching for…*

"Constables," she whispered back to him, struggling for clarity. *A tencount of white headbanded men at Zeted's pavilion.*

"What do they want?" asked Tayre.

*"To speak to your Arunkin, Domina. Just a few questions."*

*"My guests," Zeted would say, furious.*

*A small room. A dark room.*

"We must go," Amarta said, standing.

Tayre went to Zeted: "My dear, we must depart. Too soon, I know."

"Pah!" spat Zeted with a grimace, seemingly about to object, but with a flickering look around the terraces, she nodded. "This is the last time I give Timurung my coin," she muttered. A gesture to her retainers. "Show them the back way. Get them a fast carriage."

"Yes, Domina."

Zeted stood, took Tayre's shoulders in her large hands, and kissed him. On the lips. "When you grind that little toy into dust, you come see me, hmm?"

"My dreams are only of you, Zeted," Tayre said, giving her a look of naked desire that far outshone his last lecherous look at Amarta. Envy shot through her.

Then they were moving, hustled out by Zeted's men. Up one level, through a narrow aisle, down narrow stairs. A winding passageway, a door, and they were on the large boulevard outside. Above them towered the walls of the amphitheater.

---

"THE DOMINA graciously offers you her best carriage," said one of the retainers who had led them from the amphitheater.

A stocky Perripin woman stood by a small, lacquered lavender carriage. She bowed to Amarta and Tayre, then turned to four leather-clad men, chaining them to a harnesses. She opened the door, inviting them inside.

Amarta stared. The chained men were Arunkin.

Noticing Amarta's expression, the woman said, "They're well treated, sera, really they are. Look—" she grabbed one of the men by his brown hair, turning his head around to show her the mark on his forehead. "See? A criminal. But the Domina believes in second chances, so we took him in. By the seas, he's so well fed—" Here she gave the man's solid-looking stomach a playful slap. "Hear that? He eats better than I do." Her smile turned wry. "I beg your pardon for saying so, sera, but I think your countrymen would not be so good to him."

For a moment, the Arunkin slave met Amarta's eyes, gave her a small, private look of sardonic amusement before his face went blank again.

"Relay my grateful thanks to your Domina," Tayre said to the retainer, pressing Amarta into the carriage.

The doors shut and the carriage lurched forward. Tayre gazed intently through the curtained window to one side, then the other.

"We are away," he said at last as the carriage achieved speed.

Amarta could not clear from her mind how he'd looked at Zeted. What was their history? *Who is she to you?*

"Zeted," Amarta began, "she—"

"She's astute, but she did believe me when I told her you were not the Arunkin being sought. Still, we now know for certain that there's a contract on you, and we should expect hounds on your trail. Very well-paid ones, if Zeted's attention was snagged."

Amarta could not seem to summon concern about being chased. She was always being chased.

"I suppose we must leave Senta, now, too," she said wearily.

"Maybe not. If I were leading the effort to find you, I'd have watchers at all city exits, as I did at Munasee." He regarded her. "A good plan, that, what you did then: hiding from pursuit by staying in-city. And it's a good plan now. Senta will be packed until the Festival is over. Though…" He took her hand in his, rubbing the back of it with his thumb. "We can make you look a little less Arunkin." He returned her hand to her leg, patted it once, then poked his head out the window, calling directions to the woman driving the carriage.

Amarta swallowed the mix of feelings swirling through her. He had reminded her of Munasee, and how he had hunted her. He had taken her hand and rubbed it. It tingled where he had touched her.

"In eight days," he continued to her, "when the Festival ends, that would be the time to leave, under the cover of the masses returning to various homes in all directions. Though —where to go?" He looked at her. "There is still time to go north to your sister's wedding, Amarta. The letter of credit will fund the journey. Be certain of your choice, before you forgo that option."

Amarta looked out her side window, through the sheer curtains. A sliver of ocean glinted occasionally at cross road.

Could she go to Arunkel, to see Dirina wed? Hold Pas, perhaps for the last time? She could almost feel Arunkel's black and red fingers grope toward her as she considered the question.

She exhaled, sat back, let vision answer.

*A great, crowded hall. The deep and ponderous sounds of well-ordered Arunkel music. Red and black draped from every balcony.*

*Dirina smiling. Pas, a year older, now and heartbreakingly handsome. He gripped her hand tightly, looked up at Amarta, his smile like the sun.*

*They would return south on the Great Road. Unlike last time, no mage at their side. Then…*

*Campfires lined the dark ridge between them and the road. Tayre yanked her back. Neither had slept in days. Out of food, the horses long gone. "We need to separate," he whispered. "Find a place to hide. I'll lead them away and circle back later."*

*In this future, foresight told her that there would be no later. In a small, stone room, stinking of mold and rot, there would be questions. So many questions.*

*And Tayre—she would not see him again. Lost, dead, or walked away, she did not know. Would never know. Months and years forward, and still she was in a dark stone room.*

"Amarta?"

What if they took the mountain passes south from Arunkel instead?

*Predawn lit the sky. Silhouettes rose, armed with sticks, blades, bows. Twenty, thirty, fifty. Cautious in their approach to her—they'd clearly been warned that she was dangerous, though now she felt anything but. "We can take you, Seer," one said. "Give up now—you live. Ah, she needs convincing. Bring him." A body dragged forward. Bound, tied. For a moment she felt a flush of hope then saw his fixed look and the dried blood across his neck.*

In the carriage, a whimper escaped her.

"Amarta. What are you are seeing?"

"A ship south," she said, under her breath, ignoring his question and the tearing feeling in her chest.

*From the boat's railing, they watched the crew tack into a shoreline cove. No one had explained the unscheduled stop, and Tayre's gaze flickered across the crew, then back to the shore, where there stood some sixty armored and weaponed men. "I can't take them," he said softly, with a rueful smile. He turned to her, came close enough that she saw nothing but his eyes. "Surrender and live, Amarta. Unless you see another option?"*

She did not. This path, too, led to a small stone room.

Arunkel was a trap, she saw with sickening certainty. They could go to the Yarpin wedding. They could not leave Arunkel.

"Amarta?" he asked gently.

She blinked herself into the present, into the dim carriage in motion.

His hand held hers. So deep in vision had she been that she had not even noticed. Now, in spite of herself, she flinched. He released her hand. Regret was sharp, followed by a tinge of despair.

"There is no going north," she said heavily.

Her head and spirit ached, but she pushed herself to foresee one more time.

*From a huge tree, a massive pendulum swung across a white sand clearing. The scent of sage and cinnamon smoke filled the air.*

"Can we make Atudaka's Xanmelkie Valley by Autumn equinox?"

"YOU LOOK RATHER in the pink for someone who's been out all night, Lord Commander."

"House Murice," Innel said, ignoring Mulack's familiar approach to fishing for information by making insinuating comments.

Their feet crunched over ice and frost. Innel's breath fogged the chill of dawn as he broke into a light jog around the garrison's outer road, hoping Mulack, in his fancy purple velvet and white ermine cloak, would sensibly decide not to follow. Instead, the smaller man double-stepped to match Innel's pace.

The jog was harder than Innel remembered and his limbs felt heavy. It had been too long. His middle was thickening. He resolved himself to take regular and vigorous exercise.

The queen was still bedridden, and Innel must stand in for her wherever he could, while acting as though he was unconcerned about why she was not yet present.

Innel's own work was piling up, too, and it was harder to get away from people and papers and meetings. Now, at dawn, was the only time he could find to exercise. He would have thought himself immune to Mulack's company; the man was notorious for his late nights.

"To what do I owe this unequal pleasure?" he muttered.

"Out to count every star, they say, Lord Commander. But not with us, your Cohort sibs, at the Pig's Ass. Imagine how hurt we are."

The bait was wiggling.

"They say lots of things."

"Maybe it's Tokerae dele Etallan, eh? Might be a bit awkward, running into him over drinks." Mulack was grinning. The man loved to make trouble.

Innel shrugged wordlessly, hoping to hide the laboring of his breath and pushed himself to a faster pace, yet again hoping Mulack would fall behind, yet again being disappointed.

The purple-and-white clad Mulack glanced around, his smile thinning, his voice dropping. "Listen, Innel. Etallan wants you…" He slowed to a walk.

Innel grimaced at this obvious ploy, but slowed anyway to match him, his tencount of guards doing likewise.

"…dead?" he finished quietly.

"Pah, of course not. That would be entirely too—" *convenient*, Innel thought, finding himself glancing at the high palace windows and towers surrounding them, wondering who might be bribed to take a shot at him.

They'd be captured or dead in moments—taking out the Royal Consort was a high crime—but Innel might not be alive enough to care.

"Ill-considered and short-sighted," Mulack continued. "Unhappy, Innel. They want you unhappy."

"Then they'll have to work harder. Tell me something I don't know, Mulack." Despite the frigid air, Innel was sweating as he began to trot again. He took out a handkerchief, wiped his brow.

"Nital wants an increase in amardide holdings," Mulack said, somehow keeping pace.

Mulack's house—House Murice—also known as the House of Dye and Weave—and House Nital were rather friendly for Great Houses. No doubt Mulack was dealing in favors for them.

Properly softened amardide wood could be reformed into nearly anything and was, from mats to layered, lacquered armor that could stop a crossbow bolt. House Nital held charters for wood products, from furniture to barrels to paper to arrows and used a great deal of amardide. So did Murice.

The two Houses shared a passion for amardide forests.

"Everyone wants an increase in amardide holdings," Innel said warily.

"And Phaltos at the Charter Courts."

Ah, there was the hook. "Kincel will never let Phaltos go."

There was humor in Innel's phrasing; House Phaltos made lacquer and waterproofing agents for wells and cisterns, but also, famously, glue, and that made them popular with every House. The strange story of how Kincel—the House of Stone—had taken Phaltos two Charters ago, had been a tenday-long study in the Cohort.

House Phaltos should have been made a Great House from the start, though Innel knew better than to voice that thought.

"Is that the queen's will?" Mulack asked, entirely too eagerly.

Innel felt a dull alarm, and reviewed his words for any crack. "I have no influence in the Charter Courts. You know that."

Waving this away, Mulack said, "But you have queen's bed—er, ear—Lord Consort. Father to the heir, after all."

"The queen is pleased to anticipate the possibilities that the Charter Court engenders. You were saying, about Etallan?"

"Watch your back, Innel."

"I have a quid of guards for that." He glanced back. "Two of them."

"Tell me straight out, brother," Mulack said, "when will we have the privilege of gazing upon the excellent heir?"

"Soon." Innel hoped it was true.

"Bring up Phaltos with her, won't you? Nital is a much better fit as their patron House. You might not know this, but I have a lovely villa no one is using, north of the Sennant River."

Innel blinked at this abrupt change of subject.

"Are you trying to bribe me?"

"Pah. It's only a bribe if you don't take it. If you do, it's a gift. A gesture of…hmm. Goodwill? I am about to become eparch, you know. This year, maybe next. Last thing I want is for you to be lopping off the head of *my* kinsmen." Mulack laughed.

Innel refrained from giving Mulack the incredulous gape that the man so enjoyed. Mulack liked to be so shocking and outrageous that you might miss the obvious.

Which was what? Well, Phaltos and the Charters was a political hot rock and one Innel could not afford to even touch.

"It's small by my standards," Mulack added. It took a moment for Innel to realize that he meant the villa, not his kinsman's head. "A place for you to retreat to. A break from your hectic days." His eyebrows drew together. "I don't believe you own any land, do you, Lord Commander? Surely you should, a man in your position."

"I don't need a villa."

"So sell it. One never knows when one might like to have a bit of extra coin tucked away. Just in case."

*Just in case what, Mulack?*

The threats had never been subtle, not since the moment he and his brother first entered the Cohort two decades ago. In a way, Innel found it reassuring that his new titles had not changed this, at least not with Mulack.

"She did actually marry me," Innel said. "You were at the ceremony. Perhaps you remember it."

"Oh yes, quite vividly."

Was there a hint of envy in that smirking reply? If so, good. Cern was the target of every boy in the Cohort, aimed for day in and day out through the many years of study. But it was Innel, who had applied every bit of cunning and verve he could find, who had finally snared her.

Still, Innel did find the offer tempting. He knew the very villa, with a high fenceline of woven amardide, thick with gray-thorned Demon Claw in brilliant yellow flowers. Mulack was right: it would be a fine place to retreat to.

No, it would not. Should things go badly enough for him to need to retreat, it would not be far enough. He would need to cross borders. He knew too much. He had made too many enemies.

But Mulack was right about the money: the sale of that villa would be a buffer against bad fortune. Right now, Innel had very little untracked coin, and could use more.

He knew how to get coin, to take a little from this account or that one. The bits and drabs he had been redirecting from various budgets could have been going directly to him, stashed somewhere far away against need. Instead he had been using it to follow—and fund—various plots, to give the traitors rope enough to hang themselves.

A lifetime's goal achieved, marrying Cern. But now he

had a child, and she was beyond all price. He would spend every coin he could to keep her safe and whole.

"Tempting," Innel admitted.

But it would put Innel squarely into Mulack's debt. Mulack wanted…what?

Lesser House Phaltos chartered to his own House's ally, House Nital. But any such promise was beyond Innel's ability to deliver. The Charter Courts were a melee of House negotiations and leverages, a mess of favors promised, called, demanded, and invented—but nothing Innel could affect.

At the last Charter Courts, king Restarn had kept a tight leash on the proceedings. The Cohort, close by and watching, had learned a great deal. This time, Cern would be holding the reins.

Innel imagined her on her throne, the Great Hall full to bursting, scribes at desks, arguments filling the air.

His daughter would be nearly five by then, certainly old enough to watch and learn. He could envision her at Cern's side, Innel next to her, quietly explaining how the Courts worked. His daughter would nod soberly, curious and clever. He would be so proud.

He and his brother Pohut had been just that age when they entered the Cohort. Then, Pohut had been the one to explain to Innel how things worked. Only a little older, his brother must have struggled hard to understand, and worked even harder to protect the younger Innel.

A deep, cutting ache went through him, mixed with the memory of a dark night, of two men fighting in the mud for their lives. He pushed it away.

Would she call him "papa"? Well, what else?

A giddy sense of joy washed over him. He found himself grinning. Yes, Etallan would need to try a lot harder to make him unhappy.

"The villa comes with a full staff of servants," Mulack added.

"Naturally," Innel said pleasantly. "Alas, I can promise nothing, Eparch-heir."

"That sounds a bit like a no, Lord Consort."

"But I won't forget that you cared enough to offer."

"That'll have to do, then." Mulack said, his smile wide enough to leave Innel with a vague sense of ill-ease, fast replaced by a vision of his baby daughter.

Innel felt a powerful tug to look in on them both. He waved at the departing Mulack then turned back to the palace.

"SOMETHING FOR YOU, SER," Nalas said, blandly, which told Innel it was important. He gestured for Nalas to speak, but Nalas looked sideways at Srel, giving the steward an apologetic smile.

"Of course, Deputy Lord Commander," Srel said smoothly, bowing as he exited the office.

Innel watched his steward's bow, which Innel realized had changed when he had become Royal Consort, Srel adding a subtle additional twist, a one-handed way of opening the door as he bowed to let himself out, a move so smooth that he must have practiced it.

That was part of why Innel and his brother had taken Srel in. They'd been so poor that they could barely afford to keep the commoner adolescent who was only a few years older than they were, but Srel was diligent and precise. And not aristo.

"Wasn't sure," Nalas said, when they were alone, "who you wanted to know what." Nalas handed him a many-folded piece of paper. "A queensguard found this."

As Innel unwrapped it, a thick twine of thread fell onto the desktop. A few inches long, dark brown and ash colors interwove. It was a thread from a garment of House Nital.

"Where did you…?"

Nalas cleared his throat a little. "In the queen's room."

His daughter's face swam into view, eyes green flecked with gold. Innel felt rage rise and for a moment, thought fled, and all he wanted was to find the person who had dropped this and tear them apart. He stared at the thread in his fingers, his free hand making a fist.

"Does the queen know?" he asked, when he felt he could speak evenly.

"The guard thought it best to tell me first."

"Don't tell her." If he worried Cern with every possible plot, she'd be a ruin. "Say nothing. But keep a watchful eye."

"Yes, ser. What does it mean, do you think?"

Innel's mind spun through all the reasons not to reveal his thinking on the matter, even Nalas.

"It's a message," he said cautiously. "It says, we can get inside, even with the Queensguard." He looked hard at Nalas. "Maybe because of the Queensguard."

Nalas's eyes went wide, then his expression turned uncharacteristically ugly. "I'll talk to every one of them, find out who has connections to Nital. They'll be sorry. They—."

"No, no—don't. Probably a false flag. Not Nital at all. Too obvious."

"Oh," Nalas said, his anger quiescing into confusion.

"Either way, someone got inside the queen's chamber, and wants me to know about it."

"A thread."

"A message."

"Well," Nalas said slowly, "Just to say, ser. It might be a message, I don't know, but it's not a weapon. Not something that might hurt her majesty or the child. *That* we would have caught."

"Would you?" Innel asked sharply. "Even so, no need to —" Replace the entire guard. Again. "Act in haste. It could even be an accident, someone wearing House colors under palace colors." Strictly against the rules, but possible. "A thread dropped from a pocket. Dragged in by foot unintentionally."

"You don't think that, though, do you, ser."

"Not for a moment. From now on, no one goes in without being fully searched."

"Even the queen's chamberlain?"

Innel gritted his teeth his daughter's face in his mind.

"Excepting Sachare, of course," he said, knowing the futility of attempting to keep her out.

He peered closely at the twined colors in his fingers. If Sachare were the threat, they could perform guard interviews and body searches for years to come, to no advantage. He could not imagine what Sachare would have to gain by sending him this message, though—she could not possibly be on the succession list.

Or could she?

Damn it.

Whatever he did, it must be subtle. "No interviews," Innel said. "No searches. Tell no one."

A secret, the adage went, was only as secure as the first ear's mouth.

"Yes, ser," Nalas said. "Then..." his tone was confused, "what do you want me to do?"

"Nothing. Nothing at all. Forget you saw it."

"Yes, ser," Nalas said, though he didn't sound happy.

Innel wasn't either. But it wasn't enough to act. Not yet.

He tucked the thread back into the envelope and put it in his vest pocket.

CERN'S HEAD THROBBED. It seemed to her that the light coming in through the edge of the drapes pulsed likewise. She groaned.

"How long have I been asleep, Sacha?"

"A whole two hours, Your Grace," said Sachare, pausing from shaking out a small, soft pink blanket edged in black, and folding it neatly to set it atop a pile of more of the same. "It's good that you sleep. You are recovering."

"Am I?" asked Cern bitterly.

Sachare turned to examine Cern critically. "Your color is slowly improving, and you're finally putting on some weight. Speaking of which…" She took a tray of food from near the door and moved it to the table by Cern's bed. From each of the carefully arranged, elegantly arrayed food, bites had been taken.

"Any good?" Cern asked.

Sachare gave a delicate belch and smiled.

No fewer than three people tasted Cern's food directly from her plate before it reached her room. All but the last—Sachare herself—were watched closely by two witnesses.

So much trouble to make sure Cern didn't die as she lay here, feeling wretched.

It was hard to imagine Niala esse Arunkel troubling this much to be certain she wasn't about to be poisoned. Then again, it was hard to imagine her doing otherwise.

In any case, if Cern's great-grandmother had endured such difficult pregnancies, she hid them well: Niala had five children in quick succession. While somehow managing four empiric border expansions.

The baby began to cry. Cern pushed herself to sit up against the pillows, suppressing a wince, and took the baby in her arms. She wanted to feed, and so Cern brought her small mouth to her nipple. The baby latched on enthusiastically, making happy slurping sounds.

"Perhaps I ought to bring you one of your gifts, to cheer you up," Sachare suggested.

"I'm cheery," Cern said dourly.

"Had to open another inventory room to store them all. Wait until you see them."

Cern snorted. Most likely, she never would. They would be sorted, cataloged, and warehoused long before Cern had time. At some point, she'd have to address the most important ones. The political ones.

"The boys' gifts especially," Sachare said. The Cohort boys, she meant. Men of the Houses, now. "So many pretty things with letters and entreaties tucked inside. Such flowery language."

Cern heaved a sigh, and tried to focus her mind on anything beyond her own exhaustion and the creature in her arms. She was coming to feel more and more like her father must have, chained by illness to a bed. It was not a comfortable thought.

"If I make any one of them welcome, the rest will demand the same. I could invite them all. Line them up and make them watch me feed the heir."

Almost on cue, the baby began to push away and complain.

"Here, let me," Sachare said, taking the baby to a side table to change her.

"They would, you know," she said, returning the baby to Cern's arms.

"Probably." It was tempting. Almost. But Cern knew how she looked—it would also reveal how ill she was. She needed more time.

"And if she is the heir, Your Grace…" said Sachare. "Perhaps it's time to make it official."

It sounded so simple: just put a mark on heavy parchment and send it to the Ministerial Council for ratification. Simple, if she ignored the succession list entirely, and what notes her father might have left in the lockbox under the bed. She could not make the child the heir without a list, and she could not construct one without knowing her father's thoughts on the matter.

*You're being childish, she told herself sternly. Surely, you can look in the box.*

She was no longer a child. The baby at her breast proved that, if nothing else.

"Tell me about the gifts," she said.

"Mulack sent a full set of amardide armor, in royal colors. It even has room to be let out here." Sachare patted her lower belly.

That message was clear enough. Of course she must try for another baby, but she cringed at the thought. Not quite yet.

"Etallan?" she asked.

"An elegant display plate of silver, your visage flatteringly inset in red and black metal. And for the child..." Sachare raised one eyebrow slightly. "The usual."

"Ah. Is it sharp?"

Across generations, Etallan's traditional gift to the heir was an exquisite child-sized sword. Cern's own sword had been dangerously sharp by the time she'd been allowed to touch it, but whether it had been sharpened to that keen edge by Etallan or her father, she did not know.

"It is not, Your Grace."

And what did that mean? *We mean the heir no harm,* perhaps. Or *your child can do us no harm.* She snorted softly in dark amusement at the other message it might carry, that an edged weapon would be wasted on her daughter.

Her daughter, she resolved, would be capable with all weapons, as Cern had been trained.

Who knew which message was actually intended? Maybe all of them. Not all gifts were blades, but so many nonetheless had sharp edges.

Cern wrapped the baby in a small, soft pale red blanket, and let her down to sleep.

"It must have taken you days to examine them all," Cern said as she stroked her sleeping infant's head. So soft.

"Not at all."

At Sachare's tone, Cern looked up. "What?"

"Innel is taking care of it. He insisted, so I let him."

Cern frowned. "Isn't he rather busy for that?"

"I would have thought so, too."

"Sacha? What happened?"

A thoughtful sound. "He has an understandable and passionate concern for your welfare, Your Grace."

"Will you make me repeat my question?"

Sachare took a breath. "I was at the inventory, directing my staff to wipe for residue and look for hidden mechanisms. Innel ordered them all out, said that it was his duty, as Lord Commander and Consort." Sachare shrugged very slightly. "I asked him to tell me when he was done, so I could select a few items for you, thinking they might do you some good. He wanted to know which ones. A few strong words were exchanged. I left."

"Does he not trust you?"

"Trust? Innel?" Sachare grinned but it faded fast. "Rumor is that he's up all hours. Doesn't sleep much." Sachare tilted her head. "Perhaps he's troubled by these gifts so fine that he himself could not afford to give them."

"He has coin."

"Not his own," Sachare said.

"Pah. If he's that fragile, let him be troubled." Cern

groaned. "I must get out of this bed and be seen." Even the thought was tiring. She lay back again. "But not like this."

"You'll be better soon."

Cern took a breath.

"The lockbox," Cern said. She had tried to pull it out by herself from under the bed, grabbing hold of the gem-crusted sides, but would not budged. So like her father to give her an impossible task.

Sachare dropped to her knees by the side of the bed where the box lived, and reached under, pulling. After a few minutes, she sat back on her heels and looked at Cern.

"Rather heavy."

"It is, isn't it."

"I'll get someone stronger, Your Grace."

"No," Cern said firmly. "This must be kept between us."

"As you say." Sachare went around the other side, wriggled under the bed, and began to push. After a few moments, Cern lowered herself to the floor, wincing at the pain through her abdomen.

Together, they worked the box for a while, pushing and pulling, until its grip on the floor began to loosen. It slid, slowly and gratingly, out from under the bed.

They stared at the jewel-wrought metal box. It was about the gaudiest thing Cern had ever seen, and given the many items that had passed through her hands and sight, that was saying a good deal.

Lifting was entirely out of the question. Just seeing the damned thing, Cern thought, was exhausting.

With Sachare's help, Cern climbed back in bed, the ache in her belly now insistent.

"Maybe tomorrow," she whispered into the pillows.

"Maybe tomorrow, Your Grace."

THERE WERE a number of ways to leave the palace grounds unseen.

It was a popular late-night hobby among the adolescent Cohort to explore all possible ways, with the exception of dropping off the high back wall into the great Sennant river below, which even the most daring of them declined to try. Many had fallen prey to the seduction of following the hidden passageways that snaked under the palace.

No one in this Cohort had been lost to that seduction. Previous Cohorts had been less fortunate.

With the right clothes, correct time of day, and perseverance, getting out of the palace grounds was not so difficult.

In those days, getting back in was the trick. It was easy if you didn't mind repercussions, and some didn't; all but Innel and Pohut were important House scions who, by that time in their education, knew that their absence would be more of a problem than their return. With the right inducement, the Cohort Master might be willing to overlook the lapse.

These days Innel could leave and return any time he wanted, but doing so unnoticed was far harder.

This night, though, weather and timing were on their side. The sky was pouring forth. In hooded, oilskin cloaks, he and Nalas left by the side gate quite anonymously, in the company of tens of others similarly dressed, their clothes proclaiming them to be from the Trades, heading home, unlucky enough to be caught out in the squall.

And squall it was: at times the wind drove the rain sideways. They hunched, striding down hill to the Broken Prayer.

The back room of the Broken Prayer was blissfully dry. Warm, too. Relatively quiet: raucous sounds from the large, main room were muffled by a wall.

Innel accepted from the server a single mug of what was

colloquially called seawater and tasted quite a bit like it. Only the one, he promised himself.

The meeting time came and went. Innel drummed fingers on the table, weighing the many things he should be doing at the palace against the promised information about the Queensguard.

Distantly, the hour's half-bell sounded.

A knock at the door. Nalas opened it to an elegantly clad woman.

"Unexpectedly detained, ser," she said, smiling brightly. "I've come to apologize on his behalf."

"Whose?" asked Innel.

The woman sat next to Innel. "I have a snug room at the top of the stairs. Let me show you how lovely my apologies can be."

"No," Innel said reflexively.

He'd been saying that a lot these last months, to attractive palace servants, beautiful slaves offered by royals, and even tart young aristos. Everyone wanted him to say yes, to have him in their debt.

But no, and no again. Not even slaves. Innel had seen what old king Restarn's slave had done for him; they were canny and too clever. Innel had resolved to stay entirely unentangled, at least until Cern was restored and could make her will known to him.

And thus it had been some time—since the child's conception, in fact—since he'd coupled with a woman in bed. Or in a closet. Or an alleyway. A basement table, even.

His mind took off like a squirrel, eager to climb the trees of possibilities. His body began to respond. The woman's lips were parted and on her face was an attractive intensity.

Would it really be so risky, here, so far from the palace? Who would fault him for taking an hour for himself? Who?

Anyone who found out.

But Nalas could be counted on to keep his tongue. And the woman—

*A secret is only as secure as the first ear's mouth.*

"No," he repeated, hearing in his voice a distinct lack of conviction. He could not seem to look away from her. Something about her face, the way her hair framed her eyes…

"Oh, please reconsider, good ser." Her voice was heavy silk, sliding over naked skin.

"Who sent you?" he demanded weakly.

It was the eyes, he realized. Her wide-set pupils, ringed in gold, hair cut short at a slight angle—she was a fogged mirror-version of Cern.

Someone had chosen her, very specifically, to tempt him.

Alas, this insight did nothing to douse his body's interest. It had simply been too long.

Maybe she saw it in his face—or somewhere else— because with neither warning nor request, she moved to sit herself firmly on his lap.

It was something that Cern would never have done, never, but knowing this affected his response to the warm creature squirming deliciously in his arms not at all. He wanted to shove her away, make her as unsteady on her feet as he felt sitting under her, but his hands seemed incapable of even this simple motion.

She twisted, brought her face close to his. He could smell her. All thought fled.

His hands were on her shoulders, stroking her arms. He just wanted to know if her skin was as soft as Cern's.

"Top of the stairs?" he managed.

"I could show you," she whispered.

"Ser, don't we need to…go?" Nalas's voice, rather too loud. Annoying, like a rough blade. "To get back, ser?"

Innel shook his head. Back to what?

To the palace. To his queen. To his child.

What was he thinking?

He wasn't.

And then it came clear to him: whoever had lured him here had never intended to show up. The true goal was to have this woman seduce him here in this mid-city inn and have it witnessed. He had no doubt that there were aristos in the main dining area, who would be encouraged to walk by just as Innel followed the woman up the stairs. Or maybe they would be invited to quietly watch through a hole in the wall or ceiling.

It was what Innel would have done, if he had wanted to sully the reputation of the Royal Consort.

*Common, they would say. Bedded a commoner. You should have seen the action. Quite the doggie show.*

Innel stood, pushing her off his lap. He accepted the cloak Nalas quickly held out and went to the door.

"Don't go," she said. "Please."

He paused, looked back over his shoulder. Her face was still enchanting. They had chosen her well.

"Tell whoever sent you that I have better things to do than fuck an unlicensed whore," he said, then had a thought. "Or did House Kincel send you?"

Her eyes narrowed, her pretense strained to the breaking.

"Working outside the charter, eh?" His lip curled, and he made a scolding sound. Was she wondering if he would report her? He could land her in a great deal of trouble.

Good. Let her wonder.

Angry and full of inconvenient desire, Innel left the Broken Prayer, Nalas following him into the stormy night.

"ONLY A FEW MOMENTS," Innel told Nalas, as they splashed uphill, the rain so heavy it flowing over their boots in the street.

An infuriating waste of time and effort, but he might redeem it by stopping at a tavern to talk with one of his informants. He motioned to Nalas to wait outside while he entered a door under a sign that clacked in the hard wind. On it was painted a long-limbed dog curled around a terrified-looking rabbit.

Inside, a warm hazy smoke washed over him.

It didn't take Shae long to stop laughing at some joke by a woman to her side and glance across the room. She gave him a gap-toothed smile and tilted her head to indicate that she'd meet him in the usual place. Innel looked around at the elbow-to-elbow patrons, as if evaluating his chances of getting served, shook a head, and left to walk around the back.

In an alleyway, under a small overhang that kept off the worst of the pouring rain, Shae waited.

"Evening, ser," Shae said, huddling against the brick alongside him. She turned her head so she could see him out of her good eye. The other pointed off into the night.

A man, she'd once told Innel over a drink, who had thought he might rename her. A fool, she had added, who now had no name at all.

It was that night that Innel had bought her loyalty—rather expensively by the standards of in-city informants—by funding her parents' escape from the dirt and illness of Yarpin streets to a modest cabin in a hilly, outlying region.

She was worth every nals.

Shae spoke. "Some awfully bright shine being spun past your sharp-toothed Rusties."

Rusties were the royal guards. The Queensguards. Closely

vetted, hand-picked, and well-paid, they were supposed to be unbribable.

No one was unbribable.

"Where is it coming from?" he asked.

"Stinks of aristo to me, but I couldn't trace it if my last eye depended on it." She laughed a little at her own joke.

"Bribed to do what?" he asked.

She shook her head. "Don't know."

Get information on the queen's health? Look the other way? Something worse?

He felt an urgency to get back to the palace.

"You find out more, you let me know," he said.

Her expression went odd around her good eye. Her voice dropped. "Just want to say, ser, a lot of us think you're fair brave, what you been doing lately."

"Brave?"

Innel considered the Queensguard. If someone was making a concerted effort to bribe them, maybe it was time to conduct interviews after all.

Or would that send whoever was spinning the shine into hiding? Innel needed to track the traitors, find out who and what they were about. How best to tap into that line of coin?

Shae's voice dropped until he could barely hear it over the pattering of rain. "Got support in the commons, you have, ser. Saying things like you do."

Innel nodded. Who was it, trying to bribe the queensguards? Which of the royals might be eyeing a succession bid? Who was both wealthy enough and foolish enough to make the attempt?

House Etallan, he found himself thinking. Would they really risk it, with the charge of treason still echoing in the halls?

For that matter, were any of Innel's own guards taking the bait? Was he in danger himself?

Too many possibilities. Too many questions.

Adjusting his oilskin hood, Innel turned to the gusting rain, feeling the distance between himself and his child like a gash through his belly. He needed to look in on them, and now. He needed to see them to reassure himself that they were well.

"Be careful, ser," Shae called out from behind him.

"Always."

Innel splashed through puddles and pattering rain to where Nalas stood waiting for him.

## Chapter Eleven

PAS WAS SUDDENLY EXTREMELY happy that he was small for his age.

As far as Pas was concerned, the best thing about the queen's palace—which was also called the Jewel of the Empire—was all the ways in which it didn't fit right. Nalas had explained to Pas that the place had been built across centuries, added on to bit by bit.

It was true: sometimes you could look up and see how one part of the ceiling was lower than another, or a wall would jut out at the join, maybe curve instead of cornering.

It was wonderful.

Draped alcoves could be full of treasures. Despite having explored the palace, Pas had just come across one he had never seen before. He glanced around to be sure he was alone in the wide hallway, then slipped behind the heavy velvet fabric.

There he found an ill-fitting join that had left a gap just wide enough for a small child to squeeze into, between the two walls. So he did, giggling quietly in delight.

He heard footsteps approaching and held his breath.

"Won't give up my Garaya contracts," said a man's voice. "The Ministerial Council can suck my hairy balls. We should petition the queen direct."

"Good luck to you. She's still in bed."

"What? The grandmother queen was up the very next day after each one that she squeezed out."

"Different times. Maybe...not made of...the same stuff, eh?"

A chuckle as the footsteps neared.

"The Consort, then?"

"Wouldn't go near him, if I were you. Drunk and down city the nights, they say."

"Can't he find any slits in the palace?"

"Beyond whores. He's got himself a following. Down-city dirt. Saying things. Making promises. You haven't heard?"

"No! Tell me."

The voices dropped to whispers and were already passing, so Pas couldn't make anything out. Soon the hallway returned to silence.

Pas looked up. Overhead, the drapes stretched high, fading into darkness. Grinning with pleasure, Pas took hold of the material, waved it slightly, tracking it upwards into the ceiling overhead to see how high it might go.

All at once he was flooded with hallway light as someone yanked back the drapes.

"Pas?"

"Da!"

Nalas began to laugh, but caught himself, a serious curtain coming down over his face. It reminded Pas of the masks everyone wore at winterfair a few months ago.

"Found a good hiding place?" Nalas asked.

"Yes!"

"Come on out now." Nalas looked up and down the corridor, holding a hand out to Pas.

For a moment, Pas forgot he was tightly jammed between two walls, and tried to do as he was told. He merely twitched in place.

"A good spot," Nalas said. "Used to be a favorite of the Cohort when they were about your age. Outgrew it, to all our relief. Too bad you're out of range for the princess's Cohort. Wouldn't it be something, to have you alongside those high-born brats?"

Pas wriggled free of the walls, bounded the few steps to the large man, gripped his hand, looked up.

Nalas looked down and his smile vanished.

"What are you wearing?"

Pas looked down at himself curiously. He had been playing with a boy his own age in the lower levels, who'd shown him the cold kitchen storage rooms and the stacks of food crates there. They'd pulled an apple out of a box and shared it. It was delicious.

Then they'd swapped shirts, which had fit so well that they did the same with their trousers. Pas's pale red outfit in exchange for the other boys' cream-colored one, his black pants for the other boy's dark green.

Then Pas had wandered the halls in that outfit, keeping his face very dour and not meeting anyone's eyes. No one noticed him in the servant's colors.

It was so much better than when people looked at him in that sort of odd way they had here. It was more like being invisible. He loved it.

Nalas sighed heavily and Pas attempted to look properly abashed at whatever he'd done wrong.

"All right, let's get you changed. I'm sure your mother's missing you now that it's dinner time."

"Oh, it's that late?" Pas grimaced and Nalas echoed it sympathetically.

They walked the hallway toward the apartments where he

and his mother lived.

"Pas," Nalas said softly, "it's not a good time for you to be hiding, certainly not dressed like that. Not with how things are right now. You understand?"

"Yes. Is it Amarta?"

"What?" A surprised frown. "No. Why would you think that?"

"Usually when things are some way that we have to be really careful about, she's the reason."

Nalas made a thoughtful sound. "Not this time."

"Good." He missed her, his aunt Amarta. "Then is it because of what I might hear?"

"Did you hear something?"

Pas nodded. "Two men talking about their hairy balls."

Nalas made an odd sound in his throat. Another swallowed laugh. Pas smiled. He liked making Nalas laugh.

"You know not to repeat things like that. Except to me. Yes?"

Pas nodded. "I know. I didn't understand everything they said, and I know not to tell anyone but you. But it was something about Garaya and the queen in bed and not going near the Consort because of down-city dirt."

Nalas stopped in his tracks, turned, dropped down to meet Pas eye to eye. "That's some good listening you did there. Did you see who they were?"

"No. Should I have looked?"

"No and more no. Stay out of it."

"I will."

"And don't get caught."

"I won't."

They arrived at the apartment. Nalas nodded to his guards as they opened the door.

"Misplace something?" he asked Dirina, ushering Pas to

her. She picked Pas up, groaning at his weight. She inhaled to speak.

Pas had a pretty good idea of how cross she would be, and how bad he would feel after.

"Sorry, mama," he said to head her off. "I got distracted. But I made a friend!" It had been nearly impossible for them to make any friends here at the palace, so that caught her attention.

"A friend?" Her wide smile faded as she took note of what he was wearing. A questioning eyebrow at Nalas, who replied with a bemused shrug.

She set Pas down. "Go get changed into your own clothes, and we'll eat."

"Yes, mama."

Pas left to the other room, but stopped just inside the doorway to listen.

"Did you ask him?" his mother asked.

"Diri, it's just not a good time for that." Pas heard the particular silence that his mother made when she was upset. Apparently Nalas recognized it, too. "I will, though, I promise. He needs me at his side now. More than ever."

"I don't like it here, Nalas."

"I understand that and after the wedding, when the queen is fully recovered—when he can spare me—I'll bring it up. But you and Pas could stay at the house he promised us as a wedding gift. I'm sure he'll say yes to that. Lovely country. The snow's clean. You'll be safe. You'll—"

"Nalas." A sharp tone.

"Diri, you are my life and my breath. You and Pas are the world to me. But I serve the Lord Commander, and he's a good man. My honor demands that I not desert him now."

His mother made a frustrated sound. "I want to be angry with you. Then you say something like that. My sweet, you melt me. How fortunate I am to have you."

"Yes, you are." Nalas laughed softly. "And I you." He took a breath. "Dirina, my heart, it really might be best if you two went away soon."

"No."

"Just until the wedding."

"Be parted from you? Never. Who would do this, that you like so much, if I were gone?" A pause. "And this?"

Nalas made a wordless sound. They were kissing, Pas was almost certain. He slowly moved one eye past the doorway.

Yes, they were. He backed away, relieved and happy, and began to peel out of his clothes.

The people who lived here in the palace—aristos, royals, and even most of the servants— were not very friendly. Like the odd walls and ceilings, Pas and his mother did not seem to quite fit.

But the palace was warm and dry, and food was good and plentiful, and that had not been true most of the other times in his life. Until recently, Pas's whole existence had been about leaving, suddenly, to escape something worse.

Thinking of it that way, the palace wasn't so bad. The house in the country might be fine, too.

He doubted they'd be staying long in either place. It was just a matter of time before they would be on the road again.

After he had put on the boring red and black he always wore, he considered the pile of green and cream on the floor, then toed it between a chest and the wall, out of sight.

———

MULACK WAS BEGINNING to regret having said yes to this particular ride.

The carriage clattered roughly across wet cobblestones and finally slowed to a stop. His host, Tokerae, pulled back the heavy curtain and slid the window open. Frigid night air rushed inside, seeming to worm its way through to his skin.

"Must you, Etallan?" Mulack muttered crossly, pulling his scarf tight against the air. Outside he glimpsed a lamplit street, an open area in one of the dirtier down-city slums. It was not a place he went often.

Tokerae handed him a small flask. "This will keep you warm, Murice." He gestured through the open window. "Watch closely, Cohort-brother."

The square was packed. People held candles and lamps and huddled together. At the far end, a figure stepped up onto a platform. A man. He held up his arms and cheers followed. In the shadows of torch and lamp, Mulack could still see that the man was well-dressed.

He pulled back a hood and Mulack's jaw dropped.

"Is that…"

"Just listen."

From the crowd, encouraging calls. The man began to speak. At this distance, Mulack could only catch a few words, here and there. Then the wind shifted and he could hear all of it.

"And who is it doing the filth-work of the city? Who digs the sewers? Empties the chamberpots? Butchers pigs? No aristo, I can tell you that. You, is it not? Hired to work the Houses and paid a pittance to do it. I know your struggle because I grew up as one of you. I know your suffering because I was born into it, too."

"By the seven Hells," Mulack whispered, still staring. "That's not Innel. Tok, is that Innel?"

"Looks like him, doesn't it? Dresses like him, too."

Mulack watched in fascination. The man continued, detailing the struggles of the common born, and how, with their support, he would change everything.

"No. Innel would speak better than that," Mulack said. "That gesture he just made—Innel would never do that."

"What can I say, Cohort-brother? Looks like Innel to me. Certainly the crowd thinks it's him. The more important question surely is, does Cern know about this, because everyone else does. Does the queen truly lie abed, recovering from the birth of the heir, or is she being hidden from us?"

Mulack frowned, finding this thought disturbing. "You don't think that."

"I haven't seen her since that wretched day when the mutt slaughtered my kinsman in front of my family and my queen. Have you?"

Mulack shook his head slowly, thoughtfully. "Every time I try, Innel and his people intercept me instead, saying that she cannot be disturbed."

"Same as what he said when Restarn was ill. Then he died." Tokerae paused to let that sink in. "I am concerned, Cohort-brother, but Etallan can barely venture into the palace as things stand."

"What do you want from me, Tok?" Mulack asked. "I don't like being cold."

Tokerae yanked the heavy drape down, muffling the sound of the speaker. He bent his long frame forward to take a wrapped sack of small, heated stones from his feet, handing it to Mulack, who gratefully stuffed the warming bundle under his cloak.

"Ah," he said, with pleasure.

"What if the child didn't survive?" Tokerae asked quietly. "Who witnessed the birth? Are the Ministers being bribed? Something is being hidden here—what is it? We are the Houses, and we are entitled to know what has happened to our queen."

Mulack shrugged, not disagreeing. "And you want me to —what?"

"I want you to tell her what you've seen and heard." Tokerae gestured to the draped window. "Make sure she knows."

How odd, Mulack thought; he had been approached by Helata just a few days ago, with a very similar request.

"Let me see if I understand you," Mulack said. "You want me to risk my reputation, by telling the queen about the various, damning rumors regarding her Consort? And what great prize awaits me should I accomplish this, House Etallan?"

"Well, what does House Murice want? What favor might Etallan gratefully provide?"

Mulack lived for such questions. They were the creak of an opening door on the other side of which could be anything.

"I want Phaltos."

Tokerae laughed. "That's quite the ask, my friend, for a mere visit to the queen."

In fact, Mulack did not want Phaltos at all. It was House Helata who wanted Phaltos, and very, very badly.

"Aim high," Mulack retorted, quoting one of their arms masters from Cohort days. He grinned back at Tokerae, who had on what Mulack always thought of as his deal-making face. "You agree not to oppose me—or whomever I designate —if I make a bid for House Phaltos. That will suffice."

"Easily done," Tokerae said graciously.

"And."

"And?"

When Taba had come to him similarly, Mulack had come out and told her what he wanted. He had then found it astonishingly difficult to say aloud.

It was not, to his chagrin, much easier to say now.

But it was not a confession of desire. Nothing at all like it. Simply an advantageous angle that House Murice might pursue, should Mulack—as eparch-heir—decide to do so. That was all.

Every boy in the Cohort had been expected to court Cern. It was part of being educated alongside the heir, the chance to become Royal Consort. Mulack had done his part to charm her with his joking manner. Later he had joined in the grousing when she clearly favored the mutt brothers, Pohut and Innel. Commoner boys who had somehow survived the Cohort alongside proper aristo blood. How could she?

It was a shock, an outrage, and then, finally, over years, a certainty.

Mulack had done his duty to court Cern, but in truth, not with much passion. Even when she had married Innel, Mulack had not felt the least twinge of envy. She was his queen, yes, and his Cohort sister, and she should have married an aristo. That was all.

Then Cern had become pregnant. When Mulack had heard the news, something had shifted inside him. He felt a tearing jealousy rip through him like a deep wound.

He hadn't known, until the very moment when he realized that he had lost her in this most intimate manner, how much he had always wanted her.

And now, alone or in the best company his coin could obtain, he spent his nights circling the question of how Pohut, and then Innel, had succeeded where Mulack himself had faltered. Was it their rude, sincere gifts? Their plain-spoken words? Their commoner good looks?

Or was it some flaw in himself?

He thought back over the many things across the years he had not done to vie for her interest. Actions overlooked. Moments unused. Regret plagued him like an itch he could not scratch.

But now he had a new chance.

"What is it that you want, House Murice?" Tokerae asked again.

"It is obvious that you are taking Innel down, and hard. When he is gone, I want a clear shot to court Cern."

Tokerae looked surprised. "You think she'd take *you*?"

Well, and so, that was the game.

Mulack shrugged. "Let me fail, then. But you give me your absolute word not to challenge me in my cause."

Tokerae seemed to consider. Then he nodded. "Etallan will not contest a bid for Phaltos should you or your designee make one, nor will we court queen Cern once the mutt is removed. Unless, of course, you fail to win her favor, and step out of the way."

"I accept. I shall be pleased to go to the palace, inquire as to the queen's health, and relay to her what I have seen and heard so that she may be…best informed."

"A pleasure, Cohort-brother."

"Every time, brother."

RADELAN HUNCHED over the long bar at the Mother's Secret Tavern, keeping his head down, trying to look smaller than he was. A lifetime's habit. He had been too big for as long as he could remember.

But then, years ago, he had gotten lucky—astonishingly lucky—and gained employment with the palace guard, where everyone liked his size.

In any case, despite his size, no one would recognize him here at Mother's, not wearing his queensguard livery. He'd be in trouble if they did—queensguards weren't supposed to leave the palace grounds. Their lives were to take place in the confines of the palace.

But some things had to happen elsewhere. Like getting as

drunk as he needed to.

He'd had three already, but barely felt them. As the barwife passed, he held out his mug, flashing what he knew was a decent smile.

She gave him a look of pity. "You owe too much, my friend. Pay down the tab. Then I can refill."

"Just need until the end of my tenday, gal. Get current with you then. My word."

"Your promises have…lost their way," the woman said gently.

"Ah. I'm sorry. But this time, this time—"

A hand fell on his shoulder. He tensed, fighting the reflex to whirl and knock whoever it was back, or to grab for his dagger.

Which, fortunately, he didn't have on him. Flash a queensguard dagger in a place like this? Gone would be Radelan's fine position and pay. Then who would keep his father off the filthy streets of this wretched city, him with his bad lungs? Who would keep his sister and her passel of children fed? His brother, who was nearly blind?

And besides, Radelan had a pretty good idea who was standing behind him.

"His tab is paid," came a woman's authoritative voice. "Forever."

Radelan felt himself go cold from throat to groin.

The barwife's eyes were saucer-wide. She bowed hastily again and again. "Your Illustriousness, Helata."

The woman dressed in a fine blue-and-green cloak stepped to Radelan's side, stepping between him and an oblivious man at the next stool, his head tucked drunkenly into his arm. The man looked up, blinking in astonishment.

House elites didn't come to places like this. The man twitched, thrust himself backward off the stool, and lurched away.

The barwife refilled Radelan's cup and withdrew.

The woman at Radelan's side brushed clear the recently vacated stool and perched on it, then turned to Radelan.

"You do remember, yes?"

Radelan took a deep swallow of his full mug and nodded.

"Shall I name them again?" she asked.

At their first meeting, before she said anything else, she had spoken names. His parents. His brother. Two sisters. Eight children. A woman Radelan had been eyeing for years, without once having spoken to her.

"I know the list."

"Don't forget," she said quietly, "the sparkling coin coming your way."

"I won't."

"You don't seem very grateful for this opportunity, Radelan," she said, her tone edged. "Convince me of your enthusiasm."

Radelan forced himself to turn and look at her. The Helata face. The clothes as quality as anything that ever made its way into the queen's room.

To be a queensguard was a glory beyond his wildest dreams. He remembered the day he had first been accepted into the palace guard, how it felt in his chest and his belly and arms and legs. It was as if he were made of pride. He gave himself to the queen's service for years. Bit by bit, his loyalty and devotion had gained him status.

Then it happened: The Queensguard.

Now his honor was gone. His life might be over soon, too, but if he failed in this, every name on the list would die.

On one side of the scale lay his honor. On the other, family and friends. There was no question which side was heavier.

"You may count on my devotion, Illustriousness," he said.

She smiled but without warmth and her voice dropped low. "I don't give a shit about your devotion, boy. You make a mess of this, you'll watch every person on that list die slowly. Obey is the word you want. Do as you're told and you'll be so well compensated that you can forget that this ever happened."

She waited a moment for his reply, then clasped his shoulder once and left.

After a long moment, Radelan downed the rest of his mug.

There were no more decisions to be made. There was only the practical matter of what to do in the meantime. He would return to the palace by dawn, of course.

But now?

The barwife was very carefully not watching him.

No reason to leave yet. Plenty of time before dawn.

Radelan held out his mug. It was filled.

Why not? His tab was paid. Forever.

***

THE PAPERS and envelopes on Innel's desk were multiplying.

"Srel."

"You wanted them to come to you directly, ser."

True enough. Innel sighed heavily, then took the top most, thick set. He struggled to focus on the script, and reached for his phapha tea.

Empty. He thumped the glass.

"More."

"Yes, ser." Srel poured a remaining dribble in to the cup from a decanter. "I'll return shortly."

He left and Innel stared distantly, thinking. Someone was bribing the Queensguard, but it could just as easily be Nital as Etallan, though Nital's history did not include challenging the monarchy. Or both of them together?

He thought not. Etallan got along with few other Houses. Sometimes it aligned with Helata, but only when they weren't fighting, like lovers who got along splendidly in bed but couldn't share a meal.

Innel blinked, his eyes felt dry from lack of sleep. The papers in his hands described a new lamp oil from Lesser House Chandler, vassal to Elupene, an oil supposedly better than any made before. Chandler would be ever so pleased to present some to the queen for her evaluation.

While the Greater Houses offered Accounts and Petitions, the Lesser Houses served up innovations they'd been working on since the last Charter Courts, in order to try to impress the monarch with their value and virtue, in case the Lesser House wanted some help changing their patron House.

Chandler had been making lamp oil for hundreds of years. Something was wrong with the entirety of the matter —Houses and Charter Courts—if the only time a House was willing to show off its production was just before the next Court.

Innel must talk with Cern about this, when her reign— and thus his own standing—were more firmly established. At the very least, after Garaya was resolved.

Garaya. He pushed the thought away.

Srel returned and refilled his cup with tea.

The next set of papers, nearly two inches thick, came from a box. Sketches of a villa from every imaginable angle. For a moment Innel stared in confusion, then snorted in amusement.

"Ser?"

"House Murice has an expensive sense of humor. Set it aside somewhere safe."

"Yes, ser."

Sleep had been hard to come by lately. It wasn't only tracing the handfuls of schemes against Cern, and it wasn't merely the phapha's stimulating effect. It was that Innel had the sense that he was missing something. Something important.

But everything was important.

The next envelope was flat, sealed, and addressed to him personally. It seemed empty, or nearly so. Bemused, he slit it open and turned it upside down. Something fluttered to the desk.

A thread, black twined with muted red. The queen's colors.

Innel's heart began to pound.

He lifted the thread, turning it between his fingers to examine it closely. It looked to him to be the same length as the one found in the queen's bedroom.

He forced himself to think the matter through logically. All the queen's retinue wore these colors. It would be easy to come by such a thing. A maid working the queen's laundry. A garment maker under the queen's tailor. A servant changing the washwater.

For that matter, anyone across years, sweeping low in a bow as Cern and her entourage passed, might pick the thread from the floor. Innel could even imagine that something of a market for such collectibles might exist.

But none of that was the point; this thread had not been found in the queen's room, or the laundry, or in some aristo's treasure box. It had been sent to Innel directly. A message.

"Ser?" asked Srel.

Innel held the thread and stared distantly.

"What does it mean, Lord Commander?"

"A threat against the queen and my child."

Whoever had sent this thread knew about the other one.

From a practical stance, there was only one person who could legitimately wear both of these colors, and that was Sachare.

He remembered his discussion with her about increasing the guards. *The move is to get you to react, Innel. And behold.*

A mocking reply, intended to make him think he might be over-reacting, which he clearly was not. Had Sachare been trying to distract him from the truth that the situation was exactly what it seemed?

"What shall we do, Lord Commander?"

Innel's mind leapt to the inventory room of gifts and his argument with Sachare about who should inspect the expensive items piled there.

A contact poison. A spring-loaded dart. So many ways to get a deadly item close to the queen and child.

Sachare was uniquely positioned to walk away from any assassination attempt; any deadly gift could be pinned on whoever had sent it.

A clever plan.

Or it would have been, if Innel hadn't insisted that he be the one to check the gifts.

His daughter's face came into his memory, fast followed by wretched, vivid imagination: he saw a toy, heard a click, as a pin popped out of a brightly painted hole. A cry. A fast poison.

A dead child.

Alarmed, he stood.

The gift inventory. He would check it again.

---

CERN WAS WRENCHED from a dead sleep by loud voices in the antechamber. She rolled over, as Sachare went to the door, listened, then opened it a crack.

Cern reached behind the headboard and pulled a knife.

A whispered discussion ensued between Sachare and someone else, a discussion that Sachare wanted Cern to hear, since she didn't leave the room to have it.

And that meant it was not an invasion. Cern carefully put the knife back in favor of the baby.

"Asleep," Sachare whispered, fairly loudly.

"I have a message from her," someone whispered. "She needs me. It's urgent."

"She doesn't, it's not, and I would know."

"Maybe you wouldn't. Fates and Hells, Sachare, let me by." This, nearly shouted. It was Innel.

Backlit from the lamps in the antechamber, Sachare was framed in the doorway.

"Come on, Innel," Sachare said, matching his volume. "Show me what you've got."

Oh, no. That would lead to nothing good.

"Sacha," Cern called sharply. "Let him in."

Sachare hesitated, then stood aside, angrily gesturing Innel to pass, then she shut the door behind him. She took up a lamp, adjusting it up to shed more light on the room.

In her arms, the baby began to cry. Innel's hands were kneading the air, like a sculptor up to his wrists in clay. It was a gesture Cern had never seen from him before.

She rocked the baby to mere whining. "Innel, what is this?"

"Did you send a message for me to come in all haste, Your Majesty?"

*What?*

Cern wriggled her legs out from under the covers and set her feet on the floor. Baby in arms, she slowly gathered herself to stand drawing herself upright.

"I did not."

"There you have it," Sachare said. "Asked and answered. Now go."

Innel ignored her, staring at the baby, a strange look on his face.

"Sacha," Cern said, "give us a moment."

"Your grace?" Sachare's tone and expression were incredulous, as if to say that to leave her alone with Innel in this state was surely madness.

But Innel was the child's father. If she could not trust him, she had a far bigger problem than her own recovery, or this strange late-night intrusion.

Cern tilted her head, a silent command. Sachare was clearly unhappy about it but nonetheless obeyed, opening a side door.

"I'll be back soon," she said in a threatening tone to Innel, then left, closing the door.

"Innel," Cern said. "Explain."

"A note thrust under my door." He held out a crumpled piece of paper.

Cern moved the baby to one arm, and took the note with her free hand, examining it.

Forging handwriting was not hard, and Cern's was particularly well-known. It was hardly the first time.

"A trick from Cohort days. Don't you remember, Innel?"

"It seemed…" Innel swallowed. "Genuine." His eyes flitted about the room, as if searching for something.

"It's not. Are you…in good health, Innel?"

"Yes, Your Grace. Entirely so."

In this half-light, his eyes wide, she did not quite believe him. What had happened to him while she was sick in bed?

"I must be able to rely on you, Innel."

His gaze came back to her and the baby. He almost looked afraid.

Of her? Of the child?

Of what?

INNEL LOOKED AROUND THE ROOM, a deep craving driving him to search the room, to see what was in each corner, under the dressers, and below the bed.

And in the crib that had shown up since the last time he was here.

The craving made him tremble.

"Are you…in good health, Innel?"

Cern looked so very tired. Even in this half-light, her face was sallow, almost aged. In her arms, the tiny creature seemed so vulnerable.

To worry Cern was to endanger them both. He must be confident and assured.

"Yes, Your Grace. Entirely so."

It was an effort not to think about the ways a threat could come to this room. So easy to slowly poison a baby with no one the wiser. Simply explained: a rough, early birth that left the baby frail—such a shame. *Weak commoner blood —what do you expect?*

And if Cern herself declined after that, well, she had already been sickly. *A tragedy for the realm, but who is surprised?*

Etallan was behind the plot. Innel was sure of it. But if he waited for proof, would it be too late?

"I must be able to rely on you, Innel," she said.

"Always," he breathed, forcing himself to look from the child to Cern. "Your Grace, that forged note is only the most recent of the aberrant things to come my way."

"Say more."

He blinked, considering all the potential plots he was following, all the evidence he had yet to gather. He could not mention the guards, not yet, not without undercutting his own authority. And Sachare? Dare he mention the threads and their implications?

The baby made a pleading sound and reached out an arm. Toward him.

Innel felt his stomach lurch. He resolved to take any risk he must.

"A thread has been found," he said. "In House Nital's colors."

"A thread?"

"In your room. By a guard, who brought it to me."

Cern sat on the bed, baby in her arms, as if this news had tired her completely. "I see. So you think—what? That my maid is sloppy?"

The queen's maid sloppy? Beyond unlikely.

"That could be," he said carefully. "Or perhaps it was tracked in by accident."

Cern frowned. "They're meticulous, you know."

Innel knew, all right.

"Ah, you mean to implicate Sacha."

Innel made a sound, as if the idea had only just now occurred to him. "I suppose that is also possible."

"No, it is not," Cern said firmly. "She swore herself into my service years ago. Nital is not her House."

"Yes, your grace," he said quickly. "Beyond question."

Sachare chose that moment to come back into the room. Listening at the door?

He could feel Cern watching him closely, but his gaze tangled in the baby's eyes, and he could not seem to look away.

"Do you want to hold her?" Cern asked softly.

From Sachare, a sharp, audible breath.

Into Innel's mind flooded vivid images of all the threats arrayed against his queen and child. Images of blood. Howling cries. A lifeless baby.

How could he take this small, innocent creature into his arms, thinking such things?

And what if he dropped her? What if he held her too tightly? His hands trembled.

He shook his head.

Sachare exhaled relief.

Cern inhaled. "You need sleep, Innel. I know I do. I require you to be…" she considered him. "Clear-headed and sensible in all your dealings."

"I shall be, your grace. You can rely on me."

"Keep them at bay, Innel, just a little longer."

"I will," he assured her.

"As for this—" Cern said, opening a hand to reveal the crumpled message.

"A mistake, Your Grace."

"That's putting it mildly," Sachare said.

"Sacha," Cern reprimanded. Then, "Innel…"

But he had already backed to the door, bowing quickly, leaving the room, knowing only that he must get away before the desire to hold his daughter became too strong to resist.

<hr>

INNEL STRODE TO HIS BEDROOM, pulling Srel inside with him. "Find out who delivered that message."

"Yes, ser," Srel replied, turning to leave.

"No. Wait."

Srel turned back.

Hells, but his mind was fuzzy. His gaze swept his room as he struggled to think.

Whoever had sent that note had intended, at very least, to make him look incompetent. If his own people started asking around about it, it would become entirely too clear that Innel was rattled. Better to seem unaffected.

"Was someone here while I was gone?"

"No."

"You were."

"Well, no, ser, I followed you to the queen's chambers, and stood outside in the hallway, waiting with the guards, then returned with you."

"Then you don't know for sure that no one was here. Someone could have come in."

"Has something been moved?" Once the thought was in his head, he couldn't seem to get rid of it. He began to slowly walk the room, looking in corners.

"I did lock the door behind me, Lord Commander."

"Locks can be picked. Light another lamp. A third."

Srel left, returning with more lamps.

Innel examined the room in detail, stopping at his pillow on the bed. He picked up a hair.

"Is this blonde? What was a slave doing in my room?"

Srel peered closely. "Forgive my eyes, ser, but it looks brown to me. Might it be one of yours?"

Innel turned to the table, on which was a stack of notes and correspondences. He swept it all to the floor, checking the wood for cracks, hidden mechanisms, or the oily residue that might signal a poisoning attempt.

*Clear-headed and sensible in all your dealings.*

Innel brought himself to a stop and stood upright, looking around at the disarray that his search had caused. At the center of the room stood Srel, looking afraid to move.

"Maybe I should sleep," Innel said.

"That would be wise, ser. You'll see better in the light of the day."

Sensible advice. But in the morning, he would still have made a fool of himself in front of the queen and his child, and he would still not have the traitors in hand.

## Chapter Twelve

CERN STARED over the side of the bed at the jewel-encrusted lockbox that now lived in the corner, like the most extravagant of step stools. Another day, surely, would make no difference.

Would she say that every day?

She considered what had happened last night. "Sacha, get the seneschal. I want to know what is going on."

"Yes, Your Grace."

And the baby was asleep. A rare moment. Cern quietly slid out of the bed and settled on the floor to face the huge, gaudy box.

What if it didn't open?

Of course it would open. She remembered her father's grip on her tiny finger, the painful prick of the knife-tip, the press of her blooded finger to the lock. It had opened then. Why wouldn't it open now?

She reached a finger toward the lock. Her hand stopped midair.

But what if the locking mechanism—magical or natural

—had aged in the two decades since her father had set her blooded finger against the lock? It could be rusted. Jammed.

For a moment she felt the crushing weight of failure. Yes, she had made an heir—at least when she proclaimed the child—but she could barely stand, let alone govern. She could almost feel her father at her shoulder, disappointed again.

Enough whining, she told herself. If it didn't open, she would simply pretend that it had, and leave the damned thing under the bed forever. Tell no one but Sachare.

A palace full of people whom she knew, and two decades spent in lengthy education with the scions of Houses, and there was no one besides Sachare whom she would trust with this secret. Innel was resourceful and ruthless when he must be, but months had passed since she felt sure that she knew what was driving him.

She snorted softly. This speculation was absurd: the box was blood-locked to her and would open. She was the queen of the Arunkel empire, and this box would, by the Fates, obey her command.

The baby began to wail. Cern got to her feet with a twinge of pain, climbed atop the bed, and took the small, beautiful creature to her breast to suck while she stole glimpses of the dully glinting monstrosity in the corner.

Maybe she would find the solution to the puzzle of the child's name in there.

"Do something useful for a change, father," she muttered.

Two hours later, Sachare had returned, and the baby was once again asleep. Cern sat before the lockbox. Before she could think, she pushed her fingertip to the lock.

It clicked loudly. The heavy lid popped loose of its bond and raised slightly from the lock. Breathlessly, she hinged the lid back the rest of the way and peered inside.

A thick stack of envelopes and papers was topped by a single folded note, with her name in her father's hand.

She took a breath and began to read.

*My daughter, I expect you to be secure on your throne by now.*

Resentment and anger sparked within her. Feelings she had thought buried along with her father rose, as hot as ever.

She set the vexing note aside, and picked up another one.

*I pen this after midnight, a bell since your sixteenth birthday festivities ended. What moths, these Cohort boys, flitting about you in the Great Hall, fawning over your dress and garish ornaments. You glitter like a decorated tree. I wanted to shake the baubles off you and stomp them flat. Your great-grandmother Niala was the finest monarch of our lifetime and she eschewed such glittering trifles. My girl, none of those things makes you fit to be queen.*

"You venal bastard," Cern hissed. "What makes me fit is that I am, and you are dead."

She felt herself tightly knotted. The pain in her abdomen stirred. She pushed herself to read on.

*I protect you daily while you fight me, blind to the true enemies that swirl around you. You're stubborn and will not listen to my words, so you remain naive. Thus I write, in the hopes that someday you will instead read them.*

"I read," she snapped.

*Pay heed to these gifts I leave you, Cern. Beware those who flutter too close and want too much. Use them but do not trust them. Know what nightmares haunt those you rely on most, and what would crush them. Otherwise, they are not truly yours, and they will betray you.*

Yes, this all sounded very much like her father. She had almost forgotten how much she despised him.

She put the letter down, and again picked up the first one.

*I had planned to leave for you only the letters I wanted you to see. But in the wisdom of my later years, I leave them all and destroy none. Learn from my triumphs. Learn from my mistakes.*

"Your mistakes? You admit to mistakes?"

This she had not expected. She looked, unseeing, at the wall. The tightness in her chest eased.

*Learn from my mistakes.*

She picked up another envelope.

---

INNEL WOKE as he did these days: fast and hard, shooting to his feet, weapon in hand if he could find one.

Another knock. He pulled back the lock, yanked it open. Srel.

"The queen? The child?" Innel demanded.

"Both well, Lord Commander," Srel said, stepping inside, gesturing servants forward who carried trays of food and tea that steamed.

"No one in here but you," Innel said, glowering.

"Yes, ser," Srel said smoothly, reversing his gestures to send the servants back out. "Here, give me that," he said to one of the servants, taking a tray with a mug and tea cylinder.

Innel had been dreaming about the old king, in bed, surrounded by vials and bottles of powders and ointments, complaining that Innel hadn't brought the right one.

Innel had not even told Srel how he had kept the king compliant and bedridden. No one, not until Innel had told Cern. Had that been a mistake?

He looked at Srel closely. What did he really know about the man?

No, that was lunacy, to suspect Srel.

"You taste it first," he found himself saying as Srel offered him a mug of hot phapha.

But no—he couldn't risk Srel. What would he do without him? "No, have someone else taste it. No, wait."

Damn, his thoughts were muddled.

Prudent to have his food and drink tasted, but it sent a signal to anyone who found out—and who wasn't watching how the Lord Consort conducted himself these days?—that he was over-worried.

*Clear-headed and sensible in all your dealings.*

"If I may, ser," Srel said. "I recommend food, a bath, and a change of clothes before the Ministerial Council meeting."

That's right, they'd called him twice now. He didn't dare miss another.

They would ask him about Garaya. They would ask about the queen. But Innel could do nothing about the first without the second.

"Srel. What do they say about me?"

Did his steward pause before answering?

He peered closely at the smaller man, who took a breath, as if to ready himself.

"That you speak out against the Council's sanctions against trade with Garaya."

"Not true."

"You promised Phaltos to Helata in the next Charters Court."

"Absurd."

"Yes, ser. Most of what is said is scandalous, false, and doesn't bear repeating."

"What else?"

"That you refuse the House liaisons."

"What? Have I missed an appointment?"

"Only a few."

"Make them again. There's more. I can tell from your face. What?"

Srel turned. "Let me get the food, ser. You'll think more clearly when—"

Innel found himself between Srel and the door, breathing hard. "Damn you, tell me."

Unflinchingly, the smaller man looked up at Innel. With the more sensible part of his mind, Innel felt a flash of pride.

"That you've been down-city the nights," his steward said. "Speaking to crowds and deriding the monarchy."

"That is…" Innel struggled for words. "Untrue."

Srel's eyes narrowed and his mouth went tight. "Of course it is, ser. They seek to filthy your good reputation with lies. They have always done so, since the time you and Pohut took me in. You'll feel better after some food. Allow me to start your bath so you're not late for the Council meeting."

"It's not true."

"May I pass, please, Lord Commander?"

Innel blinked, then stepped out of the way.

---

"WE HAVE a letter from the city of Garaya, Lord Commander," said the Minister of Exterium, a shortish woman with excellent diction who Innel knew could speak twelve languages fluently, including the ever-changing Timurung.

Innel had just sat down. At these words, he half rose. "You have? Shouldn't it have come to me?" At the half-placating, half-directive gesture of the First Minister, Innel resumed his seat, gritting his teeth, caught between frustration and the need to seem calmer than he felt. "What does this letter say, Minister?"

"It says, Lord Commander, that Garaya has changed its colors."

"A city has no colors," Innel said.

Some of the ministers exchanged looks. Had he said something wrong?

"Save the queen's colors, of course," he added quickly, forcefully.

"The very colors they mean to change, Lord Commander," said the Minister of Exterium.

"They claim Perripin allegiance," the First Minister said to him, tilting his bald head forward slightly. "Specifically to the Perripin state of Taluk. They claim no owed taxes for the year since…well. Since the force of arms sent there to restore order."

*That you ordered, Lord Commander,* no one needed to say. Another failure blamed on him.

The Minister of Accounts rubbed his ruddy, roundish face. "More insultingly yet, Lord Commander, they claim the crown owes them repayment for the men and material that they lost in that encounter."

"Outrageous," Innel spat.

"Treason, is what it is, Lord Commander," said the Minister of Justice tightly.

"We observe here today that the rot extends beyond Garaya," the accounts minister said. "Towns and cities along the border that have for generations flown the Arunkel flag are delaying and denying, asserting that levies will be yet sent while bemoaning insurmountable delays."

"Most unacceptable," said the Minister of Justice, eyes glittering.

"You don't have any back-channel contacts in Garaya, do you, Lord Commander?" asked the First Minister.

Back-channel contacts? What was the First Minister implying?

"I do not," he said, eyes narrowed.

"We are fast feeling the pain," said the Minister of Exterium, "of no longer having Garaya loyal to the empire. Trade along the Great Road suffers. The situation must be addressed and soon."

*And you must do it,* Innel heard clearly in the expectant pause that followed.

*You are absolutely right, Minister. Innel might answer. I will arrange another campaign to bring Garaya in hand.*

A campaign that would work better than the last one, because Innel would lead it? What a perfect invitation to Etallan to send illicit support to Garaya's rebellion.

Innel could do nothing without the queen's support. Without her, anything that went wrong they would blame on him.

Or maybe that's what the Ministers wanted.

"Perhaps we should ask the queen," said the First Minister, gaze on Innel.

"Ah, yes, the queen," added the Minister of Accounts, as if he had just now come to the idea as well. "How is her majesty, Lord Consort?"

Innel noted the title change.

*Healthier than she's been in months.*

He could not say that.

*In the pink of health, Minister.*

Then why was she still in bed?

"Recovering quickly, Minister," Innel said, putting conviction into his tone.

The First Minister spoke. "There is a delicate matter of some concern, Lord Consort. The witnesses to the birth— three, as you know, is the traditional quorum to verify the birth of a royal child."

Of course he knew; he was Cohort. He and Sachare had signed their names as witnesses, because the only other person in the room had been Marisel dua Mage, whose presence, by Arunkel law, was illegal.

A fine gift for Cern's enemies to have a mage sign the records verifying a royal birth.

No one else had been allowed inside during the birth, because no one else could be trusted to see how fragile the queen's condition really was.

But to this question, he had an answer.

"Practicality prevails over tradition. I point out to the Ministers Council," and here he made eye contact with each of them in turn, "that the monarch is also the mother, who would have little reason to proclaim a child not of her body as the heir. Since she has thus proclaimed—"

"Has she, indeed, proclaimed the child as heir?" asked the Minister of Exterium. At this, everyone looked eagerly at Innel. "In writing, perhaps?"

"Of course," Innel lied. Well, she would. Surely. Who else?

"And who is the regent, Lord Commander?"

"Regent," he said slowly, trying to summon clear thought.

"In the interests of the realm, it is entirely sensible, Lord Royal Consort, to have named a regent, to guide the child, should the worst happen."

"I know what a regent is for," Innel snapped. "Nothing will happen."

Ministers exchanged looks.

Had his tone been wrong? "What I mean to say, Ministers," he said, hoping to seem more reasonable, "is that yes, of course, to proclaim a regent. Entirely sensible."

"And, ah—who might that be, Lord Consort? You?"

That would follow naturally, since he was her father. "Of course," he said, with every confidence he could summon.

Oddly, they did not seem reassured. "The queen will ratify this?"

"Of course."

"One more thing." This from the Minister of Accounts, who pursed his thick lips twice, a sign that the man was about to give voice to something he believed was in his domain.

Innel stood. "We could, I'm sure, be here all day, Ministers, with one thing and the next, but I have a great deal to attend to."

"Yes, naturally, Lord Consort," said the round-faced Minister of Accounts, standing, too. "But there are some, ah, minor irregularities in some of the ledgers."

"Well, make them regular." Innel's mind felt like mush.

"I shall, ser. Ah. They come from your office."

The man could not possibly be referring to the funds Innel had been tapping to accommodate the many schemes against the queen. He and Srel had worked those accounting trails with extreme care.

Yet his mind failed to provide him with any details. "I have been managing a number of key issues on behalf of her majesty." There, that seemed safe enough.

"No doubt, no doubt," the minister muttered, hands up. "We simply want to be sure that they are correctly labeled."

Innel knew the Minister of Accounts had a late-night Rochi habit, and wondered how hard it would be to arrange for a suit mark to be anointed with something to help the minister sleep longer.

Or was that a bad idea? His mind was fuzzy.

"I'd be only too pleased to help you with that, Minister. As my time allows."

The man's eye twitched at this answer. "We look forward to your time allowing, ser."

"So do I."

With that, Innel turned to leave. He felt their stares until the door closed behind him.

———

THE QUEENSGUARD NAMED Radelan stood at attention. Innel, seated at his desk, looked him over.

"Yes?" Innel asked, taking the mug of phapha that Srel had left, only to find it empty. Had he already finished it? Had it not been filled? He couldn't remember.

The guard saluted, then did it again. Nervous. That got all of Innel's attention.

"I was bribed, Lord Commander," Radelan said.

*Some awfully bright shine being spun past your sharpest-toothed Rusties.*

"Say more."

"In the privy. A voice behind the wall. Told me where to find a coin, and how much more there would be if I…did the act."

"What act?"

"Put a vial of liquid into the queen's bedroom."

"Who bribed you?"

"I don't know, Lord Commander. Just a voice. A man's voice, through a gap in the wood."

"And what is in the vial?"

"Something to relax her, he said. No harm, he promised. But no, I wasn't going to do it. I serve the queen, ser. I came to you. Here it is, ser." He took a small, stopped, dark brown vial out of a pocket.

Innel stared at the brown vial in the guard's thick fingers, then gestured to a bit of open desk, where Radelan set it.

"What were you paid?" Innel asked.

"Think it's an uma-sorin, ser, but never seen one before."

On the guard's open palm was a large bronze and gold octagonal coin.

It was indeed an uma-sorin. Perripin money, and a lot of it. Enough to demonstrate that whoever was behind this was both serious and well-funded.

But it made no sense to pay in Perripin coin. Not unless…

Unless Perripur itself was aiming to unseat the Arunkel queen. Outrageous. But possible?

Or perhaps this treasonous effort came from Garaya itself, in a brazen, preemptive attempt to avoid royal retaliation, which they must surely be expecting at any time. As close as the city of Garaya was to the Perripin border, there would be sorins aplenty, and Garaya would be increasingly tight on Arunkel currency.

Suddenly Innel didn't feel the need for phapha. His mind felt very clear.

This was proof, at last.

Well, not quite. But it would be proof the moment he tracked this guard back to whoever had bribed him.

"I'll get you a new vial," Innel said quietly. "Nothing more potent than water. You will then carry out the plan as directed. When they contact you again, say that you have done the deed."

Innel would have someone watching Radelan wherever he went, privy and all. But his people must watch a number of guards, to dilute suspicion.

Radelan looked pained. "But, ser—"

"The next time the voice speaks to you in the privy, the moment you exit, give this signal." He brushed his left shoulder, as if removing dust. "Do you understand?"

"Yes, Lord Commander. But I hadn't planned to go through with any of this. That's why I came to you."

"Yes, and well done. They will have arranged for another

person to observe you—possibly another guard—to make sure you go through with it. One of your fellows, perhaps, or a servant—" His mind circled back to Sachare. "It could be anyone. So you must deliver the vial to the queen's bedroom, exactly as instructed."

"Ser, I don't understand."

With effort, Innel forced his tone steady. "I will watch who watches you. Later, who pays you. Then I can get my hands on them." Was all this not obvious?

The worried guard did not seem reassured. "With respect, Lord Commander, this could put me in a world of trouble."

"Only if you're caught."

"I'm trained to protect the queen. To give my life for hers. That I know how to do. This…?" He shook his head slowly. "I don't know how to do this, ser."

Innel sighed. "Wait until she and the baby are in the bath. Her room will be empty. No one goes in unobserved by a queensguard, but if you are that queensguard, simply say you heard something that you want to investigate. No one will question. Put the vial in the back, under the wardrobe."

"If I'm caught, ser…"

"I'll protect you."

"The other queensguards—if they think I betrayed them —they aren't the forgiving type. Blood could spill long before you show up, ser—mine."

He might well be right, but Innel needed him to do this.

Innel took out paper from a drawer, dipped a quill, and wrote a fast note, waving it dry. He folded it and handed it to the guard. "If it comes to that, show this, but only if you must. Far better not to get caught."

The guard put the paper, unread, in a pocket. His look at Innel was stark. "Are you sure you want to do this, ser?"

"Yes, damn it. The only way to find out who is behind

the plot is to draw them out. Don't you want to protect the queen?"

"I do, Lord Commander."

"This is how."

The guard swallowed, nodded. "I obey, ser."

"Good. Act as if this conversation never happened."

"Yes, ser."

Radelan saluted, turned to leave, then turned back. "Lord Commander. This coin, I can't keep it."

"What do you mean?"

"We get searched regularly." Innel knew this—he'd ordered it. "Don't know how much it's worth, but I can't imagine I ought to have it on me."

That was a fair point; if an uma-sorin was found on Radelan, he would be subject to increased attention and suspicion, and Innel's chance to track the traitors might well vanish.

"Would you hold it for me, ser?" Radelan looked unhappy as he asked. Innel could understand that: he knew it was a lot of money, and was wondering if he'd ever get it back.

"I can do that."

Innel took the large octagonal coin, examining it a moment before putting it in his pocket. He judged the guard's motivation to be weak, so took from another drawer a gold souver, offering it to him.

Radelan stared into his palm at the large coin, looking stunned. He might not know just how much an uma-sorin was worth, but he certainly knew how much this one was.

"Loyalty should be rewarded," Innel said. "More for you, when this is done. An uma-sorin's worth, at least. You know what to do now, guard, yes?"

The man swallowed, and he nodded. "Yes, Lord Commander."

INNEL SHOOK HIS HEAD, trying to clear it, staring at the papers in his hand, struggling to make sense of the flowery, convoluted language of another Account and Petition. This one was from House Elupene, who was taking an impressive two pages to describe the merits of its vassal House Equis.

Someone's idea of a joke at his expense, Innel thought sourly.

Equis should have been abolished long ago; every House had long ago demanded and been granted its own stables to keep and breed horses, and by now Equis's stock was hardly exceptional and nothing like pure. But tradition held.

It was late. He needed sleep. He just wanted to get through this one last document first.

Srel had just spoken. He spoke again.

"What?" Innel asked, looking up.

"A delivery, ser. Not a gift. Or at least, I don't think so. Not sure what to make of it, so I thought you should see." Srel took the lid off a box he held.

A glimpse was enough. Innel was on his feet and around the desk. He drew from the box what was inside.

A blanket, soft and pale, edged in black, with a silk embroidery of the Anandynar crest in one corner. A blanket he knew well: all his daughter's bedding looked like this.

A note fluttered down from the fabric. Still holding the box, Srel picked it up, read it.

"A time and location. Another hoax, like the last one, I'm certain of it, ser, and..." Srel trailed off as Innel wadded up the blanket and buried his face in it.

It had been in Cern's room; it smelled like his child, and Cern. Until this moment, he hadn't realized that he knew the very scent and could identify it in a moment.

It should be impossible to take the baby's blanket from

the queen's room unnoticed. It was exactly the sort of thing that the guards would stop, fast and hard. Even the laundry servants were supposed to be unbribable.

Were they all corrupt?

He went to the window, pulled back the drape. Overcast and cold, night clouds held only meager luminescence from the moon and stars. Innel walked back, took the note from Srel's fingers.

"Ser," Srel said with growing alarm at the look on his face. "Ser," he said again. "It might be best if you didn't go out. Not now. Not with the rumors going around. Ser?"

Innel gripped the blanket tightly, staring into the weave, as if the very fiber would reveal who had sent it.

"Lord Commander, where are you…what are you…Ser? I really wouldn't."

Innel was at the door, note in one hand, wadded up blanket in the other. Srel was speaking. Urgently, very urgently. But the words were meaningless.

Innel dropped the blanket on the floor and left.

---

SACHARE ENTERED, a puzzled, half-amused expression on her face.

"What is it?" Cern asked, sitting in bed.

In her arms, the baby was fussing, making sounds of annoyance and refusing to be soothed. Cern moved her to her other nipple, hoping that one nipple might, mysteriously, be more attractive than the other. The baby took hold.

"Have you ever known Mulack to wear anything but his House colors?" asked Sachare.

"Not since we were children in the Cohort."

They had all worn the colors of dawn, then, children as young as four, dressed in light blue and pale yellow, a heavy red-and-black cord about their waist to remind them of their loyalty to the monarchy. All but Cern, of course. She wore her father's colors.

"Well, Your Grace, Mulack is outside the apartments in green servant's livery, begging for you to see him."

Cern barked a laugh. "He is not."

"I would never disagree with you, Your Grace," Sachare said dryly, "but it does seem to be him. He wants you to know that this particular humiliation is—how did he say it? —a candle to the sun of his most great need to see you. Attempting poetry, I think."

"How interesting." Cern considered. Open the door to one, she would have to open it to them all.

Well, maybe it was time.

"Send him in."

Sachare left for a moment, returning to usher Mulack inside.

Cern stared at him in open shock. No one in the palace halls would look twice at the man who stood before her, dressed as he was.

"A privilege to see you thus," she said, amused, "House of Dye and Weave. How comfortable you look."

Mulack was gaping at the baby in Cern's arms, who had finally decided to feed. "The Heir," he breathed.

"The Heir," Cern said, realizing that her words constituted a verbal ratification. Well, perhaps it was time for that, too.

"Praise all the Fates, benign and cruel." Mulack's mouth turned down.

At the sight of her breasts? Or the baby? Either way, she didn't like it.

"What?" she demanded.

"Are there no wetnurses, Your Majesty?"

"Nothing goes into her that doesn't first go into me."

"Ah. I see. Such are the times. What a shame."

Cern sighed. "Why are you here, Eparch-heir?"

"Forgive this gross subterfuge, Your Most Excellent Majesty. I would have far preferred to come to you in my colors, keeping the honor of my House and self intact, but I had no choice: this matter requires the utmost discretion."

"Does it." Cern was already finding Mulack wearing. He had a knack for wearying his listeners, especially when he was trying to be charming. Her shoulder ached. She shifted the baby, who objected loudly to being jostled. Cern adjusted again and the baby resumed suckling. "What is it that can't wait, Mulack? I don't have all day."

Well, she probably did, as long as it was to try to sleep. Already the heaviness behind her eyes made the thought of lying back deeply attractive.

Mulack appeared to be struggling with words, which was decidedly unlike him. Mulack could be wearying, yes. Inarticulate, no.

He shifted his weight, one side to the other, and Cern wondered if he were genuinely uncertain. Mulack genuinely *anything* caught her attention.

"Whatever it is," she said, "Why not take it to Innel?"

"A finger on the very problem, Your Majesty."

"Oh?" she asked, striving to keep the concern from her voice.

"The Lord Commander has been acting...how shall I say it? Irrationally, perhaps? Some say they've seen him down-city, speaking to inappropriate people about...highly questionable matters."

Cern thought of Innel's recent midnight intrusion and the forged note. Irrational was certainly one word for it. Sleep-deprived, at least.

She drew herself as upright as she could, sitting on a bed, a baby at her breast. "You stand in my bedroom, interrupt the feeding of the heir of the Arunkel empire, to fill my ears with drivel and gossip? Beneath you, Mulack. I already know these rumors."

Well, not entirely: the seneschal told her what he had heard—including one about Innel having dealings with Garaya, which really made no sense at all—but Cern had no doubt there were more yet.

Still, to be queen meant to seem more knowledgeable than surprised.

Mulack held up his hands, ducked his head. "I just thought you should know."

From the time they were children, the stories about the mutt brothers had been as thick as flies on a carcass. Across the years, the brothers had faced all manner of tricks intended to take them down, and none had.

Until the night Pohut had died.

Innel was not without his flaws and questionable actions, Cern knew, and his brother's killing was high on that list.

Pohut had been on Cern's short list of possible mates. It still rankled, years later, that Innel had taken from her the choice.

But it was done. Another thing that it meant, being queen, was knowing when to move forward.

"I don't care for this particular game, Mulack," Cern said. "Innel has been addressing important issues while I recover. He's bound to face resistance. I'm recovered now." Was she? Well, given the rumors she was downplaying, and this unpleasant conversation, she had by the Fates better be. "If that's all you came for, you may go and change your clothes now."

Mulack nodded, appearing undiscouraged and giving no sign of leaving. "Perhaps the stresses have undone him. We all know how strong he is. No one questions this. Clever, too."

The litany of slurs had not been subtle when the Cohort were children, and became only a bit more refined as they all grew to maturity, as this conversation amply demonstrated. Cern heard the silent end of Mulack's sentence: *For a commoner.*

"I am ever so pleased by your watered-down compliments of my Consort, Mulack."

The baby pushed away. Done with feeding, then. Cern rearranged the little creature, leaning her chest against Cern's shoulder, rubbing her back gently.

Mulack took a wider stance. She knew the pose from childhood. It was how he stood when answering hard questions. His risk-taking posture.

"This much I know," Mulack said, "Innel, sworn directly to you, is taking bribes to affect the Charters Court."

"No, he isn't," Cern said. "He has no authority in the Charters Court. He knows that." The baby was nodding off. Cern gently set her down on the bed and let Sachare help her with a robe, then to stand, with subtle support hidden by cloth and angle.

Cern felt better, standing. A touch more queenly, anyway. "I hope you're not paying good money for these inane rumors, Mulack."

"Better than rumor, Your Grace. I know, because I was the one who bribed him."

"That old Cohort game? You tempt each other to see how far you can make the other lean, until someone falls over?"

"True enough, ma'am, but I think we now face adult matters, with more at stake than when we were playing for marks and meals. Does he or does he not hold a deed, with pictures, of a villa? A lavish gift of generosity, expecting nothing back. Does that sound much like me?" He paused a moment, voice quieting. "And is that the sort of man you want to be regent?"

She smiled wryly at this ploy. "I have named no regent."

His expression of surprise was entirely unconvincing. "I must be mistaken, then, ma'am, and the rumors of his words entirely false. Not even worth mentioning."

"And yet you do," Cern said.

Mulack brushed this away. This was the problem with Cohort-sibs, Cern thought sourly. Familiarity.

"This might be worth your time, Your Majesty: I have been approached by someone who says he knows of a threat against you. He has proof. He came to me, afraid for his life."

"Who is this?"

"A queensguard, ma'am. Name is Radelan. I left him in the hallway. He has something for you, if you will hear it."

Another imagined threat. She was already weary. But it was impolitic to let Mulack think she didn't care about such things.

She glanced at the room. Well, if her father could conduct business in his bedroom, so could she.

"Send him in. Make it quick."

Sachare went to the door, relayed a message down a chain of guards. In a few moments, a guard entered. She recognized him. He knelt smartly, stayed there until she told him to get up.

"Go on, Guard. Tell her," Mulack said.

Radelan took a deep breath. "Your Majesty, I am sorry to be here, saying this—"

"Get to it," she snapped, with a growing certainty that she didn't want to hear what he was about to say.

"The Lord Commander paid me to bring a vial of liquid into your room, promising me more money when the job was done. He said to put it..." he looked around, then pointed at the heavy wooden leg of the wardrobe. "There, by the wall, while you were in the bath, Your Majesty."

"No."

Radelan swallowed nervously. "He gave me a souver. I couldn't figure out who to tell, ma'am. Then—" he looked at Mulack. "His Illustriousness Murice approached me. I confided in him."

Cern felt bile rise in her throat. "I don't believe you."

"It's my life to lie to you, Your Majesty."

"And you are in danger of losing it," she said.

The guard's eyes went wide. "I have a letter," he whispered, bringing out from a pocket a folded paper. He held it out in front of him, directionless. Sachare snatched it up, read it grimly, handed it to Cern.

*By my order and for the good of the state, this man has done what must be done.*

It was Innel's handwriting and his mark at the bottom. Sleep-deprived, in the middle of the night, Innel might mistake a scrawled note as being in Cern's hand, but Cern had been extensively schooled in just such things, and she knew exactly who had penned this.

"It could mean anything," Cern said darkly, letting it flutter to the floor.

"Yes, Your Majesty," Radelan said, eyes down. "I left the vial at my bunk. Didn't dare bring it here. Of course, if any of you want it…"

Lies. It was all lies.

She was breathing hard.

"Out," she yelled. "Everyone out."

Sachare urgently gestured to them. The guard dropped, skittering backward to the door and out.

Mulack paused at the doorframe. "One more thing you should know."

"You've said enough for one day, House Murice."

"This one from my own eyes and ears, Your Majesty. If you do not want it, I will say no more."

She did not. She most certainly did not.

But of course, she had to know.

"Spit it out," she hissed.

"A late-night speech to a down-city commons," Mulack said. "On the overreach of monarchy. He promised the commoner crowd that he would change the laws for them."

"He did not."

"Well, someone did, who looked a great deal like him. Ask those you trust, Your Grace. It's not much of a secret, sad to say."

Then Mulack dropped his head low and backed out. Sachare shut the door and turned back to Cern.

Cern's fists were knotted, her breath shallow.

*Use them but do not trust them.*

"Sacha," she said at last. "You said he was searching the gift inventory to protect me from hidden dangers. What if he were instead planting them?"

Sachare inhaled sharply. "To what end? Surely he has everything he has ever aimed for."

"Some people aim too high."

"Insist on evidence, Your Grace."

"Test the guard's vial. Have the seneschal track down these rumors about speeches. I want to speak with the First Minister."

"Yes, your grace."

"And then I want to see Innel, but I don't want him warned. If he leaves the palace, make sure he's followed."

*Know what nightmares haunt those you rely on most, and what would crush them. Otherwise, they are not truly yours, and will betray you.*

"And get me dressed."

SREL WOKE to a sharp pounding on the door. A blade of morning light edged a draped window.

He'd fallen asleep, damn it. He leapt to his feet, opening the door to the Lord Commander's bedroom. There stood the queen's seneschal.

"What in the Hells are you doing here?" the seneschal demanded.

"Waiting for the Lord Commander," Srel answered. Just barely awake, the truth was the only answer Srel could think of.

"And exactly where is he?"

That was the harder question, and it sparked Srel fully awake. He had expected Innel back well before now. Before dawn, at least. Where was he?

"Running around the garrison, I expect," Srel answered smoothly. "He's quite taken to the practice, near daily. I would be pleased to notify you, seneschal, the moment he—"

"Not anywhere near the garrison. Not in the palace, or I would know about it. Care to try again?"

Srel had said and done everything he could think of short of putting his body in the way of Lord Commander last night, to try to keep him from leaving, but there was no stopping him.

He knew what the note said, location and time, but that was last night, and who knew where the Lord Commander was now?

Srel grimaced. "Ah, my mistake, seneschal, I beg your forgiveness. I admit to having fallen asleep, and a bit disoriented. It's later than dawn of course; I can see that from the light."

The intensity with which the seneschal regarded him was unsettling.

"Tell me where he is."

Srel's heart began to speed as he summoned an

affectation of casual servility. "Unexpectedly called away, ser. His mother, you see—"

"In her apartments, alone. Lie to me a third time, man, and it will be the last lie you ever tell."

Srel paused, took a breath.

"I don't know where he is, Seneschal."

"That's not good, steward."

"No it's not, ser," Srel admitted, but he drew himself up straight to meet the other man's gaze.

Srel had been born into the commons. As an adolescent, he had come to the palace to serve the two brothers. Lacking a drop of aristo blood, Srel knew that his only influence across the palace came from knowing when to back down and when to stand firm. Once an aristo glimpsed capitulation, his influence would never recover.

"You help him sneak out," the seneschal said, as they locked gazes. "You help him return. You think he's unseen? You're wrong. And now—"

"Ser, I do what I am commanded to do. With great and abiding respect, seneschal, the Lord Commander does not answer to you."

The old man came close, too close. Close enough that Srel knew what the man had eaten for breakfast.

"The queen wants him, and she wants him now. If you know anything at all, this is the time to tell me."

Srel felt the blood leave his face.

It was time to back down.

"He went last night to the Bent Nail to meet someone." With a start, Srel realized that his voice had taken on the down-city cadence he'd worked so many years to eradicate. He swallowed hard, determined to repair his accent. "Where he is now, though, seneschal, I really have no idea."

The seneschal exhaled, nodded. "That's a shame, young man. Come with me. Bring your keys. All of them."

## Chapter Thirteen

TAYRE DIPPED two fingers into a small tin, brought them
to her face, and stroked tan butter on her skin.

His expression was bland, his touch similarly so. Nothing
like the night he sat by her side, brushed her cheek, and told
her it was too soon. How could he make his touch say so
much? Or so little?

Was her face betraying desire now? *Your face is a window.*

Let him see, then, she decided disgustedly. No sense in
trying to hide it.

A slatted window let light into the room. Outside and
down two stories, the busy festival continued loud, night
and day.

Tayre stood from his work, made a slow circuit around
her to inspect, and handed her a small mirror.

He had cut her hair to subtly change the shape of her
head, then had roughed into her scalp some fine, sticky
powder that made her brown strands a lighter, dusty color.
Lines around her eyes made them look larger.

She barely recognized herself. She looked not a bit
Arunkin.

"Now you look like a Borderello woman," he said. "I wouldn't try to pass you off as one in the borderlands themselves, but it'll do while we're here in Senta, to keep people from wondering if you're the Arunkin woman they're looking for. Don't touch your face until it sets."

She nodded her understanding, still staring at herself.

"As for getting to Atudaka by equinox," he said, "that will require a sea crossing. We'll need money. A fair bit of it, for passage across the Temani Gulf, then overland travel to the Xanmelkie range and the Monks of Revelation. We'll need it soon."

He replaced the lid on the tin and set it in a bag alongside other ointments and bags of powders. "Horse is worth plenty as he stands, but Souver's younger, and top-notch royal stock. Possibly even breedable. She's the real gem of the pair. Find the right buyer, and both of them together should net us a good amount."

Amarta was lost? "What?"

"We'll need to sell the horses."

"The horses? Why?"

He sat back and studied her. "If we had half a year or more, we could ride to Free Port, hop a short-boat across the straight to Dulu, and get to Xanmelkie in time. But time is short, so we'll need to make a full gulf crossing and travel on foot. Selling the horses might cover it, along with what I have stashed away."

"No," she said, horrified.

He cocked his head slightly. "Did you have a plan to fund the trip?"

She shook her head slowly, feeling her short hair brush her ears. "I thought that you would."

"I do. It involves selling the horses."

"No. I've made money before. In Munasee. There are ways."

With her ability, Amarta had been able to navigate Munasee's big-city crowds. She had become a well-paid messenger, keeping her sister and nephew fed and housed for a year.

Then Tayre had found them again, and they had fled.

"I know what you earned in Munasee," he said. "We need a hundred times that."

She opened her mouth to ask him how he could be so sure of her earnings, then thought better of it. "There must be other ways."

"Many. But the fastest ones are both dangerous and illegal. Though…I could take a contract."

Anxiety shot through her. "You have a contract," she said, her voice a tremulous whisper. "Don't you?"

"Yes, of course. I mean another one." He was watching her closely. "A lesser one. With your approval."

She blinked, her breath coming fast.

"It pays well," he added, and Amarta realized that he already had something in mind. "It pays fast."

*You are merely a wager on the ground of some back-alley Rochi game.*

She pushed Maris's words away.

What was it, this contract he already had? She didn't want to know. And what if he were caught, doing this dangerous, illegal thing? She imagined herself waiting for him to return, waiting and waiting.

"No," she choked out. "No."

"Then no it is," Tayre replied.

"What of the letter of credit that Maris gave me? Isn't that worth something?"

"A fraction of its face value, because it's written for you. At best, we could sell it to a young woman wanting to go north to Arunkel and willing to pretend to be you. A small market, if there is one at all."

Someone in Amarta's place, sent to a precarious future? All too familiar. She pushed aside thoughts of her friend Nidem and shook her head adamantly.

"Even with money," he said, "horses on a ship is no simple thing."

"Horses must surely cross the sea."

He nodded. "On specially outfitted transport ships." At her uncomprehending look, he added, "When horses panic, they break things. Rather expensively. One horse getting out of hand could cost a ship its ability to stay afloat. They take up room. They eat a lot. They shit."

"So do people."

"Where they're supposed to, usually."

"But…" She thought of the ships she'd seen in the ports of the large cities of Kelerre and Free Port. "I've seen the crates that go on them, easily as big as a horse."

He opened his hands. "Anything, for a price. Is the ship leaving soon enough? How much to persuade an otherwise sensible captain to vacate valuable cargo space for two unknown creatures who could destroy the hold? What equipment is needed to secure them during transit?" He looked thoughtful. "We could board them near Senta until our return, depending on how long we'd be gone. If we knew. Do we, Seer?"

She looked into the future. A mash of images, too numerous and faint to draw conclusions. In many of them, vast expanses of water loomed. The gulf? The ocean? She couldn't tell. Distantly, flashes of dry, scorched land. A huge cliff of snow and ice. Glittering lines across sand.

The future spread out sloppily, explaining nothing.

She shook her head. "How could you sell Horse? He's been with you for so many years."

"Certainly, I'd rather keep him. He's a well-bred creature,

and I've put a lot of time into training him. But my contract is with you."

Her gaze slid away from his, then, and down. He was putting her before his companion of many years. Her heart sank as she realized that she was forcing them apart.

"If I had to choose between you and Souver—"

He held up a hand. "You don't. Atudaka by equinox, or north to Arunkel for the wedding, or stay here, or something else." He opened a hand to indicate acquiescence. "You decide. Sell the horses or not. Your choice, Amarta."

She took a breath, not quite understanding. Almost understanding.

"Why?"

"Because we have a contract."

*Help you learn about yourself and the world.*

"How is this learning, for me to decide?"

He seemed to find this amusing. "Your path has been constrained for so long. You've been chased. Threatened. Bribed. Imprisoned. How better to learn about the world than for you to choose our way forward?"

"What about you and what you want?"

Tayre's gaze flickered across the room, their belongings, the walls, then back to her. "I made my choice when I took your coin."

For a moment she was silent.

"The Emendi children," she said.

"That would cost more yet. But if that's your decision, we'll find a way."

Amarta felt a growing tingle of excitement, thinking of what she could do. With him by her side, what could she *not* do?

She could do anything.

As if following her thoughts, a slow smile grew on his

lips. He was so beautiful, she could hardly look away. If she could do anything…

Well, almost anything.

*Yet*, he'd said. Yet. *Yet* would have to do for now.

Flexing the fingers of her left hand, she was reassured by the sharp twinges, and finally understood her own reluctance to let Maris heal them; she did not want to forget where she had come from, or the price she had paid.

"Atudaka," she said.

"Atudaka it is, then." He patted the tops of his thighs in a gesture of resolution and stood. "I'm going out to pick up my messages, check my sources, and consider what unusual opportunities the Accord festival might provide us to obtain a lot of money, quickly, without running too far afoul of force or law."

He began to put on layers and wound a long dark scarf around his head. As she watched, he opened a tin of blacking, rubbing some into his beard, then added a bit of white to the hair at his temples.

A touch of pencil to his eyes, and he had changed into someone else. With a trickle of dread, she realized that she knew this older man—he was the swarthy Perripin ship captain she and Maris had met in Kelerre, years ago. Enlon, Maris had called him. Even his expression was that man's: weighty, responsible, sober.

It came to her that she'd been staring at him a long moment, and only now did she realize that he was staring back.

He nodded once, as if he'd been waiting for this, then left.

TO MAKE them harder to track, they moved to another inn that afternoon, and Tayre took the horses to a yet a third location.

Each time, he returned with messages, the pile thickening. Greetings, questions, rumors, offers. Payments for work completed.

"There's increasing demand for word of an Arunkin woman traveling alone," he said. "It's time to build you a new history."

He coached her in a southern Perripin dialect, and had her walk the room, changing gestures and motions. The next time he went out, he came back with new clothes, draping over the back of a chair a long blouse and flared skirt with colorful embroidery and dark piping.

"Your family are former Arunkel Borderland merchants, relocated to Venta when you were young. They took over a spice plantation, inland from Vilaros, at the intersection of the three states of Venta, Atudaka, and Timurung. A strange area, even by Timurung standards, so a good place to be from." He squinted a little at her. "I'll teach you some particularly condescending idioms that could prove useful."

He cleared the table, wiping it down with a cloth, and set out a deck of cards.

"Have you ever gambled?"

"Just once," she said.

"Munasee?" he asked.

Amarta nodded, warily.

She, Dirina, and Pas had been fleeing him—the deadly hunter on their trail. They had come to Munasee, a city larger than any they had known. While Amarta and Pas huddled in the fields outside the city, Dirina left to find food. She returned limping, hunched, her face swollen and bruised. She refused to explain, but Amarta guessed that her sister had gone to offer her body to men with money, and it had not gone well.

Amarta waited until her sister and nephew were asleep, and ventured out, using foresight to guide her to coin. On the grimy streets of the city, she found a group of women throwing dice. It was not hard to predict the roll of a bone cube.

But the women hadn't liked it.

"I won too much, too fast," Amarta admitted. "I had to throw the winnings at their feet to get away. I lost it all."

He began to shuffle the deck. "It's not enough to win the coins. You have to win the people, too."

"How?"

"People give themselves reasons for their wins and losses. Inherent skill, a lucky stone, phase of the moon, what they last ate—anything to explain. Truth has nothing to do with it. Even winning isn't as important as whether they believe the tale. So when you win, you must fit their story."

"You mean that I must be believable?"

"They must believe," he said with emphasis, "Or they will find another story, usually that your streak of wins is cheating, however impossible that might be. Weighted dice, marked cards, magery—they'll find a tale they believe." He stacked the cards, split the deck, riffled them back into one stack. "When you've lost the larger game, the smaller one— the one that includes the coins—folds with it."

She considered. "*Am* I cheating? Is it wrong, this thing I do?"

Expression amused, his eyes narrowed slightly. "That depends on what tale you tell yourself." He squared the cards neatly. "Have you seen a roche deck before?"

"In Munasee. Delivering messages to taverns." She remembered the cards across the tables, the angry swearing, elated cries, coins and stones slammed onto wood.

"Rochi uses this deck," he said. "Six suits, fifty-four cards. Anyone can play knuckle dice—street beggars, aristo brats. But across Perripur and Arunkel, high-stakes gamblers play Rochi. We're in Perripur, but if you ever play in Arunkel, this full deck is called the Black Deck, and because it includes the Mages suit, it's outlawed. They use what they call the Red Deck, which is four cards smaller, lacking that suit."

*They*, he said, and Amarta seized on the clue. Was he himself not Arunkin? He didn't really look it, but then, he didn't really look like anything. His face was unremarkable, at least until he did something to make it otherwise. A beard, a hat, some shading, a few lines. The way he held himself. His expression.

Who was he without all that?

Tayre dealt out five cards to each of them, then laid across the table the six flat stones of different colors. He looked at her for a long moment.

"I can teach you the rules of Rochi. With your ability, I can show you how to win. But you'll need to learn more than that and quickly, to keep the coin. You'll need to be able to pretend, and there is no small amount of risk with this plan."

"A learning experience," she suggested.

He smiled a little. "Certainly. But not a safe one. Are you sure you want to try this?"

She considered the Monks of Revelation and the chance —however unlikely Tayre would say it was—to find people like herself. She thought of Souver and Horse, whom she did not want to leave behind.

If coin were all that stood between her and what she wanted, then it was time to learn how to get enough of it. She lifted her chin and gave him an unblinking stare, hoping to show him just how well she could pretend.

"I am sure."

He inclined his head. Acceptance at her answer, or at her pretense—or both—she didn't know.

Taking two small bags of coins, he upended them onto the table, stacking them into piles.

"Tonight, I'll show you how Rochi is played. Tomorrow we'll study the game."

"Those aren't the same?"

"No."

"THERE IS no shortage of gambling taverns in Senta," Tayre told her. "And they multiply during the Accord Festival. But we need a level of victory that requires an establishment likely to inspire people to bring their best purses. Thus, our destination is the House of Sun and Moon, which hosts the most lucrative games for which they can take a percentage. Rochi. Rugen. Quun. We'll start with Rochi, which requires as much skill as luck, and so is played by those who imagine themselves to be skillful first, and lucky second. Rochi is both, and volatile as well. This is where your foresight gives us the advantage."

He stacked small sorin-ga and sorin-menha coins, and pushed half the stacks toward her.

They played for hours, until the Rochi pictures swam before her eyes. A break for food, then back again.

Amarta lost, repeatedly, until she finally began to understand the game well enough to sensibly weave in her foresight's clues. By the time the light and shadow through the slatted windows traversed the far wall and went dim and dark, requiring lamplight to play, Amarta was winning nearly half the rounds.

That night she dreamed about the colorful cards, each with a story of its own, the suit stacks, the cool stone of suit tokens. Even in her dreams, she could foresee the next down card to be revealed, but not always who would draw it, which mattered. What suit would cut, but not who would be holding the token when it did.

The next day Tayre brought in a larger table and four more chairs. He pointed to each of the empty seats and told her about the person sitting there—what they looked like, where they came from, how they held themselves, in body, mind, and face. What tales they used to explain their wins and losses. How all that led to their method of play.

Then he would speak for them, swear for them when they lost, rejoice when they won. He took on expressions, accents, cadences, languages. It was stunning, how well he managed it.

Interspersed into this rich set of stories was his own advice for her, in his singular, neutral tone, which she never confused with the rest.

"No," he said, abruptly cutting off the table-talk between her and another pretend player. "Too much deference in your face and voice."

She bit off an apology, blew out a long exhale. "What must I change?"

He studied her intently for a moment. "The strongest lies are the ones that live closest to the truth. A brittle and forced arrogance will fit your new self well enough."

"I don't understand."

"Don't work too hard to seem other than you are: young, uncertain, new to the game, eager to play. But do not defer."

She digested this and glanced at the one card still in her hand. *The Secret*, from the Kin suit. Vision said the next down card drawn would be *Venture*, from the Commons suit. An obvious divination story to come of those two, were she inclined to invent one. "Will anyone suspect me, do you think?"

He shook his head "That's part of why I've chosen Sun and Moon. As far as the house knows, what you do is impossible."

*Unique beyond reckoning.*

"How can they be so sure?"

"The mages tell them so. They'll have one or two on hand to check players' coins before they convert them to Taluk sorins. The mages keep order, usually just by being there. Not players."

"Mages don't gamble?"

He shrugged. "Among themselves, only they know. But I know very few Iliban who would gamble with a mage."

They resumed play. Amarta's stack of sorins grew, then shrank, then grew again.

And then, as the day slid to night, her piles of coins stayed high.

"Good," he said at last, and then again, as she correctly predicted a Commons win and took the poke.

Tayre cleared the table and populated it with another set of imaginary people, sketching them all so vividly that Amarta would swear that she could see them sitting right there.

They began again.

## Chapter Fourteen

TAYRE CIRCLED AMARTA. She felt his scrutiny as he looked her up and down, hair to slippers, cuffs to collar.

The heavy skirt flowed around her calves, the lacquered slippers reflected the lamp's flame. A knotted scarf about her head partly covered her hair. Draped around her neck were strands of semi-translucent blue stones, matching the bracelets on her wrists.

Finally, a gold ring, which he placed on her right forefinger, which had never been broken. No accident, she was sure, though as he slid it on, he said nothing.

Never before had Amarta worn so many fine clothes and so much jewelry. She felt weighted with it all.

Then he gave a slow nod, proclaiming her ready.

*We will be observed from the moment we arrive. Win or lose, the instant it's over, we must vanish as quickly as we appeared. You can play the astonishingly lucky young stranger woman only this one time.*

Tayre had arranged her appearance, but also her self. Her tale.

As the carriage lurched to a stop, he swung out and

dropped to the ground, looking about in what seemed to Amarta to be a rather obvious manner, entirely unlike him.

Amarta gathered the folds of her skirts in one hand and took his offered arm in the other, stepping down as gracefully as she knew how. Her fancy slippers scuffed the cobblestones as she stepped forward toward the House of Sun and Moon.

*You are in Senta for the Accord Festival, excited to gamble at this House for the first time. A bit nervous.*

Well, that was all true.

*Your family moved from the Borderlands to southern Perripur when you were quite young, so your accent reveals a mash of origins. Harder for people to pin you down. Or trip you up.*

Tayre gave an uncertain and clumsily gesture forward, the act a disguise all its own. As if that weren't enough, he walked differently, and something about his shoulders, the way they bunched, made him seem…what?

Belligerent. Oddly, this made him seem, at least to her, less threatening. He muttered something about the strangeness of the place, and asked her if she was certain about this.

*Not yet allowed by your parents to go out alone, you trail a servant doubling as a bodyguard. Treat me accordingly.*

"Don't question me," she snapped, glad that they had practiced this part.

He glowered, falling into step just to the side and slightly behind her as they made their way along the riverfront boardwalk. Luminous oil-fed lampposts edged the walkway, lighting a long, squat building whose reflection glinted off the dark rippling water.

*Raised in wealth and status, you expect to be treated with compliance and deference. Act like it.*

As they approached outside tables peopled by wealthy

patrons, she lifted her chin, as if she didn't care to see them. As if she weren't sure she did.

Shimmering silks and gemstones caught lamplight. Between fingers and lips, goblets sloshed drink and hookahs wafted smoke. Laughter wove across the tables as servants flitted about like moths.

As Amarta passed, faces turned to stare, unabashedly curious.

She looked back. From days of Tayre spinning stories about people and their workings, she could imagine what he might say now.

*See that man's mouth, lips tight, nostrils flared? He's got something to prove. The woman with her head craned forward, chuckling through the haze of smoke? Not a serious Rochi player, at least not tonight.*

The entrance to the House of Sun and Moon was fronted by a tunnel of heavy iron trellis, covered in thick vines of fragrant white flowers that fell open to the night like fingers. They passed through the living corridor, and were met by two large men in snug green livery that showed off their impressive bulk. Behind them was a heavy wooden door.

"May we help you, miss?" one asked in Perripin.

She said nothing as Tayre stepped forward and handed to them a purse, which they examined and handed back. They nodded politely and opened the door.

*Coin alone will not get us to the tables, but it will get us inside.*

A wide, brightly lit lobby revealed walls of muted green and a bejeweled ceiling. Underfoot, polished wood marquetry resolved into a detailed map of Perripur. Tayre walked to a wide-set counter, each step crossing hundreds of miles. From various pockets he removed four large pouches, placing them on the counter, his every motion speaking volumes about the man he pretended to be.

*They'll count and clean our money, taking a cut for the house up front. A quick polish to the metal of each, which gives them a chance to be sure the coins aren't forgeries.*

*They aren't, are they? she had asked.*

*No. Quite legitimate.*

She had looked over the coins, mouth dropping open in astonishment. *That's not all of what we have, is it?*

*Most of it, he'd said. We risk a lot. Look in to the future, Seer. Are we likely to depart the Sun and Moon with more money than we bring?*

Foresight had given her a glimpse of a large, bright room, filled with the unceasing muttering of hundreds. *Coins. Many coins. The weight in her pouch surprisingly heavy.*

*I think yes,* she had replied.

Now Tayre was talking to someone behind the counter. Amarta caught the gist of it—they wouldn't be long, just a little entertainment—but the way he said it conveyed so much about her youth and wealth.

Amarta looked down at the map under her feet, inlaid with such detail and delicacy that she feared to mar it with a leather sole. But no, of course it must be strong enough to endure many, many footfalls and hard-edged shoes.

She was standing just about where the Glass Plains should be. If that darker wood expanse there was the Mundaran sea, then the Shentaret mountains should be about there. She looked west, toward Senta, the very city in which she stood now, then north to the Arunkel border, just short of the wall, and marked with a ragged line of red wood —amardide, no doubt.

Inches beyond the border was the wall. The country of her birth was simply not here.

For a moment, vertigo caught Amarta, as she realized how far away she stood from anything like home.

Arunkel was no longer home. There was no home. There was no place to go back to.

What would it be like, to have a place to truly belong? A place from which no one could force her to flee?

From the counter, Tayre caught her eye, giving a cautionary look, lifting his chin slightly.

Yes, of course: the woman of status she was supposed to be wouldn't be staring at the ground. So she looked up instead.

Across a sky-blue ceiling, a spray of sparkling gemstones fanned, from one end of the room to the other, starting at the tip of a large, dark finger. The finger of God, as she remembered the Perripin creation tale, issuing forth the sky-seeds. At the far end, the accumulating sparks spiraled into a sphere. The sun, perhaps. Or the moon. Or an egg. The One hatching into the Many.

So many stories. Were any of them true?

"They have a mage back there," Tayre said as he returned to her side, loud enough to be heard by anyone in the room, though other than the man at the counter, they seemed to be alone. "Making sure the money is right or something." He snorted, shook his head.

Telling their tale.

And what would she do? Give him a cool, annoyed look for being outspoken, for appearing provincial?

She tried it. He looked away, frowning, as if both chastised and annoyed.

Yes, just so. She suppressed a smile at this small success.

A man in a more elaborate version of the guards' green now hurried toward them with a flowing gesture that was half bow, half invitation. A fall of green stones swayed from his ears. He spoke smooth welcomes to them and ushered them through an ornate door into a lavishly furnished hallway. From there they descended a wide flight of stairs into a large subterranean room.

Both vision and Tayre had provided glimpses of this room, but Amarta struggled to keep from gawking. Hundreds of people all across the space sat, stood, or lounged. All sorts of wealth was represented here, from all across Perripur and Arunkel and beyond to the islands, and who knew where else. All well-dressed and coiffed.

The air was thick with twunta smoke and the scent of splashed wines and spirits, the din of words, whispers, curses, and laughter.

Filigreed silver lamps hung across the high ceiling, each cleverly surrounded by mirrors that lit up the space as if it were day, as if a myriad of small suns floated overhead. At the center of the huge room was a raised area, obscured by screens and gauzy drapes, allowing a bare glimpse of figures moving within.

She knew what to look for and could identify the various game tables. The round ones were Rochi, with cards and coins and tokens spread across black cloth. The corner tables were for Quun, and the square ones with the rounded dice were for Rugen.

The long, rectangular tables with the bright grids painted onto them were the Grand Roche tables.

*The House encourages the belief that easy luck and attainable skill are all that stand between its patrons and a fortune, which most can afford to lose many times over. You must seem likewise.*

The green-clad man bowed again, gesturing. "You may join any table that will have you, Domina. May the honor of finding you a seat be mine?"

*Domina?* The title of a land-owning Perripin woman, which surely she was not. She recalled Tayre's words: *They will call you whatever they think will flatter you; act flattered.*

"Yes, you may." Her voice sounded uncertain in her ears. "Rochi. Find me a Rochi table."

The green-clad man led them to a table with five players and an open chair. Tayre dropped back, taking his place in the loose ring of surrounding personal servants whose task it was to see to their player's needs and watch the money.

The players looked her over. Summoning nerve, Amarta looked back, her gaze touching each one. Arrogantly, she hoped.

*Again, she could imagine Tayre's voice. The man with the small, pig-like nose? Sensitive about his looks. Atudakan from his clothes, not far from where you're supposed to be from, so be careful. Likely to spend too much re-buying suits. The bald woman next to him with the red-painted eyes and spiral scars is Snake Order of Dulu. Her people believe that winning and losing is a mark of their god's favor, so they tend to fold early. The small man next to her, petting his mustache…see how he hunches forward and to the left? He'll play to the middle suits. The two young men across from you are brothers, some Primeri's boys. They'll expect to win because they're aristocracy. The smaller one has a temper, and the older one's easily bored. Both more confident than skilled; that'll work in your favor, if you annoy them properly. Remember your idioms.*

Or maybe, she thought, as she took the offered chair, she had it all wrong, and he would describe them entirely otherwise. No finding out now. *Not even hand signs* he'd warned. *Every servitor is house security, and they watch closely. You must seem unsupported and impulsive. And lucky.*

She glanced at him. He inclined his head in a servile fashion. A breath and she turned back to the table, trying to emulate the snotty looks of the Primeri's boys.

Who was she, this young Ventan woman? If she didn't need the money, why was she here? Even having studied the game intently these last days, it was not evident to Amarta why other people played. To impress? To gain someone else's fancy? She looked at the older Primeri boy. He looked back, as if quickly assessing her and finding her wanting. She swallowed at the curl of his lip, and wiped sweating hands under the table on her fine skirt.

A sudden shout. Amarta tightened, looked around. At a nearby game a man hooted loudly, slapped the table in what appeared to be victorious joy.

Would her pretend-self be this jumpy?

Maybe. Though she doubted her pretend-self would be thinking about a sea voyage and transporting horses, never mind two small Emendi children. Had they already been sold? Was it too late?

Vision tried to answer, failed.

Later. When she had enough money to make the answer be whatever she wanted it to be.

Two green-clad servitors brought forward the strongbox that contained their money, presumably checked and cleaned, and set it on a small, sturdy stand, handing Tayre the key. He unlocked it, taking out coins and stacking them on the table near her right hand.

The table host shuffled the deck, inserting it into a heavy, ornately carved box, which he closed with an audible click, then tapped twice to indicate that the cards inside were ready to be used in play. From the front of the box he drew cards, dealing until each player held a hand of five.

Amarta's hand included four of the six suits. At her turn, she made a show of uncertainty, bought the Valor suit token, paying for it with a sorin that she placed with exaggerated care in the suit's poke. She looked around as if bemused.

"Domina," said the host after a moment, "you must tell me if you wish a card drawn from the deck onto the table, before play can continue."

Amarta made a thoughtful, uncertain sound. The rest of

the table looked as if they were beginning to regret having made her welcome.

"Yes," she said at last. She knew what it would be: *The Drum* from the Commons suit. And it was.

Snake Woman played next, buying the Realm suit, fingering the token. Then Pig-nose, who bought Kin. At Amarta's next turn, she foresaw the drawn card, *Apprentice*, Mages suit.

Mages, as yet unclaimed, with a win count of two, and Amarta held one in her hand. Since she could choose the order—draw or play—the cut and win was now hers, if she wanted it.

*When you win, look surprised. Charm the other players and they'll forgive you for taking their money.*

So she bought Mages, clumsily imitated someone else's finger-turning gesture to indicate that yes, she wanted the draw.

"Mages for the win," announced the host.

Amarta clapped her hands in delight and cooed over the two coins from each player. A small, fast victory.

"Borderello luck," muttered Pig-nose. A slight smile from Snake Woman and an indulgent nod from Mustache. The young men gave her twin scowls.

This all felt surprisingly familiar—they were not so different from Tayre's invented people. But these flesh-and-blood opponents were watching her in return, and telling themselves the story of who she was.

In the next hand, Kin was the popular suit. Bought, and bought again, accumulating a fast-ripening stack of cards. At Amarta's turn, she wondered which of three moves to make. Foresight said the draw card was Kin, but was predicting Realm for the cut, though it was unclear who would be holding it then.

She folded, regretting the decision a moment too late;

did it seem too sophisticated?

Suddenly foresight instead predicted World for the cut. Someone must have changed their mind about something. Again, she felt the bite of regret.

Snake-woman bought World. Pig-nose bought it back. Mustache drew the cutting World card, giving Pig-Nose the win and now-sizable poke.

*Rochi moves fast. Your advantage is a small but sharp edge; use it well.*

Amarta's next hand held four Valor cards, so she was happy to foresee Valor for the cut. On her turn, she bought the suit.

Snake Woman folded. Then Mustache, who she'd figured for a fold, bought Valor out from under her. Pig-nose bought it from him. Amarta found herself angry, determined to buy it back in spite of the increasing cost.

She didn't get the chance: it cut. The win went to Pig-nose, who cackled annoyingly.

Amarta exhaled genuine frustration, trying to regain her composure. Her stack of coins was shrinking.

*Foresight is not enough; you have to understand the people, too.*

Who were, she was realizing, rather more annoying than Tayre's invented ones.

Something was different in Snake Woman's expression this hand, but Amarta wasn't sure what. She weighed this against prediction, decided that the woman had World cards in her hand, and a lot of them.

The World suit, unwon these last rounds, now had a rich poke. Snake woman bought World, confirming Amarta's guess. On his turn, Pig-nose hesitated. Amarta foresaw that he would either play a World or Realm card, and two drawn cards hence, World would cut. That win could go to her, but only if Pig-nose didn't draw now.

How to convince him to buy Realm instead of World, but also not to draw?

"So," she said slowly, as if thinking aloud, "if all my cards were World suit cards, then World would never be able to cut. Oh, I understand now! A dead suit is like a…rolled pig." She laughed.

It was one of the idioms Tayre had taught her, from her supposed homeland. A rolled pig, meaning rolled in excrement, meaning a stinking animal that no one wants to touch.

Pig-nose blinked slowly at her, his mouth edging into a deep frown, as if he weren't quite sure if she were insulting him or not. But he played a Realm card, bought the suit, and shook his head at the host, fingers going wide to pass on the draw.

With effort, Amarta hid her delight.

The Primeri boys did what she had predicted, and on her turn, Amarta bought the World suit, taking the token, and nodding to the host.

He turned over the draw. *The Wheel.*

"World for cut and win," the host announced.

Sorins came to her from each player—plus the sizable poke—along with a delicious sense of triumph. She found herself grinning at the various scowling, hard looks, and— gods, was that really an annoying cackle coming out of her mouth?

Well, but look at that pile of coins. She had surely earned it. She'd doubled her money in just one round. Pig-nose gave her a look that bordered on suspicious.

"Table's stale," spat one of the Primeri boys.

"Two more to last hand?" asked Mustache. Nods around the table. She shrugged agreement.

This time, vision said Mages, but by the time it was her turn, vision instead flashed Valor, so she bought the suit.

Mages traded owners. Pig-face bought Valor from her with a smug expression. Part petty revenge, she supposed, but mostly the heavy poke it had accumulated. At the younger Primeri boy's turn, vision told her that the next drawn card would cut and be Valor. She caught her breath, waiting to see if he'd draw. He shook his head slightly, opening his fingers to pass.

She hid relief and looked around uncertainly. "Oh, why not," she muttered, buying the now-ripe Valor, then gestured to the host to draw.

"Valor cuts."

Amarta's excited yelp was entirely unfeigned.

No one had folded in play, so five coins apiece tumbled toward her.

How should she feel about this large win? She was caught between trying to seem arrogant, yet uncertain, and ended up looking unnerved, which probably suited the hostile looks she was getting.

*Follow a big win by an over-play, enthusiastic and losing. Seduction to those watching from the higher tables.*

This time, vision predicted Kin to cut, so Amarta bought both World and Commons instead, letting Mustache play the cutting card. He was pleased and even smiled.

The table game was over. The host divided the suit pokes into six, slid them to the players, keeping the small remainder.

As the members of the table began to stretch and stand, a servitor appeared at her side, tilted his head to her ear, speaking softly.

"Domina, the players of the Sapphire Table invite you to join them. May the honor of giving them your reply be mine?"

"THE WHAT?" Amarta in a loud, guileless tone, as Tayre collected her winnings, though she knew perfectly well what he meant.

"Ah," said the servitor, reassessing. "The Sapphire Table, Domina. They play with a higher minimum. They wondered if you might feel, hm. Constrained at this table."

"Why, yes. Yes, I do." Amarta stood, then followed the green-clad servitor around tables and their circles of patron servants, then through the maze of screens at the center of the room, stepping up and into one of the veiled sections.

There sat two men and three women in mid-game. A large, fat-necked man with many rings on all fingers leaned forward, looking her over as he stroked dark beard-braids shot through with white streaks. *Thinks he's clever,* Amarta imagined Tayre might say. *That you'll slow the game. Hopes you'll spend too much doing it.* The man next to him was dressed in an elegant maroon jacket, hems and pleats sharp and trim. *A trader from the east ports. He'll play tight.* Next to him was a Perripin woman with dark skin, high cheekbones, a younger woman by her side bearing a familial resemblance. *Mother and daughter. They'll compete with each other. Especially with the Kin suit, playing to the card's meanings.*

And finally, to Amarta's right, an Arunkin woman dressed in expensive white-and-brown livery. Aristo. Maybe even Lesser House scion. Anxiety shot through Amarta as she struggled to pretend indifference—or ignorance. Fortunately, the woman gave no indication she saw Amarta as anything but who she pretended to be.

Here the game play was slower, suit buys more conservative, players folding more quickly. More astutely. Round after round, Amarta watched the growing stacks of coins around the table as her own dwindled.

While she was cultivating a not-entirely-feigned look of dismay at her losses, she found that she was getting better at looking ahead into the labyrinth of possible card futures. Her mind spun through layers of conjecture, combined with her improving grasp of the game. Weighing the other players' styles—aggressive, conservative, vengeful, and so on—she used foresight to test her guesses. As Beard-braid played a hand exactly as she had thought he would, she found herself laughing lightly.

She stopped abruptly as he looked at her.

She would win this hand, she decided. Then she did. Also the next. Then another.

A complicated set of futures unrolled itself into her mind, and she felt that she was starting to understand. Yes—she had it now. She bought Mages for a fast win. Next hand, it would be Commons. So she would…

Tayre was at her side, straightening her stack of coins. Unnecessarily and slowly, nearly blocking her view of the players on that side of the table. She heard the host shuffle the deck and put it in the box for the next round, craning her neck to see.

For a moment she was annoyed. Then she blinked, understanding.

*Don't win too much too fast.*

She folded early, winning nothing.

Was it, she wondered, the nature of some hands to coalesce to a single suit's win, like sands through an hourglass fulcrum, while other hands had many and equally likely outcomes?

Amarta was finding that she could plan farther ahead. Not just one player forward, or two, but sometimes three and four. When she could almost hold the whole table in her mind, circling back to herself again, the game's possibilities spun out like a lattice of strings, a spreading weave of meaning.

It hit her all at once, the blinding headache. In her mind,

the carefully fabric of future play possibilities shredded. Amarta pressed a hand to her head.

"You all right, miss?" asked the east port trader.

She waved away the question, but folded the hand, waiting for the ache to subside before she resumed play.

By watching, she learned that the mother and daughter were indeed inclined to sabotage each other over the Kin suit, that Beard-braid was not as clever as he thought, and that the Arunkin woman was a solidly good player.

Amarta resumed play. By the twelfth hand in, her stack of coins was again high.

A tap to her shoulder, startling her out of her focus. A servitor bent close. "The members of the Ruby Table invite you to join them mid-game, Domina, if you would be inclined to grace them with your company. It's quite a privilege. May the honor—"

"Yes!" Amarta stood, dropping her cards on the table carelessly enough that some fell face-up. "The Ruby Table? Fortune kisses me sweetly tonight!"

The Arunkin woman spoke up. "If you leave now, you lose your share of the poke, you know."

"I don't care."

Tayre collected her winnings.

No one smiled. She wasn't charming anyone at this table, either.

It didn't matter. She'd been invited to the highest-stakes Rochi table in the house, and that was what she had really been playing for.

AMARTA AND TAYRE were led upward from this table's draped room to an even more elevated and central fabric room.

There three men and an elderly Perripin matriarch were mid-game. They gave her smiles and friendly gestures to join in. As Amarta settled into the chair, she looked around the table, quickly assigning titles: Duke's Brother, Money-changer, Wealthy Matriarch, and…

Her gaze stuck on the small man, panic lancing through her as she struggled to remember who he was. Not someone she had known in Munasee, of that she was nearly certain. Not from Arunkel, either, not with those dark eyes and heavy brows. But so familiar.

Could he be someone that she had once foreseen, years ago? Someone yet to come?

No. She knew him. In the present, not the future. But who was he? Who?

She tried to imagine him doing something. Maybe dancing about. Throwing…knives.

Knives?

It all came back at once. He was the Farliosan showman —the small juggler—with the cute, long-snouted creature.

Relief flooded her. She covered it by straightening her already neat stack of coins. The performance had only been days ago. So much had happened that it seemed longer.

Five cards were dealt to each. As she picked hers up, she felt a new fear: would he give her away?

She snuck a look at him. He looked back with a small smile and an even smaller nod before his gaze went to his own cards.

He recognized her. But if she read his response right, he would stay silent. She exhaled softly.

"Finally," she said to the table, "Experienced players!" She smiled at the old man she had dubbed the Duke's Brother. He returned a pleased, almost paternal nod. The Money-changer launched into a story about his own winnings at this very table, naming some apparently well-known players. The

Wealthy Matriarch scratched her ear and gave her cards a sour look.

Amarta began by losing deliberately, then arranged to take some of the larger pokes, feigning surprise at the cuts when they came. Between foresight and her sharpening ability to glean each player's likely strategy, she was noticing points in play that felt like knots, or forks in the road, at which the winning suit might suddenly change, or someone might decide to fold.

She would then snug her focus tight, going back and forth between the now and the soon-to-be-now. Could she, she wondered, hold in her mind—in the now—not just the win, but more than one way to achieve it?

The pattern of play drew her in—the dance of the cards, each with its own vibrant story. And the players, each with theirs. Suit stones, cool and smooth to the touch but for the fine etchings of the suit's crest. The growing stacks of glinting, polished coins, faintly smudged with fingerprints.

She was getting the hang of it. If the Duke's Brother folded now, the ordering would change thus, and if she bought the World suit here, and the Wealthy Matriarch bought it there, then…Amarta calculated the costs. A net gain for this hand, even if she didn't take the suit. Multiple ways to near-certain wins. Delight coursed through her.

Tayre brushed her hand with his own as he adjusted her stack of coins. She blinked, suddenly realizing that the other players were looking at her. She glanced at her own winnings.

That much? Already?

Too much. Time to lose some.

Folding wouldn't be enough. She had to arrange to buy a winning suit and make sure that someone else bought it from her before it cut.

She eyed her many coins. One of the bigger suits.

She glanced at the Farliosan. Olessio—wasn't that his

name? His stacks were shrinking. She would, she decided, lose to him.

Now to change the criteria by which she assessed play, and thus how she used foresight, and turn it all around. Despite her aching head, she successfully lost a hand to Olessio. Then again. Then one last time, letting her own expression deepen into an angry scowl.

Quite satisfying to see the table's suspicion and hostility split between her and the Farliosan, then moved entirely to him. He spun out a story about climbing up an open-air balcony to sleep and waking just as the owner toed him over the side, a heavy growth of foliage below miraculously saving him from injury.

"So fortunate, I thought to myself—" he said brightly. "Only to realize that I'd fallen in to poison sumac. Luck— such a fickle thing!"

Everyone laughed, and Amarta looked at how well he had charmed the table. No one was upset with him now, despite his high stacks of coins. How easy he made it seem.

Tayre slowly reached across her stacks of coins to change out some sorins and la-sorins for the brighter, larger na-sorins. As he did, he made the one sign they had agreed on, to allow themselves tonight, the one that said they were done with the Rochi tables.

*End in the middle of a hand. It's worth the cost to make you seem brittle, fickle, and disregarding of your losses. We'll need that to keep the story intact.*

At her turn, Amarta took her time, dithering in apparent indecision. She bought World, the least promising suit, gave a lazy yes to the draw, paid little attention to the game play as it continued past her. She fidgeted, rearranged her coins.

During the Duke's Brother's turn, she stood up suddenly.

She had everyone's surprised attention.

"I'm bored," she said loudly.

"Domina," the table host said placatingly, "If you leave mid-game, your share is forfeit."

"Good," she replied nastily, flicking the World stone into the center of the board, scattering cards and coins and tokens into disarray.

To the shocked muttering and chiding that followed from all but Olessio, she curled her lip and turned away.

Tayre scrambled to collect her winnings and drew back the drapes to allow her egress from the draped room into the corridor and beyond, into the greater room that stretched hugely and loudly all around them.

And now, the final part of the plan.

Chapter Fifteen

AS THEY WALKED THE ROOM, Amarta realized that there was no way to tell how long she'd been here playing Rochi in this well-lit windowless cavern. Hours, at least.

She gave a slow exhale, relieved to have accomplished the first part of the plan. But no—she must not seem to be relieved. Or satisfied. Or tired, for that matter. She must seem…restless. She ended her exhale with a guttural sound of disgust and cast her gaze around the room.

"More Rochi, miss?" A servitor asked solicitously. "Many other tables would welcome you."

A nice way of saying that she was not, any time soon, likely to be invited back to the Ruby or Sapphire tables.

"No," she said, drawing it out, wrinkling her nose.

*Act the poor loser.*

How much had she actually won?

*I won't stop you until you've at least tripled the coin we came with.*

Tripled the purse they brought with them. A fortune by most standards, and certainly at any time in her life before now.

And yet, not enough. A stunning thought, if she let herself consider it. Which she could not, not yet.

Tayre trailed her as she wandered the room. He paused to speak quietly with one of the house servitors. Arranging, she knew, to convert their collection of coins into fewer coins.

*By this time, if matters have followed the plan, we'll be carrying a lot of money, in high denominations. Call for drink and food and walk away as if you've forgotten it. Show off your wealth, then disregard it.*

Amarta did so, demanding to be brought something exceptional, unusual, that no one else here had. A female servitor bowed to her and rushed off.

*Someone is always watching. Make sure that they tell themselves the story we want them to.*

Amarta cast a disinterested glance at a dice game of Rugen and moved on. She passed another table, and another, her gaze flitting, as she muttered some of the idioms that Tayre had taught her, collecting annoyed looks.

She stopped. Tayre stood by her side.

"I have to say," she told him loudly, her voice slurred as she gestured widely to the room, "that all this is starting to seem rather tedious. I want a soak in a hot tub of scented water."

"As you say, miss," Tayre answered, bowing. There was, she had to admit, something rather delicious about having him act solicitously. Even if it was pretend. "Do you wish to leave?" he asked, as if hopeful.

"No, not yet."

Amarta trailed her fingers across chair backs, asking obvious questions but not waiting for answers. At the far end of the room, they came to some rectangular tables inlaid with elegant mosaic grids that displayed the Rochi suit symbols. No seats for these, but standing around the edges was the elderly Perripin matriarch that Amarta had played earlier. The Matriarch fingered a stack of la-sorins.

"And this?" Amarta asked. She had rehearsed the casual, bored tone in her head a hundred times.

"This is Grand Roche, Domina," answered the table host politely.

"How does it—" she waved a hand. "Go?"

"Wager what you wish, Domina, on any open square. If you like, further select the suit's Night or Day aspect. The odds depend, naturally, upon your selection. As host, I deal to the cut. If your bet wins, you will be paid as indicated."

Amarta gave a derisive snort. Her food and drink arrived. "Get rid of that," she snapped. The servitor retreated, bemused.

Without looking behind herself, Amarta held out her hand, palm up, at her shoulder. "Cowpies, servant," she said, using Timurung slang for coins. Tayre filled her hand with metal coins.

"Betting is open," the host announced, shuffling the deck, inserting it into the roche-box, and tapping it to indicate its readiness for play.

*Lose. Lose big.*

Tayre had given her five large octagonal coins. Na-sorins, they were, each worth ten sorins apiece. Hardly a small sum of money. She looked at the board, feigning indecision.

"Final bets, please."

In Rochi, her opponents were the other players. In Grand Roche, it was the table—the house itself. There were no players to change their minds. One deck, the order of cards unvarying.

This game had questions that foresight could answer with certainty.

*Valor would cut to the win, a mix of Day and Night aspect cards, ending with the Border card.*

The matriarch pushed a neat stack of la-sorins across the grid, into an open Kin square.

Amarta dropped her pile of coins noisily, sloppily, onto the open Mages' square.

*Name your bet. There must be no ambiguity.*

"Mages," Amarta snapped.

"La," said the elderly Perripin matriarch, concerned, "that's quite a lot, dear. Are you sure…?"

Amarta gave the elderly woman a narrow-eyed glare. The woman went silent.

"Very good, Dominas," the table host said to them. "Anyone else? No? Very well, then." He passed his hand over the board. "Bets are now closed."

He drew cards from the Roche-box, his long, elegant fingers flipping them over onto the space reserved for this purpose, separating them out into their respective suits as he built the stacks. The stories.

"And Valor cuts. Ah—no winner! Alas."

Disappointed mutters from the crowd now gathering to watch. Amarta recognized a few faces. Perhaps she had charmed a few of them after all. Or maybe they were eager to see her lose.

"Betting is open," said the host, shuffling a new deck and inserting it into the Roche-box, clicking it shut, tapping the top to indicate its readiness for play.

At Amarta's left, Pig-face placed two na-sorins onto the Realm square with an authoritative thunk. Just beyond the matriarch stood the Arunkin woman, in her brown-and-whites. She pushed a stack of la-sorins onto a Commons square. Behind her was the Farliosan, watching Amarta.

Amarta held up her hand, palm up, again, at her shoulder. Into it, Tayre put five more na-sorins.

She looked at the fortune in her hand, struggling to think of it as not enough, not yet.

"More," she said forcefully, putting her hand back up again. He removed the coins, replaced with three new ones.

Deep bronze, these. Edged in silver. Beautiful. Cho-sorins, each the equivalent of fifty sorins.

For a moment Amarta simply froze. There was more in her hand than they had walked in with, by far. It was more than she'd ever seen in her life. Or dreamed of seeing.

So much to wager away, just for show. Could they back off now, make some excuse, and keep what they had? This, and what Tayre still held, surely was enough. Why not be content?

*You'll be tempted to deviate from the plan. This works only if you stay the course. Hold steady to the end.*

"Final bets, please."

*The cutting card would be Serpent Moon, the World suit. A night card.*

Near-horrified as she did so, Amarta slapped the three palm-sized coins onto a square.

"Kin," she nearly shouted. Then she added, as smugly as she could manage, "Day aspect."

Sharp inhales rippled out around her. At the size of her bet, and the insensible, long-shot odds.

A small fortune, tossed away on the whims of a naive young woman. She felt herself flush hot with the fear that they were right.

"Luck favors the bold," offered Olessio from the far end of the table. With a light laugh, he tossed a la-sorin onto World.

The host stared at her coins a moment longer than he had to. He made a circular gesture over the board. "Bets are now closed."

One by one, he drew cards from the box, laying them face up in their suit stacks.

"Cut and win to World! Congratulations, ser."

Five na-sorins were pushed back to Olessio. "I must be sure to be bold again," he said. "Someday." His words were rewarded by chuckles.

As Amarta's fortune was swept away, she felt it physically, as if food had been yanked directly out of her stomach.

All around, others looked at her sideways, seeking from her face and actions a believable tale. She struggled to keep her expression between mildly irritated and truly dissatisfied.

*Lose big twice, and the stage is set.*

Now was the tricky part. She must wait for a long-shot win, while still playing, yet appearing to be losing interest.

She played another round, a far smaller bet, lost again, shrugged, watched two rounds, pretending not to notice how many eyes were on her. But she could skip only so many rounds and still keep the tale of her pretend-self intact.

So she burned through another na-sorin, in dribs and drabs, struggling to steady her breathing at the staggering amount of coin she was throwing away. One round after another, while foresight revealed nothing that she could use.

*Then, there it was: Realm would cut, and it would cut with all Night cards. Her heart sped.*

"Final bets, please."

She'd rehearsed this moment in her mind countless times. A deep breath.

"Fates and monsters," she said loudly. "Do people really play this insensibly dull game all night?" She turned slightly to see Tayre from the corner of her eye, held out a hand. "Oh, give me the rest."

He tightened visibly, eyes widening, lips thinning. "Miss? Did you say, the rest?"

"Yes, you fool. The rest."

"You can't mean all of it."

She whirled on him, fixed him with the most scandalized

expression she could. "You dare to question me? You dare? You?" She hoped her terrified trembling might pass for anger, rather than what it really was.

Seeming surprised yet helpless in the face of her furious command, Tayre handed her the single, entire, heavy purse that he held. Amarta grabbed in her hands the rest of the fortune they had built this night, which she knew included a large portion of everything Tayre owned, and turned back to the table.

There she dropped it with a clanking thud onto the *Realm* square. Grinning as nastily as she could, she pushed it onto that square's Night side.

"Realm," she said loudly. "Realm and Night. Finish this up, and I'll be done with this whole revolting waste of time."

Across the table, and all the tables surrounding, silence slammed down and rippled across the huge room. Amarta heard whispers, felt every gaze upon her.

The host cleared his throat, swallowed, then reached over to carefully upended her pouch, revealing the coins within. His eyes widened.

"Final bets, please," he said, croaking slightly. Then, more softly: "Anyone? Anyone at all?"

Amarta's was the only wager on the board.

"La," the matriarch exhaled. "La. Do you really think this is wise, dear? Do your parents—"

"By the gods," Amarta shouted, as loudly as she could, arms over her head in exasperation, "Will you all stop telling me what to do with my own damned money?"

Now no one spoke. Amarta swallowed, clinging to the edge of the table as if she might otherwise drown, and staring, as everyone else must surely be, at the coins she'd laid there.

Another moment, and the host passed his hand over the

board. The room around them was dead quiet. Everyone heard the slight waver in his voice.

"Bets are now closed."

One by one, he played out the cards from the Roche-box, turning each over, laying them out in suit stacks with slow and meticulous precision.

Amarta knew, absolutely knew, how this must go, because vision had shown her with vivid clarity how the river of the future flowed. Yet she felt herself tight with terror. Forcing herself to seem only slightly interested in the outcome was entirely beyond her.

It didn't matter—no one was watching her now. All eyes were on the board and the stacks of cards.

To win Realm's Night, not only must the Realm suit cut, with three cards, but the cut must be achieved using only the half of the Realms suit that were also Night cards. Any single Realm Day card would break the run, and lose her…everything.

One by one the host lay down the cards.

*Monarch*. A Realm card. A Night card.

"Oh," breathed someone. Awe or relief, Amarta wasn't sure.

More cards drawn. Other suits. Other stacks lengthened.

Then: *Assessor*. Both Realm and Night.

Down the table, Pig-face gave a small, nervous laugh.

More cards: *Half Mage. The Island. Aftermath. The Circle.* None of them Realm cards.

And then, the cutting card: *Consort*.

Realm and night.

The host stared at the Realm stack, full of Night cards, then looked at Amarta, his mouth hanging open. He snapped it shut, drew a breath.

"Cut and win, to Realm and Night." He held a hand high. One of his assistants quickly ran off.

*Act as if the win doesn't matter, as if the coins never have. You're done.*

"Did I win?" Amarta asked, trying for a tone somewhere between indifference and bemusement.

"Yes, Domina," replied the host in a hushed voice. "We are just fetching your winnings."

The two servitors returned, flanked by a foursome of guards. For a moment, Amarta suppressed panic—could they possibly know what she did? Did they suspect cheating?

No, they had simply brought coins. A lot of coins. The servitors held out two purses to her. She waved them off to Tayre.

There were not nearly as many coins as they had held before, she saw, as he opened the purses to inspect them. But they were the large ones. Bronze and gold. Uma-sorins. All of them.

Tayre stashed it all quickly into his various pockets, and handed her a small purse as well, which she put in to her own pouch.

*Now we must be exceptionally alert. It is one thing to win coin, and another thing entirely to keep it.*

She looked around—no, through—the faces of the many, many people staring at her.

"Now," she said, "I want my bath."

---

"THIS WAY, MISS," Tayre said, steering her by the elbow while somehow making it look subservient.

Amarta was exhausted and exhilarated. She had done it. They had won. She looked longingly at an empty, comfortable couch as they passed.

No, they were not done. Not quite.

*Another thing entirely to keep it.*

Across the room, people watched them go. Conversations quietly resumed. They were clearly speaking about her.

This was why she and Tayre only had this one chance. She was no longer anything like unknown.

*Whatever happens next, you'll be famous.*

Amarta's head ached and her stomach growled. In the tension and excitement, she had forgotten to eat.

Her work was not done. She peered into the next moment, finding a foggy soup of possibility. *A hallway, the sounds of excited chattering across the room muffled.*

Softly, for her ears only, Tayre said: "There are four exits. We are walking toward the east one now, but we'll be taking the north one we're out of sight of the room, unless you say otherwise. Look and warn me if there are problems."

*Empty passageways. Stairs. Doors.*

They exited into a long corridor and doubled back the way they'd come. The din of the large room faded, resumed, faded again.

Amarta pushed herself to foresee through the throbbing in her head. Flickering, murky images. She was tired. She tried again.

Stairs upward. Another passageway. Another turn. She clung to Tayre's arm, dipping into foresight again and again, flickering between the now and the soon-to-be.

*Well-dressed people milled outside the nearby exit. From their expressions, they had not yet heard about her.*

It was promising until an expanding set of futures showed someone shouting and pointing at her.

"Not that one," she managed.

Every exit contained possible challenges, and similarly all exits could lead to uneventful outcomes. Until they were close, she could not be certain.

Another set of stairs. An external doorway.

*Only the sound of soft rain. She nodded.*

At the doorway, two huge men who might have been kin to those at the entrance opened the double doors outward for them. Tayre led her through. Behind them the doors closed and locked.

They stood within an enclosed walkway, high windows open to the wet night. They climbed a staircase to come level with the street. There, a stone archway led to an empty, narrow alleyway. A soft warm rain was falling onto dark paving stones.

The future was suddenly clear. No time for words; she gripped Tayre's arm, sharply, once, then let go.

He moved forward, pushing her back. "How many? Where?"

"Four," she said. "Maybe five. No, I—"

Tayre didn't wait. He stepped out from under the archway, his arm moving in a circle, which seemed odd to Amarta until she saw him jerk a figure into view.

Then, from overhead, a gray shape dropped, shouting, cursing, and stumbling as Tayre twisted one way and then the other, reminding Amarta of the winterfair toy, a stick notched with rope on one end, flats of wood attached that clattered loudly, to frighten away winter's evil spirits, when you rolled the stick between your palms. She had one, once, when her parents were still alive. Even now she could remember the sound. Where had it gone?

She pushed away the memory, shocked at her distraction.

Again, Tayre spun. The two figures attempted to stand, but his timing was such that they instead fell together, heads first, in a dull crack. One staggered to his knees, the other collapsed.

A blink. So fast. Amarta was agape, struggling for focus, barely remembering that her part of this was to wrench open the door to the future. To warn him.

*Another rag-clad figure launched at him. Then another.*

"Two more," she shouted. "No, three. Northeast?" Damn, which way was north? That way, she thought. "The third from the south. Or…" she trailed off.

Shadows on shadows, sliding and grunting across the wet, dark night. Which one was Tayre? Had he even heard her?

That one. The one moving faster than anyone else.

He turned and dropped with a kicked straight back at one of the figures on the ground who had just started to rise. The man's head snapped and again he went down, this time staying down.

Two more from the far side of the alleyway, in one's hand a dull glint, in the other's, a stick.

Tayre barked loud laughter at them, the sound echoing off the walls of the alleyway.

Amarta wasn't the only one bewildered at this sudden incongruous sound. In the split-second of hesitation, Tayre closed on the man with the knife, forcing the other to try to step around his companion. A muffled crack and the man with the knife howled in pain, retreating, clutching his arm, which was bent oddly.

Tayre dropped to his hands, his feet somehow tangling the legs of the man still standing, who then tried to bend over to reach him with the stick—almost instantly clear as a mistake. His balance undone, arms waving, Tayre kicked, and he was down. The man rolled up on to his knees, readying himself to stand.

Somehow Tayre was there first, holding the knife, the blade a dim line that flashed across the face of the kneeling man like a silver paintbrush.

The man yelped and pulled back as black began to flow from his cheeks. Blood.

"Don't kill them!" Amarta found herself pleading.

"That's a bit harder," Tayre muttered, as the bleeding man stood, unsteadily. Tayre swept the knife again, and the man clutched his throat, making a mewling sound as he sat heavily on the cobblestones.

Amarta gasped, her own throat closing up in sympathy, and her stomach heaving.

Tayre had warned her. "You know what I can do," he had said in the quiet of his camp outside Maris's homestead. "Of course I do," she had replied impatiently, eager to get him back to telling her a story. "To understand my words is one thing, Amarta, but to be part of it is entirely different. To see me work is likely to be more challenging than you think." But she had shaken her head, adamant. "I've been on the other side of it," she'd said, almost angrily. "No," Tayre had answered mildly. "You haven't."

Until this moment, she was certain that he was wrong, that she understood this side of him perfectly well.

She had been mistaken.

What was she doing? *Look ahead*, she told herself fiercely.

Tayre sidestepped a weak grab from someone on the ground. Another stood unsteadily. Tayre sank an elbow into his sternum, putting him back down.

*Another figure, wide and bearded, a club in his hands, came at Tayre. Then another…Oh gods, she'd missed one. How many was it now?*

Amarta cried a voiceless warning.

Two large, bearded men were suddenly surrounding him, a third at their back.

Tayre turned. The first swung a huge club, the other a length of metal. The third came around the side.

It was too many, too close.

Her fault. Why hadn't she seen this sooner?

From the rooftop on the other side of the alleyway, a

strange sound, half growl, half scream. Dark on dark, a small shape descended straight down the far side's brick wall, and launched onto the leg of the man now lunging at Tayre.

He cursed sharply. The shape darted to the next man, crawling up his leg, causing him to fumble the swing of his club and missing Tayre. The man's cry turned to a howl as the creature clawed its way straight up his body and across his face, then launched off his head on to the third man.

This distraction was all Tayre needed; he spun like a shadowy vortex.

The club thudded to the stones, as did the metal bar. He stepped in close to the remaining men, and did something hard and fast. They dropped like rag dolls.

For a moment everything was motionless, even Tayre, frozen in a posture of quiet readiness.

Then he walked the alleyway, making a slow inventory of the prone figures, pausing long enough to stamp or heel-kick, hard and sharp. Heads, faces, necks.

A thud. A crack. A moan cut short.

Silence.

Amarta held her breath. Even the rain had stopped.

For a stomach-dropping moment, she realized that again she was so engrossed in the action that she had forgotten her part. But a glimpse forward reassured her that the alleyway was quiet for minutes to come.

She shuffled forward to steady herself with one trembling hand on the stone archway, her heart speeding. She smelled sweat. Blood. Urine.

The whole thing could not have taken more than a minute. It felt like hours.

"Are they—" she whispered.

"Doesn't matter," he said. "We must go."

"Impressive!" came a cheerful voice from behind Amarta.

She whirled. Why had vision not warned? Too much, too much—she could not see everything.

In the shadow behind her stood a figure at the lip of the descending stairs. The Farliosan.

His eyes went very wide in the near darkness, as Tayre bore down on him. He stepped to the side, barely avoiding tumbling down the stairs, his hands held high.

"Harmless! Harmless!" he squeaked.

Tayre crossed his arms lightly. The knife blade lay against his forearm, ready.

A scraping sound passed Amarta's feet. The small creature scampered up Olessio's leg and onto his shoulders. There it hunched, staring at Tayre, eyes glinting.

As the moment stretched, the small creature growled quietly, claws seeming to sink into Olessio's shoulders.

"Ow," Olessio whispered, giving Tayre and his knife a fixed, wide grin. "This here on my shoulder is Tadesh, who helped you out just now. Not that you needed it, of course, but—helped, yes? Did you hear the part about how harmless I am? I could repeat it, if you like."

Tayre turned slightly to Amarta, not taking his eyes off Olessio. "Are we clear to leave?"

Amarta glimpsed the future. Seconds. Minutes. "Yes," she breathed.

Tayre lowered his arms and the knife and stepped back. "You followed us out. Why?"

"Curiosity. Cursed curiosity." Olessio laughed nervously. "Nearly consumes me, at times. Be the death of me someday." He tore his fascinated gaze from Tayre to put it on Amarta. "What *are* you?"

"What am I?" Amarta asked, bemused.

"I saw your work in there. You—"

"Not here," Tayre said.

"Then—" Olessio smiled wide. "—elsewhere, by all means! I'll follow you, ser."

Tayre gave him an assessing look, then gestured for Olessio to go into the alleyway first.

As Amarta slowed to look at the bodies sprawled across the ground, Tayre gently pressed her forward.

## Chapter Sixteen

OLESSIO HELD Tadesh on his lap. He inspected her paw, dabbing at it with a bit of cloth wetted from a basin of warm water, to clean the blood from between her padded toes. Tadesh tolerated the attention, but barely, giving an intermittent low growl and an occasional shake of the wet paw.

"Just a scratch, my dear," Olessio told her, sprinkling onto her paw a touch of the powder Tayre had offered him. She shook the powdered paw and chittered. He held a crust of bread high in his fingers. "Will you forgive me? Just a little?"

Tadesh stood up on her hind legs, easily balancing on his thigh, her good paw extending to him to take the bread, which he released into her care.

"There, we are reconciled."

Amarta watched, fascinated, as Tadesh quickly gobbled the bread. "You trained her to do that?"

"Well, yes and no." Olessio dug inside his shirt pocket for another crust to offer. Tadesh daintily took it between her teeth, then into her mouth, giving it a cursory chew before swallowing. "I show her what I want. Then she decides if she wants to learn it."

Tayre was crouched in the corner of the room, rearranging their belongings and turned in such a way that he was probably also checking his various hidden pouches. Coins? Knives? who knew.

He stood upright again, and Amarta noted a difference in his movements. Slow. More careful. Belatedly, she realized that he had just been in what would have been, for anyone else, a very hard fight.

Easy for him, though, surely?

Or maybe it wasn't. She felt a stab of guilt, recalling the many times that people treated her as though her foresight was easy.

"Are you all right?" she asked him.

"Well enough," he replied, "but I'll take that basin if you're done with it."

"Yours, ser, with our heartfelt thanks," Olessio replied.

Tayre took the water, powder, and cloth to the wall, sat on the floor, and began to dab at what Amarta now saw were numerous cuts and scrapes.

Tadesh hopped off Olessio's lap and, limping, began to explore the room, giving Tayre a look and a wide berth.

Olessio turned a pensive look on Amarta. "Your impressive Rochi win tonight, sera. Substantial, even without the clearly intentional losses to me—thank you for that, by the way. Do you win this way often?"

"Never before," she said, only realizing now just how tired she was.

He was studying her intently. "I know a bit about how to cheat in Rochi, so I can say with confidence that you weren't. No magery there, either. But clearly you haven't been playing very long, so how…?" His gesture invited her to answer.

Tadesh completed her search of the room and managed a

three-legged leap onto Olessio's lap. There she gave a soft sigh and curled into a circle, her striped tail overlapping her long snout.

"How do you know I haven't been playing very long?" Amarta asked, feeling slightly offended. She had worked so hard to seem to be someone who knew the game.

He frowned a little. "Well…"

"How you hold and place the cards," Tayre said from the corner. "How you watch other players. Small reveals that very few will have noticed."

"Yes, exactly," Olessio said, giving Tayre a respectful nod.

Amarta narrowed her eyes at the man. *Farliosan*, whatever that really was. Why had he followed them out? Curiosity? Nothing more?

"So. What are you?" Olessio asked her, apparently done with being subtle.

*Unique beyond reckoning.*

She looked at Tayre for direction. He returned a small shrug. Her decision.

"I am—" She stopped, licking her lips. A seer? *The* seer? She didn't know, not even that. "I see the future. How things will happen."

Olessio barked a laugh, then looked at Tayre and laughed again, but this time more tentatively. Tayre's return look was bland. Olessio's amusement faded to uncertainty.

Amarta frowned. His hands came up, placatingly. "I mean no insult, sera. We all make our way through the world how we must. My people also tell futures, with cards and stones. Seed pods. I myself am not above such work, now and again, to avoid sleeping in the rain or to fill my stomach."

"I am no fraud," said Amarta, finding even her own annoyance wearying. Her head hurt. She wanted to rest. "I don't do what you do."

Olessio leaned forward, an easy grin on his face, eyes wide. "What do you do, then?"

From across the room, Tayre held up a coin. They both turned to look.

Amarta sighed. "All right."

With a flick the coin was airborne, landing on the table between them.

It was an Arunkel silver falcon. Amarta picked it up, rubbing the image of Cern's face. A new mint; the last time she'd seen a coin like this was years ago, on a cold autumn night. A pile of them on a small rough table.

Those ones had shown the king's profile, and they had been offered by a well-dressed stranger in return for dangerous answers. Innel sev Cern esse Arunkel, Amarta would later discover.

She looked up from the coin and the memory, realizing with dull wonder that she knew less about the two men sitting in this room with her than she knew about Innel, a man a thousand miles to the north. She exhaled a laugh, and flicked the coin across the wood to Olessio, who took it in hand, tossed it into the air, and slapped it flat against the back of his hand, keeping it covered.

"Falcon," Amarta said.

He looked, inclined his head slightly. Then, with a small, apologetic smile, he flipped it back to Tayre.

"Not that I don't trust you." Seemingly out of nowhere, Olessio opened his hand to reveal another coin, brassy in color, a round hole in the middle. He showed both sides to them; on one side was stars, the other fishes, swimming the brassy channel between the inner and outer circles. He flicked the disk into the air—a practiced move—and slapped it between his hands, held horizontally.

"Stars," Amarta said.

He opened his hands like a book to reveal the coin, then

nodded. Next he spun the coin on the tabletop, slapping it flat on the wood.

"Fishes."

He lifted his hand, nodded, and spun it again. Slap, hold, pause.

"Stars. Fishes. Fishes again. Stars…"

After a number of tosses, Olessio pocketed the coin, and drew out a Taluk sorin.

Amarta fell into a near trance, focusing on the near-future, calling each coin's toss, spin, or flick.

"How many tests do you need, Farliosan?" Tayre asked, standing at the table. There was an edge to his voice that brought her sharply out of her reverie.

Olessio grunted slightly and pocketed his various coins.

"You're right. Enough coins. How about this? If you don't mind? Won't take long."

He brought from his pack three small wooden cups and an ocher-colored rubber ball. He held them for a moment, as if he were performing, then placed the cups upside down on the table, one of them over the ball, and began to weave the cups around each other. Slowly at first, then faster.

Then he stopped, looked at Amarta and picked up the middle one to reveal the orange ball. He waggled his eyebrows at her as if they shared a joke. Then, with a flourish, the ball was again hidden, and he danced the cups around each other again.

He stopped, fingers lightly on the cups.

"Sera? Where will the ball be, do you think?" he asked.

Amarta frowned. "I think…I think maybe the middle one."

"You *think*? You correctly predicted over a hundred coin tosses." He smiled brilliantly, gestured at the cups. "Surely you *know*. Where is it?"

She took a breath, looked, and then—no. That wasn't right. She tilted her head to the side, confused, looked again.

"This one?" Olessio prompted, touching the middle one. "Or this one? Perhaps this one?"

A befuddled sound made its way from her throat. She was weary. Maybe that was why her vision was muddied.

There was something about his smug grin as he leaned back in his chair, hands laced behind his head, that made her loath to give up. Despite all the coin tosses, he didn't believe her.

Tayre stood at her side. "Say what you see, Amarta."

She gave a sharp, frustrated sound. "Any cup I choose—he lifts it, it's empty. But any cup *he* lifts, the ball is there. I must be too tired."

"No," Tayre said. "You are exactly right. The ball isn't under any of them." He fixed Olessio with a sharp look. "It's in his hand. A very old trick."

"A trick?" Amarta demanded.

Olessio grinned wider, holding the ball up between two fingers.

"That's not fair."

"Oh, now, don't be cross," Olessio said to her, tone conciliatory. He made a small sound and gestured. Tadesh bounded onto the table, then across to Amarta, her nose quivering as she gazed upward. "See? Now Tadesh is concerned."

Amarta felt her anger melt in the large golden eyes. She gave Olessio a wry grimace, even as she trailed her fingers down the animal's soft coat. "Another trick..." she murmured, but as a small sound not unlike a cat's purr came from Tadesh, who then climbed into her lap, she found that she didn't care.

"You can see the future. I am entirely convinced." Olessio said. "Does that mean—"

"No more tricks," Tayre said warningly.

"No more tricks," Olessio agreed. His hands made lazy circles in the air, as if he were thinking with them. "Does that mean that you know what I'm going to say next?"

Tadesh looked up at Amarta, head cocked as if she, too, were curious. Or were mimicking Olessio.

Amarta sighed.

"I've been asked that again and again. Anything that I say about what you might say will change what you say." She shook her head. "The future isn't a set thing."

"Then how can you predict it?"

"I can't always," she allowed. How to explain? "If you have an hourglass, and sand is flowing through it…" she used her hands to sketch the shape in the air. "When there's only one way the sand can flow…" She brought her hands together until they nearly touched. "Then I can predict with more certainty. Like a coin toss—one side or the other. Other times—" She moved her hands apart. "It's more like a swirl —the grains can go in many directions. And rarely—" She spread her hands even farther. "They go everywhere, like a storm."

Olessio made a thoughtful sound. He picked up one of the wooden cups, spun it midair, caught it, then tossed the cup over his shoulder. It hit the floor with a crack. He reached over, picked it up, held it out again at arm's length. "The cup must fall, yes? Or is there a future in which it does not?"

"Of course," she said. "The one in which you don't drop it."

He laughed. "But assuming I do, is there any other way it could go? Might it, for example, float?"

Amarta stroked Tadesh with growing sympathy; she was beginning to feel like a show animal herself.

"In a thousand futures, the dropped cup will fall. But

those futures aren't all the same. Little things…the direction of the wind. The path a spider walks across the ceiling." She looked up, saw no spider, and shrugged. "How long do you want to wait, while I search out some near-impossible thing, like a storm blowing open the shutters and knocking you senseless before you can drop the cup? While you wait, everything changes, including the future. We could be here until we starve. I'm hungry," she said, surprised at just how hungry she was.

Olessio's smile vanished. He released the cup and it clattered across the floor. "There. Question answered. I beg your forgiveness. I presumed upon you, caught up in my own curiosity." He stood, bowed deeply to her. "May I make a start on amends by fetching us some food? I would consider it a kindness if you allowed me to relieve myself of some of the weight of the coins you generously arranged for me to win tonight." He grinned, crouched a bit, and held his arm out and down. Tadesh launched herself off Amarta's lap, running up the ramp of Olessio's arm, then lay herself about his neck like a thick, striped scarf.

He went to the door and paused. "The failed robbery tonight? Was there no way to avoid it? Quite the show. But risky, yes?"

"Sandstorm," Amarta mumbled, feeling exhaustion piled atop her hunger.

"Sometimes the best answer is the lesser of the bad ones," Tayre said.

Olessio nodded. "Right you are, ser." Then he left, shutting the door behind him.

Amarta looked a weary question at Tayre.

He rolled a shoulder, slowly, as if it ached.

"He's held a weapon before against an attack. Not often, but enough to know how it's done. I would guess he can hold his own against the clumsy or unwise. No surprise, given his likely upbringing among the nomadic Farliosan. Still…" his gaze fell on the bag that Olessio had left behind, and he began to search its contents. "Farliosan don't usually travel alone. Is he outcast? Searching for something? Running from someone?" He finished his fast search, apparently not finding anything of note, though he took a moment to examine a knife before returning it to its hidden pocket.

"Why did you bring him back with us?"

"Another in our traveling party makes us three, and that helps our disguise."

"Do we trust him?" she asked. *Do I trust you?*

"To what?" Tayre asked.

She thought of the messages Tayre gathered wherever they went. How much was being offered for her? *You don't know your own worth.*

She didn't want to.

"To not sell me to the highest bidder."

"The Farliosan have keen loyalties," Tayre said. "At least to their own. When we came in the room, the first thing he did was to look after Tadesh's injury. Does this indicate a willingness to confer care on others? An investment in his show animal? Or something else?"

A polite knock at the door. It was Olessio, laden with an armful of packages and a tray of carafes. He unwrapped and laid on the table wraps filled with spiced bean paste, skewers of meats and vegetables, and tangles of cheese rope. The three of them—four, Amarta corrected herself, as Tadesh sat in Olessio's lap—settled themselves around the food.

Olessio fed Tadesh every other bite until she curled up in his lap to sleep. His eyes were bright with curiosity. His gaze flicked between them and settled on Tayre.

"So," he said, "she is the seer, and you are—what? I don't see a family resemblance, and you move like a big cat. Are you lovers? A hired bodyguard?"

Tayre gave a half-smile. "Something like that."

"That's rather forward of you to ask," Amarta said, embarrassed.

"It is, isn't it," Olessio said, smiling in what could only be described as delight. "I'm sure the tale of how you two met is fascinating." He trailed off invitingly.

The room was silent for a while, as Amarta reflected on how easily Tayre said nothing, and felt herself no need to speak. Olessio's smile slowly faded. Tadesh yawned, stretched, bounced out of his lap and wandered about the room, limping less.

"All right," Olessio finally said, "If not the past, how about the future? Where are you headed?"

Amarta hesitated to answer, then decided that she was too tired to be indirect.

"We think you might travel with us."

"Oh?" he asked, leaning forward in his chair, hands folded on the wood. "Am I having a good time?"

Food had restored Amarta's spirit somewhat, but the part of her that looked into the future felt sore and bruised from hours and hours in the gambling house.

Still, it seemed important, so she gazed at him while she let the question sink into her mind and let the answer come.

*"I've always wanted to see this," breathed Olessio. On his shoulders, turning, Tadesh fairly vibrated. He brushed her tail from his face, his smile wide and full of excitement.*

"You seem to be," she answered.

"And if I don't travel with you?"

She shook her head ruefully. "Much easier for me to see futures that include me."

Tadesh jumped onto the table, in front of Amarta.

"What is Tadesh's future?" Olessio asked.

"She is..." There were so many future images of this striped creature...on shoulders, in arms, curled to sleep.

Dashing from side to side. Standing up on hind legs. Making chittering sounds. And eating. So much eating. "Well-loved."

"Words to gladden my heart. Tell me, where might we all be going, in this traveling?"

"Atudaka," Amarta said. "The Xanmelkie Mountains. The Day of Revelation."

"Ah! Quite the show, I hear." His eyes twinkled. For a moment, no one spoke. "Well?" he asked with a mock-impatient gesture. "Are you inviting me along or aren't you?"

Amarta took a breath, let it out slow. She tried to foresee the many ways this might go, but it was a sandstorm. How did others like herself keep the future's many grains of sand out of their eyes?

Tadesh jumped from the table into Amarta's lap. She looked down at the small face, caught in the gaze of the large, golden eyes. As she looked down, Tadesh stretched upward to bump her damp snout against Amarta's nose.

Amarta laughed with delight. "Yes. I am."

## Chapter Seventeen

IT WAS late morning as Innel bounded up the palace steps. He hadn't meant to stay out all night, nor was he pleased to be entering the palace in full day like this, feeding the fire of palace gossip.

Still, his mood was excellent. The previous night at the Bent Nail had gone unexpectedly well. In a private room that did not entirely muffle the sounds of cheering from a larger common room beyond, Innel had an enlightening conversation with the Eparch of House Glass.

Out of an abundance of caution, Innel had drunk only water and eaten nothing, and was now quite hungry.

Food soon enough. First he must check with Srel. Poor fellow. Probably sick with worry, with Innel out all night.

Everyone would want to know where the Lord Commander and Royal Consort had been last night. He would need a plausible story. He would ask Srel. He'd have a good idea.

But it had been worth it: by the end of the late-night conversation with the Eparch of Glass, they had fashioned an agreement. Innel was elated.

Elated, but exhausted. His months-long debt from sleepless nights caught up with him suddenly and Innel could hardly stand. The eparch had helped Innel to a room, where he bolted the door, planning only a nap.

He'd slept through to morning.

Nothing for it now. Innel strode the hallway, bounding up another flight of stairs. A messenger saw him, did a double-take, and took off running.

Another one stared at him as he passed.

Only one night away, and he was getting strange looks. To the next gaping servant, Innel handed his cloak as he strode by. Better to walk the halls in the queen's colors anyway, however rumpled they might be from having slept in them.

Even the looks did not dent his good mood. A full night's sleep—the first in countless months—had left him feeling very fine indeed. His thoughts felt clear, shedding a bright light on everything, including his conversation with Cern over the forged message.

Cern had been entirely right: Innel should never have fallen for such an obvious ruse. And rested, he wouldn't have.

And Sachare? Innel's suspicion of her was at best impractical, at worst foolishly misplaced. Sachare had forgone numerous opportunities to act traitorously. At the very least she was taking her time, and Innel had better do the same. He must stay in her good graces. To protect his queen and child, he must aim his suspicion more deftly.

*You need more sleep, Innel,* Cern had told him. He now knew how right she was. He smiled a little, imagining confessing to her his obedience—albeit inadvertently—at the tavern and what he had learned there from House Glass.

It was House Glass himself who had sent him the baby blanket and the note about where and when to meet. "I didn't mean it as a threat," he told Innel earnestly, apologizing profusely. "I hoped it would bring you to this meeting, Lord Commander, but I never meant to worry you."

And what was so urgent? It turned out that House Glass wanted to escape the grip of their patron House Etallan, before Etallan forced them into a deal that would shatter the ancient House of Glass.

"Etallan is unforgiving to vassal Houses who do not obey," Glass had whispered, though the two of them were alone in the room. "We must be cautious." Glass then offered to name the Houses behind the bribing of the queensguard and to bring proof. Not only to Innel, but to the Minister of Justice. "Give me a few days to gather the proof."

To show good faith, the eparch named the guards closest to the queen. The list included Radelan.

"And will you make our case to the queen, Lord Commander? Only she can protect us from Etallan." The eparch was nearly begging. "We are an ancient House, ser. We never wanted this union."

"I will," Innel promised. Glass should never have been put under Etallan in the first place. Glass and metal? It didn't even sound right. It had been part of a larger brokered deal, thrown in at the last minute, some many Charter Courts ago.

It was understandable that Glass would want out, that the eparch would offer Innel help and support in return for the queen's attention to their problem. Innel would make the case to the queen. He would tell her about the conversation.

All of it, he decided, including the blanket.

Finally, something tangible. He would talk to Nalas. Soon Innel would be able to lay hands on the traitors.

Into his mind flashed the face of his daughter. He was already walking fast, but he picked up his pace.

Another foolish thing he had done, to refuse to take his own daughter into his arms, out of some absurd fear that he might drop her. He had a sudden inspiration: he would ask Sachare's help. Holding the child properly. Understanding her.

"Help make me a good father," he could say. That might go some way to mending fences with his Cohort sister.

And what would her name be, his child? He wished she had one, so that the first time he held her, he could address her properly. He laughed a little at the unlikely possibility that Cern had named her while he'd been gone—last night— and kept smiling.

He would hold her. Before the day was out, he resolved.

As Innel turned the corner leading to his office, he was struck by the number of guards in the hallway, then realized that they were all at his door.

As one, they turned to look at him. Some saluted.

Some did not.

Something had happened.

He pushed forward, pushed through. Uniformed guards parted to make a path as Innel stepped in to his office.

---

INNEL PUSHED INTO HIS OFFICE, taking in the scene. The room was full to capacity. Uniforms and outfits, a sea of red and black.

At his desk stood Cern, three ministers, and the queen's seneschal. Scattered about were handfuls of queensguards.

Everyone stopped what they were doing to turn to look at him. The hairs at the back of his neck rose. Cern's expression did nothing to reassure.

Innel buried the sudden urge to drop to a knee. He had yet to find out what had happened. This might not be about him at all. But it was something sobering, for his private office to have been invaded.

Whatever it was, Cern respected his confidence and strength, above all. It was a fine line, one that he had walked his entire life.

*Steady, then.*

He met her eyes, held her gaze. "Your Majesty."

"Where have you been?"

Dare he relate the discussion with Glass about Etallan, here, with all these people watching? Some of them might be involved in the very treason he was tracking. At the very least, anything he said would get back to whoever was driving the plot, warning them and sending them in to hiding.

"No matter," she said quickly, as he failed to reply. "A plot to poison me has come to light."

Innel let a look of grave concern come across him, while his mind spun. Surely she could not mean the very plot he had been following and preparing to dismantle, with the help of the queensguard Radelan?

*A secret is only as secure as the first ear's mouth.*

That's right, and so he had told no one. Not even Srel. Only the queensguard knew, only—

Only the queensguard. Innel's thoughts lurched, stopped.

What if Radelan were not so loyal, after all?

"Excellent," Innel said firmly, with all the conviction he could muster. "That plot is one of many that I have been tracking. I have details to provide." He took in the gazes of those who stood at the queen's side. Her seneschal. The First Minister. The Minister of Justice. "To all of you."

Innel passionately wished this conversation had fewer observers, but if there had been a moment for selecting his audience, it had passed.

Cern's eyes narrowed with uncertainty. Good.

"The guard names you as the origin of the plot, Innel," she said.

Innel suppressed outrage at this duplicity, allowing himself only a soft, amused snort. "Of course he does. It's the very strategy I would use, were I your enemy, Your Grace, which I am not: to create suspicion and divide you from those most loyal to you."

"He gave us a letter," said the Minister of Justice, holding up a note. "In your handwriting."

Innel struggled to recall what exactly he had written in his sleep-deprived haze, but nodded with assurance.

"The guard Radelan," he said. Time to name names. Innel only wished he had done it sooner, to get in front of this. "He came to me. Claimed he had been bribed. I instructed him to pretend to be bought and let the scheme play out so that I could identify who was behind it."

"Let the scheme play out?" echoed the First Minister, in a scandalized tone. "You mean, let him poison our queen?"

"No! I—"

"Did you," Cern interjected sharply, "pay him a gold souver to deliver a vial of poison to my bedroom?"

"Of course not. It was water, Your Majesty. The vial contained only water."

Someone exhaled sharply, but Innel kept his eyes firmly on the queen.

"What did your examination find, Minister?" Cern asked, her gaze equally locked on him.

"Upon ingestion of the substance," the Minister of Justice said, "all three birds died within a count of thirty, Your Most Excellent Majesty."

Innel's stomach dropped, as if the ground beneath him had fallen away. "Impossible. I myself put into his hand an entirely new vial, one containing only clear water. He…" Radelan had changed it, of course. "He's lying," Innel growled.

"Can any witnesses confirm this action that you say you

took to replace the wicked elixir with one benign, Lord Commander?" asked the First Minister.

Innel had kept it to himself. Could Srel convincingly lie for him under the hard questioning that would necessarily follow, if Innel named him as witness?

He doubted it.

He gave Cern an earnest look. "On my word, your grace."

She gestured to the minister at her side. "Show him what was found here."

*Him.* No longer *you.* Not a good sign.

The First Minister held up a thick set of papers. "A deed for a villa, Lord Commander?"

A villa?

"Ah—that," Innel said, shaking his head. "Sketches only, nothing more."

Then, with the ruthless clarity that a speeding pulse and a full night's sleep provided, Innel recalled that he had not actually examined the full set of papers. Would Mulack have really hidden a deed to a villa inside them?

Of course he would. It was exactly what Mulack would have done.

The minister drew out a page from the set, and held the deed high, turning it for all to see, before placing it face up on the desk.

Dread trickled down Innel's spine. "This is not what you think, Your Majesty."

"Oh? Tell me what I think." Her voice was edged.

"Mulack. His humor. You know how he is." The words sounded weak, hollow. Pathetic.

"And yet, a villa, Innel," she said. "A bribed guard. Poison. This is…" Not betrayal. Surely she would not use that word. "Troubling."

*Troubling* he could work with. "In appearance only," he

said, struggling for a calm tone while his future hung on every word. "I've been working day and night to identify your traitors, Your Majesty."

"There is also," The Minister of Accounts said, "the matter of the missing funds. Funds that you withdrew, ser."

"Yes, of course," Innel snapped. "Bait, to bring the vermin from the walls." Then to Cern: "Always in your defense, Your Majesty, always to protect—"

"Did you name yourself Regent?" she asked.

"No!" Or had he? His mind paged through memories of the Ministerial Council meeting, when his thoughts had been so sluggish. What had he said? "Not quite," he amended.

"The Ministers say that's exactly what you did."

A mistake, that, but he could not capitulate now and insist on his full innocence. He stepped to the desk—the side farthest from Cern, so as not to seem a threat—and slammed a hand flat on the wood.

"I am loyal to you. Utterly and completely."

"It's the child, isn't it?" Cern's composure broke, her voice rising. "Claim the regency, poison me, and she's entirely at your mercy. Was that your plan?"

"Never! My child, too. Cern—I would never—"

"You couldn't even touch her. What kind of father would you make? I annul our marriage."

Only once. She had said it only once.

Yes, it would cut deep into his influence. But as long as she didn't repeat herself, it could be a simple royal spat. The histories were full of such accounts—a consort publicly humiliated one day, in favor the next. The Anandynars were known for both tempers and quarrels.

He wasn't done yet. He could still win back her trust. If she didn't say it again.

Was this the moment to drop to his knees in

supplication, to beg for mercy for his missteps? He gave a fast glance at the audience, wondering if his reputation and standing could survive such a plea.

"I have a witness," Innel said. Of sorts, anyway. "Last night, at the Bent Nail, I spoke with the eparch of House Glass, who told me about specific plots against you, Your Majesty. He named traitor guards. He'll tell you."

Innel had meant to keep that to himself, to track those guards to their handlers. But he had no choice now.

Cern frowned slightly. A crack in her certainty. She exchanged a look with the Minister of Justice. "Find out," she said.

The minister bowed deeply.

Cern looked back at him. "Search him."

For a blink, no one moved. Every guard in the room was subordinate to the Lord Commander, who was still Innel, at least in name.

But the queen was the queen. They closed on him, groping through his vest and pockets. Innel's mind quickly did the same, considering what they would find.

The uma-sorin. His stomach clenched. A Perripin coin, one of great value. Innel had meant to take it mid-city and quietly change it into Arunkel currency. He hadn't gotten to it yet.

One of the guards drew it from Innel's vest pocket and set the large bronze and gold octagonal coin on the desk. The sound of metal on wood seemed to echo in the silence that followed.

"Ah," Cern said, disappointment weighting the word. "I can think of no good reason for you to have such a thing on your person."

*Would the truth serve here? The guard who lied to you gave it to me.*

No.

There were a lot of armed men in his office, all men Innel had trained. For a crazy moment he considered calling them to his side.

Memory careened across the years. Once he had entertained a strategy to unseat Cern, but that was before the seer had told him that the empire's survival required Cern to be queen, and Innel had by then believed her.

Then Cern had married him, and their child was born, and all such thoughts vanished.

He licked his lips, mouth gone dry, realizing that he must say something. "I can explain."

She was looking at the desk where lay the deed and umasorin.

"Have you ever spoken against my rule, urging sedition?"

"I have not."

The First Minister spoke up. "Tens of witnesses of good reputation swear they have seen you speaking to large crowds, on nights when you were known to be gone from the palace."

*Known to be gone from the palace. He had been so careful.*

Not careful enough.

Innel shook his head adamantly. "Cohort games," he said, quoting Sachare. "Nothing more. Cern—"

"The ministers are urging me to consider your actions high crimes." Her tone was chillingly flat.

Innel's breath caught. "I've been played, Cern," he said, voice barely above a whisper. "Set up to fall. But there are plots against you that no one knows about but me. I can explain. But not here, in front of...some of these might be..."

"First you suspect Sachare, then everyone around me? I see what you are doing, Innel: create suspicion and divide."

He opened his mouth, then shut it again, realizing that there was nothing he could say, and wondering if he should have realized that earlier. As he looked around at the ministers, the seneschal, and his own terrified staff, he could think of no words that might save this moment, but plenty that could make it worse.

He must buy time. Time for her fury to ease. Time to explain. Later, when she might listen.

Her gaze wandered the room. Assessing. Deciding. He knew what she was thinking: she could not afford to seem indecisive, not now, having been absent so long, her reign weak, not here in front of these people. She must be regal. Confident.

He understood the problem.

As her mouth moved silently, as she rehearsed her next words, his heart sank.

"Innel sev Cern esse Arunkel, I accuse you of high treason."

Innel's heart pounded in his ears. His mind went blank.

Absurdly, at that moment, he wanted nothing so much as to touch her. To stroke her face and feel her skin. Only a few feet away, a desk between them, but it might as well have been an ocean. Even if he could somehow cross the distance and lay hands on her, it would be his final act.

"Take him to the tower," she said.

As Innel held out his arms, to make it easy for his men to strip his weapons from him, he stared at her face. Committing it to memory?

His men turned him, taking his arms, pressing him out of the room.

They might have been a little slow. A little uncertain, in handling this prisoner. He'd speak to them about it later. If there were a later.

As he was escorted from his office, for what might be the last time, Innel reminded himself that he still lived. Cern could have had him run through where he stood. She had surely been furious enough, feeling as betrayed as she must.

Yes, he told himself, as he was marched forward, he still had breath in his lungs and blood in his body. His world might be crumbling around him, but it could have been worse.

Might yet be.

---

AS HE WAS MARCHED out of his office and into the hallway, his mind began to work again, the puzzle pieces slamming together, as his mind mercilessly presented clues that he'd missed.

*Out until dawn, they say, Lord Commander.*

*Got support among the commons, you have, ser. Saying things like you do.*

He'd been tricked. Repeatedly. And fallen for it. Repeatedly.

He'd been induced to leave the palace on numerous occasions, so that he would be unaccounted for during specific times. How many of these witnesses of supposed good reputation had ties back to Etallan?

The woman at the Broken Prayer hadn't been sent to seduce him and damage his reputation. No doubt whoever had sent her would be happy with that, but the main objective was to get him out of the palace so that he would have no alibi that night.

Only Nalas and Srel had known where he went those nights, and even then, not always. Regardless, both men were known to be loyal to him and no one would believe them.

The walls of the hallway were packed, people pressing themselves out of the way of Innel's escort, expressions of shock and bewilderment as they watched Innel pressed forward by—how many, now?—four guards.

Four guards, for a prisoner of such consequence, one that possibly dangerous? It should have been six. He had trained them better than this.

Nalas, pacing alongside them, looked stunned. Was he wondering how he might survive this?

"Lord Commander!"

Srel was nearly running at them from the far end of the hall, his expression full of shock and dismay. Srel strode directly toward Innel, foolishly heedless—or willfully ignoring—the armed escort. If Innel had been someone else, the guards would have kept Srel away, and not gently. But they knew him, and old habits were hard to break.

Steps away. They would not let him get closer.

For nearly a decade, Srel had been one of the few people Innel could rely on, and one of the best investments he and his brother had ever made. The man was loyal beyond reason. If Innel was going down, so was he.

Innel thought fast. He stopped in his tracks, sharply gesturing, fist held high, to signal a unit halt. To his mild surprise, his men obeyed smartly, even dropping their hands from holding his arms.

At this, Nalas swallowed a sound of frustrated, conflicted anguish.

Innel took the few, quick strides to Srel, who froze where he stood. His men, no doubt tangled by confused loyalties, let him.

Innel wasted no time. "You," he shouted, voice pitched to carry. He grabbed Srel's collar, twisted, and shook. "You bastard. This is your doing."

Expression stark, Srel shook his head adamantly in denial. Though of what, Srel himself probably had no idea.

Innel stepped him backward, slamming Srel against a

fast-vacated section of wall. He brought his mouth close to the other man's ear.

"Disavow me. Publicly," he hissed, feeling Nalas closing behind, "Say you suspected me all along."

"Ser, no. I will not do that."

"You will. I'm a hair's width from execution. Don't follow me."

Innel drew Srel back from the wall, and with a disgusted look shoved him into the open hallway, sending him backward with more force than he had intended. Well, good —the performance would be convincing.

Srel sprawled on the hallway floor and struggled to his feet, backing away, and—was the man trying not to cry? He was. That would play well to the audience.

If Innel somehow managed to return from all this, he could find a way to fix this moment. But if not, he'd given his steward a chance to get clear of the wreckage.

Srel was resourceful. If he were clever—and a bit lucky— he might survive this.

Nalas's hand was on Innel's arm. A grab, as if to exert control, but too light for that. Innel suppressed his surging instinct to fight back.

"Ser," Nalas whispered. "What should I do?"

Another man too loyal for his own good.

"Renounce me," Innel answered softly. "Protect my queen and child, at all costs. And watch your back."

Nalas's mind was clearly in turmoil. Innel shook off the grip and turned on his escort. Some of them had hands on weapons. Most didn't. None of them looked as if they knew what to do.

"What in the seven Hells are you thinking?" he barked at them sharply. "You have orders from your queen to take a prisoner to a tower room, yet you stand around like sheep, gaping at the rain." He glared at Nalas, who recovered his wits enough to gesture a command at the men.

Now it was a six-guard escort. Innel felt oddly satisfied at this. He held out his arms again, letting his men twist both behind his back before pressing him forward.

As he stumbled forward, Innel caught Nalas's eye. He mouthed: "Protect them."

Nalas nodded once, sharply, indecision clearing from his face.

Innel could see and feel, from grip and pace, that his men were now taking Nalas's commands. They were finally ready to convert their commander into a prisoner.

As he walked, he considered what he knew of the history of royal consorts, which was quite a lot. He knew that this was not the first time that a consort had been sent to the tower. Sometimes this had given the monarch a little time to recover their good humor.

But not always. Sometimes that recovery never happened. The consort quietly disappeared. Or not so quietly.

Or was executed.

But this was the first time that the consort had been born a commoner.

Everyone in the palace, it seemed, had stopped what they were doing to watch Innel marched to the tower. The walls were lined with aristos and servants and any visitors who happened to around.

Had anything really changed, he wondered, since the day he and his brother first walked into the palace, since the moment they had been inducted into the Cohort? He had always been an outsider. The higher he rose, the more enemies he made.

As he looked into their faces, full of surprise, or fascination, a fierce pride came over him.

*I rose from commoner, to Lord Commander, to Queen's Consort. I am father of the heir of the Arunkel empire. Not one of you will ever be able to claim such an ascent.*

He wanted to shout it at them, force them to understand, but he must keep his tongue and wits while he still had a chance, however slim, to return to her good graces.

He met their looks. Those who seemed most pleased, he would remember.

It was a long walk to the heavy doors that led to the tower stairs, and yet too short. They climbed, up and up the winding staircase. Step by step, Innel felt the weight of what had happened settle on him.

He pushed away thoughts of his daughter, lest grief bite through what remained of his hope.

A glimpse through a slitted window reminded him that he had never actually seen the rooms that were set aside as holding cells for those important enough—offensive enough —to await the judgment of the crown. The rooms were said to be small, made of stone. Simple rooms with heavy metal doors.

But also, it was said, the view was stunning.

## Chapter Eighteen

THE RUMOR TURNED out to be true: the view was magnificent.

Hours passed, then the night, and another day.

What was happening in the palace? What? He had to know.

His tower room faced west, providing an excellent view of the oceanside harbor, now bristling with the masts of ships great and small. Many flew the Arunkel sigil. Some flew House Helata's flag alongside.

A handful of other ships were marked by the brilliant Perripin flag. Merchants. Diplomats.

On the horizon, a huge ocean-going Arunkel trade-ship was leaving the harbor for some distant island. He watched as it shrank against the horizon and then vanished.

The harbor neatly symbolized the reach of the empire. North to the frozen continent and the Emendi lands. South to the warm states of Perripur. West across the Nelar ocean. Impressive. Enough to inspire patriot pride.

Another time, perhaps.

Innel turned away to take stock of his small room. Daily,

food and water was passed through a low, small door to the side of the larger one, an opening barely enough for Innel to exchange nutrients, when they came, for the chamber pot.

"I need to talk to the queen," he said to legs beyond.

Silence.

Innel finally had enough time to think. He considered Amarta, the seer, and wondered how different his situation might be now if he had not released her. Useless speculation, but it was better than thinking about what he should have done differently just days ago.

Cern. The things he should have said.

His daughter.

Had his last words to Nalas landed? He should have shouted them instead of whispering.

Would Nalas protect them? Could he?

Not if the man didn't know what Innel knew, and not if he were fooled by the same people who had so successfully deceived Innel.

Innel looked out the window. The sun was setting in a sky the color of blood.

What in Hells was happening in the palace?

INNEL AWOKE to the metallic sound of the door's external bolt being slid back.

His mind went to the worst—Cern overthrown, his child slaughtered. This, his last moment, the traitors tying up loose ends.

He would be snuffed without a fight. On his feet, he groped for a nonexistent weapon.

A quid of guards and a hooded figure fast filled the small room. The figure pulled back a hood.

"Sacha," Innel said, not wasting a moment. "My abject

apologies, Cohort sister. I was an idiot to suspect you, of all people. I humbly beg your—"

"Too late, Innel," Sachare said.

"No. No. Let me explain. The thread. Why I thought—"

"It no longer matters, Innel, what you thought."

"If I could just talk to her—"

"She has no choice, now, after what you've done. You must see that, surely?"

Innel shook his head. She would reclaim him, if he could ferret out and reveal the plots to her. She must.

"Sacha. You don't believe this of me, do you? Do you? Tell her."

Sachare heaved a deep sigh. "What I believe is unimportant. Innel, it might be time to confess. Beg mercy, rather than be dragged to something worse."

"Listen to me: the guard—the poison. He's the traitor, Sacha, not me. You can't let him near the child."

"More guards have come forward to claim that you bribed them."

"That I—no! They lie. The eparch of House Glass. Did you talk to him?"

"Yes," Sachare replied. Her look held an expression that he had never seen before, not in the two decades he had known her. It took him a moment to realize what it was.

Pity.

"Sacha, he and I spoke for hours at the Bent Nail. Glass wants to break free of Etallan. It's Etallan bribing the guards."

"And yet, Eparch Glass told the queen that you gave a rousing speech in the Bent Nail's common room, drank so much you couldn't stand. He says he helped you to a bed to sleep it off."

Innel made an outraged, incoherent sound. "That's not what happened."

"The innkeeper told us that you dropped this into your

empty mug." She reached into a sleeve, took out a small square of fabric, shook it open.

Innel's handkerchief. Stinking of whiskey.

Innel swallowed bile at this outrageous betrayal. He thought he could read people well—a lifetime of study—and Eparch Glass had seemed sincere. The man he had been doing his patron House's bidding after all. A performance worthy of the Cohort, Innel thought bitterly.

"Yes, I was there," Innel said, not taking the offered handkerchief, "But I never entered the common room." His voice dropped to a whisper. "Cohort games, Sacha."

"Perhaps so, but many claim to have seen and heard you there that very night."

Innel remembered how tired he had been, how deeply he had slept. He had credited it to exhaustion, knowing that he had only consumed water.

Water. Even water could be drugged.

"It wasn't me. I gave no speech. Give me time, and I can prove it."

"You are out of time, Innel, as well as liberty."

"I didn't do any of this."

"All this evidence against you, you still claim to have done nothing wrong?"

That was the problem, right there: all his own evidence had evaporated the day he had been imprisoned.

"Many things wrong," he answered, his throat tight. "I relied on the word of traitors, while suspecting those I should have trusted all along, like you. But I am not guilty of treason. Never."

She gave a small shrug. "Not for me to say. Guilty or innocent, I urge you to confess. It will be easier on her. And the child, if that matters to you."

"Of course it does."

"There could even be clemency in it for you, Innel. Exile, perhaps."

"Exile? No. My daughter would grow up thinking I'm a traitor."

"Well…she's not your daughter anymore, Innel."

"I don't accept that. I've recovered Cern's trust before."

She shook her head. There was the look again.

"You're done, Cohort-brother."

"If I could talk to her…Sacha, I know you can sway her. Please?"

Sachare put her fingertips on his lips. Her touch was so gentle that Innel felt his stomach tremble.

"If I do speak on your behalf," she breathed, "you must throw yourself on her mercy. Not merely for her sake, and the child's, but for your own. Innel, execution is not the worst horror you face."

His daughter's life was in danger from those who threatened the queen, her enemies and his, who had put him in here so that he could not protect either of them. What could be worse than that?

"Putar," she said, reading his thoughts. "Putar."

---

ANOTHER DAY and lampless night in a dark room. More than enough time to review, again and again, every slip, every ploy, every missed clue.

The threads. The deed. The poison. The uma-sorin. He was set up. All these machinations used against him, all so clear now.

But worst of all, he had played right into their plans by keeping quiet about everything he knew.

A stunningly concerted effort had been made, and an

appalling amount of coin must have been spent, to take Innel down. The plan had to be months—or years—in the building. He had known Etallan was outraged at his beheading, but to go to such lengths to exact revenge against him?

No. It had to be more than just him.

*Got support among the commons, you have, ser.*

Innel had been so caught up in his own thoughts at that moment that he had missed the significance of Shae's words.

Shae knew him, by face and voice. If she herself were convinced that Innel was the seditious speaker, whoever was impersonating him must be an impressively good likeness. But that was one more puzzle that he could not solve from here.

He walked to the window. He had been up the whole night, and the city was just beginning to lighten with dawn.

Did he still have a chance?

Cern. It all came down to Cern. He could sway her, he was nearly certain, if he could speak to her. All the nights they had spent together, all the vulnerabilities she had shown him—he still had influence with her, he was certain of it.

Sachare would put in a good word for him. Cern would come. After all the years together, she must come, even if, in her mind, it was for the last time.

Then, somehow, he would convince her.

And if he could not?

*Putar.*

He stared out the window and watched the city wake.

---

EACH NIGHT, in the small, dark hours, Innel woke, sleep giving way to an obsessive review of every misstep, his Cohort-sharp assessment of every decision finding his past self most wanting.

Again, exhaustion became his constant companion, his thoughts relentlessly replaying the past, uselessly imagining what he might have done instead. He fought a growing despair that Cern would not come after all. That in the end, she would simply throw the mutt out, the low-born dog, finally expelled from the manor into the woods where hungry wolves waited.

In the dark, his eyes shot open. The bolt to the heavy door slid back.

Lanterns suddenly lit the space as a quid of guards deployed in the room, another set hinted at beyond the doorway. In the lamplight, a figure entered. He knew instantly that it was Cern.

He rolled off the bed, onto his knees on the cold stone, and lowered his head.

"Your Majesty."

"You betrayed me."

He lifted his gaze. This was it, his last chance. He had wrestled with what to say now, what to confess to. What lie to tell to make things easier for Cern. For his daughter.

For himself.

Her half-lit face was the beautiful, now, the regal Cern whom he had forged his life to circle.

"I did none of the things of which I am accused, Your Grace."

She exhaled sharply. "Why am I here, then, if not to witness your confession?"

Why, indeed? He had constructed a story about his culpability, about how he had been weakened by confusion and fallen for the promise of secret wealth. But now his daughter's face flashed into his mind, and he could not seem to force out the words.

"I confess," he said with angry passion. "That I should have told you what I was doing and why. I should have named names. Who I suspected of acting against you and what I was doing to stop them. I was a fool to stay silent. But I did not betray you. Let me explain—"

"Plots and schemes?" she asked tightly. "Bribed guards? Evidence invented against you?"

"Yes!"

"The witnesses, from guards to eparchs—every one of them a liar. Is that right, Innel? And Etallan behind it all?"

"Yes, Etallan! An extravagant plot against me. And you. But I am not its author. With time and liberty, I can prove this."

And with her backing. It would take a lot of backing.

She was breathing hard. "Nothing has changed, then," she said flatly. "Stand for this, Innel al Arunkel."

Innel looked down again, taking in each detail of the stone floor. Could he say no? If he refused to stand, could he prevent her from saying the words to come?

Could he somehow extend this moment, this second in which he breathed, in which his pulse sped, if he simply stayed on his knees?

Many would say that was what he should have done all along.

Slowly, heart pounding in his chest, Innel made his way to standing.

"I am innocent," he breathed.

"I am still deciding your fate, damn you," she snapped, her voice shaking. "Give me a reason to be merciful."

*A reason.*

All he must do was to ask for clemency. Confess to something—anything—that a traitor would have done.

"I am innocent," he found himself saying.

*Idiot. Fool.*

Their gazes locked. Her expression went hard. She took an audible breath.

"Innel sev Cern esse Arunkel," she said, her voice steady, "I condemn you as a traitor. I say it twice. I say it thrice."

Innel gasped as if he'd been clubbed in the gut. His ears rang. He hunched around the pain, shaking his head in denial, struggling for what he might now say. But his thoughts were like birds, having flown too high, senseless and without control.

With an effort of will, he struggled to stand upright. "Cern. You know me. You *know* me. I wouldn't do those things."

She took a step toward him, then another. The queensguards tensed, wide-eyed, horrified, as she came close. Too close. The guards' hands flexed and twitched on halberds and daggers.

Innel's mind laid out plans of exactly what he could do: grab, spin her sharply, one arm fast around her neck, the other twisting her forearm behind her back. In the blink of an eye, he would have her. He'd tell the guards to back away. He'd tighten his arm around her windpipe, enough that she could not speak, could issue no orders.

Then negotiate? For what? He could buy himself minutes. An hour, if he were lucky.

An even more impressive execution, certainly. And no question in her mind as to his guilt.

He kept his arms at his sides, motionless.

Cern, shorter by a head, looked up at him, searching his face for something. Veracity? Loyalty?

Her eyes were dark green, with gold flecks. Just like their daughter's.

"I did once believe that I truly knew your character," she answered softly. She shook her head. "I should have taken a lesson from your brother's body on the floor of the audience chamber."

That had been a delicate time, figuring out how to charm

her again, after Innel had returned to the palace with his brother's body over his shoulder. Months, it had taken, to convince Cern that he had had no choice about the matter, to persuade her to trust him again. What could he say now about Pohut that he had not already said?

*I thought he had betrayed me, so I killed him. But I was wrong.*

No.

Could Pohut have said anything in those last minutes, when the two brothers had fought, to convince Innel that he was innocent?

No.

Her face had closed. She was done trusting him.

"I only wanted…" Innel whispered. "To protect you and our child. She's not safe, Cern. Not with the many plots out there, against you."

"Safer now," Cern said cuttingly. Now that he was contained. Condemned.

He knew from the histories what would happen after he was gone. Cern would remarry. She would have him stricken from the records, as if he had never existed. Their child, the union of a commoner and a queen, if she survived at all, would never know his name.

This is what it came to, his lifetime of proving himself, of wooing the princess, of climbing the ladder—nothing.

*The ladder goes up one rung at a time, Pohut used to say.*

The fall, though—that came all at once.

He thought of his mother in the palace and his sister Cahlen in Abinar. Neither of their lives would be worth much after he was dead. Cahlen had tried to kill him at Otevan, and Innel had convinced Cern to pardon her, pointing out that Cahlen's skill with birds was too valuable to lose. His sister became a bird-keeper in faraway Abinar. Captive, like the birds she bred.

His mother was fragile. She was as good as dead. But Cahlen was clever, possibly clever enough to survive her brother's treason.

"Goodbye, Innel." Cern raised her hood over her head.

"Cern, no. Please. Don't go."

But Cern was turning and turning, her back to him as he called out, again and again, the guards filling the space between them. He pushed forward. They pushed back.

In his last glimpse of her, a dark lock of hair had come loose from her hood.

*Goodbye, Innel.*

Long after the heavy metal door shut, Innel stared at it, mouth agape, the sound of it closing and her last words to him echoing in his ears.

MORE DAYS PASSED. At first Innel was grateful. One more meal. One more hour free of Putar's artful ministrations.

But the moments grew heavy and the days slowed, thick with silence and dark threat.

It was easy to imagine Putar in the rooms of the Ministry of Justice, rolling out plans on which were sketched unique tortures for the traitorous mutt who had risen too far above his station. Putar would be taking his time, getting it all just right.

Putar loved torture, much the way Mulack adored clothes. He would see this opportunity as one of his finest chances to perfect his art.

Innel began to wonder if the waiting itself, this uncertainty as to just what horrors awaited, was part of Putar's elaborate torture, a ramp of tension to make Innel's eventual misery even more acute.

He paced the small room, lurching from regret to anger

and back again. He reviewed all the plots he'd fed so that they would fatten enough to be run down. He imagined them running free across the palace. He cursed Etallan, the Cohort, the old king, and himself. He could not quite bring himself to curse Cern.

Would Nalas realize that the plots that Innel was accused of championing were still alive? He was smart, Nalas was, but Innel should have told his second-in-command everything. What a fool he had been.

For that matter, where was Nalas, or whoever was now in command? Innel would have spent a great deal of time with anyone charged with high treason, finding out every detail of what they knew.

Who had decided that the former Lord Commander was not to be questioned? Someone high enough in the palace to convince the queen. Or to stand between her and the prisoner, because of what he might know.

The ministers.

Innel pounded on the door and howled his frustration.

It came to him with despairing certainty that whoever filled the void that Innel left—whoever Cern married— would find no reason to keep the daughter of a traitor whole. Her next consort would want their own child as heir, without competition.

So easy to slip poison into the queen's room. How much easier to slay an infant?

Innel had been overconfident, passing by the simple baits, stepping over the obvious traps, all of which were there to distract him with false successes and make him think himself clever. Maybe they were right after all, the aristos who had his whole life whispered that his blood was too common to thrive at these high levels.

He went back further in time. Perhaps he and Pohut had never been intended to succeed in the first place. Maybe king

Restarn had brought the two small boys to the Cohort as sacrifices to give the aristo children someone to step on.

Well, he was crushed now.

Soon, anyway. The execution would, no doubt, be legendary, as executions of those closest to the monarch always were.

What would it be? Torn apart by dogs? No—too obvious, too common. Perhaps something more traditional: snakes, cougars, and falcons, as the Arunkel sigil depicted. But slow. It would have to be slow. Perhaps a feast of many parts—fingers one day, toes the next. Bits of this, and bits of that.

A dark humor took him as he realized that he would provide one last service: entertainment. Or maybe that was what he had provided all along.

More days passed. Innel found himself rewriting the past. What if he had not gone to Botaros that night and taken the seer's advice on how to kill his brother? What if Pohut had lived?

A sob escaped his throat.

"I am sorry, brother," he said to the air. "If I had it to do over again—"

If death were a door to the Beyond, as was so often advertised, then Innel would soon be able to apologize to him directly, to make things—not right, surely not that—but at least to offer his heartfelt remorse.

The next day Innel sank into self-pity, then he viciously refused any such thing to himself. He sank again.

The morning was bright outside, a beautiful day, achingly warm and full of summer. It was suddenly all too much, and Innel found that with enough rage, he could lift the solid wood bed on which he slept. He slammed it against the stone walls, again and again, until his grief and fury were replaced by exhaustion.

When at last he let the bed back to its feet, it wobbled, one leg's tip ruined, the shards of wood spread across the floor. He felt an unreasoning satisfaction.

What was taking so long? Why the delay to begin his torture and demise? By now his treachery must be old news. A traitor sat breathing in the tower. His enemies would be in a lather of anticipation.

Putar had had more than enough time to construct a fabulous mechanism by which Innel might slowly be eaten, cut, impaled, crushed, or dragged to a slow, excruciating death.

Innel knew one thing for certain: it wouldn't be hunger. A starving man was simply not that amusing.

No, his execution would be about humiliation and pain, drawing low the wretch who had thought himself worthy enough to rise so high above his station. Putar would find a way to strip him naked in every way possible, to slowly grind him into an agonized lunacy, keeping him alive long enough to exhaust every possible means of unpleasantness.

And his Cohort would be there to witness it.

At night, Innel woke to every sound, in a stark, sweat-drenched panic. It was one thing to know death was coming, but another thing entirely to breathe it in and out, every moment, across days.

"Get on with it, damn you!" he shouted from the window, and howled until his throat was raw.

Only the seagulls heard, and they ignored him.

What in Hells was taking them so long?

## Chapter Nineteen

INNEL GAZED down at the morning below, at the various ships in harbor, some readying to leave. He found himself reviewing Arunkel's trade agreements with Perripur, chewing over the problem of Garaya, and speculating as to how all that would play into the upcoming Charter Courts.

He blinked with the realization that none of it mattered.

The day was clear, the sun picking out spots of color across this vast city in which he had spent nearly his entire life. Tiny carts and carriages made their way through narrow streets. People the size of ants went about their uncomplicated lives, lives that weren't ending in an execution destined to be among the most famous in living memory.

*Did you see it? Tremendous! Why, it went on for months.*

When at last the sky turned orange and pink and gold, the sun sinking brilliantly into the Nelar ocean to die along with the night, he wondered if he was ready.

He was, if not truly ready to die, something like resolved. Sachare had been right: his time was over, and by the very moment that he had walked into his office for the last time, there had been nothing more that he could have done to save anything he thought he had.

He could have begged Cern for clemency when she came to see him, giving her some vague half-truth about his culpability. He knew how to lie—he had been schooled in the Cohort, after all.

But in the end, he had discovered, it was not in him to lie about his own treason.

As the light faded in his lampless room, he reclined on the bed and stared at the ceiling, thinking about what it would be like to die.

There was no pride to be had in Execution Square. He had watched hundreds die there, and he knew that the right sort of lethal artistry would make crying babies of even the bravest souls.

His mind, undaunted, sketched huge scaffolds and winches, barrels of scorpions and fire ants, and rivers of centipedes.

Putar would be ecstatic.

Innel must have dozed, because a sound brought him awake as he leapt to his feet.

The bolt slid back, the metal door cracked open. A bar of flickering lamplight. A whispered conversation.

Not the sound of guards. Hope lit within him, hope he had thought properly and fully extinguished.

Two large men entered, a third one following—nearly a giant—carrying what looked like a rolled-up rug.

No one brought a condemned man to an execution in a rolled-up rug. Were they here to rescue him?

More likely, someone had decided that execution was a bad idea, and they were here to kill him, the rug a means to hide his body.

"We can do this one of two ways, ser," said the first man in a down-city accent, his hands out in a nearly friendly gesture. "You can let us tie and gag you, because we got to do that. That'll be the fast way. Or you can fight us and we'll take you down and tie you and gag you just the same. Up to you, ser. We're not choosy."

The three men watched Innel, waiting.

"Who sent you?" Innel asked.

"Ah, well, no. Not here to answer questions. Got a job to do, and that's the sum of it." The man nodded. "What we don't have, ser, is a lot of time. So I'll give you the count of three. Then we'll knock you down, tie you up, gag you." He gave a short nod. "Right. One."

The giant holding the rug turned, eyeing the room, as if to gauge where best to unroll it.

"Answer one question," Innel said, "and I cooperate."

"I guess we can skip two, then," the man said, and shrugged.

The three of them rushed him.

It didn't take long, not with the giant on their side, but it was obvious that they didn't expect it to be as difficult as Innel made it. He drew blood on one, gave another an eye-bruising hit, and kicked the giant nearly in the groin.

Some groaning, some swearing, but they brought him to the floor. As Innel struggled under the giant, who was now half sitting on him, the other two tied his hands and feet with leather straps, then wrapped more leather around his head, gagging him.

"That hurt," the man on top of him said to him in a petulant tone.

"Good," Innel muttered around the gag.

His last fight, perhaps. Considering the odds, he felt good about his performance.

"Right, then," the first man said dryly. "All working together, now."

They laid Innel on the rug on the floor and rolled him. He was hefted and taken from the room.

To die, surely, he told himself.

But hope gnawed at him, taking larger and larger bites.

---

THE RUG MUFFLED SOUND, so Innel heard little as he was carried along. Motion and direction told him where they were going. Down the winding tower stairs. Along a hallway. Down a level. Another hallway.

A faint scent told him they were at the kitchens. Then a long, straight walk and down and somewhere cold.

A tunnel. One of the many that riddled the underside of the palace.

Another door, then another, then a muffled roar, which at first Innel did not place. Then he did.

It was the great Sennant river that flowed around the backside of the palace, far below the high stone palace walls that rested on granite cliffs.

His captor's voices were louder now, to hear each other over the sound of the roaring river. They had carried him outside the walls, and were making their way along descending, uneven paths along the bluffs of the cliffs.

Escape or execution?

"Here," one man said.

"Still seems pretty high," one said.

"Don't see how we can get much closer."

"Glad it's not me."

"You always are. Do it."

Innel felt himself being rotated.

"All right." Then: "Well, ser, this is it: off you go!"

With great force, Innel was snapped into the air, the rug unrolling to spit him out.

All at once he understood: this was no rescue. He was being dropped into the Sennant river far below. Death, but for a man not even worthy of a true execution. Thrown into the sewer like trash.

As the rug unfurled around him, he sailed into the air and plummeted into the dark.

He spun down, falling and falling, his gag-muffled screams nowhere near as loud as the river that was rushing up toward him.

He hit the river as if it were solid ground, then slid into the roil of dark, watery expanse. His mind careened with panic and he bucked and struggled against the leather that bound his hands and feet as he sank.

Crashing, rushing, the river water filled his ears and mouth. He spun and tumbled, helpless, tossed by the current. The river dragged him under.

He would drown. He would die.

The last thing he saw was his daughter's face.

---

SOMETHING CAUGHT Innel hard around the waist, dragging him against the tremendous pull of the river, as if trying to cut him in two.

More sharp tugs. He broke the surface of the rough water, bobbing and sputtering, trying to suck in air around the wet gag. A sharper pull and hands grabbed him and drew him up into a longboat.

He struggled to breathe around the sopping gag. A knife flashed, and it was cut off his head. As he eagerly inhaled, he was pushed to the bottom of the boat, down to wet wood slats. He gasped and retched.

Many minutes later, he felt recovered enough to turn his head.

A figure sat over him, giving hand signs and silent directions to others in the boat. She looked down.

"Stay quiet," Sachare said.

He nodded his understanding, then shivered, coughing out more river-water.

Above them loomed cliffs and bluffs. They were heading toward the ocean.

When he could, he summoned the strength to climb the bench on which Sachare sat. When she didn't object, he inched closer to her, risking a whisper.

"Her decision? Yours?"

She spared him a glance. "It's an exile that you don't deserve," she said softly. "Don't come back."

A moon, shy of half full, lit the night, water, and shore, as they rowed the widening expanse of the Sennant. They passed through the channel and then to the harbor, full of the ships that had seemed so small from the tower.

They came alongside a coastal vessel, its sides rising like walls.

Sachare held up a hand to signal someone above and a net was lowered over the side, to hang just short of the boat, making a seat. Innel, still bound, was hefted and placed inside the net, hanging.

Sachare met his look one last time.

"Tell her—" he said urgently. What? *I'm sorry.* "Tell her, thank you."

Sachare gave a very small nod.

Then Innel was drawn upward like a net of fish, pull by pull. At the top, strong hands yanked him onto the ship. A large sailor threw him over his shoulder and he was carried across the deck, then down into a small, windowless cabin. He was tossed on a bunk, a blanket thrown on top, and left, the door barred.

He stared into the darkness. The room stank of mold and brine.

Whose ship was he on? And where was it going?

*An exile you don't deserve. Don't come back.*

Innel tried to work his hands free, or his feet, but the soaked leather straps had swollen, tightened, and would not yield.

An hour and more and the ship began to move, then slowly left the harbor. Judging by the rocking of the bunk under him, they were finally in open waters.

More hours passed. Innel huddled, wondering why he was alive.

The door opened. A large figure entered and shut the door behind, hanging a lamp on a corner hook.

She took the room's single chair, turned its back toward Innel, and sat, facing him. Her face broke into a wide grin.

He blinked.

"Taba?"

---

"TABA," Innel said. "Thank the Fates…" He drew himself to sit up straight on the bunk, facing her.

"You look like you've been dragged through the sewer, Innel. Twice."

"Whatever you've heard about me," Innel said quickly. "It's not true. I was set up, Taba. I am loyal to the queen. I am no traitor."

"No?"

"No! I was played. A deck was stacked against me. I was tracking various plots against her, working to protect her and —" *My daughter.* "The child. Taba—Cohort-sister—you know how loyal I am to Cern."

"Ah, so you are innocent!"

"I am. Entirely so."

"You did not betray the queen, then?"

Innel blinked. Hadn't he just said exactly that?

He was still so cold, shaken from the last hours. Perhaps he was not thinking clearly. He exhaled.

"Yes, exactly. I did not betray the queen. I'm grateful for your rescue. So very grateful."

"You say the rumors are false. Interesting, because House Helata, we have people—servants, spies—just as you had, Lord Commander. Ah—forgive me. Former Lord Commander." She paused.

"Yes," he replied, uncertain.

"And what they tell me, Cohort-brother, is that you bribed a queensguard to poison our queen, my Cohort-sister. My sovereign. I am told that you said to the guard, 'You must deliver the vial to the queen's bedroom, exactly as instructed.' Is that untrue?"

"Well, yes, but there was more to that conversation..." Innel trailed off.

She had quoted him exactly. Another piece fell into place, heavily: House Helata.

"Not how it happened, you say?" Taba asked, still grinning.

Now Innel heard, quite clearly, her mocking tone.

"No. Those are my words, but out of context."

"What?" Her expression was one of pretend surprise. "But I am told that you paid the guard a gold souver."

"So that he would lead me to whoever hired him. I was drawing out the plot."

Taba nodded. "I understand entirely, Innel. Of course you yourself would never take money for such a scheme, would you?"

"Of course not."

"You were only playing the part. A small amount then. A

few falcons, perhaps? Just enough to convince everyone that you were on the take? Yes?"

The uma-sorin. She knew.

Innel looked around the small cabin, then back at her. This was her ship.

"Taba, what do you want?"

"Now you try to bribe *me*?"

For a moment the only sound between them was Innel's breath.

He summoned a contrite tone. "I wouldn't be here, still alive, Taba, if there wasn't something you wanted from me. Name it, and it's yours."

She rolled her shoulders, regarding him with a sort of fascination.

"I already have it. I've been waiting for this day a long time, Cohort-brother. So long. How long? Since the seventh day of the hunter's moon, empire year nine-hundred and eighty-two. Astonishing how that sort of detail stays with you."

The seventh day of the hunter's moon…?

She was watching him now, very intently.

He quickly searched his memory. What had he been doing then?

A hard ride. A fast horse. Mountain roads. A small town. A child who supposedly could see into the future.

*Pohut.*

"Ah, you *do* remember," Taba said, sitting back, giving him a satisfied smile. "Good. I would be so very disappointed—" Her smile vanished abruptly. "—if you had forgotten."

She slowly stood and kicked her chair to the floor. Her first hit opened Innel's lip. He tasted blood.

Then she did it again, hard enough to knock him, still bound, off the bunk and onto the floor. He turned his head to look up, saw a heavy, booted foot coming toward his stomach.

Years of beatings in the Cohort playyard had taught him a great deal. He curled to tense against the kick, while knowing it would only help a little.

## Chapter Twenty

TO ONE SIDE of Amarta stood Tayre. To the other, Olessio. She cautiously leaned on a chest-high railing that threatened splinters and stared at the harbor and the Mundaran sea beyond.

"Horses." Olessio drew the word out, as though it were new to him, and he was trying it out.

From his pack, slung over his shoulders, Tadesh snored gently.

"What about that one?" Tayre asked Amarta, nodding at a large ship at dock. Like most of the ships here, it flew the Perripin flag.

Longshoremen hauled boxes up a ramp on wheeled flats, calling to each other over the sounds of surf against distant rocks. On the dock, a pretend fight broke out between two of the sailors. A small crowd of them gathered around, laughing. "La las" followed, and the two men hugged.

Amarta held Tayre's question in her mind, then sent it to go into the haze of the future. Conflicting images. Souver and Horse might indeed walk up that ship's ramp. It was at least possible, which was better than most of the Atudaka-bound vessels they had considered.

Tayre, it turned out, was right: not many ships wanted to take horses anywhere.

"I think yes," she said uncertainly.

"I had a horse once," Olessio said. "A big dun boy, he was. Ornery as the sun is high." Olessio chewed one side of his mustache thoughtfully, his bottom lip protruding on the other side. His eyebrows drew down. "Tell me, Amarta, are these *magical* horses?"

Amarta blinked away the hazy half-view vision provided, of the horses being cajoled and pushed up the ship's ramp. She looked at him.

Olessio's eyes were pale, one a sort of watery gold-green, the other a slightly richer, mossy color. His gaze was only a little higher than her own. Short for a man. Odd that she hadn't noticed that before.

"I don't think so," she replied, confused.

"Ah," Olessio answered, nodding. "Then I most humbly beg you to enlighten me as to why you are spending the better part of the fortune you nearly lost outside the Sun and Moon to…" he gestured at the ship. "Hmm. Torture them."

"Torture?" Shocked, she gave Olessio her full attention. "What do you mean?"

The smaller man looked over his shoulder at Tayre, and smiled warily. "None of my business?"

Tayre shrugged a little. "Her decision, not mine."

"Oh, now *that's* interesting. So…" He waved a hand in the air, making a large circle.

"Explain yourself," Amarta said tightly.

Olessio put his wandering hand on the splintering railing. "Imagine being tied, hand and foot, then suspended in a sling in a dark cabin, pitching and rolling, for ten days. It's not the open ocean, of course, but the

Mundaran sea provides plenty of up and down and sideways excitement all on its own. It sounds like torture to me."

"Valerian and skullcap," Tayre said. "They'll settle. They'll sleep."

"For ten days? In their own piss and shit?"

"They'll be kept clean," Amarta said, then looked at Tayre. "He's wrong, isn't he? Are you sure they'll sleep through it?"

Tayre shrugged. "Are you?"

Overhead, a seagull shrieked. Amarta looked back at the ship, then at Olessio.

"I don't want them to suffer. That's the last thing I…You think this is a poor plan?"

"Well." Olessio scratched his nose. Then, brightly: "Perhaps I am wrong. The intoxicants—hanging in a sling in a dark room for days—maybe it's all fine. Now me, I'd try it myself first, just to be sure." He shrugged. "But I'm an odd one. There's a reason I pull my own cart."

Amarta stared at the ship, the dockworkers, porters lugging bags, cargo managers arguing with harbor officials.

At the bow of the ship, a single sailor dropped a rind of bread over the side. A seagull dove and grabbed the scrap midair, screeching victoriously as it trailed a handful of other gulls into the sky.

"I want to see how they would travel," Amarta said.

A short nod from Tayre. "I'll go talk to the captain."

"He'll want to see the glint of a la-sorin, just to come aboard, I'd say," said Olessio. "At least."

"At least." Tayre agreed, and walked off.

AT THE TOP of the ramp that led to the ship they paused, grabbing the rope railing. There stood a thickset, heavily bearded Perripin man, a captain's wrap around his head.

"Captain," Tayre said, "we wish to inspect the equine accommodations to be sure they are sufficient for our needs."

It felt such a precarious place to stand, here, so high above the churning water that separated hull from dock. Amarta tried not to look down.

What would the horses think, when they were led up this same ramp?

"Come aboard," the captain said, standing aside, an amused look on his face. They were led across the wide deck and into a narrow door, then down a passageway.

As she followed, Amarta trailed her fingers on the planked walls, looking for a future in which Horse and Souver would not only enter but come back out. *Flickers of people, of sad, worn faces. One man in particular, sallow and thin, his hair and beard a dark, tangled mess, his eyes oddly familiar.*

She frowned. Who was the man? Someone she'd met? A future—a vision once glimpsed—now remembered? Sometimes it was so hard to tell.

But no, it didn't matter. Only the horses mattered. In what future were they brought safely off the ship?

One image after another and then she found it: Souver and Horse, walking toward her in this very passageway, heads low to clear the ceiling.

They looked sick. Amarta's heart sank.

"This way, sera," one of the sailors called sharply, as Amarta, distracted, missed the turn. She doubled back to follow.

The party descended a steep ramp into a dark hold that smelled of mildew, brine, and sweat. The small crowd of sailors gathered around a door.

"In there," said the captain. "Your horses go in there. We'll use the big slings. Be just like hammocks. Cut some leg-holes, some padding, and your four-legged friends will be as comfortable as babes in cradles. They'll barely know they're on the water!" He laughed.

Amarta stared at the barred door. "I want to see the room."

The captain heaved a sigh. "All right," he said to his sailors. "Get them out."

The sailors drew from their belts what seemed to be short sticks, but flexible. Heavy leather, Amarta realized.

Amarta looked bewilderment at Tayre. His expression told her nothing, but he stepped close and put a hand on her shoulder.

The door opened. A powerful stink wafted out. A couple of sailors, faces wrinkling at the stench, stepped inside and pulled from the dark room into the hold a pale-haired man, his hands and feet shackled, and pressed him along what was now a row of sailors who sent him into another room, just opened.

Another blonde man was drawn from the dark room. Then a woman, her hair damp and lank about her shoulders. She looked around wide-eyed as she was thrust into the other door.

Emendi. Amarta's mouth was open in shock.

"Hurry it up," one of the crew snapped at another woman as she resisted being pushed along.

"Na to worry," the captain said. "We'll get that room clean and clear by the time your horses come aboard."

Amarta felt hot, her skin prickled all over. A slave ship. They were going to transport the horses on a slave ship.

She tried to speak, failed, tried again.

"Where—are they going?"

"Atudaka. Same as you and your horses, sera."

"No," Amarta breathed. Two were drawn from the room —a man and woman—hands gripped tight despite the shackles binding their wrists, forcing their outer arms across their bodies.

A face at the edge of the doorway. A girl's face, eyes wide. Then gone.

"What's she doing in there?" the captain said. "Youngers in the far cabin, I told you!"

"Stop! Stop!" Amarta cried out.

At this the sailors paused. The captain motioned them to continue.

"Stop what you're doing to these Emendi," Amarta shouted.

"These what?" the captain demanded.

She whirled on him, struggling to keep her voice steady, and failing.

"You don't even know who they are?"

"They're money, is what they are." The captain looked to Tayre in annoyed confusion. "You want slaves, too? Can sell you some." He looked back at Amarta, his own expression hardening to match hers.

Amarta was shaking, her fists tight. "These accommodations are not sufficient," she bit out.

The captain's expression went from hard to sour. "No? All right, then." He gestured abruptly to his men, who reversed the flow of Emendi into the room from which they had come.

"We go," Tayre said into Amarta's ear, pressing her toward the exit door and the ramp that led topside.

She resisted. "The girl. I want to buy her."

"I won't sell her, not to you," the captain spat.

He was wrong. It was clear to her, the future in which the captain—if not happily, at least willingly—handed the girl to Amarta. It was slippery, that future. She struggled to find it.

Then it wasn't there at all.

She rifled through, trying to weed out the futures in which yelling at him—which she very much wanted to do—failed to gain his compliance. What about the various entreaties she might make? How would they feel in her throat? She began to sound one out, to make it real enough to feed foresight what it needed in order to give her clear answers.

"Get the hell off my ship," the captain's voice cracked.

Amarta blinked back into the present. The crew all stepped forward in a closing circle.

Tayre moved, fast, standing between the captain and Amarta. He held up a coin, at eye level. It glinted a deep bronze, edged with silver.

A cho-sorin. A lot of money.

"Perhaps this will change your mind, captain," he said, in a tone that was, somehow, both fearless and nonthreatening at once.

The future shifted again.

The captain's face was twisted in anger, but he held up a hand to stop his men from closing.

"Could be a virgin, the girl," the captain said, eyeing the coin. "Worth a hundred times that."

"Doubt it," Tayre answered with a thin smile. "Not the way you stored them together. In any case, this is twice the going price for a girl that thin. One less mouth for you to feed on the journey, yes?"

The captain considered, then nodded sharply at Tayre, and gestured to his men. "Get the girl, take the coin, and get these dirty landlubber Arunkin the hell off my ship."

Two of the crew entered the lightless room with a lantern. "Come on, you." He pulled the girl from the room, but something held her other arm.

"Hoi, you," yelled the sailor, pulling her from the room. "Let go!"

"Mama!" cried the girl, arms stretched, looking back.

Now, framed in the doorway, leaning backwards to hold the girl, was a woman, her eyes wide, face etched with a hard determination. "Don't take my baby," she cried.

"No, no, no!" Amarta cried.

Suddenly everything was closing in on her. The tight quarters, the sailors, the future. A problem she did not understand, could not fix. She could not breathe.

Too much.

She thrust her way through the people now thick around her—Tayre, the captain, the crewmen, ignoring everything but the next split instant, pulling it around herself like a tight cloak. She ducked and twisted between bodies, sliding through hands reaching for her, then ran up the ramp, through the corridors, and across the deck

Unbidden, a wail came from her throat.

She recklessly sprinted down the ramp, barely keeping her feet. She did not slow at the dock, weaving her way through knots of people. Only escape mattered.

A longshoreman reached out to stop her. She stutter-stepped, leaned, slid by him.

Up the steps. Into the city. Forward.

High buildings rose overhead. Twisting streets were thick with festival crowds.

Only then did some small, reasoning part of mind her suggest that she wait for Tayre and Olessio.

Stifling sobs, she attracted little more than curious looks. In Senta, during the Accord festival, there were far stranger and more riveting entertainments than a gasping, crying woman.

She slowed to a walk, sense finally permeating the worst of her panic. She put her back to a sun-warmed brick wall and bent double, sucking in air, foregoing foresight and thought alike, letting herself be settled by the scent of grilled fish, the loud chatter of crowds, the distant music.

Only days ago Senta's festival had been overwhelming. Now it felt like a haven, assuring some part of her that all was well.

*Please don't take my baby.*

All was not well.

She forced herself to think through what had happened. She had no obligation to these enslaved Emendi. They were not her friends from the hidden city of Kusan. Why did it hurt so much?

Did she carry some part of Kusan with her, as if the stone dust from underground had embedded itself into her spirit?

Her breath had begun to steady when Tayre and Olessio arrived.

"I need more money," she told them. "How much to buy the whole ship?"

Olessio's eyebrows shot up.

Tayre gave her a thoughtful look. "And the next one? The one after that?"

Amarta slowly lowered herself to the cobblestone, feeling inexplicably tired. "How many are there?"

Olessio crouched down next to her, letting Tadesh out of his pack to roam the street. He took a hesitant breath. "A very good many. Alas."

"How many?" she demanded, her voice breaking.

When Olessio did not answer, Amarta looked up to Tayre, whose gaze was sweeping the crowds. "One a month, I'd guess," he said. "Peak season, maybe two."

"There's a peak season for slaves?" Amarta asked, voice rising.

Olessio put a hand on her shoulder, the sorrow on his

face echoing her own. "It is a sad thing, I agree. But it is also the way of the world, I fear."

She wiped her eyes, shook her head, snuffled. Was this maturity, to accept such horrors? She searched his mismatched eyes for a moment, then slowly stood, the aches of her body and spirit making her feel old.

Festival crowds passed them by, happy and loud. Amarta stared distantly.

"Those two Emendi children being sold," she said to Tayre. "There must be something we can do for them, at least."

Tayre gave a thoughtful nod. "Zeted, perhaps."

"Zeted? What does she have to do with this?"

"I've seen how she treats her slaves at her mansion in Bayfahar. They are well-fed. Respected. Given work that suits them. If you like, I can recommend to her that she purchase those two in particular, here at the festival."

Amarta recalled how he had kissed Zeted. She had no doubt that he could convince the merchant of anything.

"She won't use them for sex, will she?" Amarta asked.

Tayre shook his head. "Her tastes don't run that way."

Amarta wasn't sure she liked the implication of his confidence, but decided not to pursue that.

"Will you do this for me?" she asked.

Tayre nodded. "I'll need a few hours to take care of it."

From above, a scratching sound. Tadesh had managed to climb most of the way straight up the ragged brick wall where Amarta had leaned and then sat, and was now slipping downward, her back feet first, looking worried.

Instead of falling, Tadesh somehow twisted, then launched herself onto Olessio's shoulders, landing there with a meaty thud.

Olessio exhaled a sharp hiss, while Tadesh changed direction, her tail at one shoulder, her head at the other.

"I may need a new shirt," Olessio said softly. "One made of leather." Tadesh then turned again, nosing her way into his pack.

Olessio offered Amarta a hand, and she took it. The three of them began to wind their way through the crowd.

"The horses," Amarta said heavily. "We'll have to sell them after all."

"Aha! Now there I may be of some use." Olessio wrapped a gentle arm around Amarta's shoulder. "Such a fine creature, your Souver. What kind of horse is he? He likes to run, yes?"

Amarta nodded uncertainly.

"I thought so! It happens that some of my people live just up river on a sizable homestead called The Bogs. Isn't really. Just a name to discourage folks from coming too close, you know? They raise bees. Hogs. For the wax and the wine, they say." He laughed lightly, then frowned. "The bees, not the hogs. The hogs are to entertain and to eat."

"So?"

"They have pasture to spare. I'm sure mama-Jurdje would board your horses and keep them safe while you travel. Worth asking, anyway, yes? Shall I send word?"

Amarta looked at Tayre, whose expression told her that he had no particular objection. It was up to her.

She examined Olessio carefully. He seemed sincere, but if she had learned nothing else in Senta, she had learned how easily lies could come to some people.

"First I need to see it, this homestead."

To make sure the accommodations were sufficient.

---

THEY LEFT Souver and Horse to explore in one of the large pastures, then walked to the main house of The Bogs.

There were no bogs to be seen. Tamarind trees waved in

the breeze. Stone-edged footpaths led them through high grasses and around lush fruit trees to the house, a large, sprawling structure. Coming toward them was a small group with an old woman at the center. She walked slowly, steadying herself with a carved cane in one hand and a sturdy young man in the other.

Olessio made introductions. The woman was the family matriarch, called mama-Jurdje. Was she Olessio's aunt? Sister? Distant cousin? Amarta could not tell.

The group doubled, then tripled, speaking a fast mix of Perripin and Farliosan that Amarta could not follow.

Younger children flooded the group, pressing greetings and hugs on Olessio, then Amarta. Even Tayre, who seemed not the least discomfited by this outpouring of affection. Then the youngers began the whole process again, as if they'd forgotten who they'd already greeted.

Mugs were passed around. Some sort of honey-mead that fizzed slightly, and cups of fruit mash that tasted like fermented lilikoi.

The youngers knew Olessio well enough to demand that he entertain them. They eyed Tadesh, on his shoulders, jumping and begging to hold her. She looked back warily.

Then Olessio spoke to her softly, and she stood on her hind legs and waved down at them. Delighted, the youngers cheered.

Mama-Jurdje waved her hands and everyone moved forward, beginning the tour. A few young men and women about Amarta's age proudly showed off the new barn, the coops, and offered varying, colorful accounts of the two babies born to the family this year.

There was so much shouting that it took a little bit for Amarta to realize that no one was actually upset. They simply spoke at volume. A joyous din, is what it was.

Tayre raised his voice to match theirs, smiling and

laughing, making jokes. Did he fit in everywhere? Was any of it genuine?

Amarta stepped near Olessio. "Are you really related to all these people?"

He waved a hand. "Cousins, no doubt. We don't keep careful track. We're all family."

Then a loud clanging of pots and a repeating high, trilling call, in what Amarta gathered was Farliosan. They were led to the far side of the house, where long tables were heavy with dishes and baskets of food.

"An ancient call of our people," Olessio told her behind a hand. "It means: Come-now, come-now! Wait longer and the food will be gone, and your stomach will hurt empty. Only you to blame!" He laughed.

Everyone found seats, but most sat only long enough to fill cups and bowls before wandering around the table to chat and share food from their plates.

The sun set. Musical instruments were brought out. The elders leaned back in their chairs, some smoking small pipes, others passing around jugs. Small children climbed into laps. One boy looked up at the woman holding him and smiled.

The ache hit Amarta all at once. Her throat went tight, her eyes stung. Pas used to climb into Dirina's lap just the same.

A fire-pit was burning, warm and bright in the cooling evening. A woman with bells on a hand-hoop began to tap out a rhythm, accompanied by a man with a lap-lute. One voice began, high and clear, then another, and another, until it was too many to count, while others danced.

Overhead, the evening star brightened. For a time, Amarta lost herself in the music and joy.

Olessio gestured to her and Tayre to come and sit close by him and mama-Jurdje.

He had been talking with her and had come to what he

thought might be a suitable arrangement. "They'll store my things as well," he told them. "They'll keep your Souver and Horse safe. Until we return." He waved at the land and grinned at Amarta: "So much room to run! I wish I were so fortunate!"

"Not to sell," Amarta said urgently.

"Never to sell," mama-Jurdje assured her. "We care for them, like our own."

"But what if…" Amarta struggled to keep foresight muffled as she struggled to find the words, as it offered up a hundred conflicting answers. "What if we don't come back?"

Mama-Jurdje tilted her head, spread her hands. "Who can say what tomorrow brings? Our brother Olessio asks us to give them a temporary home, and we are only too happy to oblige."

"Thank you," Amarta said.

Olessio cleared his throat. "There should be a bit of, ah, sweetener? For the effort? And the feed?"

"Oh," Amarta said, looking at Tayre.

Tayre nodded. "I'll take care of it."

The sky darkened, and the stars brightened. Amarta dipped into vision, holding rein on its tendency to spread branches into horrors and heavens alike.

Just this one place, just this one question: Would Souver and Horse be happy and healthy here, months and years to come?

Months, vision could say yes to. Years were another matter. There, vision was a gibbering, mumbling pile of flashes, most of which made no sense.

"Never mind," she muttered to herself, brushing it all away. "Months will do."

That night they slept under the open sky, the stars bright, in the company of many youngers who brought soft bedding and blankets for them and pointed out their favorite constellations.

"Tell us yours," one said to her.

Amarta pointed. "The scales. When you die and go to the Beyond, they weigh the good you've done against the bad."

"What, that, there?"

She nodded. "In Perripur it's called the flying fish."

There was tittering. Then, after a time, there was sleep.

The next morning, Amarta slipped away and went to the stables, where Souver and Horse had spent the night.

They looked happy. They looked content. She caressed Horse's soft snout and he exhaled, making her hand moist.

She stroked Souver's neck, scratching the spot under her ear that she liked best.

Then she spoke to them quietly, explaining to them the situation, telling them how well they would be cared for. Hoping they would understand.

Hoping they would believe.

"I'll come back for you," she said to them earnestly, her eyes stinging.

Horse turned his head, a large brown eye on her. For a moment she imagined that his look was skeptical.

"It's not a prediction," she admitted. "But I will."

She put her arms around Horse's neck. He nuzzled her hair a little, and she brought her head closer to his ear.

"I name you Promise."

# Read More!

Be sure to read all the books in The Stranger trilogy!

*Unmoored*
*Maelstrom*
*Landfall*

Available at your favorite retailers!

**It's True. Reviews Help.**

IF YOU LIKED THIS BOOK, please consider giving a rating and a review. Even a short "Can't wait for the next one!" will do nicely, and help the author to make more books for you.

## About the Author

Sonia Orin Lyris's stories have appeared in various publications, including *Asimov's SF magazine*, *Wizards of the Coast* anthologies, and *Uncle John's Bathroom Reader*. She is the author of *The Seer*, an epic fantasy novel from Baen Books. Her writing has been called "immersive," "ruthless," and "unsparing."

Her passions include martial arts, partner dance, fine chocolate, and the occasional human critter.

She asks questions and gives answers, but not necessarily in that order. She speaks fluent cat.

### A note from Sonia

Thank you for being part of my creative process. I have regular chats for subscribers, on my Patreon account, here:

**https://www.patreon.com/lyris**

### Never miss a release!

I announce new projects on my Facebook feed:
https://www.facebook.com/authorlyris

You can also sign up for my newsletter:
https://lyris.org/subscribe/

### Connect with Sonia

Web: https://lyris.org

facebook.com/authorlyris
goodreads.com/Sonia_Orin_Lyris
twitter.com/slyris